TIME NEXT

CAROLYN COHAGAN

D1114314

Copyright © 2017 by Carolyn Cohagan
All rights reserved.

No part of this book may be reproduced in any form or by any electronic or mechanical means, including information storage and retrieval systems, without written permission from the author, except for the use of brief quotations in a book review.

Published 2018, Girls With Pens, Austin, TX
Printed in the United States
ISBN: 978-0-9995624-3-7

This is a work of fiction. Names, characters, places and incidents either are products of the author's imagination or are used fictitiously. Any resemblance to actual events or locales or persons, living or dead, is entirely coincidental.

ALSO BY CAROLYN COHAGAN

The Lost Children

Time Zero

For my husband,
who has to listen to more weird facts about
fundamentalism than anyone you know.

AUTHOR'S NOTE

The religion in *Time Next* is fictional, but the cultural practices and beliefs are real. Teenagers all over the United States are currently asked to abide by similar rules and suffer the same punishments that Mina witnesses and experiences throughout the story.

For more information, please visit:
www.timezerobook.com/religious-rules

I distrust those people who know so well what God wants them to do, because I notice it always coincides with their own desires.

—Susan B. Anthony

ONE

I'm not in the van for long. My eyes have barely adjusted to the dark when the doors are flung open and sunlight pours in, blinding me. A male voice says, "Let's go."

Several figures are backlit by the morning light, but I can't make out faces.

"She isn't moving," a woman's voice says.

"Maybe she doesn't speak English," says the man. I can understand him, but he's speaking with the same odd accent as Beth, like he's got a mouthful of honey. I suppose I should speak up, tell them I can understand, but I keep my mouth shut. I might learn more this way.

"Poor thing," says the woman. "She's probably frightened to death."

"Or she's waiting to kill us."

"Luke! Bite your tongue." The woman gets closer, sticking her head in the van. Her face is pudgy and pink, her hair cropped short and streaked two different shades of blonde. "I'm Bithia, honey. Bithia Dixon. Now come on out. No one's going to hurt you."

She reaches a hand toward me, and I shrink into the corner of the van.

"Gilad!" she shrieks.

A large man appears beside her. His face is also pudgy, but pasty instead of pink, and his eyes have a startled look, like he's just stepped on a nail. His large bald spot is shiny with sweat.

"You'd better go in and get her, hon," Bithia says.

Gilad scowls. Lifting a chubby leg, he heaves his enormous frame into the back of the van. As he hoists himself up, the foot of his other leg catches on the edge of the platform, and he comes tumbling into the cargo hold face-first. Laughter comes from outside.

"Good heavens, Gilad! What are you doing in there?" Bithia says with irritation.

"Checking the floor for weapons," Gilad says dryly, then slowly stands. He moves his knee around a few times, wincing. *I could rush him*, I think, *try to knock him out of the van and onto the ground*. But he's awfully big. It would be like rushing the side of a house.

Gilad doesn't move any closer to me. He puts his hands in front of him, moving them up and down as he talks. "Sweetheart, you need to come with me."

Why am I his "sweetheart?" I try to pull back more, but I'm as far into my corner as I can get.

"We're your friends." His hands still bob up and down, like he's trying to close a car trunk.

I shake my head. I may not know much about the Apostates, or Queens, or this strange man, but I do know he is *not* my friend.

He takes a few steps closer, approaching like I'm a tiger who will pounce at any moment, but he's so large, I'm more like a kitten who can only attack his pant leg.

He smiles, and I'm frightened by his rows of huge white

2

teeth. I'm still staring at them when he shoots out his hand and grabs my wrist. "Got her!"

Without a thought, I bite his hand as hard as I can. The metallic taste of blood fills my mouth.

"*Goddammit*!!" he cries, releasing me. I sink back into my corner.

"Gilad! Language!" Bithia leans into the van.

"She bit me!" he says, holding up his hand.

"She doesn't know any better. Think what she's had to endure. Poor lamb."

"More like a wolf if you ask me," Gilad mutters. He peers down at me. "Listen here, girlie—and I know you can understand me. They're still speaking English over there, and we know it. You better come with me. Otherwise, I'm gonna get Jeremiah in here, and he's got a big ol' gun, and none of us wants to use force. So let's just do this friendly-like, okay?"

Squinting out the van doors into the light, I can make out a figure holding what appears to be a very large weapon.

Maybe I'll let Jeremiah join Gilad, and then I will bite Jeremiah, and then he'll have to shoot me. The idea is almost . . . relaxing. I'm so tired. All I want is to go to sleep. I don't want to talk to these people. I don't want to be anywhere where Juda and Grace and Dekker and Rose are not.

"Where are my friends?" I hear myself blurt.

"See now? Was that so hard?" Gilad says. He turns to Bithia. "I told you she knew English!"

"So I owe you a donut," she says. "Big deal."

"Where are my friends?" I repeat, wildly impatient now that I've decided to speak.

"Why don't you join me and we'll find out?" Gilad offers me his hand.

His face is solemn and I trust him more without the smile. I

3

don't take his hand, but I stand and walk to the edge of the platform, shielding my eyes with my hand.

To my surprise, we've arrived at another neighborhood full of brightly painted houses. I'd expected a prison or even gallows, but I don't find the picturesque neighborhood reassuring.

A small crowd of Apostates is gathered around the van—adults and children—watching expectantly. Everyone's clothing is one solid color: green, blue, yellow, purple. Standing in front of the vibrant houses, they look like a wall of colored pencils.

Like a switch has been hit, they all smile at me, and I'm assaulted by more big white teeth like Gilad's. A little girl waves but stops when I don't wave back.

Bithia, who wears royal blue, says to them in a low voice, "Remember your training." She smiles up at me. "Come on out, dear."

Hopping down out of the van, I see a few people step back, and one man pulls his daughter into a close embrace, as if I might breathe fire. *I wish I could.*

Bithia snaps her fingers twice at a blonde girl my age, the only one in the crowd who looks bored. The girl steps toward Bithia holding up a shiny silver blanket that blinds me as it catches the sun.

Snatching it away from her, Bithia throws it around my shoulders. "There, there. You're safe now."

The blanket crinkles loudly and makes me feel uncomfortably hot. Is this part of my punishment for believing in the Prophet?

"Are you hungry?" Bithia asks.

Am I? I was starving when we emerged from the subway, but I don't think I want to eat with these people. "Where are my friends?" I ask again.

Bithia smiles with closed lips, pity in her eyes. "They're with other families, guests like you."

This is how they treat guests? They assault, separate, and terrify them? "What kind of people *are you*?!" I ask, my fear turning to anger.

No one speaks. The little girl who waved stares at the ground.

"I demand to see my friends!" I say, frantically looking around, wondering where I can run. I throw off the silver blanket. "I DEMAND TO SEE THEM NOW!"

Jeremiah, the one with the big gun, approaches on my left.

I'm shrieking now. "YOU'RE HEATHENS! ALL OF YOU! YOU'RE EVIL, JUST LIKE MY MOTHER SAID!"

Out of the corner of my eye, I see Jeremiah raise his arm above me. The light catches a needle in his hand. I turn to flee.

And then there is darkness.

TWO

When I awake, I'm in a bed, a large fan spinning lazily above me. The room smells fresh, like a spring day. Every surface is covered in vases of flowers: roses, daisies, tulips, and others I've never seen before.

The quilt that covers me also has a flower pattern, as does a stuffed armchair in the corner. The crisp white walls look as if they were painted yesterday and the wood floors are light and creamy. Several large windows show treetops; I must be on the second floor.

All the floral patterns make me think of Sekena, my best friend, in her pajamas. I'm miserable with the knowledge that I won't ever see her again. I would never have come here if I'd thought for a second that I would end up alone. I was only brave because of the others.

Trying to sit up, I realize I can barely move, because the sheets are tucked so tightly under the mattress. I wiggle my arms, trying to free myself.

Looking to my left, I'm startled to see Bithia sitting silently in a wooden chair near the door. She smiles without showing any teeth. "You're awake!"

I glare at her, but her smile persists.

"Welcome to Kingsboro! I know you're going to love it here." Her voice has a practiced quality. "We celebrate freedom and encourage our boys and girls to be anything they want." She wears a loose dress in the same royal blue as yesterday. "How did you sleep?"

I continue to give her the meanest look I can. A voice inside of me is telling me to stop, that I need to not antagonize these people, but I can't help it. We went through so much to get here—this self-satisfied woman couldn't possibly understand.

"You've been asleep for more than twelve hours. You must be famished!" she says.

I turn my head away.

"I'm sorry—Jeremiah is sorry—for what he did. But you were agitated, and he panicked. It wasn't dangerous or anything. It was just a sedative. Heck, I take one myself to help me sleep at night." She smiles that closed-lip smile. "You'll feel a lot better after breakfast. Silas is making pancakes."

I won't look at her.

"How about a little juice?"

When I don't answer, she says, "You've got to eat something. I just won't forgive myself if you make yourself sick."

The idea of taking anything this woman offers is what makes me sick.

"This is your room, dear. Isn't it pretty? I cut the flowers fresh this morning."

I don't respond.

"Will you eat if we talk about your friends?"

I turn to face her again.

"That's what I thought." She scratches her hand. "I'm not

supposed to say anything, but I get why you're upset. So, um, I'll tell you what I can."

I hold my breath.

"They're safe. No one's hurting them. They're in homes just like this being looked after by people just like us." She grins as if she's just delivered the best news I've ever heard.

"Will you take me to them?" I sit up as best I can.

"Uh, no. That's not allowed yet."

"Not allowed?" By whom?

She scratches her hand some more. "This is why I shouldn't have said anything. You'll understand everything soon. I promise, it's *wonderful*. Really. I'm just not the best person to explain it." She stands to leave. "So let's get you that food."

"Bithia?" I say.

"Yes?" she says, apparently surprised to hear me use her name.

"I won't be eating until I see all of the people I arrived with."

She sighs. "That's a shame. Silas is famous for his pancakes."

I cross my arms to let her know how serious I am, while inside I wonder how long I can hold out. I'm so hungry, I feel nauseated.

"You're only hurting yourself," she says. "It's no skin off my teeth." But I can tell she's anxious. After a moment of silence, she adds, "I'll tell the others what you've said. But I can tell you, it won't go well. Ram doesn't respond to blackmail."

Is Ram her boss?

"In the meantime, there's a bathroom here, if you need it." She points to a door by the window.

I don't want to comply with Bithia in any way, but I really need to go. I try to push back the heavy quilt. She comes over to help me, adding to my suspicion that the tightly fitted blanket was meant to hold me in place.

When I stand, I realize that I'm no longer in the Twitcher

uniform that I arrived in. I'm wearing a long white nightgown, thin and sheer. "Who changed me?" I say, horrified.

"Me and my daughter, Tabby. Don't worry. There weren't any men around."

"Who gave you the right?" I ask, feeling violated in a way I can't express.

She seems taken aback. "Your clothes were disgusting, child. Ready to be burned, in my opinion. We were doing you a favor."

"Don't do me any more favors!" I say, walking into the bathroom and slamming the door.

I burst into tears as soon as I'm alone, but I cover my mouth, determined not to make a sound.

Who are these people? What do they want with me? When I remember Nana and her words—"thinking of you out there, *free in the world*, will keep me alive and smiling"—I can't stop crying. I gave up so much to be here. I gave up *Nana*.

But she also said that whatever is here can't be worse than what is there. Rayna said we had to leave because of the coming war between the Convenes and the Deservers. If she's right, then I should be home helping my people—my family, Sekena, the Laurel Society—not wasting time with shady Apostates.

I shake my head. Why am I torturing myself with these pointless thoughts? I can never go back. Damon and Mr. Asher are dead. Mr. Asher was working *directly* with Uncle Ruho. The Twitchers will never stop looking for me. Mrs. Asher will hunt me down until her dying day. The thought of her—her beautiful face and cruel smile—makes me cold with fear.

I stop sniveling. I've got to be realistic about my situation. I don't like Bithia or Gilad or the strange way they're treating me, but they haven't put me in a cell, beaten me, or cut off my head. I should be grateful for that.

And I have nowhere else to go.

I have no intention of trusting them, but perhaps I should

give them reasons to trust *me*. And then they will tell me about Juda and the others.

After I use the bathroom, I open the door and face Bithia with my head turned slightly down. I try not to grit my teeth as I say, "Can I please have some pancakes now, Mrs. Dixon?"

She walks over and takes my hands, which I find disconcerting. "Of course, dear. Of course. And just call me Bithia!"

I nod and force a smile.

"Tabby found some old clothes—I mean, old to her. They're very nice—and everything's in the closet over there." She points to a door by the window. "Help yourself to whatever you want and then come downstairs. I'll tell Silas to heat up the griddle!"

She saunters out the door.

That was it? All I needed to do was agree to eat, and she would leave me alone?

I explore the room. I'm able to open a window, but I'm too high to climb down or jump. A large lawn spills out beneath me and big colorful houses stand to the left and right.

All the drawers in the furniture are empty—I find nothing I could use as a weapon.

I go to the closet, having decided to follow Bithia's instructions for now. I discover a space as big as our kitchen at home. Stepping inside, I see more clothes hanging on the upper and lower racks than I've ever owned in my life. And everything—pants, skirts, blouses, T-shirts—is the same horrible shade of yellow-green. Does Tabby like to walk around looking like a giant asparagus?

In addition to the wretched color, many pairs of the shorts and skirts are cut above the knee. I can't possibly wear them. The tops are mostly sleeveless and many of them look like the undershirts I wore when I was too young to wear a bra.

The closet has a strong, musky smell. Sniffing the sleeve of a blouse, I realize that it's the clothes. The blouse smells slightly soapy, so I know it's clean, but it also has a rich, brassy smell. Tabby must use a lot of perfume. I don't like the idea of wearing her clothes or her scent.

Looking down at my gauzy nightgown, I know that I have no choice.

I finally choose a pair of green pants in a thick, heavy fabric and a top with long sleeves and a high neck. Surprisingly, all the clothes touching my skin, no matter their texture, are silky soft.

The top is tighter than I would like, and I'm relieved to find a loose sweater folded on a high shelf. The sweater is navy blue and reaches nearly to my knees, making me feel almost like I'm wearing my cloak, which makes me calmer.

My feet are too large for any of the closed-toe shoes, so I have to settle on a pair of sandals. They're white with silver buckles, the same as the ones Beth wore—Beth, the young girl who turned us in so easily.

Remember not to trust *anyone*.

I don't have a hair tie, so I use the mirror in the bathroom to finger comb my hair as best I can. I barely recognize myself. My eyes are lined with dark circles; my skin is so chalky it looks gray. Bithia said I was asleep for twelve hours, but I look like I haven't slept in years. Perhaps food will help.

I say a silent prayer to the Prophet before I leave the room.

A little boy stands in the hall gaping at me. He must be only four or five, and his hair is so blond it looks white. When I walk toward him, he makes a little squeaking noise and goes running down a flight of stairs to my right.

Bithia told me to come downstairs after I was dressed, so I follow the strange boy. The floors and walls are the same out here as they were in the bedroom: creamy wood and brilliant white, although I see a few tiny handprints along the stairwell. Light splashes over everything, and I look up to find a skylight over the stairs.

I've never been in such a large house; I've never really been in a house at all. The Dixons must be very wealthy. Why am I here? Is Mr. Dixon the leader of the Apostates? The thought makes me frightened. I certainly wouldn't want to be a guest of Uncle Ruho's for any reason.

The walls of the staircase are lined with family photos. I see Bithia, Gilad, the girl who held the silver blanket (Tabby, I assume), the white-haired boy, and an older, teenage boy I haven't met yet. In one picture, they smile hugely, hands upon one another's shoulders. Each child has Gilad's dauntingly large, gleaming teeth.

My family doesn't have any pictures like these. Not many people own cameras, and it's considered prideful to display photographs of oneself in one's home. Still, I wish I had a picture of me and Nana together.

"Mama says you should sit down at the table," a voice says.

The white-haired boy stands at the base of the stairs. As soon as we make eye contact, he runs off again. Walking down from the landing, I discover a huge living room full of more furniture covered in flowered fabrics. An impressive dining room table stands solemnly in front of a vast picture window.

The scent of butter and something sweeter than bread makes me weak at the knees.

Sitting in one of the upholstered chairs at the enormous table, I look outside at Bithia's vibrant green lawn. The flowers that line the edges are so perfect, I wonder if they're plastic.

After a few minutes, Bithia appears. "Well, for goodness' sakes. Honey, we're all waiting for you in here!" She points behind her.

She isn't angry exactly, but she sounds like someone who expects things to go according to plan.

I stand. "I'm sorry," I say.

"Don't apologize. You didn't know," she says, waving me toward her.

I pass through a door into a huge kitchen. Every countertop is covered in food. On my left sits Bithia's entire family. They're crowded around a circular table that's much smaller than the one in the next room. Tabby and the little boy gape at me, while Gilad seems to stare right through me to the other side of the room. The teenage boy looks down at the table so that I can't see his face.

As if sensing my confusion, Bithia says, "We only use the dining room table for special occasions."

"Nice, Mom," says Tabby. "Now she feels totally un-special." Tabby has white-blonde hair like her little brother. It's short above her eyes, but long and straight on the sides. Light dances off of it like liquid, and I find it mesmerizing. Her eyes seem kind of small for her large mouth and teeth, but her nose is turned up and adorable. She wears a short-sleeved canary yellow blouse that compliments her long alabaster arms. Overall, I think she would fetch a very large bride price.

"Oh, dear. I'm sorry," says Bithia. "Was that rude of me? We can go eat in the dining room if you'd prefer."

I shake my head. There's so much food on the table it would take twenty minutes to move it.

"I'm hungry *now*!" says the white-haired boy.

"Cornelius, mind your manners." Bithia gives him a threatening look.

"Yeah, Corny, shut your trap," says Tabby.

"Don't call me Corny!" he screeches. "Mom!"

"Not today, Tabitha, *please*!" Bithia says.

Gilad doesn't seem to hear the shrieking. He stares silently into the kitchen with a contented smile on his face, and I wonder if maybe there's something wrong with him.

"What is she wearing?" says Tabby, suppressing a laugh. "She's dressed like it's the middle of *winter*."

She and her brothers look me up and down, taking in the pants and huge sweater. These are Tabby's clothes, so why is she ridiculing me?

"That's Dad's sweater," Cornelius adds disapprovingly.

The teenage boy says nothing, studying me closely as he bites his nails. He has the same light hair as Tabby and Cornelius, but not quite as white. His eyes are hazel, and his lashes are so long and thick that, for a moment, I'm struck by the thought that he's prettier than his sister. His T-shirt is the same awful green as my pants.

"The important thing is that the clothes are clean," says Bithia. "Now, say 'Good morning' to . . ." She turns to me, frowning. "Honey, we don't even know your name. Do you have a name?"

"*Of course* she has a name, Mom. She's not a *stray dog*," Tabby says.

I'm shocked at the tone Tabby uses with her family. At home, her sarcasm would get me a smack.

"Mom, can we get a dog?" says Cornelius.

"No," says Bithia. She guides me into the chair next to Tabby. "Sit here, dear."

Tabby rolls her eyes. I'm wondering if the teenage boy is as irritated by my presence as Tabby appears to be, when he leans over and whispers, "I'm Silas."

Silas? The one who made the pancakes? When I try to imagine Dekker cooking, all I can picture is a pan on fire and Dekker with no eyebrows.

Silas's voice is serene among the chaos of the others.

"I'm Mina," I say.

"That's a lovely name!" says Bithia. "Isn't that a nice name?" she asks no one in particular.

Bithia takes her seat and grabs the hands of Silas and Cornelius, who sit on either side of her. She looks at Gilad, who continues to stare off into space. Bithia clears her throat, but Gilad doesn't move. "Gilad!" she cries, and he jumps.

"Turn that thing off!" Bithia says. "We have company for goodness' sakes."

Gilad blinks slowly twice then turns to face his family. "Good morning."

They all repeat, "Good morning."

He looks me up and down, frowning. "Are you better now?"

I'm about to tell him that nothing was ever wrong with me, when Bithia says, "She's fine, aren't you dear?"

"I'm . . . uh . . . hungry, I guess," I say.

"You talk funny!" Cornelius announces from across the table.

"The feeling is mutual," I say.

He's confused but turns out his bottom lip as my meaning sinks in.

Gilad reaches for Tabby's and Cornelius' hands. I understand that we are forming a circle, like when we pray at home.

When we are linked, Gilad begins: "May the Unbound flourish and may we serve the Lord as well as he serves us. So be it."

The family repeats, "So be it," and then we let go of one another's hands.

I thought the Apostates didn't believe in God or the Prophet. It's strange to hear them praying, when I grew up believing they would spit on the Book. *But what if they're praying to Satan or some other horrible demon?* Shivers run up my spine.

"Pass the syrup, please!" says Cornelius.

"You don't even have pancakes yet," Bithia says, laughing.

She hands him a small pitcher of amber liquid, while passing Gilad a stack of golden pancakes.

"I'm getting ready," says Cornelius, dipping his finger into the pitcher and then licking off the sticky substance.

"Gross!" says Tabby, filling her plate with food.

"Children," says Gilad. "Let's please show our guest we know how to be civilized."

"Why? She's the savage one," says Cornelius.

"Cornelius!" Bithia and Gilad both shout. Turning pink, Bithia adds, "Nina, we apologize. Corny is only four, and he has no idea what he's saying half the time."

"Don't call me Corny!" the boy wails.

"I'm going to send you upstairs in about two seconds," Gilad tells him, voice severe.

Corny becomes still, and an awkward silence falls over the table.

"What's this mood about today, Gilad?" asks Bithia, passing a tray of bacon. "You've had a lemon-face all morning."

"The Elder meeting this afternoon. We were supposed to be discussing the treaty and now . . ." He glances at me. "We'll be discussing something else."

Bithia indicates me in a much less subtle way and then gives her husband a look of sympathy. "Surely today's business is more important."

Gilad tenses. "Nothing is more important than this treaty and supporting Ram's efforts. Too many people would be happy to see it fail."

"Why, Dad?" says Corny.

"We'll talk about it later, kiddo." Gilad winks at him.

I concentrate on my food, which I confess is delicious. The pancakes melt in my mouth. There's also crispy bacon, potatoes, sausage, and fresh orange juice. Bithia offers me seconds and thirds, and everyone keeps eating until no one seems to have the energy to lift a fork. The Apostates don't seem to be experiencing any kind of food shortage.

"Tabby, after breakfast," Bithia says, "I want you to take Nina to the Leisure Center."

"But I'm meeting Phoebe and Deborah!" Tabby says.

"She should be socializing. Take her with you."

Tabby looks at her father for help, but he says, "Do as your mother says."

Tabby stands abruptly, sending her chair clanging backward. "Fine." She marches out of the kitchen.

"Good luck," whispers Silas, laughing to himself.

"What about my friends?" I ask Bithia.

Bithia looks at Gilad, a frustrated look in her eyes. If she thought a hot meal would distract me, *she was wrong*.

Gilad turns to me. "We have a certain way of doing things in Kingsboro, Nina."

"Mina," says Silas.

"And we've been doing things this way for a long, long time and it works for us. We like it. And we think, eventually, you'll like it. So you're just going to have to trust us that our way is the best way."

I have no idea what he's just said. It was a lot of words, but they had no real meaning. "When will I see my friends?" I ask.

Bithia sighs as if the whole breakfast has been a disaster. Standing, she begins to gather the dirty dishes from the table and put them into a wonderful machine I later learn is called a *dishwasher*.

"You will see your friends," Gilad says, "when we say it is time to see your friends."

My body stiffens. Who are these people to say what I can or cannot do? I don't see any guns or weapons in this house. *I could just run*. I just have to reach the front door before anyone else . . .

Silas, on my left, murmurs, "It's not worth it. The sirens will sound, and you won't make it past the lawn."

I look at him, disconcerted. "How did you—?"

"You're tense as a violin string," he whispers. "And if I were you, I'd be thinking the same thing."

Oh.

"Go to the Leisure Center," Gilad says, in a reasonable voice. "Make Bithia happy. It's the quickest way to see your friends. Really." He smiles, his eyes disappearing into his thick cheeks. "This is going to be a glorious day, Nina. Today is the day that you get to meet Ram."

Bithia mentioned Ram. "Who is he?"

"He's no one. And everyone. He's the leader of our people, the Unbound. And he's going to explain it all to you, and you won't feel as confused as you do right now. Ram is the one who will show you the truth."

So Gilad is not in charge. He still hasn't told me why I'm staying in his home.

Gilad clenches his hands together under his chin and gives me a pitying look. "Nina, I'm sorry to tell you this, but your entire life until this day has been a lie."

THREE

Back in the bedroom, Tabby waits on the bed, towel in hand. "You should shower," she says.

I'm mortified. We spent a long time in the water in the tunnel, and it didn't smell very good. I'm sure I'm disgusting.

"You're probably used to only bathing once a week, right?"

"No, I—"

"Come and find me when you're done," she says, shoving the towel in my hand. She walks out before I can say anything else.

The shower is an intimidating contraption that has doors that slide open like an elevator's. With its slick white walls, it looks more like something that a Twitcher would use as a charging station than it does something for washing. I'm excited, though, because I assume that, like the Ashers, the Dixons will have instant hot water.

Once I'm inside, the doors shut swiftly. I'm baffled to find buttons instead of handles. They're numbered 1, 2, and 3.

Having no better ideas, I press 1.

Hot water comes shooting at me from every direction. I hop in alarm, as the spurting drops hit me like pebbles. Water permeating my nose and eyes, I reach out and hold down the number 2 button.

Immediately, the water changes from scalding to freezing. I cry out and try to step out of the shooting stream, but there seems to be no place to hide within the box. Once again, my nose fills with water and begins to burn. I choke.

Images of Damon flash through my mind: He's trying to swim; he can't breathe; he sinks, lifeless.

Desperate, I try to pull the doors open, but they won't budge. I don't see an exit button. Goose pimples covering every inch of my pale skin, I hit the only button left: 3.

A creamy yellow substance replaces the cold water. It coats my skin like goat's milk on a raw chicken leg. I'm frightened by what the liquid could be but relieved that it's at least warmer than the water. I shut my eyes and mouth as the sprayers reach my head. The sharp smell of something chemical lingers as the machine stops.

As the goopy mess swirls down the drain, the doors of the shower open. I dart out while I can, grabbing my towel. I wipe as much of the yellow stuff off as possible and then stand wrapped in the fluffy towel, teeth chattering. That was the worst shower ever. Not only did I feel pummeled, I never even had the chance to use soap!

I must have used it incorrectly. I want to ask Tabby about it, but I dread the look of disdain she'll give me.

When she returns, I'm dressed in the same outfit as this morning. She shakes her head, dragging me to the closet.

We have a difficult time finding an outfit that pleases us both. She wants me to wear shorts or a skirt, but I refuse to show so much skin. I want to keep on the large sweater, but Tabby insists that it's meant for a man and will make me—and by association her—look stupid.

"You can keep on the turtleneck if you want, but you're going to die of heatstroke," she says.

She's talking about my top with the tall neck, I guess. It fits tightly across my chest and I can't possibly leave the house wearing nothing over it. "Do you have another long sleeve top that might be looser?"

She chews her lip, sorting through the clothes one more time. She holds up a silky blouse. "How about this?"

It's loose but has no sleeves. I shake my head and she sighs.

"This one?" She holds up a shirt that looks exactly like the last one.

"I'd like to, uh, cover my arms, please."

"Oh. Is that like, a Prophet thing?" she asks, now a little more interested.

"I would just feel more comfortable . . . ."

"Whatever," she says, losing interest again. She grabs a long-sleeved shirt with a V-neck and hands it to me. "This should be fine." She walks out of the closet, so I guess we're finished.

I change into the shirt, which is the softest thing I've ever touched, and leave on the yellow-green "jeans," as Tabby calls them. She gives me a once-over. "We have to do something about your hair."

I touch my wet head self-consciously.

"For now, let's just put it back. Come here." She directs me to sit on the floor in front of the bed. Sitting right behind me, she proceeds to braid my hair.

As she pulls and tugs each strand, I feel her working out her frustration through her fingers. I wish I had the nerve to ask why she dislikes me so much. Is it me or all people from Manhattan? "All done!" she says, standing and heading for the door. "Let's get this over with."

When Tabby opens the front door, it isn't locked, and when we step outside the house, I see no guards. I had expected, at the very least, to see Jeremiah looming on the edge of the lawn with his enormous gun.

But there is no one but me, Tabby, and the birds in the trees. Maybe I shouldn't be surprised after what happened with Beth. It took seconds for her to sound the alarm that brought people running from every direction. Why shouldn't Tabby have the same power?

She walks several steps in front of me, shoulders back and head held high, her yellow blouse and skirt glowing in the morning sun. She's annoyed to be taking me wherever it is that we're going, but I wonder if she's normally a happy person. It's hard to imagine anything in this beautiful place that could make her unhappy.

We walk past house after house that looks just like Gilad and Bithia's, each a different color. Even the flowerbeds out front look exactly the same. *Everyone* here must be rich; I've never known anyone with a lawn. The streets and sidewalks seem brand-new, without any cracks or potholes.

The sky seems immense—a never-ending expanse of electric blue. How could it be bigger when I've only crossed a river?

The skyscrapers. They aren't here to block the view. Turning all the way around, I'm startled to see Manhattan in the distance.

The Wall doesn't seem so high from here—buildings jut out from it in a jagged pattern, and I'm struck by how black and gray the city looks, like a burnt-out stove left on the street to rot. In comparison, the town I'm standing in feels like a page in one of Dekker's coloring books.

A loud banging comes from the next street, and I whirl around to see a garbage truck. It's a much newer and cleaner version of the ones we have at home. Both the garbagemen are actually garbage*women*, with short-cropped hair and blue jump-suits. I've never seen a woman collect trash in my life.

Perhaps there are many job opportunities here for women. I allow myself a tiny drop of hope, like a dab of forbidden perfume.

As we walk out of range of the loud truck, I notice a low buzz, almost like the sound of the Ashers' air conditioner.

I stop walking. I look at the nearest house, wondering if it's coming from within.

"What's wrong?" says Tabby.

"What's that noise?"

"What noise?" she says, losing patience.

"It's like humming," I say. "It's sort of like . . ." And then, remembering Beth and the machine with the peach, I look up.

Hovering about five feet over my head is the biggest bug I've ever seen. I instinctively jump toward Tabby. The bug jumps with me, staying high above.

"*What is that?*" I ask, frightened.

Tabby takes a bored step away from me. "Did you think they'd just let you walk out the door? I wasn't allowed to go anywhere without a Bee until I was sixteen! And you're a woolie!"

"I'm a what?"

"I mean a refugee. Whatever."

Looking more closely, I see now that the insect-like object is a microscopic version of the flying contraption that we saw land yesterday. "What's it *doing*?" I ask.

"Don't freak out. It just keeps track of where you are, and you know, what you're doing. But it can't make a decision or anything. AI is against the law."

There are too many new words coming at me at once. What is AI? And *who* does this thing give its information to? "I'm feeling really uncomfortable right now," I say.

Sighing deeply (which she seems to do a lot), Tabby puts her hand on her hip. "I don't exactly *love* being your babysitter, but

Mom said I had to take you to the Leisure Center, so that's what I'm doing. Can we please make it quick?"

I look up at the "Bee." Are people watching us right now, seeing me refuse to walk any farther with Tabby?

"What is the Leisure Center?" I ask, picturing something like a bathhouse.

"It's kind of benny, I guess. It's where everyone hangs most of the time. You can eat or shop or commune."

I'm not sure what "benny" is, but by her tone, I'm guessing it means "good," or "fine."

She brushes her bangs out of her eyes. "I think Mom wants you to, you know, socialize, or whatever."

On the one hand, I have no desire to be around a bunch of Apostates. So far, their behavior has been extremely unpredictable, making me feel guarded and unsafe. But on the other hand, Bithia said that Grace and the others were staying with different families. So maybe someone will take one of *them* to the Leisure Center, too.

"Okay," I say. "We can go."

"Gee, thanks," Tabby says, turning to walk again.

I follow, the hum of the Bee setting my teeth on edge.

"You'd better get your act together," Tabby says. "Or you're never going to get out of those horrible green clothes."

I have no idea what she means, but I'm too overwhelmed to ask.

I've never seen anything like the Leisure Center. It's as big as Lincoln Center and the entire thing seems to be built of glass. The building is several stories tall, but all I can concentrate on is the atrium, which could hold twenty buses.

Seeing hundreds of people milling around inside, I'm

tempted to turn and run; but reminding myself that Juda could be inside, I walk through the enormous glass door with Tabby.

I'm sorry to see that my Bee has swept in right behind me. Looking up, I see a stunning crisscross of metal beams, but the whole space is open to the sky. Trees and greenery line the edges of the room, and roses climb up the walls. How are they growing roses on glass?

My Bee has ample room to hover above my head. I notice a handful of other Bees suspended in the air over the crowd, and my breath catches. *Maybe they're monitoring the others.*

"Let's head to the food hall," Tabby says.

She plows straight into the throng of people. While making sure not to lose her, I scan the faces around me, desperate to see Grace, Juda, or Rose. At this point, I'd even be happy to see Dekker.

I quickly realize that while I'm trying to be subtle about looking at people, everyone is gaping at *me*. Conversations near me all seem to cease, and I see a woman point at me, whispering to the man next to her.

"Why is everyone staring at me?" I ask Tabby, wondering if I should've taken more of her advice on what to wear.

She looks around, then keeps walking. "You're one of the Manhattan Five," she says.

"Huh?"

"You can't pop out of a subway tunnel, say you're a Propheteer, and not expect to get famous."

I don't like the way people are looking at me. Some of them have pity on their faces; others look angry; and others look like they're studying an exotic food they've never tasted before. Worst of all—none of them seem to realize that I can *see* them studying me.

Tabby slows down and walks taller under the scrutiny of the crowd, and I could swear she sticks her breasts out a little.

"Let's get compressions," she says as we reach the end of the room.

I deflate with disappointment. Every other Bee I saw in the atrium was monitoring children or frail-looking old people. My friends are nowhere in sight.

Tabby takes me down a tunnel with a set of moving stairs, just like the ones in our prayer center, except these still move! I get a little nervous stepping on and can see that Tabby wants to laugh at me. My Bee stays behind in the atrium.

Tabby notices me watching it. "They aren't allowed indoors," she says. "They tried it for a while and people *hated* it. Can you imagine it, like, hovering there while you tried to sleep? How feeble."

When we reach the bottom, I exit the stairs ungracefully. Hundreds of people sit at tables, eating, talking, and laughing. The noise is overpowering.

A blast of cold air jolts me like ice cubes going down the back of my shirt. This giant space has *air-conditioning*. I wish I had my cloak.

Past the tables are different food stalls. It looks like the Union Square market, but if the stalls were all made of glass and the pavement were shiny marble. Once again, men, women, and children stop talking to stare at me. I stare back, hoping they'll realize how disrespectful they're being.

Tabby smiles and in a sweet voice says, "I think a compression would be perfect, Mina. It's scrunched up fruit and pure vitamin infusions and should make you feel much better!"

I never said I felt bad. "I'm not hungry." How could anyone eat a thing after the breakfast we just had?

She glides across the room, flipping her hair. She may not like me, but she's decided she likes the attention I'm bringing her.

She stops at a stall that looks like an enormous glass strawberry. Behind the counter, a skinny boy with pimply skin and upswept hair gapes at me, then at Tabby.

"We'll have two mango ruby vitamin-D magnesium compressions, please," says Tabby.

"Uh, okay," the boy says.

"Isn't it great how actual people wait on you here?" Tabby says, watching the boy move around his stall. "Out west, some computer would just spit your food out at you. It isn't natural."

A family of six stops eating so they can ogle me.

"It's really rude how everyone keeps staring at you," Tabby says. She leans her elbows on the counter, giving everyone in the room a nice view of her bottom.

At home, her behavior would get her several lashings, if not a few days in the Tunnel, but no one seems appalled by her. The men aren't experiencing uncontrollable lust, the women aren't shaking their heads in judgment, and no Matrons are coming over to shock her with a silver tube. In fact, everyone is ignoring her to keep staring at me.

Besides the fact that they are gaping at me, something about the Apostates has been bothering me, and I've finally realized what it is: Everyone is white. All the faces looking at me essentially look the same: pale with light eyes. Is all of Kingsboro like this?

The people of Manhattan are indescribably diverse, with every kind of eye, ear, nose, neck, body, skin tone, and voice you can imagine. With discomfort, I realize that with my blonde hair, I look pretty similar to the Apostates.

Two girls approach us. They wear bright yellow clothing, just like Tabby. One girl has green eyes and wavy black hair and the other has a long face and short brown hair cut like a boy's. They're both white, like everyone else.

"Tabby, no way. Got your nod!" says one.

"Is this her?" says the other.

Tabby looks at the girl with black hair like she's a moron. "What do you think, Deborah?"

"Whoa. Weird."

"Right?" says Tabby.

Do they think I can't hear them?

"Mom said I had to bring her with," says Tabby, rolling her eyes.

"I think it's benny," says the brown-haired girl. "Everyone's talking about it."

"Really?" Tabby says, as if she's not interested. "Cute top, Phoebe."

Phoebe's face lights up. "Thanks, Tabs!"

To me, Phoebe's blouse looks identical to Tabby's, but I guess I'm missing something. I don't know why anyone would want to wear such little clothing when it's so cold inside.

Phoebe and Deborah slowly look me up and down, and I feel as scrutinized as if they had Senscans.

I wish I had the nerve to ask if they knew where my friends were, but I can only imagine this would lead to more contempt from Tabby.

The boy behind the counter announces, "Your compressions are ready." He shyly hands us metal cups that look a foot tall. Mine is so cold I can barely hold it in my hands.

After a few greedy sucks on her straw, Tabby says, "What's wrong? Aren't you gonna try it?"

I take a sip, and although it is fruity and sweet, I don't want it. I'm still full from breakfast, and the drink makes me shiver. I don't want to be rude, and I don't want to be wasteful, so I slurp down more, trying to smile.

I keep drinking until I feel a bit sick. Then I remember Mrs. Asher and how I drank her champagne because I was afraid of being rude. *I can't believe I just did it again.* I stop drinking. Tabby's attention is no longer on me anyway.

The boy tells Tabby a price and she waves her hand over the counter. After the enormous glass strawberry flickers with a pink light, the boy says, "Thank you."

She runs her fingers through her bangs, giving him a big smile. When she's not frowning, she's really pretty.

The boy blushes, reminding me of how nervous I get around Juda. He must like Tabby a lot.

Turning away from him, she tells her friends, "Let's find a table." She grabs a napkin and another straw. They begin to meander through the crowd looking for a place to sit. Assuming I have little choice, I follow them. They find an abandoned table at the edge of the crowd. I'm happy to put down the cold compression.

Deborah and Phoebe soon notice everyone gawking at me.

"Whoa, this is intense," says Deborah.

"Yeah," says Phoebe. "It's like how everyone stares at you at Promise Prom."

"How would you know?" says Tabby.

"I mean, like, how it must be," says Phoebe, looking away.

Smirking at Phoebe, Deborah turns to me and asks in an accusing tone, "Why are you wearing green?"

"I don't . . . Tabby loaned her clothes to me," I say.

She looks at Tabby like she's done something wrong. Tabby shrugs. "Mom said it was fine until she meets Ram."

"It seems weird, since she hasn't earned it, you know?" says Deborah.

"Yeah, but would you want to be her age wearing white? How embarrassing," says Phoebe.

After making a face suggesting the thought is nauseating, Deborah asks me, "How do you like Tabby's old clothes?"

Still overwhelmed by the reek of Tabby's perfume, I try to think of something nice to say. "They're very soft."

Phoebe's eyes get wide. "Holy moly. I bet the Propheteers don't even *have* spider silk yet!"

I sit back in my chair, touching my shirt. "Spiders made this?" I shudder, thinking of a factory full of thousands and thousands of spiders.

The three girls smile. Tabby says, "Yeps. It takes them years to make one piece of clothing."

"Th-that's amazing," I say, still horrified. "Please don't ever take me to wherever they do that."

They all giggle. "Don't worry," Tabby says. "We won't."

Deborah turns to Tabby, excited. "What are you wearing to Promise Prom, Tabs?"

Tabby runs her fingers through her hair. "I haven't decided yet."

Phoebe and Deborah are scandalized.

"It's *three* days away!" says Phoebe.

"Gee, thanks for the calendar update," says Tabby.

"You, have, like, a few things to choose from, right?" asks Deborah gravely, as if Tabby needs to choose between medications to save her life.

Tabby raises an eyebrow, saying nothing.

"Of course she does!" says Phoebe, relieved.

Deborah grins hugely. "My dress is fuchsia, and it's major razzmatazz."

I have a headache, and I don't know if it's from the frozen drink or the fluctuating conversation. It's like listening to squirrels discuss nut recipes. I tune out the girls and take in the room.

Lots of teenagers wear the bright yellow of the girls next to me. Some wear crimson. The adults seem to be wearing darker colors: blues, purples, and grays. What does it all mean?

I lock eyes with a man who's glaring at me with disapproval. Many people are inspecting me, but he's scowling as if he's spotted a destructive new weed in his garden. Unlike all the

Apostates I've seen so far, this man is very disheveled: His hair is white and uncombed; he hasn't shaved in several days; and his skin is awful—ruddy and pitted. Is he ill? Should he be here?

His hostile inspection makes me squirm. "Who is that?" I ask, interrupting the girls.

They turn to look.

"Who?" asks Phoebe.

The one who appears to want to stone me for being alive? "The one with the red skin," I say.

Phoebe goes quiet as Tabby tries not to laugh.

"That's my dad," says Deborah, voice going icy. "He wouldn't let me come here alone."

That's her father? He looks like a homeless man.

"Why not?" Tabby asks her, giggling. "We're surrounded by, like, hundreds of people."

"Yeah, but," Deborah says, giving me the side eye. "No one knows what she's capable of."

I almost laugh out loud. Should I bare my teeth at her?

In a voice barely above a whisper, Phoebe says, "Ram says helping our neighbors is one of our greatest callings."

Deborah leans forward, pointing at Phoebe and Tabby. "You're my neighbor, and you're my neighbor." She jabs a thumb in my direction. "This woolie is not my neighbor."

"Deb, just be benny," Tabby says, her voice clear and forceful. "Don't make a scene or everyone will think we're completely feeble."

Deborah sits back with an eye roll, admonished.

"Phoebe, what color do you think looks best on me?" Tabby says, changing the subject. Phoebe enthusiastically launches into an answer.

Resolved to ignore Deborah's father, I look around at the other tables, wondering if there are other parents worried about their children's safety. What do they think I might do? Put a curse on them? Convert them?

I'm wondering how much longer we have to stay here when my breath catches. On the far side of the room, I see the curly mop of hair that is unmistakably Grace's.

Her back is turned, but in addition to the hair, I recognize the stooped, self-conscious way of sitting that she has. She's seated with parents that look a lot like Tabby's: plump and pink with gleaming white smiles.

I stand, saying a small prayer to the Prophet: *Make Grace turn around. Please let her see me. Please!*

"Hey, what's she doing?" says Deborah.

"Do you need something?" asks Tabby.

I'm wondering what kind of scene I'll make, if everyone in the food hall will panic if I run across the room. Deborah might slam me to the ground.

"Is there a problem?" Tabby says, agitated.

"No . . . I . . . ." I don't know what to say, but I'm not going to sit back down. *Turn around, Grace!*

"The little girl's room is over there," says Phoebe, pointing toward the metal stairs.

Little girl's room? Is that a special room where young girls gather?

Seeing my confusion, Tabby says, "She's talking about the bathroom. Jeez."

"Oh," I say. "Thank you." Phoebe giggles.

I walk toward the stairs, which will take me right by Grace's table.

I have to pass by Deborah's dad. He keeps his eyes glued to mine, and when I walk by, he mutters something that I can't understand. By the tone, I understand that it wasn't nice.

I try not to stare directly at Grace, but I can't help it. What will I say? *Peace? Nice to see you?* Will the people at her table try to keep us from speaking? My heart pummels my chest like it's trying to break free.

I remember the question I've been dying to ask her: *How is your Nancy Drew book? Did it get ruined in the subway tunnel?*

I'm about ten feet away from her table, when Grace suddenly looks over her shoulder and locks eyes with me.

I feel faint. Tears come to my eyes, as I realize it isn't her. It's not Grace. This girl is much older and is looking at me with alarm.

I pass her table and keep walking.

Inside the bathroom, the sound of chatter and laughter from the hall penetrates the door. My tiny moment of hope has caused a new despair. Loneliness and dread envelope me.

Where are my friends? Remembering the look of abhorrence on Deborah's father's face, I have to wonder, are they even alive?

FOUR

On the walk home, I try to make note of certain houses, streets and numbers. I want to understand where I am. When the moment comes to break away from the Dixons, I have to be ready. I'm starting to appreciate the bright colors that everyone paints their houses, because without color, the buildings and streets look exactly alike.

The heat seems different here than in Manhattan. I'm not used to feeling the sun directly on my skin. At first, the warmth was a relief after the frigid food hall, but now I feel overly exposed, like a newborn being held too close to the furnace.

The air smells different, too, mostly in that it doesn't smell like anything. At home, a person is assaulted with scents every block—horses, uncollected garbage, spices at the market, the homeless. Not to mention the noise—the busses and cars, the people, the Bell.

It occurs to me that walking through Kingsboro, with its lack of sounds and smells, is like being locked up in the Ashers' guest room. What is it with rich people that they're so determined to shut out the world? I shudder thinking of an entire town of Ashers.

By the time we arrive back at the Dixons' purple house, I'm hot and sticky. Tabby looks fresh and dry. The good news is that I'm fairly confident I could find my way back to the Leisure Center. Ditching my Bee is a whole other problem.

When we walk through the front door, I'm surprised to find the living room filled with people. Rushing forward from a cluster of guests, Bithia embraces me. "Welcome home, Nina!"

"Mina, Mom. Her name is Mina," Tabby says. I'm surprised Tabby remembers.

"Do you girls need something to eat?" Bithia asks.

"No thanks. We had compressions," Tabby says. My stomach turns a little at the memory.

Gilad emerges from the group. "Come and meet everyone," he says, taking my shoulder and guiding me to the middle of the room. It's a gathering of around twenty men and women, mostly old people wearing gray or white, smiling at me with sympathy, as if they've heard I have an incurable disease.

One of the younger faces belongs to Jeremiah. He has no weapon, but he still looks intimidating—thickset with a torso like an upside-down triangle. His black hair and blue eyes would make him handsome if he didn't look ready to eat metal.

Two women standing in front of a couch quickly divide to make room for me. They seem to want me to sit down, but the men are standing, so I'm not sure what to do.

Bithia says, "Don't you want to sit down? Do you need to make a pee-pee first?"

I wish I could crawl under the sofa.

"She's not a baby, Mom. Jeez," says Tabby. "You don't have to talk to her like she's Corny."

For once, I like Tabby.

"Sorry, dear," Bithia says, looking around at the others as if she's offended them and not me.

"Let's all sit down, shall we?" says Gilad.

As we sit, Tabby heads for the stairs, saying, "I've got a lot to do for Prom, so . . ."

"No, Tabby. You'll stay," says Gilad. "This will be good for everyone."

Sighing one of her sighs, Tabby comes to the couch and rests on the arm, ready to bolt as soon as possible.

A bald man in glasses opens a book bound in beautiful red leather. His head is oddly shaped, with skin that's tight on top and loose and saggy at the bottom, like a partly deflated balloon.

He reads aloud. Everyone says the words along with him, including Tabby. Before long, he says, "So be it," closing the book. The others repeat, "So be it," and then relax back into the chairs and sofa. All eyes turn to me in question, but I have nothing to say.

Bithia giggles nervously. "How was the Leisure Center, Mina?"

I say what I hope will get me out of the room the fastest: "It was nice, thank you."

They all nod in approval.

The bald man says, "You have seen what our people can supply: community, safety, comfort, *ample* provisions. Life here is beyond compare."

A woman clears her throat.

The bald man chuckles. "Yes, Marjory. Life here is *almost* beyond compare, but we'll get to that soon enough." He smiles at me, and the baggy skin under his chin wobbles.

This is Ram, I assume, their leader. How can his people listen to him without staring at his jelly neck?

"Don't you look nice in green!" says a woman with big lips and long auburn hair.

Out of the corner of my eye, I see Tabby snicker. She and her friends made it quite clear that they think the color I'm wearing is repellent.

The woman called Marjory wears a white skirt, white blouse, and white cardigan. She has a perfectly clipped gray bob and sits with her back ramrod straight. She says, "How happy you must be to finally be free of that veil."

Everyone continues to gaze at me, but the smiles have disappeared, replaced with unconcealed curiosity.

Anyone would know from Marjory's tone that she expects me to agree with her and say, "Yes, I'm very happy to be free of my veil." But is it true? Ayan and Rayna would be happy that I'm walking around without it. Nana would probably be proud and a little jealous. But I don't know how I feel about it yet. I know I hated being in the Leisure Center with everyone gaping at my face.

Ayan was certain that the veil was about men's lust. But I was also taught that it was about being humble before God. And isn't it good to be humble? I've started to feel that coming to Queens was very self-important and that maybe God is punishing me. I'm longing for my cloak and veil, to pray on my own and commune with the Prophet. I know from Beth's question when we arrived that believing in the Prophet is not a good thing. Is my bedroom private enough for me to pray there? Or will the Dixons always be watching me?

Everyone is waiting for my answer. I give them a piece of truth. "I like the freedom of seeing things more clearly."

They all nod in a knowing way, as if I mean more than having better peripheral vision. I want to add: I just wish you couldn't see *me* so clearly.

"I think we should introduce ourselves," says the woman with the red hair, smiling enthusiastically. "I'll go first. Hello, Mina. I'm Rachel. I'm one year Gray. I'm the mother of four children—

two Whites and two Greens." She smiles and looks to her left at Jeremiah.

Looking not at me but straight ahead, he says, "My name is Jeremiah Benjamin. I'm eight years Blue." He speaks in a monotone voice, as if giving his information to a superior. "I'm a Sentry, like my father, and my father's father. Next week, I'll take my Black exam."

"He's taking it much earlier than most people," says a pretty older woman sitting across from him. Her bright indigo eyes shine with pride. She has silver hair and a lovely complexion. "I suppose I should go next. I'm Jeremiah's mother, Naomi. My husband is sorry he couldn't be here today, but he's patrolling the perimeter. We're both just so proud of Jeremiah we could burst!"

Jeremiah remains stone-faced, but I perceive the smallest twitch of annoyance on his lips.

"You're forgetting something," mumbles Marjory.

"Oh!" Naomi says, becoming more sedate. "I'm ten years Gray and my husband is two years White. I'm also the mother of a Green."

Marjory nods, satisfied. And then—I didn't think it was possible—she sits up straighter. "I'm Marjory, ten years White. I'm the assistant bookkeeper in the head office, and I lead a devotion group on Friday nights. My husband was Marcus and he's dead." She looks around the room as if someone might challenge her on this fact. "I live in the very simple blue house on the corner."

"Marjory, you sure take pride in not being proud," a high and surprisingly squeaky voice says. The comment has come from a man sitting across from me in an overstuffed chair. I hadn't noticed him before. He has tight curly hair and large gray eyes. He's small and boyish in stature, but something about the way he holds himself tells me he must be kind of old.

The room has gone quiet as people look at one another, and,

as the moment stretches out, I wonder if Marjory or the squeaky-voiced man is in trouble. At home, it would automatically be the woman, but I have no idea here.

To my astonishment, Naomi bursts out laughing. Then the bald man joins her, and then Rachel, and soon everyone is laughing. Even Marjory manages a smile. What just happened?

"Oh, Ram, you are such a tease," says Rachel.

The curly-haired man smiles mischievously.

This is Ram? Their great leader? The one that Bithia needed to consult before she could tell me anything? Sitting in the overstuffed chair, with his feet not touching the ground, he looks like a teenage boy who missed his growth spurt.

Ram gives me a playful grin. I try to return his look with a neutral expression, but I'm sure my mouth is agape.

"Maybe it's time for Mina to introduce herself," he says.

I don't know what to say.

Everyone leans forward in their seats.

"I'm Mina. Peace," I say. This doesn't sound right. I think of the other answers. "I'm not married . . . and I don't have children."

Some of the women look surprised, and I see Rachel nudge her neighbor.

"Tell us about your parents, then," Ram says with warmth. "Your brothers and sisters."

I think of my father and his water plant. Has it been destroyed? Or did Uncle Ruho have Father arrested before he could do anything about the bad water? And Mother. I slapped her the last time I saw her.

"I don't want to talk about my parents."

Ram nods. "That's fine. You don't have to tell us anything."

Marjory gives him a stern look. "We need to know about the electricity, Ram."

Hopping out of his chair, Ram stands right in front of me. "I'm sure we're boring this young lady to death. I suggest that she and I go for a walk while the rest of you discuss permits, land-scaping, and other topics too tedious to mention."

The men and women who have not introduced themselves look disappointed.

Ram says, "Fret not. You'll see Mina again at the Worship Hub."

Everyone seems to cheer up. Why do they care about spending time with me? One minute they're shoving my face in the ground, and the next I'm the most popular party guest in town?

I look to Gilad to make sure he approves of me leaving with Ram. He's beaming with pride.

"Madame." Ram opens the front door, motioning for me to walk out in front of him. My Bee is waiting there, buzzing happily above our heads. Ram looks at it and makes a quick waving motion with his hand. Without hesitating, the Bee flies off into the sky.

"Where's it going?" I ask.

"To an enormous metal hive," says Ram.

"Really?" I say, amazed.

"I'm kidding," he says, smiling his mischievous grin again.

"Oh," I say. "You must think I'm pretty dumb."

His face gets serious. "Not at all. In fact, I think you are very smart and very brave. What you did to get here is truly incredible."

I'm surprised. I didn't think the Apostates had any idea of what we went through.

"You and your friends are extraordinary, and I look forward to getting to know each and every one of you." He clasps his hands together. "Let's walk. There's a lovely park down this way."

We take a different route than the one to the Leisure Center. This one involves more trees and dirt paths. Ram points out a few birds, and we even see a fox hiding in the grass. He can't believe I've never seen one before.

"Kingsboro has the greenest grass I've ever seen," I say, and it's true. Each blade is so green it's almost reflective.

"You have the Elders to thank for that. We paint every two months."

"Paint?" I ask, startled.

"We can't possibly use our water on such frivolities, but the Elders think the color is a spiritual booster. I wish I could say I hated it, but I confess, I love a crisp green lawn with a nice bed of roses, don't you?"

Still absorbing his words, I murmur, "Mmmhmm."

"What did you think of the Elders?" he asks.

Those were the Elders? "They were younger than I was expecting," I say.

He smiles. "Yes. 'Elders' suggests ninety-year-old men in togas, doesn't it? But they're just a little group that the town uses for advice. And Jeremiah isn't an Elder. He's there for security."

"Why?" I ask, nervous that I already know the answer.

"Some people are unsure about Propheteers and what you are capable of. Please forgive them. I find it ignorant and rude, but at least Jeremiah wasn't armed."

"There was a man today at the Leisure Center . . ." I say, unsure if I should mention him. "He seemed to hate me, and he's never even spoken to me."

"Was he a bit unkempt?" Ram says.

When I don't answer, he says, "It means 'messy.'"

Feeling foolish, I say, "Yes. He was messy."

"Mr. Tanner. Yes. He has a particular problem with Propheteers and my decision to give you refuge, but please, ignore him and any others. They won't bother you, I promise. You are under my personal protection, and they know it."

Protection from what?

We've reached a huge expanse of open green grass with a pond in the middle.

"This is Peace Pond," Ram says.

"It's beautiful," I admit. It's wonderfully still and quiet.

"I find it relaxing," he says. "I come here when I need to get away from people."

"Don't you like the people here?"

"Of course. I love them. But just because you love someone doesn't mean they can't annoy you." He grins.

"Why does Mr. Tanner dislike, uh, Propheteers?" The new word is awkward in my mouth.

"The same reason most people hate things—you're different, your culture is unknown. Maybe you want to change the way we do things."

"No, I—"

"Of course you don't, but Mr. Tanner can't see that. All he sees is something foreign that doesn't belong, like grit in his teeth or lice in his wayward hair."

Grit or lice? Ram is not making me feel better. "But the Elders don't feel the same way?"

"No, they don't. Especially since I told them how special you are." Becoming more serious, he walks closer to the water. "Two months ago, I had a dream I was crossing a bridge, and on the other side awaited a crowd of Propheteers. It took me a long time to get across, but when I finally did, one of the men in the crowd came forward and held out his hand for me to shake in solidarity. When I looked down, my own hand had disappeared. How could I possibly unify our cultures if I could not return the simplest gesture of reception? Then I heard God's voice, and He said, 'Fear not, for I am sending you a new hand, and it will lead the way to greater peace and prosperity.'"

After he looks at me for a while, I realize this is the end of the story.

"Don't you understand?" he asks, seeing my confusion. "You, the Manhattan Five, are my new hand—five new fingers! You will lead the way to peace and prosperity between our two people."

Ram is so excited about his interpretation of the dream that I feel it would be rude to contradict him. Do I believe in visions of the future? I'm not sure. I'm especially suspicious of them if they involve me.

"Let's rest." He leads me to a huge rock by the pond, and we both sit down. As his legs dangle over the side, I can't get over the feeling that I'm with a boy and not a man. "What I'm trying to tell you is, I'm glad you're here."

I give him a small smile.

"You don't have to pretend to be happy, Mina," he says. "I know things are difficult for you right now and that you miss your friends."

He seems genuine in his sadness for me, but isn't he the one keeping me away from them? He puts his hand on my shoulder. "Stop smiling. Stop acting as if everything is okay."

I open my mouth to protest, and, to my surprise, emit a smothered sob instead. Embarrassed, I try to keep tears from following.

"Let it out," he says. "Relax, stop pretending, and just let it all go."

I begin to cry for real, with hard gasping sobs, both from the relief of acknowledging that I'm miserable and from the deep frustration of people ignoring my questions.

"Just breathe deeply," he says. "Look at the water. It will make you feel better, I promise."

"I don't w-w-want to feel better. I want to see my friends."

"Of course you do," he says. "If I were you, I would want to see them too. I would want to rip apart every house until I found them. Is that how you feel?"

Is this a trick question? Is he testing me to see how violent I am?

"And I sure wouldn't trust anyone. Not me, not Bithia, or Gilad. Or Tabitha." He chuckles. "That Tabitha. What a piece of work. I hope your trip to the Leisure Center wasn't too unpleasant."

When I don't respond, he says, "Your friends are perfectly safe. They're being treated well and with great respect."

"Then why can't I see them?" I say, voice rising.

"I'm hoping that will be a bit more clear after our talk here today."

The world seems to stop as I wait for him to go on.

"Can you breathe deeply for me again, please?" He inhales loudly through his nostrils. Wiping my nose, I imitate him. "Thank you. If you don't breathe you'll pass out, and we can't have that." He smiles, but I am sick of his smile. I want an explanation.

He surprises me with his next question. "Who is the Prophet to you?"

I continue to breathe deeply.

"Don't worry. You're free to discuss Her here." He looks around as if to remind me we're alone. "I'd really like to know about your spiritual relationship with Her."

I've never had anyone ask me who the Prophet is to me specifically. I suppose I grew up thinking that She was the same for everyone. I thought that God, the Prophet, Uncle Ruho, and the Teachers were all equal. The more Nana and the Laurel Society taught me about Uncle Ruho, and the Teachers, and how they've twisted the Book, the more they all separated in my mind. The Prophet has remained sacred among all the power-grabbing men. "She is pure," I say, attempting to explain my thoughts. "She's my Divine Mother." Her first followers called Her this, and I've always liked it.

He nods. "That's nice. Thank you for sharing." His expression grows solemn. "I have to tell you some information, and it's delicate. It's important that you and each of your friends hear this information on your own, because for each of you, the right time will be different. The others will be ready soon, I think. Grace is sharp. But you, Mina, you're special. I think you're ready now."

How does this man know if I'm special or not? He's known me for less than an hour. But I smile in appreciation, because it sounds as if the sooner we all know his information, the sooner we can all be together again.

"Mina, your people have been lying to you. And I'm the one who's finally going to tell you the truth."

"Many, many years ago, our country was headed toward destruction. The leadership was corrupt and careless. They wouldn't listen to the people, and they only followed their own personal agendas. So the people revolted. Citizens gathered up their weapons, headed to the capital and threw those degenerates out. It was a time of great glory and celebration. The revolution had many great leaders, but one in particular rose to the forefront of the movement: Sarah Palmer."

"I know this story," I say. I've been told the story of the Dividing since birth.

"I know you do, but please indulge me." He keeps talking in his casual way. "She led the new government for many years and the people were happy. She understood that God's laws should precede state laws. Those who didn't agree fled to the West. It was a peaceful, golden time."

"And then She got pregnant," I say, wanting to hurry him up.

"Yes, She got pregnant. And She announced to Her followers that it was an *immaculate conception.*" He says these last two words with an odd tone. "And She started dressing modestly and covering Her hair, like women of long ago."

"And all the sinners and people who didn't believe in God tried to kill Her," I say. "And it led to another revolution, and to protect Her and the baby, our people had to move to Manhattan and blow up all the bridges so no one could bother us anymore."

"Here is what I need to tell you, Mina." He looks deep into my eyes. "It wasn't just sinners and atheists who didn't believe Sarah Palmer. Many of Her most devout followers didn't believe Her either. They thought She'd gone crazy with power and was using Her pregnancy as a way to become a dictator. As time went on, She was becoming more and more inflexible and Her believers more fanatical."

I shudder at his blasphemy. His high-pitched voice is grating on me.

"Most of Her original followers abandoned Her. Many people cried out for Her arrest, but Her status as a martyr would've become too great, so the people decided instead to grant Her and Her people a refuge."

I don't believe a word he's saying. Sarah's people never betrayed Her.

"She led Her remaining acolytes to Manhattan, and then Her enemies built a wall around the island, blocking them inside. They cut off the water and power . . ."

I look at him, starting to understand what he's saying.

His voice is grim. "They assumed that the Prophet and Her followers would die."

"But She didn't, because She was chosen by God," I say.

"What I'm trying to tell you, Mina, is that She wasn't chosen by God. She was an ordinary person like you or me, and She made up an extraordinary story that many people believed."

I want to cover my ears and scream, anything to tune him out.

I've lost Nana, Sekena, my father, and my friends, and now this man is trying to take away the Prophet, too.

"The good news," he continues, "is that we are not the monsters you believe us to be. The Unbound are simple people who believe in the word of God. We are the people who liberated this country from the sinners running the government. And you have a home here with us." He smiles.

"You walled up the Prophet and wanted Her to die?" I ask.

"Well, not us specifically. Our ancestors. And they didn't *want* her to die. They thought that her desire to be a supreme leader was dangerous and did what they could to stop it."

I stand but feel dizzy and sit down again.

He puts his hand on my shoulder. "You've had a shock. I should take you home."

I let him lead me away from the pond, and we walk slowly back toward the road.

I look for the fox we saw on the way here and then think about the pancakes I ate for breakfast. I can't focus on the story Ram has told me. It's too much. It threatens to crush me. As we walk, I put space between us, afraid he might start speaking again.

Ram says goodbye at the front door of the house. He's smiling, but his face is more serious than when we started our walk.

"I know I gave you a lot to think about. Please come see me if you need to talk. Everyone in town knows where to find me. Okay?"

I nod, seeing he's trying to be kind.

"Don't despair. All children must stumble before they can walk on their own."

Stepping lightly off the stoop, he saunters away.

What do I do now? What are you supposed to do when you hear that the center of your life is a fraud?

FIVE

I tell Bithia I need to lie down, and, although she has lunch prepared, she allows me to go straight to my room. From her pitying tone, I assume she knows what Ram told me.

Shutting the door to my bedroom, I wish I had my own clothes to change into. Anything in my closet would do—even my most hated elastic pants.

I take off the ugly green jeans and top and crawl into bed in my underwear. I pull the comforter up over my head. I want to disappear.

Do I have a fever? I feel like death.

Ram's story shouldn't surprise me. We were arrested for believing in the Prophet, so I knew that the Unbound weren't Her followers. So why was his story so disturbing?

Because he said that She is a fake, a mortal like any other. And if She's a fake, that makes Uncle Ruho, Her descendent, a fake too.

I *know* Uncle Ruho is a big, fat liar. He was poisoning his own people. What kind of "divine" being does that?

A small groan escapes my mouth. If Ruho is a liar, couldn't his great-grandmother have been a liar too?

I close my eyes and think about the Book, which talks about doubters. Miracles take great faith, and how can you say you have faith in God and then not believe in His miracles?

What if I refuse to believe Ram's story? Will he make me leave Kingsboro? Send me back to Manhattan?

I try to imagine life without the Prophet, without the ability to turn to Her each day when things are hard. It feels impossible, like giving up water. I've simply never known life without Her.

Or is that Nana? Whose voice do I really hear when I'm in trouble? I wonder what she would think of this story. I wish she were here to help me.

Does Ram understand what he's asking of me? Of Grace and Juda and the others? He wants us to risk damnation, an eternity of unspeakable suffering, based on one stupid story that he's told us.

Even as I have the thought, part of my brain is saying, *it's not stupid,* and I want to turn my brain OFF. What if She did lie about Her pregnancy, and it wasn't an immaculate conception? Who was the father? *Why* would She lie? To grab power in the way that Nana says men are always grabbing power?

I hate Ram. I hate him for putting this sliver of doubt in my faith, like a splinter left to fester.

I hate all the Unbound. They walk around thinking they're better than me. I can see it in their eyes. I could see it at the Leisure Center, and I could see it at the meeting downstairs.

Tabby and her friends think I'm some sort of idiot. What do they know about anything? They're mean and petty. They know nothing about real danger, or pain, or death.

I should never have left Nana. In the moment it felt like my only option, but could I have stayed? Grace, Rose, and I could've returned to Macy's, and the Laurel Society would've taken us in, but Dekker and Juda would have been turned away, and every Twitcher on the island was looking for them. They couldn't have stayed hidden for long.

How soon will the war begin? How long will it take for word to spread that Mr. Asher was poisoning the water? And how soon will the Convenes connect it to Uncle Ruho? Will they blame my father? Is he in danger?

Will I even know when the war starts? We seem so close, like I'll be able to hear it or feel it if a war begins, but that's silly. Hundreds of people could be dead, and I'd have no idea.

I'd like to take a hot shower to calm down, but I'm afraid of the slick white box and its shockingly cold water.

I need help. I want to talk to Juda. The thought of his absence causes me to curl into a tight ball.

I hear a knock, and then the door opens. I don't move, staying underneath the blanket.

Bithia whispers, "Mina?" When I don't answer, she gently places something on the bedside table.

After she's gone, I peek out and see it's a package wrapped in shiny paper. An envelope is taped on top, which I peel off and open.

The note inside reads,

Dearest Mina,
I know today is not the easiest of days, but I hope this gift might make your burden somewhat lighter. I am always here for you.
Yours in light,
Ram

Opening the pretty paper, I discover a thick book of worship. I flip through it randomly. Who knows what other parts of my faith will be refuted within these pages? I slam the book shut.

Is it time to run? Get as far away from this family and Ram

and the Bees as I possibly can? Where would I go? I don't even know how big Kingsboro is. Could I find people who would help me find my friends, or will everyone be the same as the Dixons?

I can't sleep all night, my mind spinning over what's happened and what my options are. I stare for hours at the vases full of roses and daisies, watching the flowers wilt in real time.

By morning I'm totally spent, a washrag squeezed dry, but I've come to some realizations:

1. I can't run away as long as Juda and the others are still here.
2. The Dixons aren't treating me badly or being cruel, so I should try to behave well so that doesn't change.
3. I can secretly continue to honor the Prophet in my heart, no matter what Ram teaches me about his own beliefs.

These revelations make me feel better, but I still have no desire to leave my room.

I'm wondering if Bithia might bring me a meal, when there's a knock on the door. *What a relief*, I think, but she doesn't enter, which is strange. She barges in whenever she feels like it.

After another few moments, I say, "Come in," thinking maybe Bithia has sent Tabby. But to my complete surprise, Silas opens the door. I pull up the bedspread, mortified.

"Um, hi," he says. "Can I come in?"

This is highly improper, and I can't believe he would ask.

"I need to talk to you in private," he says, chewing his thumbnail. His face looks worried.

I study him distrustfully.

"Forget it," he says, starting to walk away.

"Can't you tell me downstairs?" I ask.

He shakes his head.

"You're going to get me in trouble." A boy in my bedroom at home would get us both arrested.

"I know where some of your people are," he whispers.

All thoughts of punishment fly out of my head, as I say, "Shut the door. Tell me everything you know."

He shyly brushes his blond hair out of his eyes. "A guy at Chivalry Group was saying that his neighbor was bragging about having two of the Manhattan Five at his house."

"Which ones? Who?" My pulse quickens.

"I don't know. I'm sorry." My disappointment must be clear. "I know it's two boys, or young men, or whatever."

Juda! It has to be Juda and Dekker.

"Take me to them," I say. I start to jump out of bed but stop when I realize I'm only wearing underwear.

"Whoa," he says. "You can't just charge out of the house. Remember what I said this morning about sirens and not making it past the lawn?"

The Bee. If Bithia and Gilad don't stop me, the stupid Bee will.

"So did you just tell me to torture me?" I say with hostility. "I have to sit here and do nothing?" I gather the bedclothes around me.

"I didn't say you couldn't leave the house. I said you couldn't do it *now*." When I don't respond, he adds, "They aren't far. We can walk."

"Maybe Ram told you to come tempt me, and if I go with you, I fail some test."

Silas sighs, and it is deep and dramatic, like one of Tabby's. "It's up to you. I have nothing to gain, and if I'm caught sneaking out, I'll be in as much trouble as you." He walks to the door. "You have until dark to decide."

After he slips out, my head is spinning. Why would Silas help me? His sister can't stand me, and his parents treat me like a visitor from another planet. Why should he be any different?

It must be a trick; I just can't figure out what kind.

Hearing that Juda and Dekker are not far away, that I could actually see them, fills me with a tense energy. I know nothing about Silas. I don't know if he can be trusted. Even if he genuinely wants to help me, the risk of getting caught seems huge.

I get up and put on another one of Tabby's pea-green outfits. When I see my reflection in the bathroom mirror, I stop in my tracks. Because I slept with it in a braid, my hair is lopsided and crimped. My skin is pink from the blaring sun yesterday, making me appear permanently embarrassed, and my eyes are bloodshot from a lack of sleep. I look *bizarre*.

I can't believe I just sat in bed, looking like this, talking to Silas. How humiliating.

I undress again and enter the shower booth of misery. As much as I hate it, I have to do something about my hair.

That evening, Bithia is thrilled to see me come down for dinner. Making a big fuss, she heaps twice as much food on my plate than I could possibly eat. I stare at the pile of fried chicken and mashed potatoes, a glossy mushroom gravy congealing on top, and feel slightly sick.

Silas barely makes eye contact. He sits quietly, fading into the background, as he did at the last meal. His light hair frequently falls in front of his face, obscuring his hazel eyes, but when he's with his family, he doesn't bother brushing it out of the way. He's good at hiding.

I'm relieved that the family ignores me for the most part. I don't feel like talking.

I notice that Silas' parents don't talk to him much either. They say, "Pass the salt" maybe, but they don't ask him questions or start a conversation. They can't seem to get enough of Tabby and Corny and want to hear all about their days.

At home, Silas, as the oldest son, would be the most honored sibling. He would be served before his brother, sister, and mother. Not only is Silas not treated as the exalted son at this table, but when Gilad passes him a basket of bread, I could swear Gilad frowns at him.

I wonder what Silas has done to bring such disapproval. Perhaps he has refused to enter into a marriage contract, or he doesn't want to take over the family business.

Either of these things would explain Silas' rebellious nature and might explain his offer. But what if he just wants to make his father angry? That would be very bad.

I decide there's only one way to know what his motivations are.

When we're dismissed, Silas heads for the stairs and I walk up right after him, whispering, "Why do you want to help me?"

He waits until we reach the second floor, making sure no one else is coming up the stairs. "It's complicated. But let's just say I refuse to let someone be a prisoner in my home."

"Okay," I say. It's not the answer I was expecting. "What do you get out of it?"

"If I'm ever in prison, you can return the favor," he says, with a lopsided smile.

If Silas came from where I did, he would know that such a promise is nothing to joke about.

"So you're in?" he says, eyes growing brighter.

Picturing Juda's face, I nod. But Silas' enthusiasm makes me nervous. I don't trust anyone who wants to help me for no reason, especially if he's putting himself in danger. Nana would say, "Beware the beggar who's excited to give you his only coin."

After the sun goes down, Bithia checks on me three times to make sure I'm feeling okay. I assure her I'm fine, fighting the urge to tell her to get out.

I lie in bed, fully dressed under the blankets, listening to the sounds of the family settling in for the night—doors opening and closing; feet padding across wood floors; faucets turning off and on. And then, finally, the household seems to be asleep.

I wait, wondering what I've gotten myself into.

After nearly an hour, I wonder if Silas is coming. Maybe he changed his mind? Or maybe he never had any intention of coming, and he's downstairs laughing with Tabby right now?

I'm starting to get angry when the bedroom door opens, and Silas tiptoes inside, carrying a large bag. I open my mouth to ask what took him so long, but he raises a finger to his lips.

Opening the bag, he pulls out what looks like two uniforms. *Nyek.* Does he want us to imitate Sentries or something? Like Grace and I did with the Twitchers? I'm not up for that tonight. It's too much.

He hands me a uniform, which is thick but surprisingly light. He gestures for me to put it on.

I start to say, "No," but he signals for me to be quiet. I shake my head instead.

He comes in very close to me, so that I can feel his breath on my face. He whispers, "It protects you from your Bee."

I look at the uniform again. It's a dense black material with no markings or pockets. The fabric doesn't feel like fabric at all— more like fuzzy rubber—and the legs end in little sewn-on shoes, like the pajamas Dekker wore as a toddler. Weird.

Taking off his shirt, Silas starts to change in front of me.

Mortified, I rush into the bathroom. Are all Unbound men like this or is it just Silas?

I stare at the uniform in my hands. I have no idea what the

penalty will be for breaking the rules. A beating? Starvation? Worse?

I picture Juda, his face pressed into the grass as he tried to tell me something before he got dragged away. Before *I* got him arrested by Apostates.

I pull off my green clothes and put on the strange black suit. Whatever the penalty is, I'm ready to pay it. I need to see Juda. I have to make sure he's safe.

The thick material feels light and is surprisingly easy to move in, but it clings to my body in a way that makes me self-conscious. I want to put my big sweater over it, but I assume that would defeat its purpose.

When I come out, Silas has put on his suit and is holding gloves and a mask. I look away at once, embarrassed by how much of him I can see in the tight rubber. I've never seen so much of a boy's body.

Telling myself this is normal in Kingsboro, I try to make my face neutral. If Silas notices how form-fitting my uniform is, he doesn't let it show.

He puts on the mask. It fits snugly, so that I can still see the shape of his head, but it has no holes for his eyes or mouth. It looks very claustrophobic.

He hands me my own mask. Reluctantly, I put it on and am surprised to find that I can see and breathe very easily. The fabric looks thick but feels thin, just like the uniform.

He hands me gloves. Once covered, we both have not an inch of flesh showing. The Prophet would be proud.

Going to the largest window, Silas opens it, letting in a night breeze. A large tree branch is just outside, and I see immediately what Silas has in mind. But even if I manage to climb down the darn thing, how does he expect me to get back up?

Silas pulls a tiny container out of his pocket. Sitting on the windowsill, he motions for me to take a seat as well. He sprays something on the souls of my shoes and then the palms of my gloves. He does the same to his own gloves and shoes.

The next thing I know, he's swinging his legs over the windowsill and scurrying down the wall of the house like a spider! I'm too shocked to do anything but stare.

When he reaches the bottom, he looks up and waves me down. Is he *crazy*?

He waves me down again, then puts his hands on his hips, annoyed. Seeing that I'm not budging, he puts his hand on the side of the house and pulls. The hand doesn't move.

I get it. The spray is some sort of adhesive. That doesn't make his descent seem any less bonkers to me.

He looks around nervously and signals to me again.

Think of Juda, I tell myself. *Think of Juda.*

I scoot to the far edge of the windowsill, reach over, and place my right hand on the outside wall of the house. I pull back, but the hand is very firmly in place. I do a small hop and twist and my right foot lands on the wall with a *thud*. I wince at the noise.

My legs caught in the splits between the windowsill and the wall, I hold my breath, waiting for lights to flicker, for sirens to sound. But there is only silence.

I exhale.

I'm amazed that the adhesive, with just one glove and one shoe, holds my body weight. Quietly, I bring my left foot to the wall and then my left hand.

I pull away my right hand to begin climbing down, but it doesn't move. I try my left hand and both my feet, and they're stuck as if they're an inch deep in plaster.

From below, Silas whispers as loudly as he dares, "Push your hand up, not down."

What is he talking about? I'm trying to pull my hand out, not *down*. I try to pull my hand out and up. Nothing. The moon is

bright, and even in the dark suit, I'm sure I'm incredibly conspicuous hanging off the side of this house.

"Like you're washing the wall," whispers Silas.

I push up, keeping my hand on the wall as if there's a rag in it,
and my hand comes flying off. Praise God I didn't try both hands
at once.

I move my free arm level to my waist and place my hand on
the wall again, rubbing down and resticking it to the wall. Then I
slide up my left hand, releasing it. Now it seems simple.

Until I try to do the same thing with my feet. I've never used
a rag with my feet. But soon I figure out a releasing motion that is
a bit like biking backward. Once I understand how to stick and
unstick both hands and feet, it doesn't take me long to get to the
ground.

As soon as I land, Silas signals for me to follow him across the
spacious lawn in back of the house. We rush into a thicket of trees
and then cross behind a few more houses. Before long, remark-
ably, we're walking on the dirt path that Ram took me down to
reach the pond.

As soon as we're out of earshot of the houses, I hiss at Silas,
"Why didn't you explain how to climb down *before* you jumped
out the window?"

He shrugs. "I've never met anyone who didn't know how to
use StickFoot."

I scowl at him but then realize he can't see me through the
mask. "Don't assume I know anything, okay?" I say.

"No problem. You're a total moron. Done," he says.

What am I doing with this person? I'm tempted to run back
to the house and back into my bed.

"I'm kidding," he says. "Relax. Tabby and I do this all
the time."

I'm shocked. "Tabby sneaks out with you in a rubber suit?"

"We don't do it together."

"Why do you do it at all?"

"Things around here are pretty strict," he says and then his voice changes. "Sorry. I mean, not, like, strict in the way that your life was strict. But it can still feel suffocating."

I wonder how much he knows about life in Manhattan, but I don't want to talk about it. "Where did you get these suits?"

"The Smokers?" He laughs. "This kid David Pellman stole them, I don't know, maybe twenty years ago? His dad's lab was trying to create technology that would make it impossible to brainwash people. They managed to invent material that blocked *outgoing* brainwaves, but they couldn't block any information going in. His dad thought the experiment was a complete failure, but David snuck out a handful of masks before they were destroyed. Kids have been handing them down ever since. I think there are maybe, like, ten of them floating around. Very benny."

"This suit is blocking my brainwaves?" I ask.

"Just the mask—and yeah, it is."

"My Bee reads my mind?" I say with unease.

"Not really. It's *connecting* to your mind. Your brainwaves are as unique as, say, your fingerprints. So when your Bee senses your brain in action, it can find you instantly."

"If it's just the mask why am I wearing the rest of the suit?"

"It's black and makes you hard to see at night," he says matter-of-factly.

Now I feel dumb.

The wind rushes through the trees with an eerie whine. Could someone be following us?

"Why do you call them 'smokers'?" I ask, distracting myself.

"Oh, uh, I think because in olden days people used smoke to calm down bees."

I nod. "Oh, yeah. They do that with hives on the island."

"You have live hives in Manhattan?" he says, incredulous.

"Yes." I didn't know this was remarkable.

"Wait until I tell Mom. How's the honey?"

"Expensive," I say, not wanting to admit I've never tasted it. "How far are we going?"

"Not far at all," he says. "Just across the park."

Before long, I see Peace Pond. The fastest way across the park would be to run across the huge expanse of grass, but Silas takes us around the perimeter, sticking close to the creepy trees. It's hard for me to go slowly, knowing Juda is close by.

"Do you know the family who has them in custody?" I ask.

"You mean who's 'hosting them as guests?'" he says, correcting me. "A little bit. You know everyone around here sooner or later. The Delfords—parents of the *otter daughters*."

"The what?" I ask.

"Oh, um, well, they're both kind of round, and they have these kind of strange short arms." He turns toward me and pulls in his arms. "You know, like an otter?"

"That's so mean!" I say, stifling a giggle.

"I know," he says, shrugging. "Everyone might stop saying it if the girls were a bit nicer to people."

"Or maybe they'd be nicer to people if everyone stopped saying it," I suggest.

He sighs the Dixon sigh. "You're probably right." He stops walking. "We're here."

Looking around, I see a dozen houses. "Which one?"

He points to an emerald green house that overlooks the park, and although the color is cheerful, the house seems menacing.

"What do we do?" I say, feeling nervous now that we've arrived.

"We can't make contact yet. You can only watch and hope to see someone."

If I can't make contact why did he bother bringing me? "I need to talk to them!"

"No way. Not tonight. We'd be caught immediately."

I'm sure he's right, but I can't imagine seeing Juda and then just walking away. "Let's get closer," I say.

We stay in the cover of the trees, approaching slowly. We pass a blue house with all its lights on, and I can hear a baby screaming. The sound frays my nerves. All I can think about is Beth and the sirens and how quickly we were surrounded by dozens of men.

Silas kneels behind some bushes, so I do the same.

The green house has two large picture windows on the first floor and two small windows on the second. A faint light shines on the first floor, but we're too far away to see inside. Upstairs the rooms are dark. Won't this family be asleep like the Dixons? What's the point of coming after bedtime?

"I want to get closer," I whisper. Silas shakes his head.

We wait for movement downstairs. We wait some more. Nothing happens.

"My legs are cramping," I say.

"Then stretch them," Silas says without sympathy.

"This is pointless," I say. "We should get *closer*."

"Trust me. We should *not* get closer."

"Why?"

"Because the Delfords own an uzi."

I don't know what an uzi is, but I'm guessing it's very bad.

"Look!" says Silas.

In the bottom left window there's movement. My breath catches, but I can only see a shadow.

I can't stand it. I have to see more.

Rising, I run to the next cluster of trees. I hear Silas protesting behind me, but I don't care. I can still only see vague shapes in the window, so I dart behind a tree that's even closer.

Breath catching, I peek around the trunk and look into the house.

In the middle of a sofa, in a living room that looks exactly like the Dixons', sits Dekker. He wears black pants and a black shirt and he looks freshly bathed, his hair combed and parted to one side. He sits with a large, very fit man, also in black, who speaks to him forcefully. I can't hear the words, but his body language suggests he's very confident about his lecture. Dekker nods and smiles at him. At one point, Dekker *laughs*. Then the large man, who I guess is Mr. Delford, laughs as well, and pounds Dekker on the back.

Leave it to Dekker. He's playing along and doing whatever they want, because Dekker will always do whatever is best for Dekker.

I feel disgust, but then . . . isn't that what I'm doing? Going to the Leisure Center and taking a walk with Ram and eating my meals and saying "thank you"? I'm just as pathetic as Dekker.

I watch them for a while, the two of them chatting like old friends. I wait breathlessly for Juda to enter the room. Feeling a tap on my shoulder, I nearly scream.

Silas stands an inch behind me. His words tickle my ear. "We have to go."

I don't budge. I haven't seen Juda.

He pulls my elbow. "*Now*. We've been gone too long."

He's gotten us this far without getting caught, so I know I should listen to him. *Nyek*. I turn away from the house in angry frustration. "Fine," I say, a little too loudly.

He sprints back the way we came. I follow.

On the way home, there's no conversation. We run the entire way. When we finally reach the tiny grove in back of his yard, Silas looks at the wall of his house and says, panting, "You go first."

"No way," I say. Is he trying to sacrifice me or something?

"If you start to fall I can help," he says.

I nod but hesitate to cross the lawn, where we're clearly visible.

"Let's go," he says, grabbing my hand. He darts across the grass, leaving me no choice but to join him.

When we reach the wall, he gives my hand a squeeze of support.

I don't stop to think; I just climb. I *rise* up the house. The natural movement of climbing creates the push-down, pull-up necessary to stick and unstick my hands and feet. Why couldn't we have started with a climb up instead of a climb down?

Within no time, I've reached my window. I swing my left leg over and then my right and I'm back inside. I'm relieved to find no one waiting in my room.

I look back out the window. Silas is making his ascent. He's quicker than me, of course, and he's incredibly graceful. He's almost to the window when his left foot pushes up instead of down. Instead of sticking to the wall, his foot comes free and his leg swings backward. His balance completely thrown, he grasps for the windowsill, but he isn't close enough to grab it.

I reach out my hand, but it's too late. As he plummets to the ground, he cries out, "Mina!"

The scream is loud, causing houselights all down the street to flicker on.

Silas lies on the ground, his arm at an odd angle.

"I'm coming!" I say. I'm not sure what to do. I could climb back down the wall or run downstairs and out the front door—I don't know which will be faster.

It doesn't matter, because the Dixons heard Silas' shout, and Bithia and Gilad are already searching for him.

Within seconds they're outside, discovering their injured son. Bithia takes off his mask and his face is a grimace of pain. She strokes his cheek. "Oh, baby boy. You'll be okay. I promise, Honeybear."

Silas looks up at me and we lock eyes, just for a second.

Glancing up, Gilad sees me crouching in the windowsill. "What did you *do*?"

I'm filled with misery and regret. Silas was only trying to help me, and I'll pay a large price for what's happened.

Sitting on the bed, I hear Tabby outside and then other neighbors, as they gather to ask what's happened. Soon a car or van pulls up, and I listen as men talk to Silas about his injuries. They must move him, because I hear him shriek out in pain. Then the van drives away, and there is silence.

I wait for Gilad and Bithia to come punish me.

I replay Silas' fall over and over in my head—the way his foot detached, when he'd seemed so experienced. And how, when our eyes met, there was pain, but there was something else: apology.

I can't explain it, but I could almost swear he fell on purpose.

SIX

The next morning, Bithia and Gilad walk me through the quiet streets of the neighborhood. They haven't spoken to me since last night when Silas fell. They didn't offer me breakfast or tell me where we were going. They waited for me to be dressed and then led me out the door.

I'm used to my mother's screaming. As soon as I broke a rule, she would screech, frequently slapping me. Done. This silence is really frightening. Perhaps they're walking me back to the subway tunnel, and they'll just point at it. I'll have to climb down the stairs and swim back to the island alone, without a raft. I think I would rather be shot here than drown alone down there.

After several blocks, I realize we're headed for the Leisure Center. I recognize a few of the houses and numbers from my first day. I relax a bit. Nothing about the Leisure Center seems to be about torture or punishment.

My Bee hums above me, seeming louder than before. My imagination is telling me that it's angry about last night and my achievement of sneaking out undetected.

When we arrive at the Leisure Center, we don't go to the

atrium like before. Instead we head to a set of metal stairs that loops around the side of the building. Climbing up the stairs, Gilad has to stop to catch his breath.

Hands on hips, Bithia sighs, and I see where both her children get it from. "If you walked around the block everyday like me, you wouldn't be huffin' like a hundred-year-old man on a hamster wheel!"

I should run. Whatever is at the top of the stairs will be my punishment. And watching Gilad wheeze, I know he can't catch me. But my Bee hovers nearby, ready to sound the alarm. I'm stuck.

After a minute's rest, we continue up the stairs, and soon we've reached a glass door that says, "Let in the Light." Bithia pushes it open and cold air rushes out.

We enter a room that's all white—white desk, white chairs, white walls. It reminds me of Mrs. Asher, and I shudder. Each wall contains a door with no handle, which I find disconcerting.

Marjory, the woman who sits very straight, stands in the middle of the room as if she'd been expecting us. "Welcome, Dixons."

"Morning, Marjory," says Bithia.

"Have a seat. Ram will be with you shortly."

Ram. The man who said I was "special." He probably won't be thinking I'm so special today.

After we sit in a row of white chairs, I turn to Gilad. "I'm very sorry about what happened last night. I never meant—"

"No talking," says Marjory crisply.

On the wall above Marjory's head is a long, old-fashioned gun in a glass frame. Inscribed into the glass are the words *semper paratus*. I have no idea what that means. Is the gun being commemorated, or is it being held there until Marjory needs it?

I sit with my hands in my lap, staring straight ahead. I'm freezing in my green jeans and thin green blouse. A sign on the wall says, "Savor His Blessings." I read it over and over, until the words become gibberish.

Time goes slowly. Bithia and Gilad don't even speak to each other.

Finally, Marjory, for no reason I can observe, says, "You can go in now." The handleless door on our left swings open on its own.

The three of us rise.

Marjory says, "He just wants Mina."

Bithia and Gilad look at each other in surprise.

"He was quite clear," Marjory says. "You're free to wait."

They sit back down, clearly irritated.

I head for the open door, not sure if I'm relieved or frightened to be free of them.

Inside the office, Ram is wearing the same white pajamas as the last time I saw him. His brown hair looks more tightly curled. He sits on the floor with his legs spread in a V. All over the rug are hundreds of little pieces of wood in weird shapes.

After a moment, he looks up and says, "Aren't you going to say 'hello'?"

Embarrassed, I whisper, "I was waiting for you to speak first."

"Of course you were. I'm sorry! Women don't have to wait for men to speak here." He shakes his head at the ridiculous notion. "Please join me."

I don't see any chairs, so I sit next to him on the floor. Without warning, a huge yellow dog leaps out of the corner, knocking me over. She licks my face and ears until I think I might drown.

"No! Jezzy, down!" Ram cries, leaning forward to pull her off me. He manages to subdue her but only barely. I can't imagine Ram weighs much more than she does. "So sorry. This is Jezebel. She's a total princess and also the devil, right, Jezzy?" He sticks his face in her neck and kisses her fur. "Get in your bed! Go on. Bed!"

Jezzy looks at him with soulful brown eyes, slowly turns around, and lopes to a much-chewed-on dog bed in the corner.

"Do you like dogs?" Ram asks.

Not a lot of people keep dogs as pets on the island. They're too expensive to feed. Cats keep away mice and rats and feed themselves. "I don't know," I say. "Jezzy seems nice."

Ram laughs. "Jezzy has horrible manners and old-cod breath. But you're sweet."

I smile, almost forgetting that I'm in trouble.

Ram's office is very odd. Where the reception area was pristine and white, this room is cluttered and every color of the rainbow. A desk is piled sky-high with books, papers, and a stuffed bear. Shelves are full of books, knickknacks, and what appears to be bags of candy. The walls are covered from floor to ceiling with photographs of people—families smiling and waving, their arms around Ram as if he were their favorite son or brother. Most bizarre of all, an enormous white wheel sits in the corner of the room. It's taller than any man I know and looks like the tire of a giant car.

Concentrating once again on the wood pieces on the floor, Ram says, "This is what people used to call a 'puzzle.'" He connects one piece to another. Holding up the top part of a box, he says, "This one is called 'Wicker Kittens.'" He shows me the picture. "See? It's cats in a basket!"

"What's the point?" I ask. I just want to get my punishment over with. Why is he toying with me?

"The point?" he says, confused. "Recreation, I suppose." He inspects the pieces, fitting two more together. "I confess, I find it very relaxing."

This is why we were waiting all this time? So he could put together a picture of kittens?

"Do people work in this town?" I exclaim without thinking.

He looks up, startled. Then he grins. "Our way of life must seem very odd to you."

"Everyone seems to sit around eating all the time," I say.

Who's growing the food? Who's transporting the water? Who's driving the taxis and busses?

He laughs. "Yes, it must seem that way. But we actually work very hard. And we all have the same job."

I wait for him to tell me what it is.

"But let's talk about that another time. This morning we're here to talk about you and a little incident that happened last night."

I become very interested in the wheel in the corner.

"That's my desk," he says.

When I look at him with bafflement, he stands and crosses the room. "I don't like sitting still." Stepping inside the wheel, he begins to walk. Screens appear around him. "It's one hundred percent human powered. Very efficient. Neat, huh?"

I nod.

When he stops walking, the screens disappear.

"Let's get comfortable," he says, stepping down. He goes to the corner and plops down in what looks like a gigantic red nest. He points to a blue version against the wall. "It's a 'beanbag,' and you'll love it."

Rising, I approach the big blob and descend awkwardly. I'm surprised to find it is soft and conforms to the shape of my body. Not bad.

"Why are you called the Unbound?" I ask, hoping to keep him distracted.

"We're not attached to earthly pleasures. We're ready to rise quickly and easily to the Lord's kingdom." He frowns. "So you tried to see your friends last night, but it didn't go very well, right?"

73

Silas has probably told everyone everything at this point.

"The Dixons are very upset," he adds. "Poor Silas has fractured his wrist."

"I'm so sorry," I say. And I am. I didn't mean for anyone to get hurt.

"He says it was his idea to sneak out of the house. Is that true?"

It is true, but poor Silas already has a broken wrist. What else will he suffer if he takes the blame for our misconduct?

"Tell the truth, Mina. I'll know if you're lying." Ram looks into my face, and something about his strange gray eyes makes me believe him. He *will* know.

"Yes. It was Silas' idea." I feel bad being disloyal to Silas, but I feel good about being honest.

"Wonderful. Everyone agrees on the story." He shakes his head. "I can't believe kids are still using Smokers. We had those when *I* was a teenager."

"Is he in terrible trouble?"

He looks at me like I'm not as bright as he thought. "Shouldn't you be worried that *you* are in terrible trouble?"

I shrink into the beanbag chair. I'm not used to this. If I'm in trouble, why is he being so friendly?

Wiggling out of his beanbag, Ram walks to a shelf and picks up a box similar in shape and size to the puzzle box. He hands it to me. "This is for you."

I don't take it. "Does it have to do with my punishment?"

"Yes and no," he says.

When he sits back down, Jezebel rushes over and puts her head in his lap. He strokes her ears as he waits for me to open the box.

The logical part of me says there can't be anything in this box that can hurt me, but I'm still wary.

"Go on," Ram says.

When I don't think I can put it off any longer, I take the top off the box. I move aside pink tissue paper to find a beautiful white dress.

"I don't understand," I say. My punishment is new clothes? Holding up the dress, I see delicate lace cutouts around the shoulders and hem.

Ram laughs. "I love your face right now! I should have taken a picture."

I try to smile, but I don't understand the joke.

"Sweet Mina, this is an exciting day!" He stands and comes to sit on the floor by my beanbag. "I know you've noticed the clothes we wear, the colors. You must've been wondering what it all means."

"I guess I—"

"It's all very simple. When we're born, we're innocent, sweet little babies, and we have no sin. Life is very straightforward—eat, sleep, poop—that's it. And that phase lasts a long time. We put our children in white to represent that innocence, that precious period. It's a time to savor. Life becomes more complicated when we reach adolescence. Our thoughts become less pure. We are tempted to defy our parents, to question the society around us. This is why children going through puberty wear green, to signify growth."

The green I am wearing right now, the color that Tabby and her friends despise, is the color of adolescence?

"Next there is yellow, red, purple, blue, black, gray. Each level becomes harder to achieve, requiring a spiritual and inner awareness that tests your morality and sincerity. And if you work very, very hard, one day you can achieve the highest level, which is white."

"I thought the beginning level was white," I say.

"Yes! It is every man and woman's goal to return to the state of innocence and lightness of their birth." Ram is very joyful as he says this. "Today is an important day because you'll be conse-crated as a 'Day One White,' like a newborn baby girl. All your sins will be washed away, and you'll start fresh. I can't imagine the lightness you'll feel."

He gazes at me with complete delight.

"Thank you," I say.

I *am* grateful if this gift means I won't endure any punishment.

"You are so, so welcome," he says.

Jezzy sniffs at the new dress, then returns to Ram.

"Mina, what do you want?" Ram asks. "And don't say that you want to see your friends. I know that. I mean, what do you *really* want, in your life?"

His question throws me off guard. I take a full minute to think about my answer, then say, "I want to be safe."

He frowns. "You *are* safe. You couldn't be safer. This is the problem with life in Manhattan: a girl's life shouldn't only be about 'staying safe.' That's a crime. What do you want to *be*? What do you want to *do*? Do you want a husband? A family? A calling?"

"I don't know," I say, and it's true. People tried to force me to have a husband and family before I was ready, and now those things seem like shackles.

"I've been told that you can read," he says.

Shaken, I almost drop my box. *Dekker.* Dekker must've told them. Grace and Juda never would've betrayed me.

"Congratulations," says Ram. "It's an extraordinary accom-plishment when you're living in such dire circumstances."

I don't move. I let my face betray nothing.

"You might be interested to know that when you reach the level of green, you'll be allowed to attend school."

The Dixons haven't mentioned school.

"The new session starts in four weeks. Boys and girls attend.

We teach reading, writing, history, math, science . . . Are you smiling, Mina?"

I hadn't realized I was. "Won't I be behind?"

"I'm sure the Dixons could arrange for a tutor if—"

"If what?" I ask, trying to contain my excitement.

"If you're behaving well. Level Green will get you in school, but I imagine level Yellow would get you a tutor, extra books, and whatever else you might need."

Level Yellow. Tabby and her friends all wear yellow, so how hard could it be?

"How long does it take to be Yellow?" I ask.

"That depends on you. You're a bright girl, and I know you'll work hard. You need to listen to the people around you, especially Bithia and Gilad, read your Book of Glory, visit the Worship Hub regularly, and, most importantly . . ." He leans in. "Bring biscuits for Jezzy every time you visit."

I smile.

"Are you ready to open your heart to us?" he asks. "To obey our rules, respect your neighbors, and *let in the light*?"

I hesitate. Am I ready? He's asking me to be open, to be respectful, and to obey the rules. These all seem like reasonable requests, and he hasn't specifically asked me to *stop* praying to the Prophet.

"Yes," I say.

"Great!" he says, clapping his hands together. "Now, let's go to the house of God!"

When Ram opens the office door, I walk out, and Jezzy darts straight into Gilad's lap. Gilad seems very unamused by the face-licking he receives.

"Sorry, Gilad. Down, Jezzy!" Ram cries.

"He doesn't mind," says Bithia, smiling hugely at Ram.

"Mina and I are going to the Worship Hub."

"Are you sure she's ready?" asks Bithia.

Ram's smile disappears. "Has God given you a better plan?"

Bithia stutters. "N-n-no. I just meant, after last night—"

"I'm kidding, Bithia," Ram says. "Trust me on this one, okay?" Walking to her, he gives her a large hug. His head only reaches her chest, and I'm embarrassed by how his head rests on her bosom.

People touch one another so much here. It's weird.

Releasing her, he says, "You go on home and take care of Silas."

"But the service—" Bithia says.

"God will understand," Ram says. "I'll look after our girl. Don't worry." Putting his arm around me, he turns to Marjory. "Marjory, will you please arrange for delivery of Mina's dress after the service?"

Marjory frowns at me but nods. She obviously doesn't think I'm worthy of the white clothes.

Her and me both.

SEVEN

When we arrive at the Worship Hub, I'm stunned by the number of people filing inside. The building is gigantic, definitely bigger than any prayer center in Manhattan. It's made of brick and concrete, but to get inside you have to walk through a massive star-shaped balloon. The star is yellow and spiky and when you walk inside it, light filters through the material, giving everyone a golden glow.

"This star is a filter," says Ram, with Jezzy loping next to him. "It helps clean the contaminated air from your people's horses and busses."

Does he want me to apologize for the pollution?

We enter a lobby with blue walls and paisley carpet. The smell of disinfectant clogs my nose. Families wave at Ram. A few people approach him or Jezzy for hugs. He smiles and attends to them all.

Finally passing through the crowd, we reach the main auditorium, where an entire country seems to be congregated. A massive stage fills the north end of the room, while hundreds and hundreds of chairs fill the rest of the space.

Ram says, "Find a seat here in the back, and I'll find you after the service."

"You're leaving me alone?" I say, overwhelmed.

"Well, I have a couple things to take care of," he says, winking. He and Jezzy head back to the lobby. I look around the enormous room.

Someone waves at me. Squinting, I realize it's Phoebe, Tabby's friend from the food court. She's motioning for me to sit in the empty chair beside her.

Having no other place to go, I join her.

"You came with Ram! Very benny," she says.

"Yes," I say.

"You look pretty. I like what you've done with your hair," she says.

It's in a plain ponytail. "Thanks."

Turning to the man sitting next to her, she says, "Daddy, this is Mina. Mina, this is my dad."

He's chunky with hair in a bowl shape. After smiling briefly, he goes back to his conversation with the man next to him: "How can they not understand that the treaty is the only way to reach our salvation?"

"How many people are here?" I ask Phoebe, still staggered by the huge arena.

"I never really thought about it," she says, looking around the room. "Like, five thousand maybe? And there's another service right after this one."

Wow.

She touches my arm. "You must have had a really fascinating life. I'd love to hear about it sometime."

I smile politely, unsure how to respond. She's being much nicer than she was at the Leisure Center. Why?

She leans in, whispering, "Is it true you get married at nine?"

"Uh, no. We—"

"And that you always cover your face? Does your husband even know what you look like? And do you really throw away female babies? I heard a girl's mouth will be sewn shut if she talks back to her father!"

"What?" I say, horrified. "That's not true."

"Which thing? I *know* you throw away babies."

"No. We don't." I look around for another seat but don't see one. Is this what all the Unbound think of us?

"I heard that if your husband doesn't like your cooking, he can cut off your head. I'm a terrible cook, so that is major freaky. I also heard—"

Before I get to hear what other delightful thing she's heard about my people, the lights go out. We're thrown into total darkness. I'm becoming distressed, when huge beams of light appear on stage: white, red, pink, and purple. They wave, flash and criss-cross. I'm entranced.

Minutes later, when the light show has finished, a giant screen descends from the ceiling. A booming voice comes from all around and then images appear on the screen. A *movie*! My first one!

The thunderous voice says, "To follow God is not a job, it is a calling. To follow God is not a burden, it is the source of joy. To follow God is not a choice, it is a destiny."

While the voice speaks, images of mountains and clouds appear on the screen, like I'm a bird flying high above. I dip up and down and twirl through the air. My stomach drops, as if I were actually up there swerving in and out of trees and not sitting here in my seat.

Next I'm approaching an enormous canyon. It's so beautiful, I want to cry out. Instead of skimming across the top of the canyon, I'm suddenly diving toward the bottom. My stomach drops again. We keep diving. I go faster and faster. I wait for the bird to pull away, but it's not changing course. I'm headed for the rocks. As I'm about to hit the bottom, I see an enormous burst of light.

Lights all over the auditorium flare as the color beams return to the stage. Everyone applauds.

The screen rises, revealing a group of men and women with instruments. People clap harder.

A woman begins to play the piano, the notes echoing throughout the enormous room. The sound is unfathomably beautiful, like raindrops dancing on glass. This is *music*—banned for nearly one hundred years by the Teachers. I want to sit here all day and listen to this instrument. This is what I will tell Ram that I want.

And then, *then*, other instruments join in that I don't recognize; the group of women and men create all sorts of incredible sounds—strumming, plucking, and tapping. Paradise must sound like this.

"Are you crying?" asks Phoebe, amazed.

I wipe my eyes. "It's breathtaking."

People in the audience wave their arms to the music. I'm too self-conscious to join, but I'd like to.

When the song ends, a hush comes over the crowd. Excitement fills the air. After the movie and the music, I can't imagine how the spectacle could get any better.

A hole opens up in the middle of the stage and up rises Ram, holding a microphone like the Heralds sometimes use.

I want to giggle. He's so small on the big stage and the red lights are making his curly hair glow pink. After welcoming everyone to the Worship Hub, he says, "Give yourselves a hand for being such good citizens this week!" The crowd applauds. "And give yourself another hand for *always being prepared.*" Everyone claps more.

"Take this moment to remind yourself that this is YOUR house of God. You built it with your contributions and your love.

The more you give to God, the more He gives to you. It's that simple. And the Unbound are the most giving people of them all, am I right?" People stomp their feet. "What you give to God today, you will see tenfold in Heaven!"

A man to my left whoops loudly.

"Earthly suffering is worthwhile. I know you don't want to hear that, but it is. You must suffer, so that you might understand the beauty of Heaven when the day comes to sit beside the Lord. And that day is coming my beauties. It is coming! So make every moment count. Love thy neighbors. Be fruitful. Be generous. And show God that you love Him EVERY day."

The audience cheers more while many people stand up to holler their approval. I've never seen anything like this. When we pray at home it's a serious occasion, and yelling would be considered insolent.

"I've been telling you for years now that a special time is coming, and I'm pleased to tell you that I've had a VISION that the time is nigh. The holy destiny of the Unbound WILL be fulfilled soon!"

The band plays music again while people jump up and down, some dancing in the aisle. Ram motions for people to sit down. "We have a special event today! Everyone's favorite! That's right. It's someone's DAY OF VALIDATION!"

The people go crazy.

"And this isn't just anyone. This is a very special girl. She's risked her life to reach us. She's endured years of oppression and abuse, and yet she still manages to find God in her heart. Isn't that amazing?"

"He's talking about you!" Phoebe says, eyes big as hubcaps.

I feel sick. What is Ram doing? Why didn't he warn me he was going to talk about me?

"Let's get her down here and show her the love of the

Unbound!" he says. "Brothers and sisters, I give you MINA CLARK!"

"I have to leave," I say, rising.

"No way!" says Phoebe, grabbing my arm. "This is your moment!" She turns to the people around her. "THIS IS HER! This is MINA CLARK!"

Before I know what's happening, I'm surrounded by Apostates. They're grabbing and pulling at me. All I can think about is the stoning I saw, and I feel faint. I want to kick and spit at them.

Despite my protest, a big man seizes me and lifts me in the air like he's going to launch me across the room. He flips me until I lie horizontally, facing the ceiling. The others get underneath me and support my weight with their hands. They carry me a few feet, and then they pass me off to another small crowd. Dozens and dozens of strange hands pass across my back and legs to keep me from falling.

"Stop wiggling," says a woman, "or we'll drop you."

"Keep stiff," says the man next to her.

Flexing my muscles, I feel my carriers' relief.

I'm passed from group to group to group. I close my eyes, thinking it might be better for me not to see the faces of the strangers who are groping me. I feel humiliation at being touched and dread at being dropped.

Finally, we reach the front. Someone below me says, "We're putting you on the stage. Don't try to get up until we're finished."

They slide me onto the stage, and I just lie there. After a few seconds, I hear laughter.

Ram says, "Is she dead?"

More laughter.

I open my eyes. Ram stands right above me, offering his hand.

Taking it, I stand, feeling mortified after being passed around like a bread basket.

"Let's give her a hand, brothers and sisters."

The people clap. From here, the crowd looks even bigger. I don't like these people ogling me.

"Mina, everyone is carried to the stage on their Day of Validation. It tells you that our community has got you, you can trust us, and no matter what happens, we won't let you fall."

Through the applause, a girl yells, "WE LOVE YOU, MINA!" I think it's Phoebe.

Ram says, "I'm full of surprises this morning, because we have not one, but TWO Days of Validation happening today!"

The crowd goes crazy. Some people stand and pump their fists in the air.

I scan the audience. Who's he talking about? Is it another one of us, the Manhattan Five?

"This boy also risked his life to reach us. He did everything he could to protect his little sister and make sure she left an unjust society. He is the ideal big brother. He's DEKKER CLARK!"

What?

Standing from a seat near the back, Dekker's got a huge grin on his face. He waves at the crowd. People swarm him just like they did me. Dekker doesn't panic. He puts his arms by his side, closing his eyes in submission.

Three men lift him with great effort. Many more people get their hands on him so they can lift him above their heads. When he's finally high enough, they walk several feet and the next group surges forward to take him.

Dekker's arms are crossed peacefully on top of his chest, like a corpse. The third group gathers, ready to take him, but the woman in front is not strong enough for his weight. She falters, dropping his calves.

"Hey!" he yells, trying to sit up.

But sitting up is the worst possible thing he could do. The people who have his rear end can't possibly carry all of his body weight. Dekker croaks out one more, "Hey!" before he hits the ground.

A collective gasp fills the room, and then, there is silence.

Ram speaks into his microphone with a whisper. "Brothers and sisters, please reach down and help young Dekker. He needs your assistance."

But the people around Dekker just stare at him, as if he were a wounded animal who might bite.

"Somebody help him!" I yell, thinking of Silas' broken wrist.

A man rises from the back of the room, where Dekker was sitting. As he walks closer, I recognize him from the house where Dekker is staying. It's Mr. Delford.

Reaching Dekker, he bends down and helps Dekker to his feet. Dekker puts his arm over Mr. Delford's shoulder and they head out of the auditorium. Dekker doesn't appear to have broken anything, but he hunches as if his back hurts.

"Let's give a hand to Dekker Clark for his fortitude," says Ram.

Applause fills the room.

As Dekker disappears from view, I wish I could talk to him. How is he being treated? Has he seen the others?

"Brothers and sisters, we have witnessed something here today," Ram says. "God has a plan for each and every one of us, and He knows what's in our hearts. God saw that Dekker Clark's heart was not authentic. God saw that Dekker Clark needed more time before his Day of Validation. What a wonder to behold. I love seeing God at work, don't you?"

The crowd claps and yells, "Yes!"

"But God told us Mina Clark is righteous; she is ready." He places his small hand on top of my head. "Lord, lead this new servant into righteousness, for she has lived a life of ignorance and misery, like a worm who knew not that there was sunlight above the dirt."

Did he just call me a worm?

"May the Unbound be that sunlight. May we be her friends, neighbors, and counselors as she embarks on a new journey toward edification."

A woman's voice screams, "So be it!"

Ram says with gentleness, "So be it."

Everyone in the Worship Hub repeats the words. Do they mean it? Will they be my friends and counselors here? They seem so joyful and ready to help me in this moment. I hope they're sincere.

He turns to me. "Mina, are you ready?"

I wish I knew what I was supposed to be ready for.

"Do you swear to honor the rules of the Unbound? To confess your sins, commit yourself to our Savior, and move forward in reaching the Ascension?"

The enormous crowd grows quiet.

Commit myself to their Savior? This is different than what he said in his office. I don't know anything about this Savior. And what's the Ascension? My throat goes dry as I look at the thousands of people waiting for my answer.

I thought I could follow Ram's rules and remain loyal to the Prophet, but I see now that he was never going to let me have both. If I want an education, I have to choose.

"Are you with us, Mina?" he asks.

Feeling my heart break, I say, "Yes, sir."

"Wonderful!" he says, taking my hand and moving me to the side of the stage.

The floor slides open where we were standing, and two men in purple rise up, just as Ram did earlier. They stand on either side of an enormous water-filled tank twice the size of the Dixon's living room.

I'm disturbed to see ladders perched on either side.

Ram still has my hand. He walks me to the tank, stopping at a ladder.

"Mina Clark, if this is to be your Day of Validation, if you have an honest heart and truly mean to follow our rules and worship our Savior, then you will climb this ladder and walk across this water!"

What?

The crowd screams in excitement.

He can't possibly be serious.

Holding the mic away from his mouth, he whispers, "I have faith in you."

"I can't swim," I say.

"God will guide you," he says.

He said if I have an "honest heart," I'll be able to cross. What does that mean? If I still believe in the Prophet, will I fall in? What if I have undisclosed sins? My legs wobble.

I sense that if I leave the stage without trying that the reaction will be much worse than if I fail. But if I fail, will someone jump in the tank after me? Or will the congregation watch me drown through the glass?

"Let's give her some encouragement," Ram tells the people.

They begin stomping their feet.

"It's time," he tells me.

Looking at his boyish face and steely eyes, listening to the bellowing crowd, I don't know what choice I have. I turn to the ladder, putting my shaking foot on the first rung. Turning back to Ram, I say, "You'd better jump in after me."

He smiles his mischievous grin, and I worry it's the last thing I'm ever going to see.

I climb up the ladder, the noise of the crowd growing fuzzy. I feel woozy and wonder if I'll even reach the water. If I fall off the ladder, will they forget about the rest?

I find a tiny platform at the top. Standing on it, I stare across the tank, which now seems twice as long as it did from below. Ram is *out of his mind.*

"God has given me many signs that you will be able to complete this test, Mina." Ram speaks more to the audience than to me. "You just need FAITH!"

After everything Ram has told them, he'll look foolish if I fail. Perhaps he actually thinks I can do this?

I *do* need faith—faith that Ram will save me when I fall into the tank.

I close my eyes and take my first step.

EIGHT

My foot splashes into the water.

I surge forward, but then, I stop. My foot has found grounding. I look down. I see nothing but water. I bring my other foot forward, and it, too, sinks several inches below the surface and then stops.

I look at Ram, amazed.

"Walk," he says. "WALK!"

I slowly pull my foot out, taking another step. And then another. I start to thank the Prophet and then realize that this is now blasphemous and could cause me to fall. I focus on walking.

I continue to find a toehold. I move slowly, afraid that any second I'll be pulled under. The farther toward the middle I get, the farther I am from the edge of the tank, where I have something to grab onto.

I'm not moving quickly, but I'm so tense, I'm short of breath. What's *happening*? There must be something helping me, something in the tank . . . but I can't *feel* anything. I can only describe it as stepping on thick water.

I keep walking, as the crowd screams my name in ecstasy: *Mina! Mina Clark, we love you!*

I grin, but Damon's face suddenly appears in my mind—the sin I've never confessed. I tilt to the left. Sure I'm about to fall, I throw my arms out to the side to catch my balance. The congregation gasps as they watch me right myself.

Concentrating on nothing but my legs, I resume a steady pace, and they yell support. I'm going to make it. I'm going to reach the other side!

One of the men in purple who waits at the top of the ladder takes my hand. He helps me onto the platform, then descends, leaving me alone. The audience claps louder, stomps their feet more. I wave at them. For the first time, I notice that the movie screen has lowered above me and there I am, walking across water, and I'm as big as a poster of Uncle Ruho!

Watching myself is disorienting, and I start to lose my balance. The man darts back up the ladder, grabbing my hand. "Careful there, honey!"

It's time to get down. I carefully descend the ladder, aware of my wet feet. I don't want to land on my rear end now. *How embarrassing.* I think of Dekker and want to giggle. Poor Dekker. He tries so hard.

When I reach the bottom, Ram gives me a huge hug. "Nice job," he whispers.

"Isn't she special?" he says into the microphone. "And aren't we lucky to be witnesses to this marvelous day?

Two girls in yellow come out from the sides of the stage with big, fluffy towels. They each wrap me in one, although only my feet and ankles are wet.

"Smile at the camera," whispers the one on my right.

When a contraption that looks like a huge beetle flies in front of us, the girl gives it a toothy smile. I try to imitate her.

"Now wave," she says.

I wave my hand. People stand and clap.

I can't believe how good I feel! Elation, joy, and relief flow through me. I want to run up the ladder and walk across the water again! Was I successful because I swore to follow the Savior? If I'd refused, would I have fallen in?

"Time to go," says the girl who told me to wave. Pulling on my hand, she and the other girl lead me off stage as Ram and the audience wave goodbye.

As soon as we are out of view, the girl says, "I'm Susanna, and you were wonderful. *Major* benny." Susanna is small and delicate with cropped blonde hair. She walks with the confidence of someone a foot taller.

"Totally razzamatazz," says the other. "I'm Frannie. We're your Hub escorts." Skinny and awkward, Frannie has weird metal bands across her teeth.

We enter a hallway, passing tall men standing by large equipment, many of them wearing headsets.

"Were you scared?" asks Frannie. "I would have been terrified."

"Can you not swim?" I ask, happy that she understands.

"Of course I can," she says. "It's all those people. Ew."

Susanna says, "Frannie's mother makes her volunteer on stage every week to get over her shyness, but I *love* it. I plan to be in the band one day."

Frannie's fear seems completely sensible. My whole body pulses with adrenaline from being in front of so many people.

"Susanna has a beautiful voice," says Frannie with admiration.

We walk through several large hallways, and the girls continue to chat at me, but all I can think about is the miracle that just occurred. I want this feeling to last *forever*.

I will study the ways of the Unbound. I will learn everything I can about the Savior and the Ascension. I will read the book that Ram gave me, front to back, as many times as it takes. I will keep coming back to the Worship Hub. I want to watch more movies, hear more singing, and be part of this crowd of passionate, happy people.

Looking at the girls to my left and my right, I wonder if they will be my friends. I can have friends here and a real life, that is what Ram was trying to tell me.

And school. I can go to SCHOOL.

I walked on water! Maybe I'm as special as Ram said I was.

Why was I risking everything by breaking their rules? It has to stop. I have to be a model member of the Unbound from now on. I'm getting my whites today, and I will get my greens as soon as possible and then my yellows. I want to be one of the distinguished women walking around in black or gray. I bet they go to the library *all* the time.

Once everyone respects me, they'll let me see Juda and the others as often as I want. I just need to prove myself. Walking on water has to be a huge step toward that, right?

"Here we are!" says Susanna, stopping at a green door. She opens it, revealing a small room with a dressing table and several clothing racks. Once we've entered, I see the dress Ram gave me hanging in the corner.

"It's so pretty," says Frannie, touching the material. "I love eyelet."

"You should change out of those green clothes," says Susanna.

"I have to?" I ask. The dress is lovely but is much less modest than I would like—short sleeves and only knee length.

"It's a gift from *Ram*," says Frannie, bewildered by my question.

"It's a real honor," says Susanna with gravity.

I take the dress with reluctance. "Where should I change?"

"Right here," says Susanna, like it's obvious, but there's no privacy in the room.

When I don't begin to undress, Frannie seems to sense the problem. She says, "Hey, look Susanna, there's makeup over here!"

Frannie joins Susanna at the dressing table and while they examine the contents of the drawers, I quickly change into the dress.

When I'm finished, I say, "Okay," and the girls spin around.

"Oooh!" says Frannie. "You look beautiful!"

"It's not too revealing?"

"I think it's perfect," Frannie says.

Susanna inspects me. "Adorable." Turning back to the table, she grabs a small brush. "But I think you're missing something."

"Susanna, you're so bad!" says Frannie.

"It's just blush!" Susanna slowly sweeps the brush across my cheeks. "Have you ever worn makeup before?"

"It's, um, not allowed where I'm from."

"It's not allowed until level Yellow here," says Frannie, raising an eyebrow at Susanna.

"The band members wear it on stage. And I've even heard," Susanna says, lowering her voice, "that Ram wears it during the show."

"Susanna!!" says Frannie, looking at the door. "You're so going to get us into trouble."

"You're major boring, Fran." Susanna puts the brush back on the table.

Feeling the soft, smooth fabric of my new dress, I ask, "Did spiders make this too?"

Susanna and Frannie stop what they're doing. "Spiders?" asks Frannie, a grin forming.

"Yeah, uh," I say, getting nervous. "Tabby said her clothes were made from spider silk."

"They were," says Susanna.

I relax. "Oh good. I thought I'd said something stupid. When Tabby told me, I said I *never* wanted to go to where all the spiders were. I would be completely terrified."

They burst out laughing.

I *have* said something dumb.

"It's spider silk," Susanna says, catching her breath, "but it's not actually made *by spiders*. It's synthetic. Like, a hundred years ago, a guy figured out how to imitate what a spider makes, and it's super strong and soft and stuff, so it's all we use."

"No need for blush now!" says Frannie. "She's gone pink for real!"

I'm mortified. Why did Tabby and her friends let me think that the Unbound kept thousands of spiders somewhere?

I don't need to ask. Tabby loves humiliating me.

"Let's get going. It's almost time for class." Seeing my confusion, Susanna adds, "'Refinement Training.' Ram wants you to join us."

"It's pretty yawny, but at least you get to hang with friends," says Frannie.

Having decided to be more well behaved, I nod with enthusiasm.

We walk out a back door, avoiding the crowd. My Bee swoops in, and to my surprise, two other Bees arrive for Frannie and Susanna. They must be under sixteen.

We walk toward a neighborhood I've never seen before, but it looks just like the one the Dixons live in.

I ask Susanna, "So do, um, a lot of people walk on water?"

She thinks for a moment. "Like, maybe five in ten?"

"So five people fall in the tank?"

"Yeps," she says. "It can be pretty funny."

A tremor of fear ripples through me, as I imagine pounding on that glass, trying to get out.

"Did you walk?" I ask them.

"We don't need to," says Frannie, as if it's obvious. "We were born innocent, into our whites. We don't need a Day of Validation."

"So everyone who goes in the tank is from Manhattan?" I wonder how many of us are here.

"No," says Frannie. "Sometimes people really mess up, and they have to start their levels all over again."

"You have to do a test to get your final whites," says Susanna, "when you're old and stuff, but that's a completely different test."

For several blocks, I can still hear Ram's voice rumbling out of the Hub. Part of me wants to go back.

"Are there always movies during the service?" I ask.

Frannie giggles. "What movie?"

"With the mountains and clouds and stuff." Maybe the girls were backstage and missed it.

Susanna puts her hand gently on my arm. "That wasn't a 'movie.' That was just like, an intro, I guess."

How many times will I embarrass myself today? "So what's a movie?"

"It has like a big, long story, and beautiful people, and a lesson at the end," says Frannie.

"Like you've seen one," says Susanna.

"I have!"

"Have not."

"I have . . . sort of," she says. "My grandfather saw one, and he told me about, like, every detail from start to finish."

"You don't have them, then?" I ask, deflating.

"No. Ram doesn't like them," says Susanna. "He says atheists made them."

"What's an atheist?" I ask.

"Someone who doesn't believe in God," says Susanna.

"You know—the people who live in the West?" says Frannie.

"People who don't believe in God live west of here?" A chill creeps up my back.

"Don't worry," says Frannie. "It's really far, like, days and days and days far."

"Can we stop talking about yawny stuff and start talking about what's major important?" Susanna's face and body go slack with impatience.

When neither of us answers, she says, "Silas Dixon! He's, like, the most beautiful guy in Kingsboro, and Mina is living with him."

Frannie wags her finger. "*Ram* is the most beautiful man in Kingsboro—"

"You have to get over it, Frannie. He's a billion years older than you." Susanna turns back to me. "Tell us about Silas."

"He's nice," I say.

"No way. You're not getting away with 'nice.' What does he look like when he wakes up? Have you seen him with his shirt off?"

Looking up at our Bees, Frannie exclaims, "Susanna!"

"I heard he *major* likes you," Susanna says, her eyebrows shooting up.

My whole body goes hot. Just listening to her feels like a betrayal of Juda.

Susanna drops her voice to a whisper. "Is it true you got caught sneaking out with him?"

Frannie gasps.

How does Susanna know? Does everyone know?

"You don't have to answer," she says, "but if you don't say, 'nope,' I will assume the answer is 'yeps.'"

What do I do? At home, my reputation would be ruined forever if it was known I'd been alone with a boy at night. But the rules seem to be different here, and I don't want to be caught in a lie. Before I know what's happening, I let the moment pass without saying anything.

"Wow," says Frannie.

"I knew it!" says Susanna. "This is gigantic. Silas has never liked *anyone* this much."

"He's your boyfriend?" Frannie's voice is full of awe. "Grats."

Grats? "It wasn't like that," I say. "He was trying to help me find—"

"I think it's romantic," she says. "An Unbound member and a woolie."

"What's a woolie?" I ask. Tabby used that word.

There's an awkward silence, then Susanna says, "It's a word people use to describe refugees from the island. It's not very nice." She gives a scolding eyebrow-raise to Frannie, who looks mortified. "It means, um, people who've had the wool pulled over their eyes."

I see. It means *fool*.

"Oh," I say. "Thanks for explaining."

"I'm sorry, Mina. It was an accident," says Frannie, who looks close to tears.

"It's okay," I say, my mood ruined. When people are being nice to me, I can easily forget what they must really think of me. Think of my opinion of them before I arrived: vicious, savage Apostates ready to gleefully murder me. I guess I'd hoped that once I started to change my mind about them, they would change their minds about me.

"I was just trying to say that I'm happy about you and Silas," says Frannie.

"There is no me and Silas," I say with sharpness. "Why would he like someone who grew up so *stupid*?"

Neither of them responds.

We arrive at a cute peach house with white curtains in the

windows. "This is it. Gentility Gardens!" says Susanna, trying to be light.

Before we walk inside, Frannie hugs me. "I'm so sorry. Please forgive."

Susanna hugs me too, and in a serious voice, different than the one she's been using all morning, she whispers, too low for Frannie to hear, "Be good to Silas. He needs your help."

We walk into the house, and I'm more confused than ever.

NINE

Walking into Gentility Gardens, I see no flowers, only a reception area with a table and a fancy carpet. When I ask Susanna where the garden is, she stands tall, saying, "*We* are the flowers, here to be tended to."

They walk me back into a larger space full of desks and chairs which is decorated sweetly in pink and green. The smell of luxurious soaps fills the air—so strong my eyes water. The room is surprisingly packed and everyone seems to be around my age. I spot Deborah, Phoebe, and Tabby against the far wall, and in the front row, I see a big bush of hair. It looks like Grace, but I refuse to be fooled again.

Susanna, Frannie, and I take a seat in the back row. A girl who doesn't look much older than us stands at the front of the class. She's as dainty as a little bird, with huge eyelashes, curled red hair, and perfect cupid bow lips. Her purple dress poofs out from her tiny waist. I doubt she's ever worn anything with a wrinkle or had a hair out of place.

"Pssssst, Mina," someone whispers. I look up. It *is* Grace in the front row. I can't believe it! She has a huge smile on her face, her hair is as big as ever, and she looks positively radiant in yellow. She waves at me. I wave back. Can I go sit by her? There doesn't appear to be a seat. I can't believe she's here! My heart swells with relief.

The bird girl in front starts speaking. "Good afternoon, girls. My name is Mrs. Prue." Her voice is so light and airy, it could be carried away by a breeze. "Welcome to class. Today is very significant. We have two special guests: The refugees Grace and Mina. Let's give them a round of applause." Several girls applaud loudly and smile, but I notice a few of them glowering. "Some of you more experienced girls will have to help them out today, okay? Joanne, posture please."

A girl in the third row sits up straighter.

"A lot of the ideas we talk about today might be new and some might be old, but it's important that we have a refresher as Promise Prom approaches."

Tabby rolls her eyes toward Deborah.

"Everyone is looking very fresh and pretty today, but I suggest that you all search the room for eye traps."

I freeze, having no idea what she's talking about.

The girls scrutinize one another as if they might discover bits of dirt. Several girls scan me, sneering. Are they checking to see who did or didn't bathe?

The girl named Joanne raises her hand. "I see one, Mrs. Prue."

"Very good," Mrs. Prue says, blinking her lashes. "Where?"

"Phoebe's shorts don't reach her knee."

"Excellent."

Phoebe squirms while the other girls look at her with disapproval. She tries to pull the shorts down a bit without much success.

"Phoebe, you've been warned before. That's a demerit." Mrs. Prue searches the room. "Anything else?"

"Yeps," says a girl in my row, raising her hand.

Mrs. Prue frowns. "Nice young women say 'yes,' not 'yeps,' Jane."

"Sorry, Mrs. Prue," Jane says. "*Yes*, I see one."

"Go ahead," says Mrs. Prue.

"The new girl, I forgot her name. I can see cleavage." To my horror, Jane turns and points at me.

I look down at my pretty new dress. I was worried it was too revealing, but I didn't want to be rude, so I put it on, and now I'm being reprimanded. Why can't I learn to speak up for myself?

Frannie has an apologetic look on her face, while Tabby smirks with pleasure.

I say, "Ram gave me this dress."

"What's that, dear?" Mrs. Prue says.

I clear my throat, repeating, "Ram gave me this dress."

"That was very kind of him, but what do we say to this, girls?"

As a group the girls say, "A woman is responsible for her own modesty."

Phoebe raises her hand, concerned. "Even when it's Ram?"

"Mina, dear, has Ram seen you in this dress?"

I shake my head.

Mrs. Prue is triumphant. "If he had, I'm sure he would've had you change immediately. He probably didn't realize you were so far along in your womanhood." She says to the others, "Let's explain *eye traps* to our newcomers."

A girl with freckles raises her hand, shaking it with enthusiasm.

"Yes, Louise, you may tell us."

"An 'eye trap' is any piece of clothing or lack of clothing that attracts the eyes of a male."

I'm confused. Everyone I've met seems so horrified by the veil, and yet wouldn't the eye trap problem be solved if everyone threw a cloak over their clothes? This is why we wear them—to contain the lusts of men.

"Very good!" Closing her eyes, Mrs. Prue pats her chest. "The men of the Unbound are honorable and devout, but men by nature are not very strong when it comes to the opposite sex. We don't need to tempt them. Offering temptation is as much a sin as the sin itself. We can live in harmony as men and women and not divide our society as the Propheteers do, because we know how to protect our femininity." She opens her eyes. "Mina, this was your first infraction, so you will not get a demerit, but next time you will." She looks around the room. "Promise Prom is coming up, and I know you're all very excited about it. Who here will be participating?"

Several girls, including Tabby and Deborah, raise their hands. The energy in the room is now buzzing. I've heard several people mention the Prom since I arrived, but I still have no idea what it is.

"I remember my Prom day," Mrs. Prue says. "It was so beautiful. My father and I still talk about it. I keep my necklace in a shadow box in our living room. I love that my husband can look at it and know I waited for him."

I don't see her hit any buttons, but the lights turn off. A 3-D image of a strange green fruit appears next to her.

"Look at this avocado. Isn't it beautiful? When you first cut into it, it's creamy and green and incredibly delicious."

The image changes. "This is the avocado on the second day. Its green fruit has turned brown. Maybe there is still a little of that beautiful color underneath. Maybe."

A new image comes into view. "The third day. The avocado is now black and rotted. You do whatever you can to keep it fresh, but nothing works. It's ruined. You only have one chance to cut into it and find ripe, beautiful fruit."

The lights come back up, and the avocado disappears.

I wish I could see Grace's face to learn what she thinks of this lesson, which reminded me of something one of my aunties would say.

"I'm not worried about you girls," says Mrs. Prue. "I look into your bright faces, and I know that none of you wants to let your husband discover rotted fruit."

Tabby guffaws.

"Miss Dixon, do you have a problem?"

"No, Mrs. Prue. I'm sorry. I just never thought of avocados as being very, um, sensual."

A few other girls giggle.

"Miss Dixon, I am a little concerned that you *do* know what is sensual. Would you care to explain to the class where your vast knowledge comes from?"

Everyone stops giggling. Tabby glares at Mrs. Prue. "I didn't mean to say that I know about sensual things. I just think avocados are vomit-inducing."

The laughter starts again.

"Okay, Miss Dixon. That's a demerit. Now, let's move on," says Mrs. Prue.

As Mrs. Prue introduces the topic of proper makeup techniques, I watch Tabby. Is she upset about the demerit? I can't tell.

I try to refocus on Mrs. Prue, who is saying, "Rouge should only be heavy enough to look like you are flushed from a long walk, no more. Mascara should be applied to make eyes look innocent and sweet. Eye pencil should be avoided unless you have particularly deep-set eyes. If you think you fall under this category, please see me after class. Questions?"

I have a lot, including *what is a demerit*, but I'm afraid if I ask, I'll get one.

"Okay," says Mrs. Prue. "Let's take a five-minute break while I set up the cooking demo."

The girls immediately begin to huddle and whisper. Grace rushes to me, almost knocking me over with her hug.

"Oh, Mina, I am SO happy to see you. I have so much to tell you, and I know you have so much to tell me! Isn't it amazing here? Just everything you ever dreamed of?"

"Are you okay?" I ask.

"I saw you walk on water! I didn't even know you were there, and then, all of a sudden, Ram was saying your name! It was, like, the most magnificent thing I've ever seen." She squeezes my arms. "How did it feel?"

"Pretty incredible," I admit. "I was terrified I would fall in."

"Of course! And that crowd was major immense."

I smile. Her halting, shy way of speaking is gone.

"I'm staying with a fabulous family," she says. "There's a son, and I'm allowed to sit and play games with him after dinner in the *same* room. Can you believe it?"

Seeing her, with her frizzy hair and big glasses, fills me with joy.

"Ram says my Day of Validation will be next week. Then we'll both be wearing white!" She must be borrowing the yellow clothes. "I'm so grateful to the Unbound for opening my eyes."

"So you're not upset about the Prophet?" I ask. Her tone suggests she hasn't been struggling with the news.

"It was a rude awakening, but the more I thought about it, the more it just made sense, you know? In all of my reading in the library, I never read anything that really *proved* that Sarah was divine. A lot of academics spoke out against Her, but most of their work was burned."

"But that's the point of faith, Grace. You have to have it even when there's no proof!" I surprise myself with this outburst. Didn't I just promise to follow the Savior?

After a few girls turn to stare, Grace pulls me into the corner, whispering, "You can't talk like that."

Is she telling me not "to talk like that" in this room or in front of her? "Sorry," I say.

She smiles. "That's okay. It's not an easy evolution."

It seems to have been for her. The lightness I felt after walking on water disappears. What has happened to the Grace from the Laurel Society who wanted to question things from all angles?

She rocks on her heels. "Are you excited for Prom? I can't wait. It's like a ball out of *Anna Karenina*. The girls will be in gorgeous dresses, and all the boys will want to dance with them. I wish we could be part of it, but at least we'll hear the stories the next day."

I nod with what I hope is enthusiasm.

"Don't you love the food?" she says. "And the showers?"

"I hate the showers," I confess. "Why is it so hot and then so cold?"

"For your health!" she says, as if I should know. "The cold water stimulates your immune system—adds years to your life!"

I would rather have lovely hot baths and a shorter life.

"What happened to your Nancy Drew book? Did it survive?" I say, happy to finally ask.

She frowns. "It got drenched, and then, like, quadrupled in size. My host-mom says I can find another one in the library, but I don't want another one."

"Of course you don't," I say. It's her only relic from the Laurel Society, plus her parting gift from Rayna. It's priceless. "Now it's just more unique." I smile.

She gives me a doubtful look. "Now it's more of a doorstop than a book."

I laugh. Looking around the room and trying to keep my voice light, I say, "Have you seen any of the others?"

"No. Well, I saw Dekker at the Worship Hub, getting passed around before he fell."

"No one else?"

She shakes her head. "You?"

Disappointed, I say, "No." I lower my voice. "I'm worried about Juda."

"Why? The Unbound are . . . are . . . They're generous and kind and would never want to hurt anyone."

I'm unable to bite my tongue. "Then what were all those guns when we arrived? And why did they throw us to the ground and separate us?"

"That was really intense and scary. I basically peed myself. My host-dad explained that they've had really dangerous people show up through the years. Some people from the island want to do them harm, and so they're really, really careful. They have to do extreme vetting."

Grace is really smart. She's read a ton of books. She's really educated, and I'm not. I want to believe her that these people are good and kind and have my best interest at heart. I want to open myself up to them, have a normal life, and go to school. But why have I walked around with such an uneasy feeling the whole time? "How did you decide you could trust them?" I ask.

"Because they don't walk around shooting each other in the streets! They aren't dragging each other into the Tunnel or poisoning each other's water supply!" She is indignant. "Look around, Mina. These people are living a civilized life. They're offering us everything—food, shelter, love—and asking nothing in return."

I gape at her blissful face. What's *happened* to her? "What if they decided Juda didn't pass their 'vetting?' What if they think he's dangerous? He had a gun on him."

"So did Dekker and I, and we're okay."

In Manhattan, when someone disappears, it always means the worst.

"You're going to see him soon. I know it," she says. "And

when you do, it will be so romantic! Like Heathcliff and Cathy meeting on the moors."

"You know when you say those things, I have no idea what you're talking about, right?"

"But you will! Did you know that the Unbound have a fabulous library? My host-mom keeps telling me about it. When I reach level Green, I'll be able to go, and when I reach level Yellow, I can check out books! We can read novels together!"

I confess, this sounds great.

"My host-mom was *so* impressed that I already knew how to read. I told her you could, too. She couldn't believe it!"

Grace is the one who gave me away? I can't believe how incautious she's being.

She removes her glasses to clean them on her shirt. "The higher level you are, the more freedom you have and the more school you can participate in. The lower you are, the more you're stuck at home with host-parents and Bees watching your every move. It's very well-thought-out."

"Okay, ladies, back to your seats," says Mrs. Prue.

Hugging Grace, I say, "I've been so scared." Even if she's changed, I'm still incredibly happy to see her.

She squeezes me back. "Stop that. You have no reason to be frightened. Everyone loves you. Everyone's on your side."

I whisper into her ear, "When can we talk alone?" The girls in the room, especially Deborah, keep glancing our way.

She replaces her glasses. "Next class, I guess?"

This isn't what I meant. I want privacy.

Moving back to the center of the room, I remember another question I have for her. "What's a demerit?"

"I'm not sure exactly, but I think you have to help the Fallen for a few hours."

"The Fallen?"

"The women you see picking up garbage. They've sinned,

and they have to clean up after the Unbound for the rest of their lives."

"That's awful," I say. "What did they *do*?"

"No more talking, please," says Mrs. Prue.

Grace returns to her seat, while I sit back down in mine. If Grace is correct, then freedom comes from attaining higher levels, and Ram said this requires a "spiritual and inner awareness." I'm afraid I need a *lot* of classes.

TEN

When class is finally over, Susanna and Frannie escort me home (with our Bees darting overhead).

"What did you think?" Frannie asks.

"I, uh, think I have a lot to learn," I say, distracted by my conversation with Grace.

"You'll be luminary. Don't worry!" Susanna says.

Frannie loops her arm in mine (I think she still feels bad about calling me a woolie). "Susanna's right. You'll have the hang of everything soon, and you'll have lots of friends, and everyone will love you as much as we do!"

"You know, Ram is working on this, like, peace treaty thing with your people, right?" Susanna says. "So maybe one day *you'll* be giving *us* a tour of Manhattan!"

I can't say I see this happening.

"That would be so benny!" Frannie says.

"You want the treaty?" I ask, surprised.

"Of course," Frannie says. "It's God's will."

"How do you know?" I ask, hoping I'm not being rude.

"Because Ram told us," she says, as if it's obvious.

God wants the Unbound to make peace with Uncle Ruho? Does that mean I might see Nana again? Or Sekena? Or my father? If Frannie and Susanna can picture themselves traipsing around Manhattan one day, then maybe it's not impossible.

"How often do we have refinement classes?" I ask.

"Wednesdays and Fridays," Susanna says.

Today is Friday, so I have to wait *five days* until I see Grace again? We came through the tunnel on Tuesday. So much has happened, it feels like a lifetime ago.

As we walk past a block of multicolored houses, I ask, "What do the colors of the houses symbolize?"

"What do you mean?" Phoebe says.

"Does the color of your house represent your relationship to the Savior?" The Dixons have a purple house, so I'm curious what that means.

"No, silly, it just means it's a color your family likes." Susanna laughs, but it's not mean.

I don't understand why this is silly considering the requirements for their clothing, but I say nothing. No one wants to hear their rules are random.

We arrive at the Dixon house, and the girls stop at the door to say goodbye.

"Do you want to come in?" I ask, smiling. Surely Gilad and Bithia would be happy to see me making friends.

"Susanna sure would!" Frannie says with a big smile, and Susanna smiles demurely.

"We can't," says Susanna, "but thank you. We're helping the decorations committee with Promise Prom."

"Okay," I say. I'm sad to see them go. They're nice, and they actually answer questions.

Inside the house, I find Silas sitting on the couch in the front room. With his green clothes and yellow hair, sitting against the floral couch, he looks like a big dandelion. He's staring into space, oblivious to my entrance. He must get it from Gilad, who also stares into space a lot.

"Hello, Silas," I say in a quiet voice. I'm still getting used to being able to speak to a male before he's spoken to me. It feels impertinent.

He blinks slowly, then turns to me and smiles. "Mina! You're back. How was worship?"

"Good, I guess. I'm one-day White—or one-morning White—or whatever."

"I see from your dress," he says. Cringing, I want to cover my exposed chest. "How do you feel? Different?"

"It was pretty amazing." I assume he's seen people walk on water before, but I wish I could convey how spectacular it was. "I didn't drown, thank the Proph—I mean, thank the Savior." Is that a thing people say? "How's your wrist?"

He holds up his arm, showing me a thin rubbery cast that covers his hand to his forearm. It's a creepy flesh tone and looks nothing like the thick, rough cast our doorman got when he broke his elbow. "They fused the bone back together, so it'll heal quickly." Seeing my astonished face, he adds, "They use lasers. It's major benny. Plus, they have good meds at the hospital." He grins. "And it's nothing compared to what's going to happen to me when Tabby hears the Smoker suits are gone."

I wonder where she goes when she sneaks out? "Maybe she'll feel sorry for you."

"If you think so, you don't know Tabby very well," he says, looking more tormented by the thought of his sister than by his wrist.

I sit by him on the couch. "Silas, I have to ask you . . ."

"Anything," he says.

"Have you heard anything more about Juda?"

He frowns. "Hmmm. Judaaaaa . . ."

"One of the boys in the house," I say, frustrated.

"Nooope. Sorry."

"Is there someone you can ask? The same person who told you where they were staying?"

He seems irritated. "No. There's no more information." He leans in, grinning. "You maybe want to go to the Leisure Center later?"

"You're acting strange," I say. I think it's the medication.

"If you're going to be yawny, I'm going back to my Tact."

He's acting like Tabby—bratty and mean.

"I'm dumb, remember?" I say. "I don't know what a 'Tact' is."

He gasps. "But they're the best thing ever! You *have* to get one. I was watching mine when you came in."

Looking around the room, I see nothing. "Where?"

"No, it's here." He points to his eye. "You have it installed at the Leisure Center. I upgrade about every two years, but people do it more often if they can afford it."

"What's it for?" I ask, astonished.

"Everything! Sending nods, scoping vid, touring the 'scape. You *have* to have one!"

"Silas?" Gilad's voice comes from upstairs. Immediately, Silas becomes less animated, leaning back into the couch sleepily, letting his legs drift apart.

Gilad appears at the bottom of the stairs. When he sees the two of us on the couch, he grins. I think this may be the first time I've seen him genuinely smile. "What are you two up to?"

"Talking, Dad. Just talking." He produces a goofy grin.

Bithia comes stomping down the stairs behind Gilad. "Stop being nice to them, Gilad. They're in trouble!"

We are? I thought taking my pledge and getting my whites was my absolution.

Bithia wags her finger at us. "Ram might think you're reborn and all that, but we have rules in this house, and you both broke 'em. There are consequences to such things."

"But Mom—" Silas begins.

"Don't 'but Mom' me. You knew exactly what you were doing when you climbed out that window."

Silas says nothing more, and the two of us sit on the couch, staring at our knees as we wait for her pronouncement.

"Tabby needs help getting ready for Promise Prom, and you're going to help her. Whatever she wants for an entire day."

"But that's cruel and unusual!" says Silas, misery entering his voice.

I say nothing, thinking that this is the lightest sentence I've ever received for anything.

"Listen to your mother," says Gilad. He heads for the kitchen, giving Silas a wink before he leaves the room.

Bithia rubs her stomach, while her eyes narrow. "Mina, I need you to come with me. There's . . . a situation, and you've been requested."

"What is it?"

"That's not really your place to ask, is it?" Bithia says.

Exhausted by the long morning, I'd been looking forward to time alone in my room. Resisting a heavy Tabby sigh, I leave Silas sitting on the couch and follow Bithia.

She marches me out the door at a fast pace.

My Bee hovers overhead as I hurry to keep up. "I wanted to say how sorry I am about last night."

"I should hope so," she says, not looking at me. "We've sacrificed quite a bit to have you and disobedience is no way to thank us."

They seem to have so much of everything—enough for three families. Am I really a burden to them?

"Becky Houseman wouldn't even say hello to me at the hospital last night."

"Because of me?" I ask, confused.

"Of course, child. Not everyone is as open as Mr. Dixon and me."

"Like Mr. Tanner," I say, understanding.

She gives me a sideways glance. "Yes, like Mr. Tanner and other Purists. They have strong ideas about your people and no amount of chitchat from you is going to change them."

"But why are they being rude to *you*?"

We walk past a blue house with green trim and then a purple house with an enormous bed of orange flowers. I think Bithia isn't going to answer me, when she says, "Some of them have the idea that you'll spread your beliefs—your old beliefs—that anyone who spends time with you will end up believing in your Prophet."

"So they think you and Gilad are people of weak faith?"

"No!" she says, mouth twisting in annoyance. "They're worried about *anyone* who spends time with you."

Picturing the faces of the girls at Gentility Gardens, I wonder how many had been warned not to speak to me. And why was the crowd at the Worship Hub so enthusiastic if they don't believe my pledge? "Everyone here seems so confident in their faith. Why are they threatened by someone else's?"

She stops walking. "Don't be smart with me. We believe in equality and all that here, but we also know a woman's place. She shouldn't overstep her bounds, and that's exactly what you've done, missy. You need to learn to talk less and listen more. Pull another stunt like last night, and we won't hesitate to send you to the Forgiveness Home." She starts marching again.

I was only asking questions. How is that "overstepping my bounds?" I wish she would explain, but, chastised, I stay quiet.

Soon we reach a faded yellow house. A man opens the door.

His face is tired and grim, his hair gray. He wears a frown that mimics the sad slump of his shoulders. "You're late," he mumbles.

"We came as quickly as we could manage, Horton," Bithia says.

Horton takes me in from head to toe. His expression suggests he shares a lot of opinions with Mr. Tanner.

"May we come in?" says Bithia.

Opening the door wider, he reveals a dining room and living room identical to the Dixons' and the Delfords'. He points up the stairs. "She's in the first bedroom on the left."

"Thank you," says Bithia, brushing by him.

I follow, not wanting to be left alone with Horton for even a moment.

Despite the daylight, the bedroom is completely dark. Only after blinking a few times do I finally see a figure sitting in a chair in the corner.

"Rose!" I cry, rushing to her side.

She turns to look at me, but her head moves slowly, carefully.

Her face is ashen, her brown eyes large and bloodshot. Her full lips are chapped and cracked, and her plump body seems to have shrunk in on itself, like fruit going bad.

"What's wrong?" I ask her, horrified.

"She won't eat. And now she's stopped drinking water," says Bithia, behind me.

"Rose, is that true?" I kneel at her feet. "Are you doing this to yourself or are they hurting you?"

She studies me for a while. "Mina . . ." is all she'll say.

"Yes, it's Mina!" I say, taking her hand in mine. "I'm here."

"No one's hurting her," Bithia says. "This is all her doing."

"Why won't you eat?" I ask.

She turns away from me, closing her eyes. She seems to go to sleep.

I don't understand how she could look so terrible when I saw her less than a week ago. Her tongue is yellow, the corners of her mouth crusty.

She's scaring me. How long can a person survive without food or water? When the Ashers locked me in a room for twenty-four hours without either, I felt like my insides had been scraped out by a nail file. "You have to eat or you'll get really, really sick, Rose."

Her voice comes out as a scratchy whisper. "Where is my son?"

Sadness overwhelms me. I can't bear to tell her I don't know. "He's coming," I whisper.

"When?"

"Soon. Probably tomorrow. He . . . has a little cold, and he wants to be well before he sees you." What am I saying? I can't magically make Juda appear.

"That sounds like him," she says, smiling for the first time.

I squeeze her hand. "He misses you."

Her dark eyes expand as she says, "Ask him to forgive me for lying about his father. I can't go to my grave knowing he's angry at me."

"No one is going to their grave, Rose. You're going to get better. How about we eat something together?" I look to Bithia. "Can we get some food from Horton?"

She shakes her head. "I'm not supposed to leave the room."

"Please. I don't think she'll eat otherwise."

Bithia stares at Rose, unsure.

Rose nods, saying, "Yes. With Mina."

Encouraged, Bithia agrees to go downstairs. "I'm leaving this door open, Mina. So don't you try anything."

I have no idea what she thinks I can do, but I nod.

As soon as Bithia is gone, Rose leans in, saying softly, "He's trying to poison me."

"Horton?" I ask, taken aback.

She nods.

The man downstairs was unnerving and disdainful, but is he really trying to kill Rose? Her eyes dart at the open doorway and back to me. She's acting deranged.

"Will you eat Horton's food if I eat some first?" I ask, desperate. She shakes her head. "What if Bithia does?"

Shaking her head again, she says through closed teeth, "I heard them talking downstairs. They hate us. Me and you. They want us dead."

"What?" My voice rises. "Who do you mean? Why?"

Bithia is back holding a tray with two bowls. "Here we are! Some delicious potato soup." She places the tray on a small table next to Rose.

"Go on, Mina. Show her how delicious it is!" says Bithia.

Sitting up, I take a bowl and stir the soup with a spoon. "Mmmm. It smells delicious. You should have some, Rose." My voice is not as confident as before.

Tightening her lips together, she shakes her head.

Lifting my spoon to my mouth, I see her eyes bulge. Could she be right? Could there be poison in it?

Bithia grins at me, waiting for me to try it. She wouldn't let me eat something that would hurt me . . . right?

I breathe deeply and swallow a big spoonful.

I immediately cry out, and Rose screams.

"It's hot! Scalding hot," I say, waving my hand in front of my mouth. "It's fine. I just burned my tongue."

"No need to be so dramatic!" says Bithia.

"It's good," I say, eyes watering. "You should have some, Rose. *Please.*" Dipping my spoon back into my bowl, I blow on the soup and take a second mouthful.

I'm about to take a third, when suddenly Rose's arm flies up and sends the tray tumbling to the floor. The crack of ceramic bowls is followed by the deafening clang of the metal tray.

"This is unacceptable behavior!" screams Bithia.

Horton appears in the doorway. "What was THAT?" he screeches. He sees the mess. "You're going to clean that up, Mrs. Alvero!" he yells at Rose.

"Visiting time is over," says Bithia. I don't want to leave, but she pulls me out the door.

"I'll be back, Rose. I promise!" I yell, as Bithia marches me down the stairs.

I can still hear Horton hollering, as Bithia closes the front door. Once outside, Bithia starts complaining about how rude Rose was.

"She needs her son," I say. "She'd be fine if you'd let her see him, I promise."

"That's not my decision to make," she says, as she leads us home.

"But you could ask Ram, couldn't you?"

Without answering, she quickens her pace.

I jog to catch up to her. "Couldn't you?"

"Why would I do you any favors after you've treated my family with such disrespect?"

I have no answer for her, and we walk the rest of the way in silence.

By the time we reach the house, I feel an uncomfortable tightness in my stomach, but I have no way of knowing if it's stress or something more ominous. Deciding I don't want to wait to find out, I run upstairs and force myself to throw up in the toilet.

ELEVEN

The next morning, Bithia cooks a breakfast large enough for the whole block. She claims she wants us all to have plenty of fuel for our day of Prom preparation; however, the copious amounts of biscuits, butter, eggs, and plump meats make me want to crawl back into bed.

The conversation is dominated by Tabby's experience working off her demerit. Before dawn, she was forced to wake up and visit the small compound in the East where the Fallen live.

"It was major feeble, the worst," she says, slumping in her chair.

"Did you have to touch garbage?" asks Silas, enjoying himself.

"I wish," Tabby says. "Anything would've been better than being lectured by a woman that looks like Dad."

Bithia and Gilad laugh.

"I hope they taught you the importance of refinement," Bithia says.

"Those are the least refined women I've ever met. They live together like animals."

"What do you mean?" Silas asks, interested for real now.

"One of them burped, and the rest of them laughed and laughed. It's like they aren't women at all anymore. They curse and yell. It was just . . . pathetic."

Corny burps loudly.

Silas laughs, as Bithia and Gilad frown. "That is unacceptable, Cornelius. Say 'excuse, me,'" Bithia says.

"Cuse me," Corny says. "Why do the ladies live and burp together, Mom?"

"Because they didn't behave like nice young women," Bithia says.

"Two of them were woolies!" Tabby says.

After Gilad raises an eyebrow at her, she says, "They were refugees, I mean. And get this, they *want* to be Fallen. They *like* living there."

Giving Bithia an annoyed look, Gilad says, "Surely the point of the demerit system is to demonstrate the humiliation of joining the Fallen?"

"Yes, dear," Bithia says.

"Don't worry, Dad," Tabby says. "Just because the Fallen live better than the Propheteers doesn't mean it's not major disgusting. I wouldn't live with them for all the Tacts in Kingsboro."

"I'm sure there's no danger of that, Honey Bunches," Gilad says. "Just stop talking back to your teachers and you'll be fine." He smiles at her. He seems so sweet when he talks to Tabby.

"What happened to your new dress?" Tabby asks me, all innocence. She was in class yesterday when I was told it was an "eye trap."

"I'm altering it," Bithia says.

I am back in the green clothes until Bithia can modify the dress and find me other white ones. I'm sure Tabby is thrilled to see me back in the sickly pea green.

Silas wears the same unsightly color, and I wonder why he hasn't progressed to yellow. I'll have to remember to ask.

Finishing her food, Tabby stands, throwing down her napkin and looking at Silas and me. "Okay, freakos. Time to be my servants for the day!"

Silas and I look at each other with dread. Maybe this punishment is going to be worse than I thought.

Silas and I sit on the cold floor inside the atrium of the Leisure Center constructing flowers out of tissue paper. Every Unbound kid under eighteen must be here. The younger children run around laughing and blowing up balloons, while the older ones, like us, take care of the more complicated decorations.

We have to make the paper flowers exactly as Tabby instructed us: "layer the white tissue paper, fold it like an accordion, attach the pipe cleaner, and fluff the paper out. The *fluffing* is the most important part." Because of his broken wrist, Silas can only layer the paper and place the finished flowers into piles. I would never say it, but I think these flowers look like big wads of toilet paper.

"You're quiet today," Silas says.

I've spent the morning worrying about Rose and wondering how on earth I can get Juda to visit her. If he knew she was ill, he would be there in a heartbeat. So either he doesn't know, or he can't reach her.

Looking around at the dozens of paper flowers, I ask, "Did Tabby say how many she needed?"

"No, which is a bad sign. She probably wants all the guests chin-deep in flowers."

"It looks like wedding decorations."

"Yeah, but it's not. All of the Promise girls will be celebrating their honor."

"Their family honor?" I understand this. A family's name is all they have in the end. Sadness drifts over me as I think again of the dishonor I have done to the Clark name.

"Yes, but more than that," Silas says. "It's about a girl's . . . you know . . . her *purity*." He smiles shyly.

His embarrassment finally makes me realize what he's talking about: Tabby's virginity. *Of course.* Mrs. Prue talked about Prom and then showed us pictures of the avocado and what happens when you cut into it too soon. This party will celebrate Tabby's untouched femininity.

Seeing all the teenage boys who are helping to decorate, I ask, "Are boys invited to the party?"

"Yeah," he says. "It's, like, the biggest party of the year."

I make another flower without speaking. I'm horrified. Women gather together in Manhattan to celebrate things such as the arrival of menses, but we would never do such a thing under the gaze of men. It would be humiliating, to say the least. I'm embarrassed for Tabby and wonder if her consistently foul temper is about the shame she's about to endure.

Tabby works across the room, separating twinkly lights. She doesn't look ashamed or uncomfortable. On the contrary, she's giving orders to two girls in green who seem very afraid of her. The nervous girls have stringy brown hair and buck teeth.

Silas follows my gaze. "Those are the *otter daughters*," he says. "I told you about them."

With simpering looks, the girls take strings of lights from Tabby.

"I feel bad for them," I say.

"You shouldn't. Growing up, they liked to bite people. And look at those teeth!"

Dekker and Juda are living *in their house*. Maybe they can get a message to Juda about his mother! I'm wondering how to approach them, when a familiar voice says, "Here you two are!"

I look up to see Susanna and Frannie. Susanna grins madly while Frannie grows shy, unable to look at Silas.

Susanna sticks out her lower lip, pouting. "Silas, I thought you were going to help me wrap the pillars in ribbon."

"Sorry, Susanna," he says. "Tabby put me on flower duty."

Susanna glances at me. "Or maybe you like the company over here a bit better?"

Silas, not looking up from his pile of tissue papers, whispers, "Maybe I do."

My whole body goes red and hot, as if someone shoved me in front of an open oven. I keep folding the flowers.

Frannie nudges Susanna with her elbow. "Let's find Marjory and ask her what she needs us to do."

The girls walk away, Susanna looking back over her shoulder at Silas. Reaching a group of girls arranging chairs, Susanna speaks in an animated fashion. She then points to me and Silas. No doubt she is telling them what Silas just said. Why did he have to do that?

Silas and I sit in awkward silence. We continue making flowers, avoiding eye contact. I'm still figuring out how to talk to the "otter daughters," when Silas says, "So, uh, do you know why virginity is even a thing?"

"*What?*" I can't have heard him correctly.

"Chastity—the reason people started caring about it. Do you know why?"

Silas seems determined to embarrass me at every possible moment.

I say nothing, but he continues anyway. "It's about property. Like, thousands of years ago, the land and cows and stuff were handed down through the men, and they had to be sure they were giving their stuff to *their* kids, and the only way of being sure a kid was yours was if your wife had never slept with anyone else."

I feel so out of place. The only person who speaks this way with me is Nana. I can't believe a boy would even say the *word* virginity to me, let alone converse about it. *Please stop talking.*

"Like, think about what might've happened if people had decided that property should be handed down through women, you know? Women knew exactly who their kids came from, right? Men would've like, constantly needed to behave well, so that the women didn't say, 'Maybe you're *not* the dad.'" He grins at the thought.

"But if a man thought he wasn't the dad, wouldn't he just leave?" I ask, surprised I've entered the conversation.

Silas stops arranging flowers, contemplating. The sunlight catches his long eyelashes. "But if it's a matriarchy, then she could just find a new husband, and no one would judge her."

"Matriarchy?"

"A society ruled by women."

I've never heard this word before. "Where is the matriarchy?"

He smiles. "I don't actually know any. I've just read about them in books."

Of course it doesn't exist.

Silas makes it sound like *matriarchy* would solve a great deal of problems, but would it? A lot of women raising children without fathers doesn't sound so perfect to me. It sounds hard.

"I know of one," I say, thinking that this is what the Laurel Society must be—women in charge, raising children, without the guidance of men.

"You do?" he says, amazed.

"Yes, it's, uh . . ." I want to say that Grace lived with them her entire life, and that the women are strong and amazing. I want to explain the horrible price for living with them is abandoning your family, living underground, and deciding you hate men.

"Does it count if there are no men at all?" I ask.

"Only women live there? How is that possible, with babies and stuff?"

I can't risk betraying the Laurel Society, even to this striking boy. "Never mind. I'm confused about the word."

His face sinks. "That's okay. It's a complicated concept." Trying to keep the conversation going, he says, "There's no animal in nature that cares about virginity, so why do we make such a *big deal* out of it?"

Silas seems like he's read a lot of books. "No boy has ever spoken to me this way."

"Oh," he says. "I'm sorry."

"Don't apologize. It's . . . different, but I think I like it. I like learning new things." Silas speaks with me like I'm another male. Ram treats me like I'm special, but I feel his authority over me. I don't feel that way with Silas.

"I'm not always great with people," he says, less confident than when he was talking about history. "A lot of people, uh, don't like me."

I look at Susanna across the room. "I don't think that's true."

"Do you like me?" he asks.

I'm thrown. I want to tell him about Juda, but I've tried hard to keep my feelings for him private. "I . . . uh . . ."

Seeing my discomfort, he says, "I mean *like*, Mina, nothing more."

"Oh. Yes. I like you."

He smiles. "Good. I like you, too." He leans forward, squeezing my forearm with his good hand. "A lot."

I feel the watchful gaze of every girl in the room. I look around to see Susanna, Frannie, and a dozen other faces gaping at an action that at home would mean I was now engaged.

Uneasy, I hop up, heading to Tabby. I hear Silas say, "Don't go over there!" but I ignore him.

When I reach Tabby and the "otter daughters," I say, "Is there anything I can help you with?"

"Are you done with the flowers?" asks Tabby, glancing at Silas in doubt.

"No, but I, uh, need a break."

"Yeah, my brother is annoying," says Tabby.

The otter daughters giggle. Tabby stares at them and they stop.

"Hello," I say to them.

They stare back at me, mouths open.

"Mina, meet Ginnie and Delilah. Ginnie and Delilah, meet Mina."

Smiling, I say, "Nice to meet you." They say nothing, apparently struck dumb by my presence. "Are you part of the celebration tonight?" I ask, but they continue to stare.

Looking away from my face, Delilah says, "We're not allowed to talk to you."

I don't know how to respond.

"Not allowed," Ginnie echoes.

Handing them the remaining lights in her hands, Tabby leads me away. "Don't freak out. They have a refugee in their house, and you're a refugee who breaks rules. Their dad would kill them for talking to you."

"You mean they have *two* refugees," I say, correcting her.

"Huh?" she says, ready to go back to her task.

"There are two boys staying at the Delford house."

"No way," she says. "Families are only allowed to have one Propheteer at a time. Everyone knows that."

Completely confused, my head whips over to look at Silas. Why did he say he was sneaking me out to look at *two* boys?

But I have no chance to ask him, because Silas is gone.

He must have known I would ask the Delford girls about

Juda and Dekker. He knew I would figure out that he deceived me. *Why would he lie?*

Running out of the Leisure Center, I don't see him. My Bee follows me outside, humming louder than ever. I head in the direction of the Dixons, and, before long, I spot Silas' hurrying figure in the distance.

"Silas!" I shout. He looks over his shoulder but doesn't slow down. He can't possibly think he can avoid me. We live in the same house.

Silas breaks into a run. I jog after him, wondering if there's a rule against refugees running. Will my Bee sound an alarm?

Before long, Silas reaches the Dixons', rushing through the front door. I'm right behind him, racing across the living room, when Bithia appears. "Mina. I was about to come find you."

I try to step around her. What if Silas locks himself inside his room? He could stay in there for days, and I need answers *now*.

Bithia puts her hand on my shoulder. "I need you to come with me."

"Sorry," I say, "but I really need to talk to Silas."

"Your friend Rose is in the hospital."

My body seems to sink into the floor. Rose. I'd stopped thinking about her. "What happened?" I ask.

"I don't know. Horton didn't say."

Horton—the man Rose said was trying to kill her.

"Can you take me to her?" I ask.

Bithia nods, sympathy on her face.

As we leave the house, I look up and see Silas watching us from the upstairs window. I give him a look that I hope he can understand: you can't avoid me forever.

TWELVE

Bithia leads me to a car sitting at the end of the block. I've never known anyone who owned a car. This one is shiny red and looks like an enormous Twitcher helmet on wheels. I'm not entirely sure how it keeps its balance.

As we get close, the top of the car buzzes opens, revealing two seats. Bithia digs in her purse and pulls out an enormous pair of sunglasses. "Get in, honey."

I'm not sure how. I watch Bithia use a small step near the front bumper to climb inside and then mimic her rather awkwardly.

"I hope you don't mind that I have to drive," Bithia says, pressing a button. "We don't believe in AI here."

Tabby has used this word before. "What's 'AI?'"

"Artificial Intelligence," she says, backing up the car. I'm mesmerized, never having seen a woman drive before. "The spirit can't work through technology."

Turning the wheel, she directs the car forward and into the street with surprising speed. She says, "You can program a robot to believe in whatever religion you want, but you can't give it a soul. Faith without the hand of God is blasphemy."

I'm confused. "So . . . um . . . your car used to hold religious beliefs?"

"Imagine if your Bee started to say it loved you. Wouldn't that be strange?" she asks.

"Yes. Very." I try not to laugh.

"Exactly. Because it's a piece of metal. We don't believe in technology or machines having emotions or trying to manipulate us. It's just common sense. God is the only One who has the right to create life. Not man. Out west they don't have the proper respect for God, and let me tell you . . . "

I wait for her to tell me, but she doesn't finish the sentence.

I'm glad she stops talking, wanting her to concentrate on steering. She behaves as if operating a car is as easy as fixing tea.

We arrive at a street with tall office buildings, like the ones uptown that house government agencies. We stop at a round one that looks like half a tomato dipped in silver.

"You go on inside. I'll be back in an hour," Bithia says. I get out, trying not to fall, and as I'm walking away, she adds, "Behave in there. We don't need any more trouble."

My Bee arrives just as she zooms off. The tomato building isn't very welcoming, but if Rose is here, I have to go inside.

The front door is open, and I'm surprised to find an empty room—no people, no chairs, nothing—just a silver room with a round ceiling. The front door shuts behind me.

A female voice from above says, "Please prepare for your exam."

"What exam?" I say, turning my head to find the person speaking.

"Stay still," the woman says.

Her voice is so authoritative that I freeze. But when red lasers start shooting from every direction, I duck.

The lasers disappear. "Please stay still, Miss Clark. This will only take forty-three seconds." She sounds irritated.

I remind myself that if the Unbound wanted to kill me they've had plenty of opportunities. I stand straight, trying to be still.

The lasers return, flicking over my toes, climbing my ankles, and creeping up my thighs. As they ascend my abdomen and chest, my stomach flutters thinking of a Senscan. Surely this technology is more advanced than ours. What can this red light see? *What if it can read my mind?*

After the laser has progressed over my neck, face and skull, the lights disappear.

"Proceed to the waiting room," the voice says. A door opens to my right. Everything inside the next room is made of the same silver material as the last—the chairs, tables, floors, even the doorknobs. I take a seat.

An athletic woman in gray scrubs enters the room after a few minutes. Although her hair is clipped back in a girlish ponytail, her expression is very serious and professional. She wears red glasses that are wider than her angular face. "You are infection free," she says and I realize she was the women talking to me through the speaker. "You had to be cleared before we could let you in."

She sits in the chair next to me. "Your blood pressure, CBC, and immune responses are perfect; I'm pleased with your overall lack of sun damage. The cloak and veil really protect your skin." She leans toward me. "But they aren't allowed here, and I can see that you're already experiencing dilation of the cutaneous blood vessels and recruitment of inflammatory cells."

"Huh?"

"Sunburn. You're wearing sunstop every day, right?"

I'm not sure what sunstop is.

"Step three, in the shower," she says. "Never skip it."

"I've been wiping it off," I say sheepishly.

She frowns.

"Sorry," I say, as if I've wronged her personally.

She stands. "Follow me." We walk down a long corridor, her soft shoes making a squishing sound on the silver floor.

Stopping at a sealed door, she puts on a mask and hands me one as well. "This entire facility is made of antibacterial nano cones. Germs and bacteria can't survive on any surface. That means that the dirtiest objects going into this room are you and me." She points to a bottle of milky gel attached to the wall. "Cover your hands well. It forms a coating that works better than gloves."

The gel goes on wet but dries immediately, creating a film that reminds me of egg whites. She presses a big button to open the door.

Unlike Rose's bedroom at Horton's, this room is very bright. All the surfaces are silver and shiny, the air cold and sterile. Strange equipment and unnerving instruments are spread around the room, like aliens lying in wait.

Rose lays in a bed in the center of everything. Her eyes are closed. Her face is pale and her forehead is drenched in sweat, her breathing fast and labored.

Anyone can see that Rose is very ill.

A thin man hovers behind her looking bored, checking computers. He also wears a mask and gray clothes.

"She just fell asleep," the woman with the glasses tells me.

"I'd like to talk to the doctor," I say, indicating the man.

"I'm the doctor," the woman says.

"Oh." First Bithia drives the car and now this.

"I'm Dr. Laban, but you can call me Dr. Rachel."

"Okay," I say. I want to ask her how she became a doctor, but I'm too worried about Rose.

"She's stable," says Dr. Rachel, gently taking Rose's hand. "But her refusal to eat is making her condition much worse."

Her condition? "I thought she was sick because she was starving herself," I say, panicking.

"Her host thought so, too, but she's having spasms, which isn't consistent with the symptoms of starvation." She touches Rose's temple. "We found toxins in her blood."

I feel faint. "She told me she was being poisoned. She told me Horton was trying to kill her, and I didn't listen!" I want to kill him for hurting Rose.

"Horton?" Dr. Rachel says. "He's a bit crabby, but he wouldn't hurt a fly. He was very upset when he brought Rose in."

"No! Rose was sure, and I didn't believe her. I should've listened to her!"

"It wasn't Horton. It's impossible," Dr. Rachel says.

"Everyone hates us here!" I say, with increasing dismay. "He's a Purist like Mr. Tanner, and he wants Rose dead! When I met him he—"

"He's from Manhattan," she says, cutting me off.

I stop speaking, dumbfounded.

"I'm not supposed to tell you. You have to be level Yellow before any former Propheteers can reveal themselves to you. But I guarantee Horton Groodly was not harming Rose. The man takes in more refugees than anyone I know."

"How many are there? Where are the others?" I ask, hope swelling in my chest.

"I can't tell you. I shouldn't have told you about Horton."

I hope my dirty look lets her know how tired I am of secrets.

With sympathy, she says, "I asked for you today, Mina, because I need to talk to you about the tests I ran on Rose. The results are . . . odd. They showed traces of mercury in her blood."

Dizziness forces me to sit down on the cold floor.

"Mark, get her some water," Dr. Rachel tells the man in the room. He hurries out.

"You seem to know what that means." She crouches down next to me. "Is mercury poisoning common on the island?" she asks.

Covering my mouth with my hands, I nod.

Mark returns with a glass of water and hands it to me. Dr. Rachel says, "Please give us a few minutes," and he leaves again.

"People stopped using mercury over a century ago," she says.

I take a sip of water and then hold up the cold glass, admiring the clarity of the liquid. These people can't understand the preciousness of what they possess. My father spent his entire life working toward one glass of water this pure and delicious.

Putting down the glass, I say, "It's in the drinking water." Dr. Rachel's eyes gape. How much should I say? "It's only been going to the Convenes. Uncle Ruho put it there."

"But . . . why?"

I only know what Rayna and Ayan told me. "Uncle Ruho thinks we're running out of resources. He wants to make the population smaller. He wants to destroy the Convenes and save the Deservers." Does Dr. Rachel even know the difference?

Dr. Rachel has gone pale. After a moment she says, "Ram is negotiating a treaty with Ruho. They've been working on it for years, and Ruho is the one who's holding out. Why would Ruho hurt your people rather than sign an accord to get supplies and food?"

I have no answer for her.

"How many people are ill?" she asks.

"Hundreds. Maybe more. They call it 'the plague.'"

"Horrifying," she whispers. "I don't understand why any leader would harm his own people."

"What about Rose?" I say, looking up at the bed.

"It depends on how long she was exposed. Right now she's

very ill because she hasn't been eating or drinking. It's hard for me to separate her symptoms. Once she's had food, I'll be able to see how bad the mercury exposure was. I won't lie. Even if it doesn't kill her, it could make her ill for a long time."

"What can I do?" I want to pray, but to whom? A prayer to the Prophet is a betrayal of the Unbound. Is there a specific way to pray to the Savior? I've never felt so isolated from God.

"You can help me persuade her to eat. I can force nutrients into her body, but eventually she needs to eat solid food."

"Does Juda know?" I ask.

She looks confused.

"Her *son*. Does her son know that she's ill?"

"I . . . I don't know. I'm sorry," she says.

"Why is everyone here so cruel?" I ask, unable to look at her anymore. "He needs to know. He needs to see her. Wouldn't you want to see your mom if she were sick?"

"What you're asking is not my area. I'm sorry. Ram is in charge of refugee relations. I don't have the authority to ask where Rose's son is."

"But you're a doctor," I say. "Who could have more authority than you?"

"You have a lot to learn about the Unbound," she says, looking sorry for me. "I see you got your whites. *That's* the way to gain authority. The best thing you can do for Rose, her son, and yourself is to go to the Worship Hub as often as possible, to obey Ram, and to ascend to Green as soon as possible."

I can't think of anything I care less about right now than "ascending to Green."

"And try to find her son," she adds.

As if this isn't the one thing I've been trying to do since I arrived.

THIRTEEN

By the time I get back to the Dixons, my head is so full of Rose, Juda, and Dr. Rachel that I've forgotten about Silas. But when Bithia and I walk inside and find him sitting on the couch, his treachery comes rushing back.

Blinking slowly, turning off his Tact, he turns to look at us. "Hi, Mina. How was your afternoon?" he says, innocent as a lamb.

With his mother standing beside me, all I can say is, "Busy. Yours?"

He smiles. "Pretty good. Thanks for asking."

Bithia squints at him suspiciously. "Did you finish your tasks for Tabby? You came home very early, young man."

"We finished the flowers, didn't we, Mina?" He looks at me, eyebrows raised.

I give him a mean look. Why does he keep dragging me into his lies? What happens if I say it isn't true?

Seeing my expression, Bithia says, "What's going on with you two?" She smiles. "Lovers' quarrel?"

I'm dumbstruck.

Silas brushes his hair out of his face. "Something like that."

Hands on her hips, Bithia says, "The best remedy for that is conversation and prayer. How about you two take a walk?"

"I would love to," I say.

Silas' mouth falls open, as he tries to think of a way out of the walk. He knows I have questions for him, and, once we're alone, he'll have to answer them.

"I thought you wanted me to check with Tabby? Make sure she didn't need any more help?" he says, a little too eagerly.

Bithia chuckles. "This must be a real doozy of a fight if you're volunteering to help Tabby. No. You go on down to the pond with Mina and sort things out. Your sister will be fine."

Silas grimaces as I smile smugly.

Unsurprisingly, Silas doesn't speak after we get outside. He also doesn't walk in the direction of the park. Instead he heads east, striding quickly.

"Silas, slow down," I say. When he doesn't, I add, "You have to talk to me eventually. I live in your house!"

He mumbles something.

"What?" I ask.

He spins around, a vein throbbing in his forehead. "I said, 'Shut up!'"

I take a step back, stunned. Why is he being so hateful?

He starts walking again.

"STOP!" I yell.

He freezes, probably startled by my volume. I run forward, blocking his path. "I know you lied. About *everything*."

His jaw tightens.

"I—I'm so confused," I say. "Do you just enjoy messing with me? Getting me into trouble?"

He stays silent, but he doesn't look away. He stares deep into my eyes. Then, he says very loudly, "I've never lied to you. You're being a silly little woolie, and you're confused." He continues to look at me intensely, then he widens his eyes and briefly rolls them upward.

Glancing up, I see my Bee. He raises an eyebrow.

He doesn't want to talk in front of the Bee. Oh.

I give him a small nod of understanding.

He gives me a tiny nod back.

We continue to stroll. He says, loud enough for the Bee, "Why do you care what the other girls think? I like you; you like me."

He glances at me, and I can see he wants me to respond, but I can't imagine what I'm supposed to say. I don't understand the game he's playing.

"But . . . I want them to, uh, be my friends," I say, hoping this is good enough.

"They're just jealous of you," Silas says.

The whole charade reminds me of walking with Juda through the Theater District, pretending to be his wife. I was uncomfortable acting as if I were something I was not, but I knew what the rules were. Here, I feel like people are constantly telling me how free I am, while putting me in a smaller and smaller cage. I hate being so ignorant.

The Leisure Center comes into view. I assume this is where Silas was headed all along.

Spotting the large crowd in the atrium, I feel exhausted. The day has been long and stressful. I want to go back to Rose. Whatever is going on with Silas feels draining. I don't want to go inside the Leisure Center and keep playing this game.

We enter and, like last time, my Bee follows. We pass through the throng of people standing, gossiping. As usual, many of them stare.

Silas takes me to the entrance of the food hall. When we step on the escalator, my Bee stays in the main hall like last time. Silas smiles at me.

"What's going—?" I ask, but he raises a finger to his mouth.

When we reach the food hall, the noise is deafening. He whispers in my ear, "Now we can talk. Let's get some food so we look casual."

He puts his hand on my back, steering me toward a glass stall that sells what seems like entire loaves of bread stuffed with melted cheese. He orders two, and while we wait, he leans in and says, "Sorry about all that. It's important no one hear us."

Still annoyed, I ask, "Why?"

As if it's obvious, he says, "Because I don't like being called a liar in public?"

"Then why do you keep lying?" I say, trying to control my temper. "Why did you say Juda was with the Delfords?" I'd also like to accuse him of falling on purpose when he broke his wrist, but I can't prove it.

"I never said Juda was at the Delfords. I said 'two boys' were there."

"Dekker is there, and you *knew* there could only be one boy in the house!" I say, voice intensifying.

Women at a nearby table look at us.

"Shhhh," he says. The boy behind the counter hands Silas our bread puffs. Silas waves his hand over the counter, just like Tabby did. After the counter flashes pink, he leads me to a table in the noisiest part of the food hall.

In a whisper, he says, "Would you still be angry if the one boy had been Juda?"

"Well . . . I . . . Of course!" I wonder if it's true. If I'd seen Juda that night in the window, would I have started worrying about where Dekker was? Surely I would've eventually. "That doesn't matter. Why did you want to sneak out with me at all?"

He rubs the back of his neck. "I can't tell you."

I throw my hands in the air. "Then why are we here?"

"Because I feel bad."

"Not bad enough to tell me the truth."

"It's complicated."

"I bet."

"Mina, please," he says, and for the first time, his voice is gentle. "You said this morning that you liked me, and I think you meant it."

"I don't like people who use me."

"Me neither."

"So tell me why you did it."

"I . . . can't."

I lean in very close. "Then tell me where Juda is."

"I told you, I don't know."

"I don't believe you."

"There's a chance he's . . . Never mind."

"What? What were you going to say?"

He picks at his bread. "It's just that . . . no one's mentioned having him in their house. People really like to brag about housing Propheteers, so I sort of think maybe he isn't in a house."

"So where could he be?"

"Before I tell you, I need you to do something for me."

I can't believe his nerve. "Why do I owe you anything?"

"You don't. I know that. But . . . please." His eyes are soft. He takes a big breath, brushing the hair off his forehead. "I need you to go to Promise Prom with me tomorrow."

Laughing, I say, "You're kidding, right?"

"I'm very serious."

"Silas—" I don't know how much I should say. "Juda and I . . . We, uh . . ."

"I know you're involved," he says, his forehead creasing.

"How do you know?"

"Every time his name is mentioned, your face wakes up, like you haven't really been listening to anything anybody says until that moment."

143

I look away, deeply embarrassed. I thought I'd been keeping my feelings a secret.

"I don't care," he says, putting his hand on mine. "You can have feelings for Juda and go to Promise Prom with me."

"Any of the Unbound girls would be happy to go with you. I see the way they look at you." Susanna would eat tissue flowers if she thought it would get her time alone with Silas.

"I don't like those girls," he says, as if the idea is distasteful.

"I'm flattered, but—"

He removes his hand. "The place they have Juda isn't very nice."

Dread rising, I say, "What do you mean? Where *is* he?"

"Are you going to the Prom with me?"

"I won't forgive you for this blackmail, Silas," I say, and I mean it. He knows I have deep feelings for Juda, and he's using it against me. I no longer think he's a nice person.

"Yes or no?" he says.

Can a "Promise Prom" really be that bad? I have no desire to spend more time with Silas, but, for the most part, the event should be painless, right? It seems like a small price to pay to find Juda. Seeing little choice, I say, "Yes, okay, fine. Where is he?"

"I think he might be in the Forgiveness Home."

"What's that?" Bithia threatened me with the Forgiveness Home yesterday.

"It's hard to describe, but it isn't a place where anyone wants to spend time."

"Why wouldn't he be with a family like the rest of us?"

He chews a nail. "People tend to get sent there when they're, uh, uncooperative."

Nyek. That sounds like Juda. "Is it a *prison*?"

"There aren't cells or anything. There's a lot of praying and, um, listening."

I exhale. "That doesn't sound so bad." He isn't being beaten or abused with Tasers.

"Yeah," he says. "Not so bad." He gives me a big smile, but I can tell he doesn't mean it. The way he's gnawing at his nails tells me whatever is happening in the Forgiveness Home is more than praying, and it's bad.

"Where is it?" I ask.

He pulls off another bite of bread. "I don't know."

"How can you not know where the big prison is?"

"It's *not* a prison, and I never said it was big. Ram likes to keep the location a secret. So it's more, um, disorienting for the people that end up there."

"So the information you've given me is really no information at all." I push the bread he bought away from me. "I don't think the Prom thing is going to work out."

His eyebrows shoot up. "Don't be that way. It will be really benny."

I let my face go blank, trying to express my feelings about all things "benny."

He leans in closer. "Tabby knows where it is."

Tabby? "Why?"

"Getting her to tell you is a whole other problem."

Tabby can't stand me. Why would she help me with anything?

"It's time for dinner. We should go," he says, standing.

We abandon the uneaten bread puffs. When we reach the metal stairs, he says quietly, "Sorry I lied to you. Please forgive?" He smiles and those long lashes flutter in the light.

I could be a lot more forgiving if I knew why he did it, but he's made it clear he's not going to tell me.

I nod in resignation, knowing I can't keep up a war with someone in the same household.

As our Bees find us, he gives me a large hug. "I care about you so much. Let's never fight again."

I've never had a friendship like this before—where one minute a person adores me and the next is lying and avoiding me like a disease. It makes me feel more off-balance than Kingsboro already did.

"Make sure you go to bed early tonight," he says as we leave the Center. "Tomorrow will be a long day, getting ready and everything."

"How long do people usually take to get ready?"

"The girls? Around seven or eight hours," he says. "It depends."

Eight hours? What could they possibly be doing to themselves for eight hours? I look at Silas, who has a big smile on his face.

What have I gotten myself into?

FOURTEEN

The next day, I'm steeped in misery. Prom prep has taken over the Dixon household like a tornado, but I'm consumed with worry about Rose and how to find Juda.

As soon as Bithia hears I'm attending the Prom with Silas, she's all smiles and exuberance (she seems to have forgiven our late night excursion). She begins digging into Tabby's old dresses to find something suitable.

She locates a long, blue gown that Tabby wore to a Promise Prom when she was thirteen.

"Don't I have to wear white?" I ask.

"No, dear," she says with excitement. "Promise Prom is the only night of the year you can wear any color you want!"

"Then can I please not wear blue?" I ask. The dress reminds me of the one I wore to my Offering, and I have only bad memories of that night.

Bithia looks astonished. "I can see what else we have, but you don't have all the choices in the world, child."

She comes back to my room twenty minutes later with a

bright red dress. "I think this one is just stunning! It will be perfect!"

"Won't everyone . . . look at me in that color?" Mother says red is the color of harlots and demons.

"Yes! And that's what every young lady wants at Prom."

It is? I thought I was supposed to avoid "eye traps."

Taking it to her sewing room, Bithia lets out the stitching so it'll fit me. After lunch, she tells me to get into the shower (which still terrifies me) and then to cover my body in something called talcum powder. Smelling of geraniums, it clouds the bathroom and makes me sneeze as I shake it from its container.

Next, she puts me into a robe and uses a loud "blow-dryer" to form my hair into some sort of big bubble. Much to my embarrassment, Silas enters the bathroom, says the bubble is awful and that Bithia needs to let me wear my hair down.

After some protest, Bithia stops using the blow-dryer, spraying something that smells like grass all over my head. She uses her hands to tousle my hair in all sorts of directions. After that, she curls my lashes and puts some sort of gloss on my lips.

She then brings me the red dress. "Here you are, honey," she said. "I hope it fits. You're slightly larger than I was remembering." She smiles. "But you're probably being fed properly for the first time in your life, right?"

"My mother is a very good cook," I say, feeling defensive for her. She was difficult in many ways, but she always made sure we ate well.

Bithia nods, but I can see she doesn't believe me. "Now this has a satin top and a chiffon skirt. See how the bottom has all these pretty layers?" She holds out the dress.

The skirt fabric is transparent but there are so many layers no one will be able to see my legs, which is a relief. The satin top goes up to the collarbone but has no sleeves, which is worrying.

I let her help me put it on, since there are hooks and zippers I can't reach. Once everything is fastened and closed, I have a hard time breathing.

Bithia beams at me. "I'm going to allow myself a moment of pride here and say *not bad* for one day's notice!"

Tabby walks in. She's wearing a stiff white skirt made of many layers which shoots out horizontally. The tight-fitting top hugs her breasts and shows her ribs. Her hair is piled on top of her head like the bread loaf Silas bought me. The high hair accents her sharp cheekbones and tiny features.

Bithia inhales sharply, saying, "Don't you look gorgeous!"

Tabby looks down at herself without smiling.

"Turn around!" says Bithia.

Tabby obeys.

"Doesn't she look stunning?" Bithia asks me.

"Yes," I say. "She does."

"What do you think?" Bithia asks Tabby, gesturing to me.

Tabby crosses her arms, studying me like a hard word. She comes closer, touching my hair. "Her hair is not bad, but . . ."

"But what?" said Bithia.

"Her forehead," said Tabby.

Bithia inspects my forehead, searching for flaws.

"She has pimples," says Tabby.

My hand jerks up to feel my skin. What's she talking about? Just as I'm about to tell her to go away, I feel them: little bumps just below my hair line.

"I would give her bangs," Tabby says.

Bithia squints at my face and a moment later says, "Yes! You are a genius, Tabby."

Tabby then eyes my red dress. "That dress is perfect on you. The style was really popular last year."

"Thank you," I say, knowing she thinks I'm too stupid to understand the insult. I tell her, "Your gown is pretty too."

She smirks. "This dress is for the pre-show. It's not my *gown*."

"Oh. Sorry," I say. How will I ever get information from this girl? She doesn't like me. She doesn't seem to like anyone. I don't have anything she wants or needs. My search for the Forgiveness Home is hopeless.

As I agonize over my problem, Bithia takes scissors from the drawer and begins cutting the hair that falls in front of my face.

When I start to protest, she says, "Sit still or I'll mess up!"

Five minutes later, I have a short shelf of hair above my eyebrows, just like Tabby.

"Very nice," says Bithia. "Now let's find you some shoes."

She rushes out of the bathroom, while I stare in the mirror. It hasn't been very long since my Offering, but the girl in the mirror looks completely different than the one that Mother prepared for suitors.

Instead of a tight bun, my hair is loose and wavy with "bangs." My face seems rounder and has more color from my time walking around uncovered in the sun. The mascara has made my eyes look wide and alert and the gloss gives my lips a wet effect. The red dress is flattering to my figure, but I can't help but worry that if Mrs. Prue is there, I will be getting demerits for calling attention to my body. It's all so confusing—look pretty but not so pretty you create lust.

Bithia returns with a pair of black flats. "These are mine and they should do—probably a little big, but I always say better too big than too small, right?"

Once I have the shoes on, I go downstairs, where Silas waits. He wears an olive suit and shirt that bring out the green in his eyes. His wrist brace is perfectly hidden under his clothes.

Grinning when he sees me, he says, "Gorgeous. I knew you'd clean up well."

He looks good, too, but I'm still too annoyed with him to say so. "How much time do we have?"

"Ten minutes at the most."

"I need to talk to Tabby."

"This really isn't the best time," says Silas. "She's jumpier than a cricket."

"She won't hate me any less tomorrow."

Smiling again, he says, "That's true."

I clunk back up the stairs, not wanting to waste one second.

From outside of Tabby's door, I can hear Bithia fussing over Tabby's hair and telling her to pull her top up higher. She then says, "Hurry up. Don't make us late!"

When Bithia leaves the room, she sees me hovering. "What are you doing here?" she asks, looking suspicious.

"I wanted to tell Tabby good luck," I say, not exactly sure what Tabby is doing tonight but knowing it seems a lot like an Offering.

"Well, be quick," says Bithia. "We can't be late!" She walks to the master bedroom, shrieking, "GILAD! You READY?"

Bithia has left the door open, so I walk inside. I've never been in Tabby's room before. I'm not sure what I expected, but it wasn't this. Everything is baby blue: the bed, the walls, the curtains, even a little skirt around the dressing table. At the top of the bed rests a teddy bear wearing a baby blue beret.

Next to the blue bed is a night table, and the top is covered with straws, just like the ones we used in our fruit drinks at the Leisure Center. *What an odd thing to collect.* Is Tabby commemorating how many compressions she's had? Or is she on some strange diet where she needs to keep count of them?

To my right, Tabby looks into a full-length mirror, tugging at her top and skirt. She seems unhappy with the way she looks.

Seeing me in the reflection, she turns around, her wrinkled nose suggesting a bad smell has entered the room. "What?"

"You look great, Tabby," I say.

She turns back to the mirror. "Gee, thanks, woolie."

I want to walk out, but I can't. She's my last hope. "Uh, I have a question for you."

"Yes, my brother is a turd." She laughs at her own joke. Seeing my serious face, she says, "Lighten up, Mina. You're major uptight."

I laugh a bit, trying to show her how "normal" I am, then I dive in. "So, uh, can you please tell me where the Forgiveness Home is?"

She stops smiling, turning to me again. "Who told you I knew?"

"So you *do* know?" I say, pulse racing.

"*Who* told you?" As her eyes narrow, she takes an angry step toward me. I stumble backward, instinctively throwing up my hand to protect my face.

She stops. "What's wrong with you? Freak."

My face goes hot.

She stares at me like I've thrown up all over her carpet.

"I just wanted—" I say, determined to ask again.

"I don't know where it is, and whoever told you I did is full of twaddle. Besides, if you really want to go there so major badly, why don't you just sneak out again? I'm sure Mom and Dad would *happily* lock you up in the Forgiveness Home, and then we all win." She brushes past me to the open door.

I follow her, despising my weakness. I blew it. Now she hates me more than ever. I'm no closer to finding Juda than I was before I agreed to go to this stupid event. I wish more than anything that I could walk out of this house and never see Tabby again.

FIFTEEN

As I walk outside with the Dixons, I'm surprised when Gilad leads us in the opposite direction of the Leisure Center. I'd assumed Promise Prom took place in the atrium where we were making decorations.

We stop at the corner of the next street, and I survey our group. Bithia's bright pink dress is covered in ruffles from top to bottom, and she resembles one of the tissue flowers we made this morning. Gilad looks more restrained in a dark plum suit. Cornelius' hair has been parted severely down the middle, doing no favors for his big ears. His lemon-yellow suit is adorable, but I can't imagine it will stay clean for long. Tabby picks at a bead on her skirt, avoiding eye contact with me.

A green bus comes into view.

"Finally!" says Corny.

When the bus stops right in front of us, Silas takes my hand and leads me on board. The affection makes me uncomfortable, but I don't feel like I can say anything in front of his family.

Naomi Benjamin, Jeremiah's mother, is the bus driver. A woman! She wears a bright yellow gown, and her hair is pulled up into an elegant twist. Smiling, she waves hello. I'm glad my misdeed with Silas hasn't soured the Elder's opinion of me.

The seats are packed, leaving standing room only. The Dixons don't seem to mind. They chat and laugh with the families already aboard.

The men wear silky thin suits and the women all wear long gowns like mine. The colors are dazzling.

When the bus starts moving, we're all thrown backward for a moment, and everyone bursts into laughter. I'm so mesmerized by people's exuberance that I don't notice that Silas is staring at me. He's standing so close, it's disconcerting. "What?" I ask.

"You look different."

"How?"

"It's the first time I've seen you in a dress."

"Oh."

He studies me more. "You look terrific, but . . ."

I knew it. Something about me looks weird.

"You're still in Tabby's clothes. I'm curious to know what you look like in your own clothes, how you are when you're really *you*."

I stare out the window at the houses whizzing by. If Silas saw me at home wearing simple cotton clothes, or a cloak and veil, would that be the real me? Someone else chose those things, too. I don't know that clothes have anything to do with who I am. The last time I felt completely like myself was when I was reading the *Time Out* with Nana and Grace.

"I feel like myself when I'm reading," I say.

His eyebrows go up in surprise. "Me, too."

I want to smile, but I remind myself that I'm going to this event against my will.

The bus stops. The tight crowd makes it impossible to see where we are. Only when I step out of the bus am I able to take in our surroundings, and I'm pretty sure we've arrived on another planet.

An expansive lawn stands between us and a huge . . . structure? Building? I don't know what to call it. It's round with massive concrete columns and no walls, like the world's largest gazebo. The circular roof is made of pink and yellow glass and might break during a hard rain. The edge of the roof is bright yellow and covered in spikes that look a bit like fangs.

And that isn't even the weirdest part. There are three towers next to the round building, each one taller than the last. The tallest one must be ten stories high! What are they for? No one could be living in them. They're skinny with a wide platform on top, like someone has balanced birthday cakes on top of broomsticks.

Gilad sees my wide eyes. Chuckling, he says, "The New York State Pavilion. Nearly two hundred years old."

Older than Time Zero!

He points to the roof. "We replaced all the stained glass up there. It looked like a big, sad bicycle wheel when I was a boy. Wait until you stand underneath it." He beams at Silas and me. "See how the bottom of the building has red and white stripes all the way around? I think the architect wanted the whole thing to look like a merry-go-round, but that's just my opinion."

I nod, not sure what a merry-go-round is.

"Let's get in there before it starts," Bithia says.

Bithia and Gilad give hugs to Tabby, who leaves our group to join a couple of girls dressed the same as her. Other Promise girls I assume? We walk across the grass toward the pavilion, while Tabby's group heads toward some trees.

The sun is setting and the sky has turned peach and rose. The smell of oak trees and damp grass fills the air. As we get closer to the pavilion, I hear music, and it's so heartfelt and lovely that it sounds like every emotion I've ever had put to sound. I can't imagine paying attention to anything else, but next I'm marveling that the twinkly lights that Tabby worked so hard on are magically reflected in the grass. However, Gilad explains that these are "fireflies." Silas says he and Tabby chased after them as children.

Families arrive from all directions, and I'm sure every member of the Unbound is here. Up close, the red-and-white-striped band at the base of the pavilion is twice as tall as any man. A double door has been opened to let in the crowd.

Once we've passed through, I feel as if I've entered a fairy paradise. The sunset causes the stained glass to sparkle in every shade of orange, pink, and yellow you've ever thought of. The white tissue flowers we made this morning wind around every pillar, while white balloons float up from long tables. Across from us, real white roses shroud an enormous doorway with a pointed arch, and above us, what must be thousands of lights are strung between pillars, a galaxy of stars close enough to touch.

Gilad and Bithia happily greet more friends. This is the happiest I've seen either of them. Many men clap Gilad on the back. Corny squirms under Bithia's hand until she finally releases him. He runs into the crowd, seeking other boys his age.

"You look perfect," Silas tells me.

I was fussing with my dress.

"All the other girls are jealous. That's why they're glaring at you." I look around, and, sure enough, several girls are giving me nasty looks.

"They're glaring because I'm a woolie."

He wiggles his eyebrows. "Well then, let's show them how razzamatazz you are." Head up, he puts his hand on my back and leads me further into the crowd.

I'm having that off-balance feeling again. Is this the real Silas? Or is he being fake again? I'm so overwhelmed by the event and my surroundings that I think I have to trust him for the next few hours. I need an ally.

"Silas, why—"

I stop speaking as the lights dim and a hush falls over the crowd.

New music fills the room. Seeing musicians in the corner, I ask Silas, "What are those?"

"Violins," he says.

I'm mesmerized by the movement of the musicians' hands. I notice a man playing a huge harp, something I've only seen in illustrations of angels. He plucks and runs his hands over the strings, creating a dreamlike, tinkling sound that gives me chills. I'm so caught up in the music that I don't notice that everyone else is looking at the entrance of the pavilion.

When I finally look away, I see a dozen girls in white dancing through the door. They're twirling, leaping, tiptoeing their way inside. I spot Tabby. She's a model of concentration, bending at the waist, swaying her head and shoulders along with the music. Her hair maintains its tower-like construction.

Eventually, the exquisite figures convene in a circle in the middle of the floor. They join hands, spinning around, their stiff white skirts floating as dreamily as snowflakes. The adults around me gasp in adoration.

The music gets louder, more furious. The violin players seem angry as they saw at their instruments. The girls shake their hands above their heads while the rhythm explodes. Finally, the girls collapse onto the floor, their heads bowed in subjugation. They look like dead swans, asking God for permission to enter Paradise.

The people around me burst into applause. Silas nudges me, so I clap, too.

One by one the girls peel themselves off the floor and flutter away through the enormous doorway covered with roses.

People around me mutter about which girls were the strongest dancers and which had the most beautiful smile.

Young men to my right elbow each other, giggling, like the young boys at my Offering. I'm sure they aren't comparing the *smiles* of the girls. I become more self-conscious of how I look tonight, and then I feel angry. How can a group of boys with no power over one's life still manage to make one feel so small? Maybe Nana could explain it to me.

A new song begins.

"May I have this dance?" Silas asks.

Panicking, I say, "I don't dance."

"I'm sure you're not that bad," he says, smiling with kindness.

Feeling as if everyone in the pavilion can hear me, I say, "It is —I mean, it was—forbidden. I don't know how."

Silas, embarrassed, says, "Of course. I'm sorry. Let's get some food."

He leads me to a buffet on the outskirts of the room. Like at my Offering, the table is piled high with food, but this table is twenty times the size of ours. There's enough food here to feed my family for years.

Silas picks up tiny, intricate pastries that I don't recognize and hands me one. I taste mushrooms and spices and maybe cheese? It's incredible. As we nibble, we watch the couples dancing.

I spot Susanna dancing with a boy I suspect is her brother. They have the same short blond hair. Susanna glances over at Silas a few times, and I can imagine she would rather be dancing with him.

"Isn't that your brother?" says Silas.

I search the room. "Where?"

"With the otter daughters."

"Please stop calling them that," I say.

"Over there." He points to a group of families gathered in the corner and sure enough, Dekker is standing with Ginnie and Delilah Delford.

He's wearing an orange suit. *Orange.* His hair is slicked back, and he's grinning like someone told him he's secretly heir to Uncle Ruho's fortune. He talks animatedly to the sisters, his hands making grand gestures as if he were telling the greatest story ever told.

He looks so bizarre; I can't stop staring. Eventually, he glances up and spots me. He makes a little wave, as if we see each other every day at Apostate parties.

What's he up to?

When it becomes obvious he's not coming over to speak with me, I cross the room. I tell Silas it's best if he waits by the buffet table.

When I reach Dekker, he throws open his arms and embraces me the way he only embraces Mother. "Mina! How wonderful to see you!"

"Peace," I say, smothered.

Ginnie giggles, seeming much more relaxed than when I met her with Tabby.

"You don't need to say that here, goose," says Dekker, releasing me. "I was just telling the girls how much more fun life is here, and how much they would hate life on the island. Isn't that right?" He looks at the sisters, and they start giggling again.

"Yes," says Delilah. "Dekker was just telling us about your Offering. It sounds just . . . medieval. I can't imagine not being able to choose the man I marry."

"No," says Ginnie. "I need to be madly in love." She looks up at Dekker, batting her lashes.

"May I speak to you in private?" I say, trying to keep a smile on my face.

"Why? The girls are my friends," says Dekker, hugging them both around the waist as they giggle more.

"It's personal family business," I say, trying to indicate with my eyes how serious I am. "I just need a moment."

"It doesn't look good," says Delilah.

"What?" says Dekker.

"Woolies talking to one another," she says in a disapproving tone.

"We'll see about that," Dekker says, chest puffing up. Ever defiant, he now wants to talk to me. He releases the girls, puts a hand on my shoulder and leads me to the edge of another group of partiers.

"Dekker—" I begin.

"Isn't this great?" he says. "These people . . . They really know how to live. Tons of food, they barely work, they practically throw their daughters at you—"

"Stop talking," I say, realizing already how annoying this conversation will be.

He shakes his head. "Typical Mina. Miserable no matter what's happening."

I ignore my urge to fight with him. "Have you seen Juda?"

"That guy needs to lighten up, too."

"Have you seen him?" I ask again.

"Nope." He looks back toward Ginnie and Delilah and smiles.

"What are you doing?" I say with frustration.

"What do you think? Working on marriage prospects. Their dad is loaded. And just look around the room. There have to be plenty of rich girls here who are better-looking than those two. As soon as I complete my Day of Valida—"

"Dekker! Can you pay attention to me for one second."

"I am!"

"Juda is missing, Grace is transformed, and Rose is deathly ill. These people are not our friends."

"Maybe they aren't your friends, but they're certainly mine.

My hosts have been nothing but generous. Did you stop to ask yourself if maybe it's you? Maybe if you acted a little more grateful and less suspicious all the time, you could see things for what they are—which is fantastic! All that Ram and anybody else wants is for us to thrive and be happy. They aren't asking us to work or study or be perfect. They just want us to be happy. How amazing is that?"

He sounds like Grace.

"Then why are they keeping Juda locked up?"

"He has an attitude problem."

"You can't really believe that—"

"It's been swell seeing you and everything, but I'd rather not be chastised for talking to a woolie, so I'm going to get back to the party." He walks away without saying goodbye.

Talking to a *woolie*? I stifle the desire to yell, "Everyone here saw you fall on your butt and no one wanted to help you!"

Speaking with Dekker has made me feel worse than ever. Why won't anyone help me? When I was little, I would have dreams that I was locked up in the Tunnel for a crime I didn't commit. I would run around trying to explain to everyone that I was innocent, but no one would listen, as if I were speaking a foreign language. That's how I feel right now. I'm telling people that an injustice is occurring, but they refuse to hear it or assist me.

Don't ever desire or expect anyone to make things easier for you.

Nana said that to me. How many times will I have to learn it?

The music stops abruptly. A drum beat sounds, and the crowd moves to the edges of the pavilion. The sky has darkened to a smoky violet, making the lights inside seem to glow brighter. Wondering what's happening, I walk back to Silas.

Before I can talk to him, two small boys, no older than six, come out of the flowered doorway. Wearing long white robes, they have wings attached to their backs like cherubs. Each of them carries a large sword, the weight threatening to pull them to the ground. They march forward in perfect unison, their tiny faces solemn. After about twenty steps, they hold perfectly still.

Two men step out of the crowd—Gilad and a man I don't know. They march toward the cherubs (their synchronization not nearly as impressive as the boys), and when they reach them, they stop.

The little boys hold up the swords so the men can take them. As the cherubs skitter away into the crowd, the men brandish the swords. For a moment, I wonder if they're about to fight, but they touch the tips of the swords together and raise them to form an upside down V.

The band plays a new tune—light and airy, like what birds would create if they could play instruments. It's beautiful.

Out of the fancy door comes the group of girls who danced for us earlier, but now they are wearing long gowns. The colors of the dresses are remarkable: orange, yellow, purple, green, red. They sparkle like jewels.

I spot Tabby. She's wearing a flowing emerald-green dress that exposes her shoulders. The green is far from the sickening yellow-green of the clothes in my closet. This is dark and lush. She flashes a large smile, which exposes her perfect white teeth. Have I ever seen her smile without sarcasm or superiority? She looks stunning.

"Tabby looks beautiful," I say to Silas.

"Yeah," he says. "Tolerable, I guess."

"Tolerable? You're tough, Silas."

He laughs. "She's my sister. What do you want me to say?"

I laugh, too.

Tabby's friend Deborah Tanner wears bright fuchsia, as she said she would. She looks proud and happy.

As the girls file out, they pass under the arch that Gilad and the man have created with their swords. Each of the girls is smiling, but as they pass under the arch their expressions become serious. They form a large circle in the middle of the pavilion. The serene music stops. Gilad and the man lower the swords.

I wait for something to happen but nothing does. We enter a silence so thick, I can hear the rustling of the girls' dresses. I look to Silas for an explanation, but his head is down. I realize that everyone has a bowed head, so I tuck my chin as well. Silas murmurs words under his breath—a prayer I assume.

After a few seconds, I feel Silas look up, so I do, too.

Ram is standing in the middle of the circle of girls. How did he move so soundlessly? He wears white, as usual, but instead of his usual pajama-like ensemble, he wears a sharp suit with a tie.

"Welcome," he says in his high voice. "What a glorious evening. What a momentous occasion. My heart is filled to bursting seeing you and your families here tonight. I know that God is pleased, too. Did you see the sunset He painted for us tonight?"

After many people smile and nod, Ram says, "I know that Promise Prom is a favorite occasion for many of you, and for different reasons. Perhaps you love coming together as a community to make something beautiful; maybe you relish the opportunity to wear a new color, to try a new hairstyle; or perhaps you have an insatiable passion for dancing (I'm looking at you, Marcus McCoy)!"

Everyone laughs.

"This year is especially auspicious, as we grow closer and closer to an accord with our neighbors. Peace with Manhattan will bring us everything we've been working for."

People clap, but underneath the applause, I hear angry mutterings, and a masculine voice says, "Bomb 'em."

I don't have to search long to find the source of the comment. Luke Tanner stands with several scowling men, and they all look ready to pick a fight.

Silas reaches for my hand, and this time I'm happy to let him take it.

Ram continues. "But we aren't here to discuss politics tonight. We are here for these girls." He turns slowly, his arms outspread, indicating the twelve girls around him. His face becomes warm and loving. "Tonight they will make a pledge to their fathers, and their fathers will make a pledge to them. But you, as their neighbors, friends and mentors, are also taking a pledge. You are vowing to help these girls to keep their pledges in the face of temptation and desire. Satan lives among us—you know this. He's always here, ready to pounce at the slightest sign of weakness. And where does weakness live? In our young women. They're our most precious resource, but, bless their little cotton socks, they just don't have the life experience to understand when Satan is trying to seduce them. Their greatest quality —their innocence—is also their greatest liability. It is the father's job to compensate for the weakness his daughter possesses. He must not just look over her, but to the side of her, and under her, and through her, if he needs to!"

The crowd laughs at this. I shudder, remembering how I wondered if the Bees could read my mind.

"We understand that daughters crave attention. They need love and affection. They want boyfriends! But they don't really know what that means, so it's up to their fathers to show them. Until it's time for marriage, a father should act as a daughter's companion, adoring her and teaching her what real men are about."

Confused, I look to Silas, but he's caught up in the proceedings.

"Fathers, come forward, please."

Men of all shapes and sizes step out of the crowd. They look clean, polished, and disoriented, like their wives ran them through the dishwasher.

Mr. Tanner joins Deborah. His hair is tamed, but his face is still red and chapped, and, somehow, his dress clothes make him look even more disheveled. When he reaches his daughter, he gives her a compulsory smile. Deborah, so proud moments earlier, now looks like she'd rather be anywhere else.

Ram's voice gets louder. "Fathers, guardians, patriarchs, warriors: take the hand of your daughter!"

Taking their daughters' hands, the men look to Ram for the next step. He says, "It's time for your pledge."

The fathers fumble with their free hands, reaching into the pockets of their jackets or pants and pulling out pieces of paper.

Together, they read out loud: *I choose before God to cover my daughter as her authority and protection in the area of purity. I will be pure in my own life as a man, husband, and father as I lead, guide, and pray over my daughter and my family as the high priest in my home.*

"Now daughters, do you stand as a witness to these words?" Ram asks.

The girls nod.

Ram looks around the room. "Do you, the community that supports these fathers and daughters, stand as witnesses to these words?"

The crowd applauds and a few people shout, "So be it."

"It is time for the exchange of gifts."

The fathers pull small velvet pouches from their pockets, while the girls try to contain their excitement. The men reveal delicate gold chains that sparkle in the light.

Silas leans into me, whispering, "Necklaces with a heart locket."

Long after the other fathers have secured the jewelry around their daughters' necks, Mr. Tanner is still trying to unhook the small clasp. Ram waits for him. Mr. Tanner mutters something under his breath which, judging from Deborah's appalled face, is inappropriate for polite company.

Mortified, Deborah takes the necklace from her father's fingers, unhooks it, and places it around her own neck.

Mr. Tanner exhales with relief.

Ram says, "Now the young ladies will offer a gift in return."

Reaching into hidden pockets in their gowns, the girls pull out something too small to see. I look to Silas, who says, "A tiny key. It fits into the heart locket, and the father has the only copy. He'll give it to the girl's husband when she marries."

Thinking of the diamond collar I once wore around my wrist, I wonder if these lockets have an alarm. Or perhaps they're like Rose's necklace and contain a tracking device. Either way, I'm glad I'm not receiving one.

Once the exchange of gifts is over, Ram announces, "We will begin this covenant between daughter and father with a dance, symbolizing how a daughter is always protected and safe in her father's arms and need not worry about a thing. She can relax and enjoy herself, knowing that Daddy is there."

A dramatic song made up of many instruments begins, quite different than the sensitive melody played before. The fathers take the hands of their daughters, and the couples begin to twirl around the dance floor. They're all doing the same dance and have obviously practiced. Gilad looks a bit petrified, his eyes large and staring straight ahead, as if he were still watching something on his Tact.

Tabitha holds her head high, smiling, executing every step perfectly, but she's scanning the room, searching for someone or something. I look around, wondering what might be attracting her attention. Does she want to know how many of the boys are admiring her shoulders in that stunning green dress?

Gilad looks uncomfortable, but the worst dancer by far is Luke Tanner, who's dragging Deborah around the dance floor like she's a mop. I bet Deborah is now wishing she wore a less conspicuous color.

When the song ends, the fathers drop the hands of their daughters, and the girls get into a line and file back out the flowered doorway. Other couples crowd the dance floor.

"Hello, Mina," a voice says.

I discover Beth standing to my right. She looks sweet in a coral dress that puffs out at the sleeves, but I find myself wanting to run at the sight of her.

"Don't you look pretty," she says, smiling.

I try to smile back, but my mouth has gone so dry that my lips stick to my teeth.

Silas says, "Hello, Beth. I didn't know you knew Mina."

"Oh yes. I was the first one to find them—the Manhattan Five. Didn't she tell you?"

Silas sees my face, which must look pallid, and he touches my elbow. "No, she didn't."

"Nice to see you," says Beth. "So glad you decided to let in the light." She grins agreeably and walks away.

"Are you okay?" asks Silas.

"Of course," I say, watching Beth disappear into a crowd of children her age. But I'm not. I hate that girl more than words can say. I blame her for everything—for Juda's disappearance, for Grace's conversion, for Rose's illness. If Beth hadn't sounded the alarm, we would all still be together.

I want to follow her and shake her until her teeth clack. I want to rip her apart from her friends like she ripped me away from mine.

"You look like you just saw the Devil," says Silas.

I snap out of my daydream, disturbed at the violence I was feeling. "No, I was just, uh, having some bad memories from home."

He nods in understanding. "I think we should dance." The music has slowed to something relaxed and lazy.

"I told you, I don't—"

"It doesn't matter. I'll lead," he says, taking my hand with his unbandaged one.

As he leads me toward the dance floor, my nervousness causes me to trip in my too-big shoes. I see a few girls snicker. "This is a bad idea," I tell Silas, pulling him back.

"It's a benny idea," he says, resisting me. "You can't be any worse than Luke Tanner."

Before I know it, he's put his good arm on my back and pulled me in close. We rotate in a circle with his injured wrist sandwiched between us. My body is smashed against his in a way I find embarrassing. I'm positive everyone is staring at us, but as I look around, I see that other couples are embracing in a similar way, slowly turning. I guess Silas and I are dancing.

I try to relax and enjoy the music, which I find soothing. I don't want to focus on Silas' body or the fact that he smells like fresh, warm laundry.

"It's easy, right?" he says.

"Mmmhmm." I can't look at him. Our faces are too close.

Near us, Susanna sways with a boy several inches shorter than her and doesn't look pleased. Gilad dances with Bithia, and Marjory dances with Horton Groodly.

Marjory is surprisingly graceful. Although she wears a floor-length gown, it is white, like Ram's suit. Perhaps enjoying color is too frivolous for Marjory and Ram?

Ram stands off to the side of the dance floor, surveying it with a peaceful smile. Next to him is Jeremiah in a black suit, alert and unreadable as usual.

"Was he serious about the bombs?" I ask Silas.

"What? Who?" He misses a step.

"Mr. Tanner. He said, 'Bomb them.' Did he mean it?"

"Mr. Tanner is a bluster monkey."

I'm confused. "So the Unbound don't have any bombs?"

"We have them, I guess. But Mr. Tanner doesn't get to say if we use them."

I don't feel any better. Knowing any of these people want to drop a weapon on my home is terrifying.

"He just likes to cause trouble. No one agrees with him," he says, squeezing me. "You're as tense as a nail meeting a hammer. *Relax.*"

He's right. Closing my eyes, I focus on the incredible music. Despite Mr. Tanner, the glaring girls, and Dekker, the event is pretty magnificent—the pavilion, the music, the decorations, the gowns. It's all sort of magical. Maybe I'm not so annoyed that Silas made me come.

I wonder what it would be like to attend the event with my own father. He would make a few bad jokes and listen to the sermon while stroking his beard. I could have danced with him, which is a strange idea, but it might have been nice.

All at once, the song comes to an end, and I realize I was resting my head on Silas' chest. I pull back, mortified.

He releases my hands. "Thank you. I really enjoyed that."

"Me, too," I say, sure I'm bright pink. "I need some air."

The music speeds up, and I depart the dance floor before Silas can ask me to dance again.

SIXTEEN

I leave the pavilion, happy to escape the crowd. My Bee hums into place above me. So much for privacy.

To my right, small girls imitate the dance we saw Tabby and the others do. The evening is still and warm. I can feel the pulsing of the music coming up through the grass.

I danced. I wish I could tell Nana.

I wonder what she would think of Silas? *Stop it, Mina. Who cares?*

I walk away from the building, hoping to clear my head.

I discover Horton Groodly standing at the edge of the lawn, staring into the distance. I'm surprised to see him swaying slightly to the music. He looks better than he did at his home. He's clean-shaven, and he sports a nice gray suit, but he still looks grumpy as a bulldog. I don't know if this is his mood or the nature of his face.

Running into him seems fortuitous. I have questions I'm dying to ask him.

I approach with a smile. "Mr. Groodly, I don't mean to disturb you, but—" I lose my train of thought as I notice what he's staring at.

In the distance, lit up by spotlights, is a huge silver sphere. It's four times taller than any lamppost, and it's just floating there.

"What is that?" I ask.

Without looking away from it, he says, "The Earth."

"Why is it here?"

"Same people who made the pavilion made it. Nice, isn't it?" His voice is as gravelly and brusque as ever.

"What's it do?"

He looks at me with disappointment. "It doesn't *do* anything. It's art."

"Oh," I say. The conversation doesn't seem to be going well so far.

"How is Mrs. Alvero?" he asks.

"Not very well, I'm afraid."

"I'm sorry to hear that."

We stand quietly observing the sphere. When I feel brave enough, I say, "Mr. Groodly, how long have you been here?"

He coughs. "I assume you don't mean at the Prom?"

"No, sir," I say.

He takes so long to answer, I figure he's not going to. But after a while, he shoves his hands into his pockets and says, "Forty years."

Wow. He probably can't even *remember* Manhattan.

"Why did you leave? *How* did you leave?"

He glances at my Bee. "I'm not allowed to talk about those things."

"Can you at least tell me who else used to be a Propheteer?"

Shaking his head, he says, "Ram will tell you when you're ready."

"Okay," I say, frustrated by his stubbornness. "One last question." Surely he has *some* sympathy for a fellow refugee. "Can you please tell me where the Forgiveness Home is?"

Surprised, he says, "Why in God's name would you want to go there?"

"I, uh—a Propheteer I arrived with might be there."

He shakes a finger at me. "Anyone who's been sent to the Forgiveness Home is a troublemaker, and you're better off without them. Don't waste your time with deviants!"

"He's not a deviant!"

He takes in my new dress and shoes. "Living here means making certain sacrifices, but there are compromises everywhere. We wish it were perfect here, but it's not, because people aren't perfect. Only God is. And the afterlife. The people who made that sphere over there spent too much time focusing on this life, on their beloved *Earth*. And they didn't survive. We did. Because we know that suffering in this life means being rewarded in the next. You need to stop doubting and be grateful. Do your best to fit in and move on with your life. You understand?"

I'm fed up, with him, with Dekker, and Grace, and anyone else trying to tell me to *move on*. My polite smile disappears as my temper flairs. "Did you *move on with your life* when you arrived? Did you leave your family and friends rotting in some detainment center while you dressed up and went to parties? Is that what you're telling me?"

I didn't think it was possible, but his sad face becomes even more sorrowful.

Nyek. He *did* leave someone behind. "Who did you abandon, Mr. Groodly?"

His face changes from sorrow to rage. "You've overstepped your bounds, and that is no way for a young lady to behave! I suggest you go back inside and learn something about grace and purity while there's still time." He storms away.

That didn't go as planned.

I wander back toward the pavilion, scolding myself for losing my temper. I've aggravated yet another person who might have had the information I need. What a fiasco.

Silas finds me as soon as I reenter the building. "You okay?"

"Yeah," I say, attempting a smile. "*Major benny.*"

He raises an eyebrow, not believing me.

A figure in purple bounces toward us.

"Grace!" I say, surprised to see her.

"Mina! You were incredible dancing out there! Totally razzamatazz!"

"Thank you." I'm embarrassed to know we were being scrutinized. "I didn't think you were able to come." I remember how disappointed she was at refinement class.

"My host-mom decided it would be a good influence on me to see the community come together like this, and she was right. This is just major phenomenal, isn't it? Wow. The pledges and the dancing and the architecture. I could just die. I mean, this is a *historical landmark.*"

Grace wears a lavender gown with sequins on the shoulders. The fit is slightly big, so I assume it's borrowed from her host-family, like mine. Despite the ill fit, the color goes nicely with her brown hair, which is pulled back in a knot. Her face is so pretty when you can actually see it.

She smiles widely at Silas, and I realize I'm being rude. "Grace, this is Silas. Silas, this is Grace."

"Nice to meet you, Grace," he says, shaking her hand.

She radiates pleasure. "Nice to meet you, Silas," she says, clearly enjoying the custom of shaking hands. She raises an eyebrow at me to show her approval of him, and I frown. How can she be so disloyal to Juda?

"You look gorgeous, Mina," she says. "That scarlet is just benny!"

"Thank you," I say. "You look very beautiful, too."

She twirls in her lilac dress. "I feel like Emma Woodhouse!"

I tell Silas, "Grace reads a lot."

"I know *Emma*. Jane Austen," he says.

I think Grace is going to faint from happiness. "Have you read all of her books?" she asks. "We had a limited collection, unfortunately." Her tone suggests the Laurel Society was providing limited amounts of food. "I'm *dying* to read *Sense and Sensibility* and—" She points behind me. "The girls are back!"

I turn to see all the pledged girls coming through the arched doorway.

Not all of the girls are smiling. In fact, several of them are on the verge of tears. Deborah Tanner has a tight smile, but you can see that her eyes are puffy and red. What happened through that door? "Why do they look so upset?" I ask Grace.

"Oh, didn't your host-mom explain?" Grace says. She looks at Silas and goes crimson. Sensing her discomfort, he walks to the buffet table and focuses on some fruit. Grace whispers, "Back-stage, each of them has a little pellet injected underneath their skin, near their, uh, uh . . ."

"Yes?"

"Near the lady region."

"Why?" I ask, feeling sick.

She says, "The necklaces are only symbolic, and over the years, the Elders decided they didn't do enough. So they started injecting the girls with 'lady bugs,' these little pellets."

"What do they do?"

"They track your pulse and hormone levels, and basically report if you are interacting with a boy in, uh, exciting ways."

"They all got one?" I look at the girls, who ten minutes ago seemed so proud and happy. Now, they look depressed and dazed.

"Yep. Every one," says Grace.

"What about the boys? Do they get one too?"

"No. I guess if the girls have one, they think . . . that will catch all the boys?"

I roll my eyes. The punishment is always for the girls. I should know that by now.

The magic of the evening has disappeared like a puff of talcum powder. "Why do you like these people so much? Don't you think these 'lady bugs' are weird?" They sound like something my mother and aunties would love.

"I was pretty astounded when my host-mom told me, but then I decided, maybe it's smart. I mean, maybe it makes things easier for everyone, the boys and the girls, to know that they're there. I can, uh, imagine that it can be hard to resist temptation, right?" She nudges me, like we have a secret together.

I frown. "I don't want a pellet in my body that lets people watch me."

"No one is watching you. It's not like a Bee. It just reports your body's physical reactions to things."

I make a sound of disgust. "Same thing."

"I don't know how I feel about it yet. I loved the father-daughter dance, didn't you? There was so much love in the room; it was palpable."

"Uh-huh," I say, feeling further away from Grace than ever. "What happens if a girl triggers the lady bug?"

"She joins the Fallen," she says, her voice solemn.

"The trash women?" I say, astonished.

"Yes," she says. "And the Fallen can never get married."

Wow. At home I felt like getting married was a punishment, and here *not* getting married is. What a strange world it is.

"My host-mom is signaling me," Grace says, pointing at a waving woman across the dance floor. "I think we're leaving soon."

The woman has thin, fluffy hair and a nonexistent chin. Her

enthusiasm as she smiles at Grace suggests she's a nice person, which is a relief.

Grace gives me a big hug.

"Don't go!" I plead.

"It was razzamatazz to see you. Major benny! I'll see you at class on Wednesday."

She hurries to her host-mom. I miss Grace—the version who lived in the basement of Macy's and surrounded herself with stuffed animals and Time Zero memorabilia. I trusted her with my life. I wonder if she's gone for good. This new version disturbs me. But what do I know? Maybe it's like Dekker said, and I just need to lighten up.

Silas is no longer at the buffet table. After a bit of searching, I spot him dancing with Susanna. I'm surprised by how comfortable they look with one another. He laughs at something she says.

I should be delighted to see them together, but an unfamiliar feeling creeps through me. Could it be jealousy? That's ridiculous. Silas blackmailed me to come here. I think he's sneaky and unreliable, remember? Why would I want to dance again with someone like that?

Even as I comfort myself with these thoughts, I'm filled with guilt over Juda. *He's* the one I care for. *He's* the one I'm trying to find. I can't just leave people behind like Horton did.

I have to come up with a new strategy. If no one will tell me where the Forgiveness Home is, then I have to get there another way . . .

With a sinking stomach, I realize that I'm going to have to talk to Tabby again.

As the night grows long, I search the pavilion. The dance floor is packed. Ginnie Delford tries to teach Dekker to dance, and now he's the one that looks like an otter. Silas dances with his mother and doesn't seem to have noticed my absence.

I finally catch sight of Tabby as Gilad approaches her for a dance. She gives him a tight smile. They sway around the dance floor, his broad face radiating pride. Tabby looks unhappy, even more than usual, because of the lady bug I assume? The whole thing sounds painful and unpleasant. Why in the world do girls look forward to this night?

Just as she did earlier in the evening, Tabby scans the room. After a few spins, she seems to locate what she's looking for. She smiles briefly, and each time she and Gilad turn, her eyes land in the same spot.

The only person in her eyeline is the gawky boy from the food court—the one who obviously had a crush on her. He's gazing at her as if she were a pancake he wants to dip in syrup. I look back at Tabby. She holds her chin high as she dances with Gilad, but each time she turns, she looks at the skinny boy with the same longing.

The straws. They finally make sense. Tabby wasn't keeping them because of the compressions or some strange diet. She kept them because of this boy. Perhaps I finally understand why Tabby used the Smoker suit to sneak out of her house.

When the song is over, Gilad looks ready to dance again, but Tabby shakes her head and walks toward the buffet table. Gilad looks hurt, but she doesn't notice. Although she moves away from the boy, she's still aware of his presence. I can tell by the way her shoulders pull back as she caresses her elaborate hairdo.

At the buffet table, she surveys the food. She occasionally glances in his direction and tries not to smile. His eyes remain locked on her. This is a game they've played before.

I'm hesitant to interrupt her flirtation, but I need to take advantage of her moment alone. I approach her with caution.

"Tabby," I say in a soft voice.

"Oh, great. It's you," she says.

I pretend to be interested in the food, taking a plate and heaping on sliced fruit.

"Your pledge was nice," I say.

She doesn't answer.

"May I see your necklace?" She inspects a wilted salad, so I lean in and look at the heart on a chain. "It's lovely."

"Why are you always in my face?" she says.

I need to ask my question or walk away. Taking a deep breath, I say, "Earlier, you said if I snuck out again your parents would send me to the Forgiveness Home. Is that true?"

She crunches on celery without looking at me. "It was a joke."

"They wouldn't send me?"

"What's your deal?" she says, looking me dead in the eyes. "That place is major feeble. Any good will you've built up will be gone—zappo—like that." She snaps her fingers. "Why would you do that?"

"You know," I say, looking at the boy.

She looks at him and then back at me. "I don't know what you're talking about," she says. She looks around to see who might be listening.

"Don't get upset. He seems nice. And I *understand*. I wasn't supposed to have feelings for my . . . boyfriend either." Boyfriend? Is that what Juda is? I've never used the word before. "He's in the Forgiveness Home, and I need to make sure he's all right. That's why I keep 'being in your face.'"

That's it. The truth. That's all I have. If Tabby won't help me now, I'm out of options.

Tabby's mouth twists in many directions, as if she's deciding if she wants to insult me or confess her own predicament. "So go to the Forgiveness Home. Get yourself locked up. My life will be easier with you gone."

"How do I do it?" I plead.

She looks back over at the boy, who's now looking at her quizzically.

"I'll leave you alone if you help me with this one thing," I say.

She rolls her eyes, showing the boy what an enormous pain I am. Can't everyone in the room see the connection between these two?

I smile slightly at the boy, trying to show that I'm sorry to interrupt whatever it is that's happening between them. He smiles back, looking very sweet and kind.

"Stop staring at him," Tabby hisses.

"Are you going to help me?" I ask.

Finally realizing I'm not going to go away, she steers me to the end of the table where no one is standing. "If you sneak out, my parents might, like, decide to punish you themselves again."

"How can I *make sure* I go to the Forgiveness Home?"

Considering this, she says, "You need something that's bad enough to get you in but not bad enough to keep you in. No one sane would want to be there more than a few days."

"A few days would be perfect!" I say.

"You make it sound like a spa weekend," she says, looking sorry for me.

"*Please*," I say.

She chews her lip, concentrating. "There's actually this idea that Silas and I have had for a while. We always thought it would be hilarious, but we never had the nerve to try it. I think tonight might be the perfect night to give it a go." She smiles wickedly. "Before I tell you our idea, you need to understand three things. First of all, you didn't see me looking at a boy. I don't know any boys."

"Right," I say, ready to say whatever she needs me to say.

"Second: you can never say my name or say I had anything to do with your infraction, or they'll put me in there right beside you. I guarantee if that happens, I will make your life a living Hell. Do you believe me?"

I nod. I absolutely believe her.

"Third: I can't guarantee what the consequences will be, but you have to be ready to accept the punishment."

"I understand." I can't believe it. She's going to help me.

"Now, how are you with little kids?" she asks.

"Okay, I guess," I say, trepidation growing. I can't believe I'm about to collaborate with Tabby. I tell myself I'm doing the right thing, while at the same time clanging warning bells are going off in my head.

I approach a large group of children playing near the entrance of the pavilion. Many of them are twirling until they fall on the floor, while others sit shoving cake into their mouths. Corny lies giggling on the ground, a victim of too much spinning.

My nerves quiver under my skin. I don't really understand how Tabby's plan will work, but it's all I have.

I hear Nana egging me on: *Afraid of children, Chickpea? Don't be silly.*

She's right. *This will be easy.*

I rush toward the children, bugging out my eyes in disbelief. "You won't believe what's happening outside! It's, uh . . . Wow . . . I can't even describe it!!"

An apple-cheeked little girl in a turquoise dress stops spinning and says, "Is it a unicorn?"

"No, dummy. Unicorns aren't real," says Corny. "I bet she saw a scorpion. Is it a scorpion?"

"No!" I say, trying not to lose my nerve. "It's people! Floating in the sky!"

The children gape at me.

"Really?" a brunette girl says with a mouthful of cake.

"Where?" says Corny, narrowing his eyes in suspicion.

"Praise God," says the unicorn girl, pressing her palms together.

"*Can you show us?*" several children cry.

"Let's go!" I say. I run outside the pavilion, a trail of tiny children following me.

Night has fallen. The glow from the Prom illuminates the lawn around us but makes the distant woods and sky black and impenetrable. "Over there!" I say, pointing into the distant woods.

"I can't see anything," whines the unicorn girl.

"Me either," says Corny.

"You can't?" I say. "I see lots of them. Dozens! Right over there!" I point again.

"Where?" asks the brunette girl.

"Right there!" I pause. "Ram says that only the pure of heart can see miracles. Maybe you children just aren't pure of heart." I produce a loud Tabby-like sigh.

The children let this sink in, and then unicorn girl says, "I see them!" and Corny says, "Me too! Right over there!" He points to the same area I did.

Soon the brunette girl and a freckled boy have said that they see the floating people too.

I smile. "This is so special. Let's go tell the others!"

They look nervously at one another, but then unicorn girl says, "Yes! We must tell everyone about the miracle!"

She rushes back to the pavilion, and soon all the children follow her.

I exhale. It's done, and there's no turning back.

Entering the building, I see the children weaving in and out of the crowd, finding their parents and announcing the enormous news.

Many adults try to brush off the children and continue their conversations, but the children won't be ignored. Some of them shout their news. Before long, everyone at the Prom has heard: a miracle is happening outside.

Guests hurry to the lawn. When I join them, I find a crowd staring at the sky, some people kneeling and praying. One man jumps up and down, shouting with his hands in the air. The children run in circles, chanting, "It's here! It's here!"

The more excited I see people get, the more anxiety brews in my stomach. What did I do? Tabby had me set off something I know nothing about.

Out of the corner of my eye, I see Ram. He's watching with a grim look on his face. He doesn't believe the children. Not for a second. "Loving family!" He has to yell to get their attention. "Please. *Please!*"

Gradually, the crowd settles down. The people kneeling on the ground continue to pray.

"I know this is a thrilling moment. Nothing could be more exciting than the return of our Savior. But I ask you, do any of you see the signs you need to see? Do you *really* see them? Because I do not. I look into our beautiful sky, and I only see sky. As much as I pray for the day of our Ascension, I fear that today is not that day. I'm sorry, my dear brothers and sisters. Your reward has to wait just a little bit longer."

A woman kneeling to my right bursts into tears.

"Let's go back into the pavilion and finish our beautiful Promise Prom, shall we?" Ram says, using his arms to herd the crowd inside.

The mood has gone from ecstatic to despondent. Most people don't move.

Parents start gathering their children and heading home.

The girls who took their pledges look at their fathers with watery eyes, not understanding why their special evening has been cut short. A few fathers steer their daughters back inside, but it's pointless. The party is over.

Tabby strides over, surveying the heartbroken guests. "Nice job. Even better than I expected." She grins with pride. "Here comes Jeremiah," she says, pointing across the lawn. "It seems the children have already given you up."

Jeremiah stomps toward us, outrage on his face. Nauseous, I pray there's nowhere worse than the Forgiveness Home.

"Good luck," she says, walking away.

When Jeremiah reaches me, he produces an unexpected smile. He puts a hand around my wrist and says in his low murmur, "Ram would like to see you."

He leads me back inside the pavilion. Silas watches openmouthed from across the floor. Did Tabby tell him what I did? I wish I could explain.

Jeremiah takes me through the rose-covered door. We walk down a flight of stairs and arrive at a large room full of mirrors and tables. Promise girls glumly gather their fluffy dancing skirts from the floor, while one of the little angel boys skips around watching himself in a mirror.

I'm about to ask where Ram is, when I feel a jab in my neck, and everything goes black.

SEVENTEEN

When I wake up, I'm on the floor of an empty room with a round ceiling, like the one where Dr. Rachel scanned me. I'm roasting hot and incredibly thirsty.

I sit up. "Hello?" I say, assuming someone is watching me, as Dr. Rachel had been.

No one answers. I'm still wearing the ridiculous red gown; the flimsy chiffon sticks to my clammy legs. How long have I been here?

Standing, I try to open the only door, but it's locked.

"Hello!" I say again.

I beat on the door. Silas told me there were no cells in the Forgiveness Home, but I'm seized by panic. "Let me out!" I holler.

A voice comes over a speaker, muffled and metallic: *Relax, Miss Clark. Someone will be with you shortly.*

The voice isn't unpleasant. It's clipped and matter-of-fact.

I wait another ten minutes before the door opens. An older man of around seventy enters. His salt-and-pepper hair (primarily salt) comes down in a sharp widow's peak and then flops casually to the side. The perfect crease down his ironed black trousers lets me know that he's a man who likes perfection. In his long elegant fingers, he holds a sealed package.

"Hello, Mina. My name is Kalyb." His voice is calm and friendly. "I've brought you some clothes. I'll wait outside while you change, and then you can join us for session."

"Change . . . here?" I ask.

He nods.

"May I go somewhere more private?" I ask, knowing that the person who spoke to me earlier might still be observing.

"No one will be watching you get dressed, Ms. Clark," he says, and without altering his friendly tone, he adds, "but you also gave up your right to privacy the moment you crossed our threshold. I'll be right outside." He closes the door.

Helpless, I look around the room for cameras. I see none, but the hairs on the back of my neck are bristling. *I know I'm being watched.* What happens if I don't change?

I stand holding the clothes, close to tears. The voice comes over the speaker again: *You have two minutes to exit.*

I huddle in the corner of the room, facing the wall. Kalyb has brought me a pair of underwear, a bra, beige pants and a beige T-shirt. Still wearing my dress, I change into the underwear. The full chiffon skirt makes it simple to then step into the pants and pull them up without exposing any skin.

But I can't possibly get the T-shirt on without taking off the dress. Shaking, I swiftly yank the gown over my head. I hear the tear of stitches, but I can't worry about the state of the dress right now.

I try to cover my chest as I put on the bra, but it's impossible to get it on without both hands. Since it has no hooks, I have to slide it over my head. Tight and constricting, it makes my breasts flatten like pita bread.

I throw on the beige T-shirt and turn around, glaring around the room. I'm humiliated and furious at the idea of someone watching, even another woman. I want them to see my rage.

When I leave the room, Kalyb smiles at me. I don't smile back. He leads me down a series of hallways. The floors have cracked tile, and the walls are peeling. From the looks of the layers of paint, people have been painting these walls since the dawn of time.

As Kalyb strides past closed doorway after closed doorway, my anger turns to anxiety. I remember Tabby's words: *No one sane would want to be there more than a few days.* We pass a well-muscled man wearing purple, and he and Kalyb nod to one another.

Kalyb opens a nondescript door, revealing a small room that was probably at one time white but is now more of a dirty-teeth yellow. The room is as sweltering as the last one, and sweat beads on my forehead. I seem to have discovered the only unairconditioned building in Kingsboro.

In the center of the space is a circle of orange chairs filled with people. They look up when we arrive. The only person who doesn't look up is Juda.

My breath catches, and I try not to grin.

Kalyb holds out an empty seat for me and then eases himself into the chair beside it. "Good morning, residents. We have a new arrival today. Her name is Mina Clark."

At this, Juda's head jerks up. I give him the tiniest of smiles, but he doesn't smile back. In fact, he looks horrified. As he turns his head away, a fist tightens around my heart.

The rest of the group is made of young people around my age. A boy to my left slumps in his chair, looking half asleep, while a girl across from me fidgets, nervous for whatever is coming next. A boy wearing glasses with sweat stains on his shirt looks at me with distaste. Everyone in the circle wears the same beige color as I do, and they all look overheated.

"Ruth, why don't you start us off today?" says Kalyb, crossing his legs.

A girl with tan skin and dark red hair shifts in her seat. Her face is overwhelmed by an immense frown. "I, uh, had a pretty good dream last night."

"Tell us about it," says Kalyb.

"I was home, and my parents were treating me like normal," Ruth says.

The others nod.

"Anything else?" asks Kalyb.

Ruth shrugs.

"Young ladies do not shrug, Ruth," Kalyb says.

Ruth looks exhausted. "Nothing else, Kalyb."

"Did you consider the path that might have led your parents and God to forgive you?" Kalyb gestures a lot with his hands, like he's talking to someone who's hard of hearing.

"Maybe."

Kalyb tilts his head. "Do you want to tell us about it?"

She sniffs and wipes her nose. "I stopped having sinful thoughts and put myself on the righteous path."

"Very good!" says Kalyb. He claps, and the others join. He looks at a pretty girl with sandy brown hair and a pointy nose.

"Connie? How about you?"

Connie looks to her neighbor and smirks.

"Connie?" he repeats.

She looks at the floor.

"You don't want to talk, or you've had no revelations?"

"Neither," says Connie.

"I'm sure that's not true," says Kalyb with assurance.

"I want breakfast," she says with agitation.

"Good!" says Kalyb. "That's the beginning of your journey—

knowing what you want. Now you have to figure out how to obtain it. And how do we get what we want?"

Everyone but Juda chants: *by letting God's light into our hearts.*

"How about you, Mary?"

He looks at a large girl with black hair and creamy skin whose foot bounces with agitation against her leg. She smiles sweetly. "Oh, uh, I *don't* want breakfast. Is that what you want me to say?"

Kalyb doesn't falter. "I don't *want* you to say anything, Mary. I only want you to find peace in the light."

"You only want me to find peace in *being* light," Mary says.

Ruth and Connie laugh.

Kalyb waves his right hand. "I want you to unburden yourself and find happiness. You know that, Mary." His eyebrows knit together. "No more sass today. No one likes an impudent woman."

He narrows his eyes, looking around the circle. "How about you, Juda? How are you this morning?"

Juda stares at him icily.

"It's a simple question and one I know you can answer."

"I'm great. The world is *paradise.*" My breath quickens at the sound of Juda's voice, even though it drips with sarcasm.

"As you know, we don't use that kind of tone in this room. Would you like to try again?"

"Not really."

"Would you like to go have a visit with Solomon?"

Panic passes across Juda's face. "No," he says.

"No, what?"

"No, Kalyb," says Juda.

"Good. Then let's try again." Kalyb's eyes crinkle as he smiles. "How are you today, Juda?"

"Fine, Kalyb."

"Do you have any revelations to share with us today?"

Juda gives me a fleeting look before saying, "No, Kalyb."

"Are you *sure?*" Kalyb asks, staring at him without blinking.

Juda glowers back. His dislike for Kalyb is so strong, I can almost taste it in the air.

Shifting in his seat, Juda looks at the floor. "I, uh, meditated on my past sins and asked God to forgive my, uh, belief in a false prophet."

I have to fight to keep from making a sound, but I'm sure my eyes bug out of my head. A *false prophet?* Juda has converted? I've been making my own attempt to accept the Savior of the Unbound, but I never thought in a million years I would hear Juda reject his beliefs. He's so much stronger than I am.

"Very good! Thank you, Juda." Kalyb rubs his hands together. "Who's next? How about you, Mina?"

I jump a little in my seat. What does he want me to say? The same thing as Juda?

"I don't see why we have to have session with *them*," says the sweaty boy with glasses as he glares at Juda and me.

Kalyb smiles patiently. "We've discussed this, Jeffrey. And if you could let in the light this morning, I think you might feel better."

"How about you tell *them* to let in the light," says Jeffrey, pointing his finger at us.

Connie nods.

"Well, I just might if you give me the chance," says Kalyb, his eyes crinkling again.

Jeffrey blows out his lips with an exasperated sound.

Kalyb turns back to me. "How *are* you today, Mina?"

"Um," I say. I look around the room, avoiding eye contact with Jeffrey. "Nervous?" I offer, although this seems like an understatement.

"That's normal on your first day, isn't it, children?" he says, looking at the others. From their expressions, I can see that none of them appreciates being called a child.

Juda doesn't look at me. He sits with his arms crossed in front of him, jaw clenched.

"How about you tell us why you're here?" Kalyb says.

Mary stares at me, riveted.

"I played a joke?" I say.

Kalyb's smile disappears. "A joke? That's what you call it?"

Tabby thought it would be hilarious, but I can't say her name. "It was supposed to be a prank."

"Hundreds of people went home crying, and a beautiful night was ruined. That's funny to you?" says Kalyb.

Everyone in the circle gapes at me and a few lean in to hear more. The way Kalyb describes it, you'd think I threw a grenade at Prom.

"No," I say quietly. "It wasn't funny."

"No. It was not. It was shameful and wicked. How do you think you might atone for what you did?"

I pull at my shirt, wishing the room were cooler. "I don't know. I'm . . . new here."

"Yes, you are from the island. And refugees can have a difficult time adjusting. You have suffered a lot of trauma, and it can be hard, even when you're surrounded by a solid new family that loves you. But that's no excuse. We still expect you to act like thoughtful human beings and not animals." He looks at Juda when he says the word "animal."

"Who here can tell Mina what the first step is toward redemption?"

Ruth raises her hand. "She has to get clean."

"Very good," says Kalyb. "You must purify yourself, purify your soul. You'll let God into your heart and only then will you be able to tell us why you're here—what you did and how you will atone. Luckily for all of us we have a spiritual leader here at the Forgiveness Home who specializes in purification. This morning, Mina, you will have the honor of meeting him."

I glance at Juda. He looks at me with such pity and sorrow that, for the first time since arriving in Kingsboro, I become truly terrified.

EIGHTEEN

Group doesn't end until everyone in the circle has spoken, each person telling Kalyb in one way or another that they're working on repentance through thoughts and prayers.

Kalyb asks us all to join hands, saying, "God can forgive you for making mistakes. Mistakes are how we learn what is right and what is wrong. The only real mistake we can make is to remain in a state of denial and to continue to repeat our sins. God will lose patience, and He'll punish you as if you never believed in Him at all. Bless you all in this journey. May you find the strength to walk the righteous path and let in the light. So be it."

"So be it," everyone echoes.

When people stand to leave, I try to move closer to Juda, but Kalyb reaches me first, placing his hand on my elbow. His skin emits a strange smell—candied fruit on top of mildew. "Wasn't that freeing?" he asks.

"Free" is the opposite of how I feel, but I nod.

He guides me unhurriedly out of the room. "This way," he says, leading me down a hall, away from the others.

Turning my head, I give Juda the quickest of smiles. He gives me an open-mouthed look of wonder that can only mean one thing: *why are you here?*

I thought he'd be so happy to see me, and instead, he seems perplexed and sad.

Kalyb turns down another hall, stopping at a rusted door. "Think over what you learned today. I'll see you in session again tomorrow morning, and then we'll have a one-on-one consultation in the afternoon." Pushing the door open, he leads me outside. We step into a courtyard with gravel and rocks on the ground. Concrete walls surround us on each side, and the heat is as oppressive as it was inside, but the patch of blue sky above allows me to relax a little, like when I've loosened shoes that were too tight.

A man in white stands in the corner of the courtyard with his arms crossed in front of him. His enormous head appears to rest on his stocky body without the benefit of a neck. His nose is squashed at the tip, as if he just ran into a door. Blond hair is smoothed across his pink forehead, but one unlikely curl pops up above his left eye. He looks impatient, as if he's been waiting for us a long time. A metal trunk rests near his feet.

"Go to the wall," the man says.

I look to Kalyb for instruction, but he nods at the man and leaves the courtyard.

"Go to the wall, and don't make me repeat myself," says the man. His voice is deep and resonant, as if he can only breathe through his mouth.

"I don't know—" I say.

"Did I ask you to speak?" he says with more volume.

Which of the four walls does he mean? Choosing the one closest to me, on my right, I walk and stand next to it.

The man approaches, stepping so close I can smell his breath, which stinks like rotten meat. "Put your hands on the wall," he says.

My hands tremble as they touch the cold concrete. I hear him shuffling behind me. Is he going to touch me with those red, beefy hands? Bile rises in my throat.

The metal trunk opens and closes, and then he's beside me again, saying, "This is your new backpack. Each rock inside represents one of your sins. You will wear it to remind yourself of your burden and how far you need to travel to be welcomed by God into His kingdom." He grabs my left arm and slides on a strap. The sudden weight yanks down my shoulder. He seizes my right arm and pulls up the other strap, and then he steps away.

I immediately fall onto the ground, the heaviness of the rocks bringing me down like a turtle on its shell.

He laughs. "Oops. Looks like the sin is bigger than the girl." He chuckles some more. "Stand up," he says.

When I begin to take off the straps of the backpack, he says, "I didn't say you could take that off, did I?"

When I don't answer, he repeats, *"Did I?"*

"No," I say.

"No, *what?"*

"No, sir?" I say.

"I am not 'sir.' I am not your father nor your cleric. I go by the name God gave me: Solomon."

God named this man? "Yes, Solomon."

"Better. Now, stand."

I attempt to stand with the backpack on—my stomach tightening as I raise my head and arms—but it's much too heavy. I can't lift even an inch off the ground.

Solomon shakes his head, making a clucking sound. "So much burden. How can we remove some of the sin so that you might stand?"

The rocks dig into my lower back. The area only recently stopped stinging from the burn my mother caused, but the skin is still tender and sore. "I don't know," I say, and then quickly add, "Solomon."

"Let's think, shall we?" He paces around my head. "Perhaps there are some things you would like to tell God? Some untruths that you have told?"

My mind races. What does Solomon know or not know?

He bends so that his face appears right above mine. Again, I can smell his putrid breath. "Do you have anything to share, Mina Clark?"

"No, Solomon."

Walking to the corner of the yard, he grabs another rock. He unzips the backpack under my head. "That's another lie." He adds the rock and zips it back up.

I'm worried I might cry, but I don't want to give Solomon the satisfaction. I must find something to say. I consider what Kalyb said earlier about how serious my prank was. "I ruined Promise Prom."

"Okay. That's a good start."

"I didn't mean to."

"Don't make me add another rock."

I say what he wants to hear: "I *did* mean to."

"Okay. Good. Why?"

I can't say that I wanted to be here in the Forgiveness Home. He might decide to keep me away from Juda forever.

"Perhaps you hated those girls for showing their flesh?" he asks. "You thought it was shameful that they don't cover up as your people do?"

"No! I never—"

"You felt they should be punished for tempting the men around them?"

I haven't gotten used to women showing their faces and skin so easily, but I don't think I've sat in judgment.

"Did you not feel a deep sense of shame when the Dixons

made you walk around without your veil? Did you not fear your *Prophet* would send you to Hell?" When he says "Prophet" his voice is full of mockery.

As the rocks cut deeper into my back, I wonder if I'm bleeding. I look at the wall of the Forgiveness Home, searching the windows for someone walking by.

"No one there is going to help you," Solomon says with glee. "I'm in charge."

I look back at his squashed, spiteful face. How long will he make me lie here if I don't say I wanted to punish those other girls? Maybe agreeing with him is the smartest thing to do.

"I . . . I . . . I was jealous," I sputter.

His eyes flash. "Of what?"

My mind races. "Of the girls—the attention they were getting."

"You wanted attention?"

"Yes, Solomon," I say.

"From your family? Do you wish your parents had shown you love and affection like the parents of the Unbound?"

I'm not sure what the real answer is. Something about the Unbound fathers giving their daughters jewelry—it seemed caring but also sort of strange in a way I can't express. But that is not what Solomon wants to hear, so I say, "Yes, Solomon. I wish I'd had more love and attention."

Solomon reaches under my head, unzips the backpack and removes a rock. "You have admitted to the sin of vanity. Very good. God is proud." He steps back. "Can you stand?"

I lift my head and flex my legs, but I'm still unable to get up.

"Okay then, Mina. What other burdens would you like to rid yourself of?"

I take a deep breath. I haven't had breakfast. The sun is rising higher, causing the air to grow dank and hot. I might be able to stand if Solomon removes two or three more rocks. Surely I can think of three more sins to confess?

"I broke the rules at the Dixons' house," I say. "I snuck out without permission."

"Ah, yes," says Solomon. "I heard about this. I suggested that the Dixons send you to me immediately, but they insisted that you should get a second chance."

I could've been here seeing Juda last week?

"Why did you sneak out of the house?"

"I wanted to see my friends."

"Why?" he says, crunching the gravel with his feet as he paces. "Did you all arrive here wanting to hurt and deceive the Unbound?"

"No!" I say, realizing the danger we'll be in if Solomon believes there's a conspiracy. "We were running away from the island. We were trying to be safe. We hoped—we prayed—that there might be people who could help us."

"And we've kept you safe, right? Yet this is how you repay us: by breaking our rules, by lying, and by ruining a beloved occasion."

I have another idea. "I needed to see my brother," I say.

"Why?" he asks, excited at the revelation.

"He's . . . uh . . . a little slow sometimes. He can get confused in new situations." Has Solomon met Dekker?

"Why did you need to see him?"

"He finds my presence calming." This is the biggest lie I've told so far.

"So you were trying to soothe your brother by sneaking around late at night and peeking into windows?"

He makes it sound pretty stupid. "I thought he would feel better if he saw my face."

"I think you wanted to spend time out at night, in the park, with the Dixon boy," he says in a disgusted tone, as if I'm a whore.

"No!" I say. I'll confess to his fabrications, but I won't let him turn me into some sort of tramp.

"Everyone in town knows he's your boyfriend," he says. "It didn't take you long to sink your woolie claws into him, did it?"

"It's not true."

"Why should I believe you? You're a liar and a sinner, and that boy has been telling everyone."

I went to Promise Prom with Silas, but has he been telling people that I'm his *girlfriend*? Has he told so many people that Solomon has heard? Or does Solomon hear everything, like a Bee?

"I don't care what he said. He's not my boyfriend."

"So why did you go to the Prom together?"

Why does he care so much? Is he disgusted by the idea of a member of the Unbound with a woolie? Or is it an actual sin?

"Silas Dixon has not tried to be physically intimate with you?"

My body stiffens. Is *that* what Silas has been telling people? "No! Silas asked me to Prom . . . that was all."

"Have you held his hand? Or kissed him?"

"No, Solomon."

"How can you prove it?"

The only thing I can do is tell him that I love someone else, but I won't do that. "Silas is lying," I whisper.

"What's that?" he says.

"He's lying! I swear to God and the Savior that Silas is LYING!" I say, growing furious.

"Okay," Solomon says in a new friendly voice. He reaches under my head and takes another rock out from the backpack. I could weep from relief.

"That wasn't so hard, was it?" he says.

One more rock and I should be able to stand. My head spins as I try to think of something else to say.

Before I can come up with anything, Solomon says, "Why did you come here?"

"The Promise Prom. I ruined—"

"No!" he says. "Why did you leave Manhattan? And remember, I have one of you woolies in here already, so I'll know if you're lying."

Juda wouldn't tell him anything. Right?

"I told you, we were in danger—" I begin.

"*Why* were you in danger? *Why* were you running away?"

"My in-laws—my future in-laws—were after us."

"Did you steal something from them?"

"No, Solomon. They wanted me to marry their son, Damon."

"Four other people were willing to risk their lives, defy Uncle Ruho, and come through a flooded tunnel just so you wouldn't have to get married?"

Shame swells in the core of my belly. "It was more complicated than that."

"Tell me."

My eyes fill with tears. How can I explain all the things that happened that made us decide to leave? And how am I to know if he'll feel sympathy for *anything* that happens on the island? He doesn't seem like a man who experiences compassion for anyone or anything.

"My fiancé was—" I catch myself. "—is—not a nice man. He treats me very badly. I defended myself. For that, his family wants to punish me."

"*Fascinating*," says Solomon. He walks down to my feet. "Take my hands."

When I reach up, he grabs my hands and yanks me forward. The weight on my back is so great that I think my arms will be ripped from my torso, but eventually, I'm standing.

Was that it? He got the information he wanted?

"You need more time to think things over," he says. "And I need breakfast. So you're going to put your hands back on the wall."

I'm tempted to say that I need breakfast, too, but I do as he says.

"When I come back, maybe you'll be ready to tell me what really happened between you and your fiancé's family. Okay?"

He walks to the door. Before he reaches it, he turns to say, "Don't consider sitting down or moving from that spot. You're being watched, of course." He smiles, smoothing his hair down across his forehead. "See you soon." He walks out the metal door, which closes with a loud bang.

What just happened? How much did I tell him? When will he be back?

Despite the rocks that have been removed, the backpack is still painfully heavy. As desperate as I was to get off the ground, I'm more miserable standing up, the enormous weight threatening to pull me down again. What happens if I fall over accidentally? Will I still be punished? I don't want to find out.

Trying to ignore the straps cutting into my skin, I concentrate on the story I need to tell about the Ashers. How much of the truth should I share? How much does Solomon already know? Most importantly, can I come up with a story that is believable and doesn't involve murder?

NINETEEN

What makes the next hour worse is the people walking by. I can see them through the windows. The residents come and go from breakfast, and not one acknowledges my existence. Girls and boys my age chat with one another, but no one looks at the girl in anguish in the courtyard.

I feel smaller than dust.

As another hour ticks by, I accept that Solomon is not just eating breakfast. He may leave me here all day. I gradually become enraged.

I convince myself that I am strong and different from the other people here; I won't be broken by a bully with bad breath. I stand taller to show the people in the windows that I'm tough.

I think of all the sins that I'm sure Solomon is guilty of—pride, vanity, wrath. I imagine him wearing a backpack filled with rocks that are not only heavy but hot from resting in a nearby fire. I would order him to stand still against the wall even as the rocks began to burn him.

Dark thoughts like this one fly through my mind, frantic and combative as birds caught in a net. How would Solomon do with a Twitcher? Could he even survive Manhattan? After a few years in the Tunnel, I wonder how tough he would be.

The Unbound have no Tunnel. This backpack seems to be the worst punishment they have for me. *And I can take it.*

As the morning moves on, my outrage fades. The sun grows hotter and the backpack becomes heavier. I slump, trying to shift the pain away from my upper back, where it feels like someone has put clamps on my shoulder blades.

I concentrate on happy thoughts: Sekena in front of her sunlamp; Juda laughing and eating squirrel; Nana reading me the museum section of the Primer:

The opulent residence that houses a private collection of great masters was originally built for industrialist Henry Clay Frick. The firm of Carrère & Hastings designed the 1914 structure in an 18th-century European style.

What I wouldn't give to have Nana reading to me right now.

Nana. I won't ever see her again. Her plan for me has been a complete failure. I am a failure.

I keep concentrating on the Primer. I resolve to go through it page by page in my head until Solomon returns.

Eateries under the Major Food Group umbrella, the one that brought us Sadelle's and Dirty French, are equal parts sustenance and scene. This Meatpacking number, a people-watching glass box tucked beneath the High Line, is no exception.

Another hour or so passes. I can only guess the time.

How could I have possibly thought it was a good idea to come to the Forgiveness Home? Tabby told me no one sane would want to be here. But I wouldn't listen. I was sure I knew better, that it couldn't be that bad. She couldn't have known about standing outside for hours with a backpack of rocks, or surely she wouldn't have helped me, right?

But would I have abandoned Juda to rot here? Thinking that I could come in here and help him escape makes me an idiot. Who do I think I am?

Coming here was a huge mistake, but it's not my first. Why did I have to choose *this* subway stop? Maybe if I'd chosen a different tunnel, we'd all be free now. Or maybe my mistake was including other people at all. I should have left Manhattan by myself and left the others to live their lives. If I'd never talked to Juda . . . If I hadn't followed him down the stairs . . . or kissed him.

Queasiness surges through me as I consider never having met Juda. My insides knot at the idea, but at least now he would be safe at home with Rose.

I jiggle my head, shaking away unpleasant thoughts. Nana would say, "Trying to change the past is like trying to become two inches shorter. It's impossible and will just make you slump around in a depression."

The straps of the backpack dig deep, seeming to pull skin from behind my ears and down my neck. My legs are so tired, my knees are shaking slightly. I'm desperate to take my arms off the wall just for a second. They've been in the same position for hours. I need water and food.

The Prophet said, "Each person's Hell is perfectly fitted to the size of his or her sin."

This must be my Hell.

It's about time I admit that I deserve it.

I killed Damon. I spurred him on, made him walk into deep water knowing he couldn't swim.

I killed Mr. Asher. Damon was trying to kill Juda because of me. If I'd just behaved correctly, none of it would've happened, and they'd both be alive now.

My parents . . . I don't know that I can bear to think about them. Certainly Father has lost his job. They could be on the streets.

I'm a horrible, selfish person, and everyone knows it but me. God knows it, and that's why I'm here, unable to move, pain shooting through every limb of my body. I begin to sob. I don't know how much longer I can do this. Will Solomon ever come back? What if he leaves me here overnight? I cry harder.

The sobbing causes my shoulders to tremble, and the straps of the backpack slide further inward. I've been standing with my back curved, so I straighten up, hoping to help the pain in my neck. But the shift is too much, and I tumble backward onto the ground.

I land hard, the rocks cutting into my skin. I gasp at the new pain. Luckily, the size of the backpack keeps my head from hitting the ground. I lie there, my legs and arms becoming jelly now that they're no longer being forced to work.

"Don't consider sitting down or moving" is what Solomon said, but my body is so exhausted, I don't know how I'll ever get up again.

I pray, not to the Prophet or to the Savior, but directly to God.

I've been terrible to You. I've disobeyed You and You have no reason to help me, but please . . . I want to be a good person. I've been so confused. I want to do the right thing. Just show me how, and I'll never be disloyal again. I promise.

All I can hear is my breathing and crying. My nose runs, and my arm is too tired to lift my hand to wipe it.

I'll lie here until Solomon returns and then beg his forgiveness for disobeying him. It's my only choice.

"You have to get up, Mina," a voice says.

I know that voice.

It's Juda.

I look up at the sky and then the roof.

"You're being watched," he says, "but they can't hear us. Just listen," he says.

Following his voice, I notice an open window on the second floor. A shadowy figure lurks there.

Sensing I've spotted him, he says quietly, "Don't move. Don't look at me."

I glance back at the sky.

"Are you okay?" I say, trying not to move my mouth.

"Don't talk," he says with force. "They'll see you and come. For once in your stubborn life, *please*, just listen."

I almost smile.

"You have to get up, Mina," he says.

I close my eyes. I can't.

"If Solomon comes back and finds you on the ground . . . it will be bad. Worse than it is now."

I keep my eyes closed. Is Juda really here? Maybe this is a dream, like the time I thought he climbed into the bathtub with me.

"If you stand, you can talk to me," he says.

I don't move. If I can just sleep for five minutes before Solomon returns, I'll be better prepared for whatever is coming.

"Listen, to me, Clark. You're going to sit up, and then you're going to stand. You're better than this."

I open my eyes. I want him to leave me alone. I want water.

"Stand, Mina. Let's go!" He's barking at me like a soldier.

When I still don't move, he says, "Ruth told me that when

Solomon took her to the courtyard, he started yelling at her, and a bird pooped on his head."

I laugh. I can't help it.

"See? You have energy. Stand!"

Lifting my head, I look down at my body, which seems to belong to someone else. I lift my torso slightly, and my bloody back unsticks from the backpack. I begin to slide the straps off.

"No," Juda says. "Keep it on. They'll see you take it off."

I want to yell at him, but I leave the straps on. Leaning forward, I pull my legs underneath me. My balance totally off, I move like a colt standing for the first time. A small breeze will topple me right back over. My thighs shake as I straighten up.

Stabbing pain returns to my neck, shoulders, and lower back, as I return my hands to the wall.

"Good girl!" says Juda.

I don't appreciate being spoken to like I'm a dog, but this isn't the time to bring it up.

"The camera is on the wall behind you, but it's really old. If you tilt your head down, you can speak to me," he says.

Anxious, but desperate to talk to him, I tip my chin to my chest. In a low voice, I say, "I miss you."

"I miss you, too," he says. "So much."

"I've been trying to find you."

"I've been here. I ask about you all the time."

I smile, thinking that he's been as desperate to find me as I have to find him.

"Are you okay?" he asks.

He must be joking. "No, I'm not okay."

"Is anything broken?" he says with worry. "Did Solomon hit you?"

"No."

"Good. Tell him you want to repent your sins. Then he'll bring you back inside."

"I *do* want that," I say.

"What are you talking about?" he says, almost angry.

I can't answer right away, because I'm afraid of crying again. "I'm sorry I brought you to Queens. I'm sorry I made you hit Damon and lose your job. I'm sorry you had to run away. I'm sorry for everything. It's all my fault, and I want God's forgiveness."

He makes a weird sound with his mouth—"Ffftttt"—but I have no idea what it means. "I know you think you hold a lot of power over me, but if you think you 'made' me do any of those things, you've really become deluded since we last saw each other."

I wish I could take comfort in his words. "We killed a man, Juda. There's no worse sin." I don't care if Solomon or Kalyb can hear me. God knows the truth.

"He was trying to kill us!" he says. "And he killed his own father. God sees what's right and what's wrong. You know that."

I wish I were sure.

"You're tired, and you're thirsty. I understand. But you *cannot* tell Solomon about what happened to Damon."

"He wants me to confess my sins, and I want to confess them."

"No!" he says. "Do you want to see all five of us on trial for murder, when the people here can't possibly understand what we were going through or what really happened? The last time you saw Damon was when you fled his apartment, got it?"

All *five* of us on trial. I have to tell Juda about his mother. It won't be good for him—it will make him suffer greatly—but I've seen his wrath when someone keeps secrets from him. *What if Rose's illness is God's punishment for killing Damon?*

"I have to tell you something," I say.

"I forgive you, Mina. God forgives you. Stop punishing yourself."

209

"No, it's—"

The door to the courtyard opens and Solomon enters, a big grin on his face. "Where were we?" he says.

I glance at the window and Juda is gone.

TWENTY

Solomon's footsteps crunch on the gravel as he approaches.

What if he puts more rocks in my backpack? I can't possibly endure one more.

He leans into my ear, whispering, "What do you have to say to me?"

Hoping to cut him off from asking about the Ashers, I say, "I want to repent."

"God loves humility," he says with joy. "God is ready to hear your sins."

Searching for courage in Juda's words, I say, "I did not respect my parents or the decisions they made on my behalf."

Solomon circles behind me, mumbling something I cannot hear. Then he says, "What else?"

Nervous, I add, "I gave my heart to a boy who was not my betrothed."

"Did you fornicate with him?"

"No!"

"Did you attempt to?"

"No."

"Did you touch each other in inappropriate ways?"

"I . . ." What does that mean? We kissed. We held each other. Nothing felt inappropriate. "No."

"Don't lie."

"We didn't."

"Who taught you to be this Jezebel? Did your mother put ideas of the devil in your mind?"

"No."

"Your friends?"

"No one."

"You're lying. Deceit and sinfulness do not appear from nowhere. They fester where they've been planted. Who sowed these ideas in your soul?" After a moment of silence, he says, "Someone taught you to be liberal with your desire. Who was it? Some other Jezebel floozy. Your sister? Your cousin? Your grandmother?"

"She's not a floozy!" I snap.

Solomon smiles. "Your grandmother led you astray."

Nyek. How could I have given away this information so easily?

"What else did she tell you? Did she teach you that the Unbound were evil and needed to be infiltrated?"

"No—she wanted me to come here to be safe. She wanted me to escape."

"Why?"

"She knew that I was in danger."

"Did she teach you to hate men? Did she teach you how to fight?"

"No! She taught me how to read."

He sniffs. "I think you'd be better prepared if she'd taught you how to punch."

He is correct in that I would very much like to punch him right now.

"The Unbound are taught to listen to and obey their parents," he says, "but, more importantly, they are taught to obey the rules of God. You were listening to the advice of an elder, but you must understand going forward that the laws of God are paramount and that they will never let you down. You will never find yourself again in the position you are in now—confused, lonely, in pain—if you follow the Lord. Do you understand?"

I nod.

"You strayed so far from the path that suffering was inevitable. Your grandmother was a provoker, and no one blames you for listening to her, but now it's time for you to become an adult and see the world for what it really is. When you do, there will be reward upon reward. The first one will be removal of this backpack. Next will be acceptance among the Forgiveness Home community. And finally, when you are ready, you will be able to return to the Dixons. And you will feel so light, so blessed, that you will be happier than you ever thought possible."

He's smiling; his voice is calm and reassuring. "Are you ready to be blessed, Mina?"

I nod, tears forming at the thought of taking off the rocks.

"Good." He crosses his arms. "If only you had fully released your burden."

"But I told you everything! You—" I say.

He cuts me off with a brisk, "Chh." His face hardens. "You still haven't told me what happened to your fiancé."

"What do you mean? He's—"

"Don't make it worse by lying. You'll keep the backpack on until you decide to tell the truth." Walking to the door, he pushes it open. "Come with me."

He can't be serious. I've had the rocks on my back for at least six hours. Standing here was hard enough; I can't possibly walk around.

"Don't make me ask twice."

With great effort, I make my way across the stony ground. If I lean any direction, I will tumble over. Once I reach the door, he leads me down the hall. He walks quickly, and I struggle to keep up. The pain from my back and shoulders shoots down my arms and legs.

We walk through several hallways, past a few men in purple. Is Solomon finally going to feed me?

We reach a room full of empty bunk beds. *Thank the Prophet, the Savior, God, whomever.* Solomon is going to let me lie down.

"This is the girls' dorm. That will be your bed," Solomon says, pointing to a top bunk.

He doesn't have to say it. He wants me to climb up to the bed with the backpack on.

I tell myself that at the end of the climb is a mattress and sleep.

Two wide planks at the foot of the bottom bed form a ladder of sorts. I approach slowly, wondering if I still have enough strength left to climb.

I put my right foot on the bottom rung and hoist myself up, but the weight of the rocks pulls me right back down.

I try again, this time tightening my stomach and leaning forward to try to compensate for the extra weight behind me. I'm able to balance and take the second step. I pull myself up again, feeling a muscle wrench in my lower back.

One step left—less than one foot high—and it might as well be ten. I know I'm going to cry. Using all my remaining strength, I place my right foot on the plank and heave my body up and over into the bed. I groan as I feel the rocks land on top of me as I hit the mattress.

"See you tomorrow," Solomon says. "I look forward to continuing our conversation."

I roll to my right, and the rocks fall to the side. Suddenly the siege on my body ends, a thumb lifted from a moth.

I fall into a painful, fitful sleep.

TWENTY-ONE

I wake to the sounds of giggles. When I open my eyes, faces stare up at me. I can't remember where I am for a moment, but the pain in my back soon reminds me.

"It's awake." It's Connie from session yesterday, the pretty one with the beaky nose.

"Terrific," says another girl dryly.

"I was about to poke it with a stick, make sure it was alive," Connie says.

More giggles.

I sit up. My body hurts in ways I've never known.

"Tsk, tsk," says Connie. "Keep that backpack on!"

Looking down, I see the backpack lying beside me. I must have wiggled out of it in my sleep.

"Leave her alone, Connie," says Mary, the heavy girl with buttery skin who was also in session yesterday. "I seem to remember you wearing a backpack for weeks."

Connie shoots Mary a look of death. "Shut up, Meatball."

"Whatever," says Mary. "Go peck at some grain."

"Let's go to session," Connie tells the other girls.

As soon as Connie and her friends have left, Mary says, "You okay?"

I frown.

"'Okay' is about as good as it gets in this Hellhole," she says.

"What time is breakfast?" I'm absolutely starving.

"We have to go to session first. It blows."

I smile weakly.

"But here, I have a roll I stole a few days ago. It's a little stale but . . ." She reaches under the mattress of her bunk and pulls out a sad-looking piece of bread.

"Thank you so much." Even covered in dust, it's the best thing I've ever tasted. I wonder how I can ever pay her back.

"No problem. I keep food here for just this purpose. They really break newcomers down with the whole starvation thing."

I want to ask why she's here, how such a nice girl could have ended up in such an awful place, but my instinct tells me it might be rude.

"We need to get going," she says. "Session starts soon."

Startled, I reach for the backpack. My shoulders sting with the movement. I lay on the bed and put on the straps.

"I can help you get down, but you have to keep the backpack on. Sorry," says Mary.

I'm not worried about getting down the ladder. I'm worried about sitting up. "I just need a second."

Telling myself that the first time I get up today will be the worst, I slowly scoot down to the edge of the bed and put my feet on the ladder. I count to three, inhale, and lift. My stomach contracts, every muscle lighting up with pain. I strained this same way yesterday, and my body hasn't forgotten.

Despite the agony, I'm now sitting up. I carefully turn around to step down the ladder. Mary stands underneath me, putting her hands on the pack and taking off some of the weight. There's no way I could do it without her.

Safely on the floor, I ask, "Did you have to wear a backpack?"

She looks unsure of herself for the first time. "No, I, uh, got something else."

"Do you not want to talk about it?" I ask.

"Not really."

"Okay," I say, knowing there are *lots* of things I don't necessarily want to share with her.

As we leave the room, I ask, "Are we going far?" I want to know how long I have to endure walking with the rocks.

"Not really," Mary says, with an understanding tone.

First she leads me to the restroom, where I stick my mouth under the tap of the sink and slurp away until I think I'm going to burst. Then she finds me a toothbrush to use. *What a relief.*

As we walk down the hall, she explains the layout of the building. "There are two girls' dorms but four for the boys. I guess boys just get in more trouble. We all eat in the same cafeteria, and you can sit with the boys, but never one-on-one." She rolls her eyes. "We have a community room with some really lame games—the ones you played when you were, like, eight— and there's a reading room with *maybe* three approved books. The bathrooms are skeevy, and you're going to feel like you'll never have privacy again. The food is barfy, and the sessions are complete twaddle. Welcome to the Forgotten Home!"

The whole thing is smaller than I pictured it. I thought it would be a massive prison, like the Tunnel, but it's not much bigger than the basement of Macy's.

Almost everyone I've seen is a teenager, but there are a few younger kids. What could they have done to get them here? They look scared and puffy-eyed. Poor little things.

"This whole place used to be some sort of gym/neighborhood center," Mary says, "which explains why it smells like used socks. It feels like a sauna because Kalyb thinks depriving us of air-conditioning will make us 'clean' faster, but it only makes us stink faster."

I smile at her. Mary would think Manhattan smelled pretty awful, I imagine.

We pass a tall man in purple who eyes us suspiciously.

"There are always two Sentries on duty," Mary whispers. "You don't have to worry about them. Just don't start a fight or run for the door."

The Sentry's grim face makes me squirm. At least, unlike Twitchers, he doesn't appear to be armed.

We pass an office with an open door, and Solomon sits in a chair staring into the distance. Maybe he has a Tact? I turn quickly away but not before noticing that the window behind him has a view of a forest. Where *are* we?

With my head turned toward Solomon's office, I don't notice Juda approaching me until his hand is around my wrist. Where did he come from? Before I know what's happening, he's leading me away from Mary.

Mary is alarmed, but I give her a quick smile to let her know I'm safe. Juda guides me into a new hall, turning into an empty room full of plain tables, couches, and chairs. Glass panels act as walls on either side of the entrance.

Shutting the door, he presses us both behind it, so we can't be seen from the hallway. As he presses against me, I wince at the pain from my back but am far too excited to see him to care.

"Are you okay?" he asks.

"Yes. Are you—?"

"Can I kiss you?" he says.

"Yes," I say.

Before I can ask him any of the million questions I have for him, he leans in and places his lips on mine. His breath is warm, and his mouth tastes like honey, just like I remember.

I kiss him back.

I seem to relax and wake up at the same time. Is that possible? I wrap my arms around his waist.

He whispers, "I was so worried."

"Me too," I say.

He pulls me in closer, but it's very awkward with the backpack.

"You look different," he says, stroking my hair.

I touch my bangs self-consciously.

"You look good," he says. "Healthy."

I don't feel healthy. After my time with Solomon, I feel beat up and wiped out.

"You look the same," I say, resting my head on his chest. We're in this horrible place, and I'm carrying rocks, but standing here listening to his steady heartbeat, I'm calm. His presence has always made me feel like everything will be okay. I close my eyes and breathe him in. "I missed this so much," I say.

He kisses the top of my head.

We stand there, absorbing each other's warmth, until he sighs, saying, "We need to get to session."

"Do we have to?" I whine, looking up at him.

He smiles the first real Juda smile I've seen since I arrived. "Who knew this is where the bull and the boar would end up?" he says.

I stroke an invisible beard, in imitation of my father. "Probably not too surprising. They are very stubborn animals."

When he doesn't laugh, I'm embarrassed. Why am I acting so weird?

He kisses me again, and warmth surges down my body. Ok, maybe he doesn't think I'm weird.

"We have to go," he says, pulling away.

"But—"

He opens the door, checking the hallway. Before I walk out,

he says, "Go down the hall, and it's the first door on the left. I'll wait, so we don't walk in together."

Reluctantly, I leave him.

When I walk into session, I must be pink from head to toe. Mary wiggles her eyebrows at me while I take my seat next to Kalyb. I refuse to look at her again. I perch uncomfortably on the edge of my chair to accommodate the backpack.

Moments later, Juda walks in, looking bored. I want to laugh at his change in demeanor. I want to laugh at everything. I can't believe how much happier I am than I was just ten minutes ago.

I'm so happy, in fact, that at first I don't notice the new member of our group.

Silas.

He's sitting on Kalyb's left, looking pale and ill. His brow is furrowed, and his lips are pursed in hostility.

Before I can ask him what's happened, Kalyb begins talking. "Good morning. I hope everyone had a good night's sleep. Some of you might know Silas. Please say hello."

"Hello, Silas," the group says without enthusiasm.

"Who wants to start today?" Kalyb asks.

There's a long silence.

"Mina, do you have anything to share?" he says.

I search my brain for something that Solomon said the day before that might be useful. "Uh, God is ready to hear my sins, and, uh, God loves humility."

"*Very* good, Mina."

Session continues in a manner very similar to yesterday. Kalyb asks various people questions, and we answer in the way that we think will make him happy. It seems very obvious that we're all saying whatever will please him. Does he not notice or not care? Mary is good at it today, sounding penitent and sad, but the second Kalyb looks away, she rolls her eyes and sticks out her tongue. It's hard for me not to laugh.

Silas stares at the floor the whole time.

"Ruth has told me that she's having trouble sleeping. Anyone else?" Without waiting for an answer, Kalyb continues. "I have a peace and relaxation method that can help you." He looks around, hoping for enthusiasm. "First, you need to breathe in and out as slowly as you can."

My breathing starts to slow down on its own.

"You can count your breaths to relax, but I prefer to concentrate on the different parts of my body."

I don't even have to look at Mary to know she's smirking. No one wants to concentrate on Kalyb's wrinkly parts.

Kalyb's voice is now a whisper. "I think, *Toes, knees, stomach, chin, nose, forehead,* and then back down again. It's important to physically concentrate on those body parts while you think about them. It makes it much easier to stay focused. Let's all try it now with our eyes closed."

People sigh and giggle, but eventually we all close our eyes. Kalyb continues to whisper: "It's important to start by acknowledging all the sounds and distractions in the room. Once you have tallied the distractions, it's easier to set them aside and concentrate."

I check for everything in the room that's affecting my senses: sounds, smells, the heat, the pain in my back, the vibrations in the floor, the thought of Juda just feet away. Once I feel I've accepted every last distraction, I start thinking about my body. I resist it at first, because I feel the pain of the rocks more acutely.

I listen to Kalyb's voice: "toes, knees, stomach, chin, nose, forehead . . ." When Kalyb suggests it, I imagine a feather lightly touching each place. Nose. Chin. Shoulders. Stomach. Thighs. As I center on different areas, I'm able to take the focus off of my pain.

We do it over and over.

The feather in my mind is replaced by Juda's hands.

I shake my head. *Concentrate, Mina.*

Many minutes pass by. Finally, Kalyb tells us we can open our eyes. When I do, I feel as if I actually took the backpack off for a while.

I smile goofily. Juda does, too.

I glance at Silas, who still scowls. I make my face neutral again. *Why is he here?*

When session is finally over, Kalyb tells me, "Be in the dorm after lunch. I'll walk you to my office for our consultation." He smiles as if the meeting were going to be the answer to all of my dreams.

Nodding quickly, I hurry after Silas, trying to grab his arm.

"Please, leave me alone," he says.

The others stare, so I let go, but I follow him out the door. "Silas, what's going on?"

He stops in the hall while other session members file past him. "You know."

"Is Tabby here too?" Maybe they're in trouble for coming up with the idea for the prank?

"No. Just me. The greatest sinner of them all." Shaking his head and looking everywhere but at me, he says, "You ruined everything."

All at once, Juda stands between us, a hand on Silas' chest.

"This must be Juda," Silas says, sighing.

"Who is this?" Juda asks, rising to his full height.

"This is Silas," I say quietly. "He's part of the family I live with."

"You live with him?" Juda says, clearly unhappy.

"Don't worry," says Silas. "I won't be going home any time soon." He scuttles down the hall.

"What was that about?" Juda asks.

"I have no idea why he's here," I say, "but I'm afraid it's my fault. I should talk to him." I start to follow Silas.

"Wait," says Juda. "Do you have feelings for this guy?"

"It's not like that," I say, turning around but feeling impatient. "I went to Prom with him to find out where you were and then—"

Juda's face scrunches. "You went to a dance with him?"

"Not like that. It's complicated, and I can explain, but right now, I really need to find out what happened. I'll find you later. I promise."

"Whatever," he says, hurrying away.

When something good happens to me, how do I always manage to screw it up? One minute Juda and I are kissing and the next he's darting off like I've got a pocketful of rats.

Why are boys so exhausting?

TWENTY-TWO

I walk down the hallway as fast as I can manage with the backpack. I hear a loud bang and turn to see the metal door that leads to the courtyard has just closed. Would Silas have gone out there?

I push open the heavy door, afraid that Solomon's horrid face will greet me, but instead, I see Silas crouched in the far corner of the courtyard, head in hands.

I double-check that the rest of the enclosure is empty. My feet crunch loudly on the gravel, but Silas doesn't look up. Lowering myself with difficulty, I sit next to him on the warm ground. "Why are you here?"

He looks up, eyes red, eyelashes wet. "It was working. Everything was fine. Then you had to go blab to Solomon!"

"Blab about what?" I want to understand, but I'm losing patience. *What did I do?*

Picking up several small rocks, he throws them across the courtyard. "You told them you weren't my girlfriend!" he says, as if I'm stupid.

"But I'm not."

"Everyone believed you were! Even my parents."

"But you knew it wasn't true. I told you I loved someone else."

"They'll punish me. They'll . . ." As he trails off, his eyes fill. "I'm finished. They'll never let me out now."

"Because you don't have a girlfriend?" I ask, more confused than ever by the rules of the Unbound.

"No. Because . . ." He looks at me with such sadness I want to cry, too. "Because I like boys."

"What's wrong with that?" I say, relieved. "Don't your parents want you to have friends?"

"Mina," he says, irritated. "I *like* boys. I don't *like* girls."

I don't know what my face looks like as I try to process the information. I hear his words, but they don't make sense to me.

"Let me guess," he says. "In Manhattan there are no molleys."

"Women named Molly?"

He smirks. "No."

"I . . . uh . . . a 'molley' is a boy who likes boys?"

"You get smarter every second."

I am way out of my depth. I've never heard of a boy who isn't attracted to girls. It sounds odd, and if I'm honest, not quite right.

"You should go back inside," he says.

"I want to understand."

"I don't really have the patience right now to explain the history of homosexuality to a *woolie*."

My face goes hot. "Stop being nasty to me! You spread a lie about us without telling me or explaining why. You have no one to blame but yourself!"

"She has teeth," he says with surprise. "Finally."

I slump back against the wall, trying to relieve some of the burden of the backpack. "What will they do to you?"

Staring straight ahead, he whispers, "I don't know. This is my third time here."

Third?

"When I was five, my best friend was this kid named Eli. I wanted to be with him ALL the time. And he wanted to be with me. My father caught us holding hands one day . . . ."

"And he sent you here?"

He nods.

I picture a five-year-old boy wearing rocks on his back, while Solomon screams in his face. Sadness descends on me like fog.

He pushes his bangs out of his eyes. "The second time was last year. I wasn't showing enough, um, interest in the girls at school."

Interest? I'm not sure what this means. At home, young men talk about marriage and families, but they would never express interest directly to a girl—only to her parents.

"Did the girls complain?" I ask.

He laughs. "Hardly, but I was being watched closely through my Bee. The Elders decided I didn't notice girls enough—stare at them or anything."

"And they punished you for that?"

"Yeah. In Manhattan you get arrested for ogling breasts and here you get arrested if you don't."

"Wait. Men here are arrested if they don't—"

"I was kidding," he says, patting my shoulder. "Only a few of us very special guys get in trouble for not wanting to jump a girl's bones."

I'm amazed. The Unbound do very strange things. "Jump bones?"

He grins. "You're cheering me up without even trying. 'Jump her bones.' It means have sex with someone."

I shrug. "I don't know much about sex. Sorry."

"Don't be." He looks away. "And I owe you an apology. I used you. I was dumb. I should have known it would backfire if you didn't know what was happening."

Now I understand why Silas still wears green and hasn't

moved up to level Yellow. He's not living his life the "correct" way. "Why didn't you tell me?" I ask.

"I thought you were—don't take this the wrong way—but I thought you were pretty backward. I didn't think you could possibly understand."

"You thought I was an ignorant woolie," I say.

"For all I knew you would want to cut off my head."

Now it's my turn to laugh. "I'm not going to pretend that I completely understand what you are . . . ."

He cringes.

"I mean, *who* you are," I say, feeling like the moron he supposed me to be. "But I know that the world isn't what I was raised to believe—one type of person, one type of right and wrong." Thinking of the Laurel Society and Nana, I add, "I think people live many different ways, and the most important thing is that they feel loved and safe."

Silas puts his hand over mine. "Thank you, woolie. That was nice."

"So . . ." I'm not sure how to phrase the question, but this could be my only chance to ask. "How does, you know, sex work for you?"

He laughs. "Well, I've never actually had it. But the way it works . . . I think I've rocked your world enough for one day, don't you?"

"Yeah. Maybe." It's nice to see him smile. "Now what?"

He becomes serious again. "I don't know. Solomon told me there would be no third chance." He inhales deeply. "Maybe they just won't let me out again."

"Can they do that? Would your family let them?"

"My family thinks that I'm a horrible degenerate and that only God can fix me."

I find this hard to believe about Bithia and Gilad. "Do your parents know what goes on in here?"

"Yep. Solomon gives them an update every week."

"And they trust him?"

"Oh yes. They believe he channels God's wisdom."

Silas can't be stuck in here forever just because his parents have put their faith in some sicko. "What about Ram? Isn't he more powerful than Solomon?"

He huffs. "Who do you think proclaims the law? I know Ram has taken you under his wing and everything, but don't let him fool you. He lets other people do his dirty work so he can smile and play nice. I mean, I haven't seen him here shouting for Solomon to release *you*."

He's right. Ram likes to tell me how "special" I am. And yet here I sit.

"Underneath it all, Ram is as cruel as Solomon, maybe more so," says Silas. "I think I always knew I would end up back here. It was inevitable." His head sags.

I remember I have another question. "When you fell from my window, it kind of seemed like, um—did you do it on purpose?"

Looking ashamed, he says, "I wanted my parents to catch us, to think something was going on between us."

"You could've killed yourself!"

"Yeah—the whole broken wrist thing wasn't part of the plan." He chews the nail of his thumb. "But it did work. Did you see how happy my dad was the next day? That's the nicest he's been to me in years."

"Oh, Silas. I'm sorry I gave you away."

He sighs. "You didn't mean to, and Solomon is hard to lie to. I know that."

"Susanna is going to be so disappointed," I say.

He raises an eyebrow.

"She's crazy about you!" I say. "I thought you knew."

He smiles, mischief in his eyes. "Susanna is my closest friend. She helped spread the rumor about you and me."

"What?" I'm dumbfounded. "She seemed so jealous."

"She's a brilliant actress and a very good person. She'll be upset it didn't work."

I decide I'm a fan of Susanna's. "Does anyone else know?"

"Tabby, of course. She finds it really humiliating and ignores it as much as she can."

"That's why you thought she'd know where the Forgiveness Home was!"

"Yeah. She and my parents visited me a few times when I was five. It's allowed when you're little. I don't know if she genuinely doesn't remember coming here or if she just wants to pretend it never happened."

"That stinks. It's hard when your sibling isn't on your side."

"Yeah, your brother seems . . . interesting."

"He's certainly not someone you would trust with a secret."

He laughs. "You made Promise Prom memorable, that's for sure."

I cover my face. "I feel awful."

"Tabby and I talked about triggering an Ascension frenzy for years. It was pretty amazing to see it actually happen. That took serious guts."

"Uh . . . Thanks?" I'm still not completely sure what I did. "I feel really bad. I made people *cry*."

"I think it's perfect punishment for requiring lady bugs, don't you?" Laughing again, he adds, "I heard Paul Franklin stayed there all night, sure your vision was real. His wife had to come get him in the morning."

"You're terrible!" I say, but I can't help laughing, too.

"Did you see Marjory? She went full prostrate in the grass. It was *amazing*. When she stood up, her white dress was all green."

Soon we're both doubled over with laughter, and I can barely breathe. I picture Marjory on the bus home streaked with green, blades of grass in her hair. I'm laughing so hard I feel deranged, but I can't remember the last time I laughed like this.

When I finally can't laugh anymore, I let out a big sigh, drained. "I have to tell Juda that his mother is ill."

Silas stops smiling. "Is it serious?"

"Yes."

"Why haven't you told him yet?"

"I haven't had the chance."

"That's totally feeble, and you know it. You could be telling him right now instead of sitting here with me."

He's right. I left Juda standing in the hallway, and I could have told him then or before session when we were alone.

"I'm scared," I admit.

"Maybe it's better. You'll just be torturing him. He's locked in here and can't get out. Better he doesn't know."

"No. If I don't tell him, he'll never forgive me."

"So this is about you and not him?"

"No!" I use my shoe to draw a line in the gravel. "Would you want to know?"

"Hard to say," he says, furrowing his brow. "My father wouldn't want to see me either way. If it was my mom, then yeah, I'd want to know."

"Even if you couldn't see her?"

He nods.

I know he's right. I just dread the task.

"Have you eaten breakfast?" he asks. "I'm starving."

When I shake my head, he says, "Let's go." He rises. "And let me know if you need help talking to Juda."

I raise an eyebrow. "So you've forgiven me?"

"Have you forgiven me?" he asks.

After I nod, his hazel eyes regain their sparkle. "Besides, your romance with Juda is the only interesting thing going on in here."

Smiling, I let him help me up.

TWENTY-THREE

Silas leads me to the cafeteria—a big, loud room that smells like tomato sauce and bleach. Residents sit at long tables, eating and talking.

Connie and her friends sit giggling at one table, while Mary and Ruth talk quietly at another. On the other side of the room, Juda sits alone, his head down while he picks at his food.

I point him out to Silas. "I'll tell him about his mother now," I say with resignation.

"I need to come with you," Silas says.

"Why?" I ask, annoyed.

"Boys and girls aren't allowed to have one-on-one conversations. Kalyb thinks it leads to trouble."

I snort. We have the same rule in Manhattan, yet the people of Kingsboro act as though they could *never* be the same as us.

"Let's get our food first," Silas says.

He leads me to the far end of the room where perspiring, angry-looking women serve scrambled eggs that look like dry chips of paint. I'm too hungry to care. I take the eggs, plus potatoes and toast. I grab an apple from a sad-looking bowl of fruit. If any of the serving women have an opinion about a fifteen-year-old wearing a bag of rocks, they don't let it show.

We walk to Juda's table and sit on either side of him. I have to be careful not to fall backward off the bench.

Startled, he looks up, smiling at me and glaring at Silas. Then, just as I'm raising a bite of eggs to my mouth, Juda leans over and kisses me on the lips. I'm too surprised to respond. He pulls away awkwardly, and I see him cast a look at Silas, who looks alarmed.

I see. The kiss was for Silas' benefit and not mine. Juda was marking his property.

I resist the urge to chastise him, knowing I have something very serious to say.

"I'd be careful with that," says Silas, looking around the room. "You don't want to put a backpack on again, do you?"

"I really missed you," Juda tells me, ignoring Silas.

"I missed you, too," I say, knowing we've already told each other this. Like Silas, I worry that other people saw our kiss, which still feels to me like a severe crime.

I take a bite of eggs. They have no flavor. Are they even real? Dousing them with salt, I begin to scarf them down.

"Take it easy," says Juda. "You'll hurt yourself." When I keep eating he says, "How's your back?" He reaches out his hand to touch me, but looking at the Sentry, pulls it back.

"It aches," I say, mouth full.

"You have to get rid of the backpack soon," he says, "or your back will ache even when it's off."

Silas nods in agreement.

Gee, thanks guys. It hadn't occurred to me to try to get rid of it. I'm shocked to hear Tabby's sneering voice in my head. "I'm trying," I say.

"What did you tell Solomon yesterday? It obviously wasn't enough," says Juda.

236

Swallowing my food, I take a big breath. "I have something to tell you."

"What is it?" he asks, looking at Silas with suspicion.

"It's about your mother," I say.

His expression goes quickly from distrust to fear. "Is she okay? What's wrong?"

"She's sick," I say. "She's in the hospital."

He looks nauseated. "Is it the plague?"

"Dr. Rachel—her doctor—doesn't know yet. But it might be," I say, hating every word that's coming out of my mouth.

Juda puts his hands on the table, steadying himself.

"She hasn't been eating. She thought the man she was staying with was trying to poison her . . ."

His eyes narrow into slits.

" . . . but he wasn't. Something else was making her ill. But she's made herself much sicker by not eating."

"Is she asking for me?" he asks, pain and guilt breaking his voice.

"The last time I saw her, she was sleeping," I say. "Her doctor seems very smart."

"Dr. Rachel is great," Silas says. "The best we have."

"I have to go to her," Juda says.

"How will you get out of here?" I ask.

"I'll confess to whatever Solomon needs me to confess to."

"It's not that simple," says Silas, interrupting once more. "If he knows there's something you really want, he won't believe a word you say."

"How will he know that I know about Ma?"

"He'll know that either Mina or I could've told you."

"I'm not going to just sit here while she dies—"

"Maybe if you're honest," I say. "Maybe if you just ask to see her—"

"Ha," he says with bitterness. "I'm sure Solomon will drive me to the hospital himself."

"He's right," says Silas. "Solomon won't do anything unless he thinks it'll benefit him."

"Could it?" I ask Juda. "Is there anything you could tell him that he wants to know?"

"I've already told him everything I can . . . ." he says.

"There's always more," says Silas.

"I need my gun," Juda says.

"Keep your voice down," I say, scanning the room. The Sentry in the corner doesn't seem to have heard.

"I have to get out of here, and if they won't let me go peacefully, then I'll use other means."

"You'll be killed," I say, imagining the sick pleasure Solomon would get if he could actually end one of our lives. "Even if you survive, what's your plan? You shoot your way out of here, find the hospital on your own, and then just stroll inside, no problem?"

He shakes his head. "I don't know. I just—I can't stay here."

"We'll think of something," I say, although the situation is wretched.

"I need to be alone," Juda says, standing.

"Wait—" I plead.

"Maybe I can help," Silas says in a whisper.

"I seriously doubt that," says Juda, glowering at him.

"I may know a way out," Silas says.

"I don't know you. I don't care about you. I don't care what you have to say. Got it?"

Mortified, I say, "Juda! Stop being so rude! You—"

Silas shushes me. He says to Juda, "I think I know what the problem is here. You have an idea about what happened between Mina and me while you were locked up. But, um . . ." He laughs. "Nothing is going on between us. I assure you."

Juda continues to look angry.

"You see, I'm—"

"You don't owe him an explanation, Silas," I say. "Our word is enough. Right, Juda?"

Sitting back down, Juda looks at each of us in turn. Silas gives him a sympathetic smile, while I try to contain my irritation.

Juda lets out a deep breath before saying, "Okay. I believe nothing happened between you."

Silas offers him a hand, and Juda shakes it.

When Juda doesn't notice my own extended hand, I clear my throat. *I think the peacemaking should be more directed at me than Silas, no?*

Taking my hand, Juda shakes it. "Sorry I was being rude."

"You can make it up to me by listening to Silas," I say.

Juda turns to Silas and says, "You know a way out of here?"

Silas runs his hand through his bangs. "If I tell you, you have to promise to take me with you."

Juda raises an eyebrow. "Not likely."

"And Mina," Silas says. "We all go or none of us do."

"No," says Juda. "It's too dangerous."

"You're not leaving me here!" I say, horrified.

"Your crime wasn't that bad. They'll let you out soon," Juda says.

"That's complete twaddle," I say, amazed at his nerve. "I'm not wearing this backpack one more second than I have to. And you're not responsible for my safety, Juda. I am."

Juda crosses his arms. "This plan is probably crap anyway, so, yes, I promise to take you both with me."

Silas smiles meekly. Taking a quick look at the Sentry, he whispers, "The last time I was here, I, uh, I noticed that we got fresh fruit about every two weeks, so I started listening for the food deliveries. A drone arrives at two in the morning every other

Thursday to make a drop into the kitchen. If you stay awake, you can hear panels open and close."

"So if we could be in the kitchen when the delivery arrives—" Juda says.

"—the panels would open, and we could get out." Silas' smile spreads.

"That's it? That's your plan?" says Juda.

"What happens after that?" I ask. "We're on the roof?"

"The building is more than two stories tall," Juda says, annoyed.

"Yeah, it's a problem," admits Silas. "I needed StickFoot to pull the whole thing off, which is why I never tried it."

"What the Hell is StickFoot?" Juda asks.

While Silas explains, I study the fatally bruised apple on my plate. From the looks of its syrupy, wrinkling skin, the Home hasn't had a fruit delivery in a while. With unease, I say, "The next food delivery is this Thursday, isn't it?"

Silas nods.

"That's only two days," Juda says. "What are the chances we can find StickFoot in the building?"

"It's forbidden to residents," Silas says. "They don't want people literally climbing the walls, but I may know where we can get some."

Juda looks at him with intense hope, but Silas' answer has a tone of resignation: "Kalyb's office."

"Why would he have it?" I ask.

"Basic repairs, cleaning out the gutters and stuff. Most men have some in their tool box."

"Then we have to get it," says Juda. "How can we gain access?"

"I think I already have it," I say, and I tell them about my consultation with Kalyb this afternoon.

"It's about more than access," says Silas, "or I would have broken out last year. I couldn't get any time in the room *alone*."

"You weren't allied with me and Mina last year," Juda says, jade eyes twinkling. "If Mina already has a meeting, you and I can distract Kalyb so she has time to search."

Silas considers this, slowly smiling.

This is all well and good, but they seem to be ignoring a much bigger question: "What about our Bees? Won't they track us the second we leave?" I ask.

"There aren't any directly outside the Home. Solomon doesn't like to be watched," Silas says.

"How do you know?" Juda asks.

"Parents complain about it. They want to be able to watch their kids when they're here, but Solomon won't allow it."

Silas doesn't need to explain why. Parents might like the results of children being forced to stand for hours on end wearing a bag full of rocks, but that doesn't mean they'd like it if they saw it.

"That's why those prehistoric cameras are in the courtyard," Silas says. "No one can hack them."

"So when will the Bees start to track us?" Juda asks.

"I can't be sure," Silas says, "but we should count on them finding us as soon as we're a mile or two away."

"And then what?" I ask.

"Can we shoot them down?" says Juda. "With rocks or something?"

"Have you seen them?" I ask. "They're barely bigger than actual bees!"

"There's too big a risk they'd report our location before we destroyed them," Silas says.

"What else can we do?" I ask, demoralized. I lean forward as the backpack tries to pull me backward off the bench. My back is damp with sweat, and my shoulders burn as the straps dig in.

"Each Bee is programmed to connect with a particular neural pattern," Silas says. "It synched when it was assigned to you, and now it searches for your brain waves. If you can control your thoughts or change those patterns, theoretically, you can keep it from finding you."

"Theoretically?" I say.

"A guy in my school did it. We watched him walk to the park and back without his Bee locating him for ten minutes!"

"We need a lot more than ten minutes," Juda says, frowning.

"You want to get out of here, and this is what I have." Silas opens his arms as if to show us he has nothing else of value.

"How do you clear your thoughts when you're on the run?" I ask, thinking of running through the Fields. Being calm and thought-free was not a possibility at the time.

"Omming and loops."

Juda rolls his eyes. "This is ridiculous."

"What's ridiculous? Solomon's kewpie curl?" Out of nowhere, Mary is standing right behind me.

My whole body tenses as Silas and Juda go quiet.

"Whoa," she says. "Didn't know you were discussing mutiny. I'll see you back at the room, Mina."

When she's out of earshot, Silas says in a whisper, "I use omming every night. It's the only way I can fall asleep."

"How did you learn to do it?" I ask.

Silas grins. "You both already know how. Kalyb teaches it during session. The old coot barely understands how a clock works, let alone a Bee. He's teaching us to clear our brain of all thought, which *is* omming. You do it using a loop of words. The one he used this morning was the parts of the body. I prefer numbers."

Wow. That relaxation technique was cool, but we only did it for *five minutes*. I can tell from Juda's face, he's thinking the same thing.

"We can practice more before we need to use it," Silas says.

"If it's so easy, why didn't we do it the night we snuck out of your house?" I ask.

"I always wanted to try it," he says, "but I guess the Smoker masks just made me lazy."

I'm really wishing he could have found more motivation.

"Okay," says Juda. "First, we focus on the StickFoot, and if we manage to get it, then we can focus on the next part of the plan—the olming."

"Omming," Silas says.

"That's what I meant. Sound good?" He looks at the two of us.

Silas and I give him uneasy nods.

Could this be the flimsiest scheme ever?

TWENTY-FOUR

Time slows down as I wait for my meeting with Kalyb. It's as if I'm on my bike, I've decided to run a red light, and now I have to wait to see if the choice will be fatal.

If I succeed in getting the StickFoot and we escape, am I putting Juda's and Silas' lives in greater danger? The Forgiveness Home has been unbearable so far; how much worse will it be if we get caught?

I also dread an appearance by Solomon. As long as I wear this backpack, we have unfinished business. When will he take me to the courtyard and force me to discuss the Ashers again? My body is taut with agitation. Fearing my tension is obvious, I hole up in the empty dorm.

Unable to face the climb with my backpack into my bed, I lie in Mary's bunk, examining the graffiti that's been etched into the bottom of the bunk above. Names overlap names, while colorful descriptions of Solomon and where girls would like him to spend the rest of eternity take up a good amount of space.

I decide to add to the collage.

I've been drawing for around ten minutes when Mary enters

the room. Putting the pen down immediately, I try to sit up, but the backpack keeps me horizontal. "Sorry. I couldn't face getting into my own bunk."

She raises an eyebrow and joins me on the bunk. Looking up, she points to my drawing. "And you thought you would add to the gallery?"

"How did you know that was mine?" I ask.

"Please. I stare at this every night. I know it better than Ram knows his Book of Glory." She narrows her eyes. "Is it a leaf?"

Feeling embarrassed, I say, "Yeps."

"Why?"

"It's a long story, but it makes me feel better."

"Hmm." She sounds curious, not judgmental.

"How can you stand it here?" I ask, scooting over awkwardly and resting my backpack against a post.

"Who says I can?" she says.

"You just seem, so together, or something," I say.

She laughs. "Me? Together? Shows what a band of freaks live in this place I guess." She lies back on the bunk.

"You think the people who live here are freaks?"

"If your definition of 'freak' is 'an abnormal, misfit, fluke of nature,' then yes, we are freaks," she says.

"You're not a freak," I say.

"Please," she says, snorting.

"What?" I say, wondering what I'm missing.

"Uh, look at me."

"What?" I say. She doesn't have any eye traps that I can name, she's beautiful, and she has the best skin I've ever seen.

"I'm a whale," she says, matter-of-factly. "A meatball, just like Connie said."

"No, you're—"

"Don't. I *hate* it when people say, 'You're not fat,' when I know perfectly well that I am."

"But why are you here? Is being overweight a crime?"

"Is that what you think? That people are here for crimes?"

"They aren't?"

"We're here for *sinnnns*," she says, elongating the word. "And mine is gluttony."

"So if you repent, will they let you out?"

"Sweetie, they won't let me out until I'm thin as a thermometer."

Shocked, I ask, "How long have you been here ?"

"A year and a half."

Ignoring the weight on my back, I throw my arms around her. "I'm so sorry. That's so unfair."

"Yeah," she says, patting my arm. Then she begins to tremble, and I think she's crying, but I don't look at her. She doesn't seem like the type of person who wants people to see her cry.

"Is there anything I can do?" I ask after a while.

"Can you give me your metabolism?" she says, wiping her nose with her hand.

Not sure what this means, I say, "Whatever you need."

She laughs. "You're sweet. I see why your hunka hunka boyfriend likes you."

She must have seen Juda kiss me in the cafeteria. I'm about to ask her who else noticed, when Kalyb knocks on the door.

"Mina, Mary, how are you ladies this afternoon?"

"Swell," Mary says, curling up in the bed with her back toward him.

"Fine, Kalyb," I say.

"Are you ready for our meeting?" he asks me.

This is it. "Yes, of course."

Slowly standing, I tell Mary, "See you later."

"Yeps," she says.

Kalyb leads me down the hall, chatting in his even voice. "I hope breakfast was satisfactory. We have games and activities in the community room this afternoon, which I think you'll enjoy, and music after dinner, which is very popular."

He walks at the same pace that he did on the first day, ignoring the extra weight that I'm carrying. I'm sweating and in agony by the time we reach his office, which is dark and spare, with strangely tiled walls and a white treadmill that takes up one corner. After inviting me to enter the room, he steps on the treadmill. After he walks for a minute, the overhead lights come on. His treadmill must power the lights, just like Ram's powered his computer.

Kalyb steps down, goes to the wall, and presses his palm against a tile. A small door opens near the floor. He pulls out two stools, places them in the middle of the floor, and motions for me to sit down.

He sinks gracefully into a cross-legged position, while I balance clumsily with my backpack on.

"How *are* you today, Mina? How did you sleep?"

"Uh, I slept well, Kalyb," I say, scanning the bare room.

"Good. That's great." He smiles. "How do you feel about being in the Forgiveness Home?"

Does anyone ever answer this question with anything besides "horrible?" I look at him. "I would rather be somewhere else."

"Where?" he asks.

With Ayan in Macy's. With Sekena in her apartment. With Nana. "With the Dixons."

He nods, although I'm not sure he believes me.

"Solomon thinks that you have a problem with male authority." He grins. "Let's talk about it."

Why do all the Unbound smile so much? Don't they know it makes them look like simpletons?

"You left Manhattan, and we're really happy about that," he says. "We're happy you're here with us learning to let the light in, but your escape demonstrates a certain rebellious streak that is concerning to us. We have certain codes—certain standards for how we expect our young ladies to behave."

"Do you have a veil for me to wear?"

"No. We don't do that here," he says, missing my sarcasm. "It's just that, well . . ." He looks thoughtfully into the distance. "What do you know about the world before the Dividing?"

"Barely anything," I say, lying. He doesn't need to know about the Primer and what I've read about Time Zero. I add what people always say about the Dividing: "People were miserable and suffering and needed to overthrow the government to survive."

"That's true. It was a terrible time." He smiles. "Did you know that before the Dividing the president of the country was a woman?"

"Really?" There's nothing about this in the Primer, and if it were true, wouldn't Nana have told me?

"Have you ever learned about the Congress?"

I give him a blank stare.

"The president didn't have all the power. She had to negotiate with two other groups—kind of like when you have to negotiate with your mom *and* your dad to get what you want."

I can tell he wants me to smile at this, but I don't.

"Both of those groups, the House and the Senate, also had a lot of women in them."

I can't explain why this makes me feel good, but it does.

"So it was the worst kind of disaster."

Wait. "Why?" I ask.

"Mina." He leans forward, giving me a pitying smile. "Women aren't meant to lead. They have the wrong temperament. They're nurturing and pliant, which is what makes them so lovely. But those qualities are terrible in leaders."

I forget about the StickFoot. "So it was the women's fault that people were starving?"

"Yes, it was."

"How?"

"It's too complicated for you to understand."

"I'd like to try."

"Fine," he says, standing up. He grabs his first finger. "They didn't know where to invest time or money. They used their emotions instead of their brains. They stopped building the weapons that the country needed to protect itself and put the money into schools and health, which sounds like a nice thing to do, but is *totally* naive." He grabs his second finger. "They stopped importing oil, pissing off every one of our economic partners and throwing us into the Great Gas Wars of '22." His voice breaks. He's so worked up, you would think he had lived through these things. He grabs his third finger. "*Then*, in her second term, the president attempted to *repeal* the second amendment."

Second term? I'm confused. "Why would the people choose her again if she was so bad?" I know enough about history to know that people used to elect their leaders. My mother says elective government is blasphemous.

"You're missing the point! She tried to take away the right to bear arms!"

"'To bear arms?'" I ask.

"To carry a gun. She wanted to take away *everyone's* guns."

I imagine every Twitcher on the island without a gun, Damon without his rifle. What a different world it would be. "It's bad to not want guns?" I say.

"No one in the Unbound would be here today if our ancestors hadn't had guns. When that harpy came for their weapons, they said, 'No way in Hell,' and they fought back."

"I thought they rebelled because everyone was starving— because babies were dying."

"That woman overstepped her bounds."

"Why are you telling me this?"

"Women shouldn't overstep their bounds. It never ends well. You seem smart, but if God had wanted women to lead He wouldn't have given them monthly menses. No one can lead if they spend one week out of every four in bed. It makes no sense!" He puts a hand on his forehead, as if someone has suggested cats should wear loafers.

Ignoring the fact that I've never spent one day in bed due to my menses, I ask, "What about the Prophet?"

"I'm glad you asked. She's a great example. Sarah Palmer was part of the revolution, as I'm sure you know. She was one of the most vocal opponents of disarmament and fought on the front lines. She was a great hero. But She didn't know how to lead."

"Yes She did—"

"I know it's upsetting for a Propheteer to hear this, to have the wool pulled away from your eyes. But Sarah was power hungry. She lost control of Herself."

"No, She—"

"She used the greatest lie available to Her sex. She manipulated our dearest scripture with Her sin and told the people She had experienced an immaculate conception." He shakes his head, blown away by the gullibility of his forefathers. "She was evil incarnate."

I've never heard blasphemy like this before. My body reacts before my mind can, and I drop to my knees to pray. The backpack immediately pulls me sideways to the floor.

"Get up!" Kalyb yells, his smile disappearing for the first time.

"You spend your days torturing children, and God sees you," I say, tucking my head.

"You will not blaspheme in this office!" Grabbing me under the arm, he tries to yank my body from the floor.

He has a hard time getting me back on the stool with the

added weight of the rocks, and he's pulling and jerking at me, when the office door opens.

Silas sticks his head in. "There's a fight in the cafeteria."

"Get Solomon," Kalyb snarls at him.

"He's in session," says Silas.

Kalyb hesitates, not ready to end our confrontation.

"There's blood," Silas says. "It's pretty bad."

Aggravated, Kalyb tells me, "You will return to that stool, and you will not move until I return. Do you understand?"

"Yes, Kalyb," I say, gritting my teeth.

He follows Silas out the door.

I can't catch my breath, I'm so angry and enveloped by Kalyb's words. I shake my head to clear my thoughts. *Remember why you're here.*

This is my moment.

TWENTY-FIVE

I don't know how much time I have, and I have no idea where to begin. The room appears totally empty. Can there possibly be StickFoot here?

Okay, Mina. Pull yourself together. I picture Rayna, with her wild blue hair and what she would do in this situation. She wouldn't panic, and she wouldn't blow it.

Kalyb got stools out of the wall, so there could be other things in there, too.

Knowing it'll slow me down, I slip off the backpack. I hurry to the wall and place my hand on the tile like he did. The same door opens near the floor. *Thank you, God.* It doesn't have to be Kalyb's hand.

I lift my palm, and the door closes.

I slide along the wall placing my hand on various tiles. I try about ten before another door reveals itself. I find a bin full of tan uniforms, like the one I'm wearing.

I close it and move on.

Doors open every three feet. I find books and papers, extra lightbulbs, and a whole bin of toilet paper. I see more stools, the chairs we use in session, and pillows and blankets. I even find a stash of chocolate bars and a bottle of whiskey, but no StickFoot.

How long has it been? Five minutes? Ten? How long can Juda and Silas keep Kalyb occupied?

Maybe Kalyb doesn't even keep a toolbox in here. Maybe he has a utility closet somewhere else in the building.

I sit back down on my stool. Silas said that men kept Stick-Foot for cleaning gutters and things. Kalyb doesn't have any cleaning supplies in here. Maybe someone else cleans? Surely they expect women to do it.

I remember something from one of the bins. I hop up and run to the wall, praying I can remember which one it was.

I place my hand on a tile and when the door opens, I see toilet paper. *Nyek.*

I try again and find the bin I want. Yanking it out, I start pulling out lightbulbs. They're all shapes and sizes and, in Manhattan, would be worth a mint. At home, we would of course use a ladder to install them, but here . . . At the bottom of the bin, I spot it—a can of StickFoot nestled between lamp bulbs.

I grab the can and shove it into my backpack on the floor. I'm returning the lightbulbs to the bin, when I hear Silas' voice: "Great work, Kalyb."

Our signal.

They're back.

I toss the remaining bulbs in as quickly as I can, praying they don't break. I press my palm against the wall, and it seems like a lifetime as I wait for the door to close.

I leap for my backpack and the stool, but the door opens before I can make it.

Kalyb and Silas enter. Kalyb looks at me, then at the back-pack on the floor.

Silas is still babbling, and Kalyb raises a hand to cut him off. "Leave us now."

Silas says, "But I was a witness and you need—"

"You did well," says Kalyb. "Don't turn into a suck-up."

Silas gives me a look of great pity before he walks out the door.

I put my backpack on while Kalyb watches. "How disappointing, Mina," he says. "We'll have to go back to the courtyard."

"I was tired. My back—"

"Let's go."

My head drops. Do I have the strength to face Solomon again?

The answer doesn't matter. Kalyb takes me from the office and marches me to the courtyard, where I'm told to put my hands on the wall until Solomon arrives.

I'm so aware of the treasure in my backpack that I assume anyone can see that I'm carrying something of great value, as if the Stick-Foot were glowing like an enormous lightning bug. How do I keep Solomon from finding it? If I give him a wrong answer, he'll open the backpack to put in another rock. If I give him a confession he likes, he'll open it to take a rock out. How can I keep him from opening it at all?

When he arrives, I can't read his mood. His expression is as unsatisfied as ever.

"Kalyb tells me that you took it upon yourself to remove your burden," he says.

"Yes, Solomon."

He nods, walking around the courtyard with his hands clasped in front of him. "Did you feel you deserved it? Had you done something or had some revelation that made you feel that your sins had been forgiven?"

My mind races. Is there a good answer to this question? Surely it is impudent to say yes. "I was, uh, exhausted by my sin."

"Yes," he says, as if expecting this answer. "Wickedness is a relentless bedfellow." He walks closer. "But you understand the problem?"

"You told me not to take off the backpack, Solomon."

"It is more than that, Mina. You attempted to unburden yourself of your sin without talking to God. Do you think you are better than God?"

"No!"

He stands right behind me. "Do you think you're wiser than God?"

"No, Solomon."

"I think you do. I think you're arrogant, immoral, and have no respect for me or the Unbound. Do you agree?"

If I say yes will he remove a rock? If I say no, certainly he will add one. What can I do?

Before I can think about it too much, I twist around and throw up my knee, hitting him somewhere above the thigh.

He cries out in pain. "You woolie bitch!"

When he's recovered slightly, he gives me a grin that chills me to the core. Grabbing my backpack, he drags me across the courtyard, the rocks scraping my arms and legs. He opens the metal door and throws me inside the building. I skid across the floor.

He heaves me along the hallway, the straps of the backpack cutting into my skin. I see the legs and feet of other inmates around me.

"Help!" I cry. "Help me!"

But no one does.

Solomon pulls me along until he reaches the room he wants, tossing me inside.

"I told the Dixons you were trouble," he says. "They wouldn't listen to me. You're ALL trouble. Freaking woolies. Lie on the table."

A silver gurney sits in the middle of the room. Terror crawls through me, and I lurch for the door.

Solomon blocks me.

"Don't be afraid," he says, no longer yelling. "I'm going to help you unburden yourself. Take off the backpack and lie down."

I don't trust his calm voice.

"Do it, Mina. Don't make me get Kalyb."

Shaking, I slide off the backpack. "What are you going to do?"

"It's a very simple procedure. Don't worry."

I climb onto the gurney mattress, looking for something, anything, I might use as a weapon. How will I get the StickFoot to Juda now? What have I done?

As soon as I'm lying down, Solomon reaches under the mattress and pulls out several straps. He pulls two across my body and one across my chin.

I scream as much as I'm able.

"No one can hear you. And even if they could, they don't care. They have their own sins to ponder."

I scream louder.

"Mina," he says, patting my hand. "Shhhh. I'm not going to hurt you. I'm going to help you. I promise. You're only making yourself more miserable by screeching."

He goes to the wall and places his palm on a tile. A door opens up, and he pulls out a bin of wires and cables. He places it on a small table by my head.

"I'm sorry I kicked you," I say, struggling with the strap.

"I know," he says. "This isn't about that. I should have done this when you first arrived." Taking a tube from the bin, he applies a cold gel to my temples. "This is a wonderful treatment. The best way I can describe it is like rebooting a computer."

I continue to twist and turn, sure I can free myself.

He laughs. "You've probably never seen a computer. I should say, it's like going into the deepest sleep possible and then waking up again. Throwing the off switch and then coming on again. It will give you a new outlook."

"Please, Solomon. Please!" I cry. I don't want a new outlook.

He holds two metal wands to my temples. The shock that runs through my body is like the one I felt from Mr. Asher's Taser, but times ten. I twitch and shriek.

Solomon says, "Where is Damon Asher?"

I can't speak through the pain, which feels like it's turning my skin inside out.

He repeats in a patient tone, "Where is Damon Asher?"

Somewhere a tiny part of my brain is telling me that if I can manage to speak, the pain will stop. I also have a small awareness that I shouldn't speak, but the desire to end the agony is too great. "Dead!" I howl.

"Did you kill him?"

"Yes!" I say, hoping God will show me mercy for finally confessing the truth.

"Who? You and Juda?"

I don't answer immediately, and he turns a dial that increases my pain.

"All of us! Everyone!"

"You and Juda . . . and the rest of the Manhattan Five? You all murdered Damon Asher together?"

"Yes!" I scream.

Immediately, Solomon lifts the wands and the current is broken.

I can't breathe. My heart thuds—every other beat a battering jolt. My eyes are blurry with tears.

I was sure I was going to die.

"Very good," he says. "The rods are so much quicker than the rocks, but Ram frowns upon them. Unless of course a child is being violent, so thank you for that."

What have I said?

"You will feel so much lighter tomorrow. You have opened your heart to God. You have confessed your sins and He forgives you. I'm very proud."

Smiling, he lowers the wands to my temples once more. My spine seems to rip apart as the current runs down my back and through my legs. "This will ensure you don't remember our little conversation. I release you from the memory of this pain."

I focus on his voice, trying to block out the torment in my body. As I near the relief of unconsciousness, he lifts the wands and steps away. The pain stops, but my body continues to convulse.

He returns the wands to the bin. He removes the strap from my body and head. When he has placed all the supplies back inside the wall, he says, "You may return to the dorm when you feel ready."

I can't move. He's letting me go? After I kicked him, I thought I'd never see the dorm again.

He walks out the door. I want to get my backpack and go, but I can't convince my legs to step off the gurney. I lie there, shaking. My brain tries to focus on what's next, but it can't. My thoughts are fuzzy, like when I'm dreaming.

A minute later, I'm not sure how I got to this room.

TWENTY-SIX

"Mina, wake up. Mina."

I open my eyes to see a girl with bright blue eyes and raven hair leaning over me.

"Are you okay? Wake up," she says, shaking my shoulders.

"I'm awake," I say with displeasure. I turn my head to look around. Mistake. I have a brutal headache.

"Want some water?" the girl says.

"I want to sleep," I say, rolling over.

"You've been asleep for twenty-four hours already," she says. "Solomon really did a number on you."

"Who?" I say.

"Oh, Lord," she says. "Who am I?"

I blink in confusion.

"I'm Mary," she says, as if I'm a dope. "We're friends."

Is this girl crazy?

She frowns. "Do you remember where you are?"

I concentrate. I remember my apartment, and Nana, and Macy's, and swimming through a subway, and coming to Queens. "Am I at the Dixons?" I ask hopefully.

She pats my hand. "No, sweetie. You're not. Maybe it's better if you don't know."

"Why? What's wrong?" I sit up, but it makes the pain in my head pulsate, like the morning after drinking all that champagne with Mrs. Asher. What happened yesterday?

"Lie back down." Mary pulls uncomfortably at her tan top. "You sure you don't want water?"

"Where am I?" I say, growing frightened.

"You're at the Forgiveness Home. Ring any bells?"

The Forgiveness Home. I shiver. "I don't like it here," I say.

"See! You do remember!" Mary says triumphantly.

"What happened?" I ask. Shadowy memories float by.

"I'm not sure, sugar, but Solomon scrambled your eggs pretty good. You wandered in like a beat dog, climbed into my bed, and lost consciousness for a whole day."

Anxiety replaces my fear. "Something's wrong."

"Of course it is. You're being held against your will by self-righteous, militant crusaders."

"Besides that. I'm supposed to be somewhere . . . or something."

"I think you need to just lie down for now."

"No. It's important," I say, sitting up despite the pain. The vital thought flutters at the edge of my consciousness, a butterfly flapping in my peripheral vision.

"That can happen in here—a feeling like you need to do something—when there's nothing to do," Mary says. "You can't meet friends, or go shopping, or return a book. It's a life of no responsibilities, no schedule, and no joy."

"It's not like that . . . ." I insist.

"Your boyfriend talked to me during lunch. He wanted me to tell him as soon as you were awake. Is that benny?"

This girl knows Juda? How can I not remember her? "I guess so."

"I also think you need food. How about I bring you something from the cafeteria?"

I nod. "That would be nice." I really just want silence. Maybe if she leaves, I can recover the last day.

But after she's gone, all I can think about is the subway and how we escaped Manhattan—the blood pooling around Mr. Asher; rats circling us in muddy water.

My stomach convulses, and I scan the room for a trash can. Not seeing one, I race for the door, but before I can get there, I vomit all over the floor.

I'm still heaving when Mary returns. She holds a tray full of food, which threatens to make me puke again.

Seeing the mess, she says, "Great. That's just terrific." She plunks down the tray with anger on a small table in the corner. "I'll be back."

I want to lie back down, but I don't want to be sick in Mary's bed. Is one of these beds mine?

She returns with a mop and bucket.

I stand to take it from her.

"Don't be stupid," she says. "Lie down."

"I'm sorry," I say.

"For what?"

"For getting sick," I say, feeling that this is obvious.

"I'm not mad you got sick. I'm mad that Solomon screwed you up so much that you can't remember where you are, you can barely stand, and you needed to blow chunks in our room. What a dook-wad."

I almost smile. "What's a dook-wad?"

"Oh, uh, hmmm. I guess it's someone who has so much crap to say that it's like their mouth is wadded up with their dook."

Now I do smile, which makes my whole head hurt. "I understand why we're friends," I say.

"We're friends," she says, "because I am cleaning up your barf. And don't you ever forget it."

"I won't," I say, and I mean it.

After she finishes mopping up, she leaves to empty the bucket. When she returns, she offers to take me to a bathroom where I can brush my teeth and rinse out my mouth. She insists that I must first put on the one-ton backpack that I was sleeping next to.

Is she out of her everlasting mind?

"You're being punished, and you'll be punished a whole lot worse if you're seen without it. Trust me."

She has to tell me all about Solomon and how the backpack is my burden before I agree to put it on. Even then, the whole thing seems insane, but when I put the rocks on my back, I can tell from the way my back and shoulders scream, that I've worn the backpack before.

I freshen up in the bathroom while Mary waits. I can't remember the last time I was so grateful to someone.

When we reenter the dorm room, a group of girls has entered.

"Why does it smell like butt in here?" asks a pretty girl with long hair.

"Calm down, Connie," Mary says. "It's all taken care of."

"Oh, did you change your clothes, Meatball? That would definitely explain the stench."

The other girls snicker.

Mary, not flinching, says, "No, but it's no surprise you picked up on the bad smell first, Connie, with that super schnoz of yours."

Connie's smile disappears. The next thing I know, she's throwing herself at Mary, who's caught totally off guard. Connie is slight in stature, but her surge was intense, and the two of them go tumbling to the ground. Connie starts pounding on Mary's stomach. "I'm going to kill you!"

"I can't even feel that!" Mary laughs. "Because I'm SO FAT!"

"You disgusting bitch!" Connie takes her fingers and scrapes her long nails down Mary's face.

Mary is no longer laughing. Blood oozes from the scratches.

Before I know what I'm doing, I drop my backpack and dive on Connie, knocking her off Mary.

Connie lands hard on the floor, and then I'm on top of her, slapping and hitting. "Leave her alone, you Saitch!"

I've never hit anyone like this before, never thought I could, but I am SO ANGRY and releasing my anger on Connie feels good and right, because she is a terrible person and she deserves it. I want to keep slapping her until I don't have any anger left.

Hands behind me try to pull me off of her, but I keep hitting. One of Connie's friends screeches, "Stop!" while yanking my hair.

"Mina?"

The voice makes me freeze. Looking at the doorway, I see Juda. His eyes are huge.

I look down at Connie, who's squirming like a trapped animal. She's covering her face with both hands. Both my arms are now being held by her friends, and Mary is grasping my shoulders. She was trying to pull me off Connie, too.

"What's happening?" Juda asks.

"You can let go now," I whisper, going limp. "I'm done."

The girls release me, and I crawl into the corner.

Connie rises off the floor like an old lady. Her face is swollen and pink.

"I'm sorry, Connie," I say. "I didn't mean—"

"I'm going to kill you," she says. One of her friends tries to get a closer look at her face, but Connie waves her away.

Juda comes inside the room, kneeling beside me. "Are you okay?"

I shake my head. I am not okay.

"She's totally fried," Mary says.

He touches my cheek.

"We should get her out of here," Mary says.

Juda helps me to my feet. As we near the door, Mary grabs my backpack from the floor.

"Mina and I can finish this later," Connie says.

Mary says, "She'll be with *me* if you need her."

"She'll be with both of us," says Juda.

Connie watches us leave, pure hatred on her face.

Juda says nothing as we walk down the hall. What have I done? I think I'm losing my mind.

TWENTY-SEVEN

Juda suggests we walk toward the community room. In the hallway, outside of the entrance, he says, "Are you okay? What happened?"

Before I can answer, Mary says, "She's loopy as a racetrack. She's had her brain short-circuited."

"What do you mean?" he says, eyebrows knitting. He puts his hand on my shoulder. "How do you feel?"

"Sick," I say, because it's on top of a long list of feelings.

"Can I get you anything? What do you need?" He looks so worried it makes me want to console *him*.

"She already hurled," Mary says. "She might be sick again before the day is done."

"How do you know?" he asks her with suspicion.

"I've only heard of them doing this two or three times the whole time I've been here. Your girl must have done something to seriously tick off Solomon." She adjusts her top. "I can't say exactly what happens, but people disappear, and when they come back, it's like they got hit by lightning."

"Will she get better?" he asks in a small voice.

She nods. "I think so, but I don't know how long it lasts. The last two residents were guys, so I wasn't in their dorm. I just heard about it."

They're talking about me like I'm not here, and I don't really *feel* like I'm here. It's like I'm in the future recollecting this conversation, and some bits are clear, but most are fuzzy.

"What happened to your lip?" I ask Juda. His beautiful smile is marred by a cut in the left corner.

He says quietly, "I need to talk to you alone."

"Mary can hear whatever you have to say." Hands still quivering, I don't want her to go anywhere.

Juda smiles at Mary. "You've always seemed really nice, Mary. No offense, but this is a very private matter."

"No offense taken," she says.

"She stays!" I say.

He rubs his head, aggravated. "What's the last thing you remember?"

"Ummm." I concentrate, but it makes my temples ache.

"You know who I am?" he says nervously.

"Of course," I say, grinning stupidly.

He grins back, stroking my arm. "What about Silas?" he says. "And the Dixons?"

I nod slowly. "I was living with the Dixons. Why was I living with the Dixons?"

"That's not important right now," he says. "You remember Silas?"

I picture a boy with blond hair and a nice smile. "Yes."

"Good," he says, looking at Mary with relief.

"Do you remember talking with me and Silas? We had a *very important* conversation and you were supposed to do something *very important* for us."

Mary's eyebrows go up. "What did you make her do? She

268

probably got caught, and that's why she's acting like a piece of broccoli."

"Shhhh," he tells her, agitated. In a gentler voice, he tells me, "Mary could be right. You may have been caught doing something for Silas, me, *and* you. Can you remember? It's how I got this fat lip."

"Just tell her what it was!" insists Mary, agitated herself.

"As soon as you leave us alone, I will!" says Juda.

"Stop," I say. "You're both hurting my eyeballs." My headache seems to have buried itself deep inside my eye sockets, and the more they talk, the more it hurts.

"I'm staying here," Mary tells me, hands on hips. "He's haranguing you when you need rest."

He exhales loudly. "I appreciate that you're looking out for her. I want nothing more than for her to be able to rest."

"But?" Mary says.

He scratches his head and rubs the back of his neck. He's at the end of his rope with her. "If we're ever going to get out of this place, we need her to remember meeting with Kalyb."

"Get out? Like . . . ?"

"Break out," Juda says, defeated.

Mary's eyes grow wide, and she grabs my arm. "Mina, you have to listen to Juda. Where did you go yesterday? What happened?" She shakes me a little.

"Take it easy," Juda says, pulling Mary's hand away.

"I don't know," I say. "I'm really sorry." Looking at their expressions, I suspect I should feel regretful or sad, but I have no idea how I've disappointed them.

"Don't be sorry," Juda tells me. "It's not your fault."

"What was she supposed to do?" Mary says, keyed up. "What's your escape plan?"

"I'm not going to talk about it," Juda says.

"Oh no. You've told me this much, so tell me the rest," she

says. When he doesn't answer, she says, "I already know you're planning to make a break for it, so I have enough to tell Solomon, which I won't do if you tell me everything."

"*Nyek*," Juda says. "Why won't anyone just let me see my mother? Why does everyone have to blackmail and bribe?"

"Because you're in Hell and the only currency is immorality," she says matter-of-factly.

His face screws up in pain.

His mother. He needs to see her.

Mary touches his wrist. "Sorry for being such a wheedle. You don't have to tell me. Just please . . ." Now she's the one who looks pained. "Please think about taking me with you. I'd like to get out of here while I'm still a teenager, you know?"

He nods. "I get it."

"Thanks," she says. They both turn to me. Sighing, Mary says, "Now what to do about her."

TWENTY-EIGHT

"StickFoot. Did you find the StickFoot?"

This is the only question anyone cares about.

And I don't know the answer.

Juda, Mary, Silas, and I sit huddled in a corner of the community room pretending to play some card game called "Beat the Queen." Silas found us shortly after we entered the room. He was very sweet about how sickly I was and at first insisted I go back to bed. I told him I was fine and that I only wanted to recover my memory.

It's the truth. Losing time is terrifying. What could have happened to me during the last twenty-four hours? The list of answers is too horrifying to contemplate.

Silas says that the last time he saw me Kalyb had caught me without my backpack (Juda had started a fight with some guy named Jeffrey to get Kalyb out of his office, but Kalyb returned a little too soon).

The moment is a big white nothing.

"I'm really sorry, everyone." And I am. I'm letting them down in the worst way.

"Quit apologizing!" Mary says. "Let's think this through. If Kalyb and Solomon caught you with the StickFoot, then Solomon would have kept you in the courtyard until you confessed why you stole it. Maybe you wouldn't tell him, and that's why he took you to the fryer."

"Good point," says Silas. "The important questions are whether or not she found the StickFoot and whether or not Solomon has it now."

I put my head down on the table. How can I remember?

"What does StickFoot look like, Silas?" Juda asks.

"It's, uh, in a small black can. You spray it on."

I look up. "*You* put some on!" I say, delighted.

"Yeah," he says. "That's a story for another time. It wasn't here."

My head goes back down.

"I think we should reconvene another time," says Mary. "She's getting tired."

"I know," Juda says. "It's just that . . ." His voice is full of guilt. "The panels open again tonight. If we don't have the Stick-Foot, then none of us are going anywhere for another two weeks."

Mary has told me to stop apologizing, but what else can I do but say I'm sorry? I want to hug Juda, to tell him it will all be okay, but I don't know that it will.

"Do you remember about Ma?" he asks, and I can tell he feels terrible asking.

Seeing Rose lying in a hospital bed, I say, "I'll do everything I can to help you get to her."

"Thank you, love," he says.

My body grows warm at the word "love," and I know that nothing is more important than getting Juda out of this strange, horrible place.

"Are you too tired to keep going?" he asks.

"I'm okay," I say, "but are you sure I can't take this backpack off? It really hurts," I say, shifting my weight for the hundredth time.

"We're positive," says Silas.

"If you take it off, Solomon will just put another rock in it," says Mary.

"That would be really bad," I say. "It would destroy everything."

"Destroy your back?" says Mary, looking confused.

"No," I say. "More."

"Wait. It will destroy everything how?" Mary asks.

The memory is so faint, like the sound of whispering on the other side of a wall. I rub my temples. "I don't know . . . . I just . . . feel strongly that Solomon shouldn't put a rock in my backpack."

"We've all worn the backpack, and I'm sure we all felt the same way," says Silas, who looks like he's also getting tired.

"The rocks suck hard," Mary says. "but people don't really feel like they 'destroy *everything*.'"

My thoughts are going white again. "I think I should lie down."

"I'll take you," says Juda, putting down his cards.

"Let me see your backpack," says Mary.

"You said I couldn't take it off," I tell her, annoyed at the contradiction.

"You're right," she says, standing. "Come to the ladies' room." She waves to the boys. "Don't leave without us."

She leads me to a bathroom down the hall. Once inside, she checks all the stalls, and when she's sure we're alone, she turns me around and unzips the backpack.

"Thank the good Lord almighty above," she whispers.

"What is it?" I ask.

She shows me the StickFoot in her hand. "You must have shoved it in here to hide it from Kalyb. Smart."

A brief flash of bins and lightbulbs flutters by.

"Should we take it and go? We don't have to go back to the boys, you know," she says.

I stare at her open-mouthed, trying to figure out what to say, when she says, "I'm kidding. We'll never escape if I have to rely on your frizzled brain."

I give as much of a smile as I can manage.

"Let's go tell them that Operation Rooftop is a go."

TWENTY-NINE

I wish I could match everyone's enthusiasm about finding the StickFoot, but I still feel like a different person, like the real me is stuck in a bubble that no one has figured out how to pop yet.

We have a little over twelve hours until the panel doors open in the kitchen. Silas and Juda explain the plan to me carefully over and over until they're sure I understand.

Thank God they told Mary, too. She's my pillar of strength right now, and I can't imagine going without her.

She and I sit alone in our session room. She's made it her mission to return me to myself by tonight. I've had two cold showers and a cup of hot coffee, but I still have a mind full of cobwebs.

"Mina Clark," she says, "who are your mom and dad?"

"Marga and Zai Clark."

"Any siblings?"

"Dekker Clark."

"His age?"

I have to think. "Seventeen."

"Great. Where were you born?"

"Manhattan."

"How did you meet Juda?" she says, a twinkle in her eye. She's asking this one out of her own curiosity.

"He rescued me from a mob."

"Really?" she says, eyes widening. "What happened?"

"There was a woman and she, uh, was being accused of cheating on her husband. The crowd attacked her, and Juda saved me from being trampled."

"Wow," she says, shifting in her chair.

I can't remember much from the last week, but my memory of Delia getting hit with that first rock stings like a new paper cut.

"Juda is really cute," Mary says. "He's so different-looking."

"Um," I say. "When you say different, do you mean 'not white?'"

She laughs. "I didn't mean it that way, but maybe."

I have a flash of standing on a stage with thousands of faces staring up at me. "All the Unbound look exactly the same. It creeps me out."

"How do people look in Manhattan?"

"Like *people*. Brown, white, tan, black, whatever."

Mary sighs. "I think the Unbound used to be like that."

"What happened?"

She shrugs. "I'm in here because I'm fat. Silas is here because he's gay. I think the Unbound have a pretty strict definition of what 'made in God's image' is."

My mouth drops in horror. "Are you saying they got rid of people who—"

"No! I mean that people who didn't feel welcome migrated west."

Is that a flicker of uncertainty in her eye? "And only white people felt welcome?"

"No one ever says it out loud like that. The Book of Glory tells us to welcome all of God's children. But let's just say it's probably not a coincidence that Juda got locked in here and your brother didn't."

I turn away from her, disgusted. What's the point of "letting in the light" if you only bestow it upon selected people?

"There's this one black family, the Merediths, who Ram loves to mention and point out during his sermons," she says. "Like they're his best friends, and if they've stayed in Kingsboro then we must be really inclusive." She rolls her eyes.

"People are such hypocrites."

"You're telling me. I heard Kalyb keeps a bottle of whiskey in his office."

This seems vaguely familiar. "If we escape, promise me you'll get out of Kingboro," I tell her.

"Are you kidding?" she says. "If we escape, I'll carry you on my back across New York."

I smile. It's really nice to have Mary to explain things. "Why did I make everyone *so* mad with the Prom thing?" Silas told us the details of what I did.

Mary raises an eyebrow. "You mocked the Ascension." On the word "Ascension" her hands make a dramatic circle above her head.

"What's the Ascension?"

"Something I wish *I* could forget. Basically, one day the Savior will return, and all of his chosen people will float into Heaven to sit at his side. If you're full of sin and depravity like us, you're left on Earth to rot and burn for eternity. It's fun stuff."

"How did I mock that?" I ask, confused.

"You told children you had seen people floating into the sky! And then they told their parents. And then everyone at Prom thought it was *the day*, and they got so excited that most of them probably peed their pants."

"So they want to die?" I ask, confused.

"It's not death, it's uh . . . How do I explain? You know when you're a kid and you have fantasies about the best day ever with cake and chocolate and tons of friends and unicorns to ride and a castle to live in with a boy named Sean?"

I don't, but I nod anyway.

"The Unbound feel that when they get to Heaven, it will be like that. Every day will be their fantasy life, with their favorite food and favorite people, even the ones who have died. They can have whatever huge house they want and look however they want."

"When will the Ascension happen?" I ask, amazed at the idea.

She throws up her hands in dismay. "Ram keeps promising it's *soon*, which is annoying, because what does 'soon' mean? Ten years or ten minutes?" She calms. "He . . . uh, says the delay involves your people."

"It does?" I ask, surprised.

"How do I say this without being rude . . . ? We believe in a Savior, and most folks think your Uncle Ruho is the anti-Savior, and as long as he's around, our Savior won't be showing his face."

"Why do you care about Uncle Ruho?" I ask.

"He claims to have divine blood, to be a descendent of God, right?" After I agree, she says, "Yeah. That's not benny with the Unbound—majorly blasphemous—and even worse, Ram thinks his claim is postponing our beloved Ascension."

This whole story is so bizarre. Would it make more sense if my brain were functioning normally? I rearrange myself in the chair. The backpack forces me to sit on the very edge, which is tricky. Mary and I are alone, but she's firm about me keeping it on. "So you don't believe in the Ascension?" I ask.

"I did when I was little, and it was great. If there was anything I didn't like about life, I could just tell myself that the Ascension was about to happen, and that everything would change. But then day after day, year after year, it didn't happen. And at some point, I decided, this might be it, kid."

"And did you feel sadder or happier about your life?"

"Ya know, I think I felt happier, but my parents sure didn't. They would get seriously angry if I even joked about the Ascension not happening. My older brother is totally perfect in their eyes, but I'm . . . well, they think I'll be beautiful in Heaven."

"But you're beautiful now!" I say.

"Whatever," she says. "Solomon and my family beg to differ."

"Who cares what they think?"

"I wouldn't. Except for this." She raises her khaki top, revealing a leather belt around her waist that is at least three notches too tight. The skin around the belt is inflamed with sores.

My hand flies to my mouth.

"I told you I didn't get a backpack," she says with a wry smile that breaks my heart.

"Oh, Mary," I say, reaching out to her.

"No," she says, flinching. "I don't like touching."

I don't blame her. It must be excruciating when someone touches her.

"How long have you—?"

"Six months," she says. "Please don't tell anyone."

"No. Of course not." This is the first time I've seen her embarrassed. "You have nothing to be ashamed of, Mary. Solomon is the one who should be ashamed."

"Believe me, I spend a lot of my free time coming up with exactly the right kind of revenge," she says, narrowing her eyes. "But we're supposed to be talking about you." She gives me a little sideways grin. "That was a pretty clear conversation we just had, right?"

I smile, too. It was. "You think I can be ready for tonight?"

"The most important thing is going to be moving quickly and clearing your mind. Your memory won't actually be a big deal."

We had a hard time deciding who should keep the StickFoot until it was time. Any of us could be caught and have to undergo the same mind scramble as me. We voted and finally decided on Juda, since he has the most urgent need to get out of here. I was touched that Silas and Mary both agreed, even though this is all Silas' plan.

We meet the boys before dinner to practice omming. We feel safe in the session room, reasoning that if Kalyb walks in we can say we are practicing his relaxation technique. Silas leads us through several loops using numbers. The idea is to count and to think of nothing but numbers. He suggests counting backward since it takes more concentration. I try it, and he's right. We do it over and over until we have to go to dinner.

Walking down the hallway, I feel both tired and very alert. The omming had the same effect as a long nap. The nausea from earlier is gone. If only the backpack were gone, I might actually feel good.

In the dining hall, we eat as much as possible, not knowing when our next meal will be. I hope the Sentries don't notice us shoving our faces full of the disgusting food.

We're going through the specifics of the plan for the tenth time, when Mary says, "Where will we hide after the escape?"

We stare at her blankly.

"What kind of plan is this?" she asks, disgust in her voice.

"There *was* no plan until we had the StickFoot, so we didn't get much further than that," admits Silas.

Mary rubs her hands together. "I know where we can lay low for a while."

"Spill it!" Silas says.

She sits up tall, enjoying the attention. "My brother's been building a new house since February. He's written me all about it. He hasn't finished the plumbing yet, but it has a roof and a floor that we can sleep on."

"Won't he catch us?" Juda says.

"That's the thing," Mary says. "He ran out of money. He hasn't been able to build anything new for months. He's stuck living with my parents until he earns the rest of the money. It's perfect!"

Silas looks wary. "I don't know, Mary. If he finds us—"

"He won't, and even if he did, he's my brother. He wouldn't turn us in."

Silas raises his eyebrow.

"It sounds risky," Juda says.

"What's your brilliant idea?" she asks him.

"Sleep outside," he says.

She snorts. "And you think we won't get caught out in the open?"

"Not if we hide—"

"The Bees will catch you if you stay outside. You think you can control your thoughts while you sleep?"

"I think she's right," I say, liking the sound of a roof over our heads. "How about we head for the house and check it out? If it doesn't feel safe, we go somewhere else. Okay?"

Mary nods. "Good plan."

Defeated, Juda says, "Okay."

Silas, begrudgingly, agrees too.

"Next item on the agenda," Mary says, sounding very official. "Where are we going for the long term?"

We eye one another, wondering who will speak first.

"I've been thinking about this for a long time," says Silas. "And I think we should head west." His voice gets wispy on the word "west."

"What's west?" I ask.

"A fantasy," says Mary.

"No," says Silas emphatically. "It's real. It's where the people went who lost the Dividing. Even Ram says it's true."

"It's a fantasy that it's any better than here," Mary says.

"At least it will be different."

"Do you know how far it is?" asks Mary.

"Not exactly, but—"

"Far, like really, really far. We'd need a car or train or something."

"There are cars all over the place," Silas says.

Juda interrupts them. "I don't know whether 'the West' exists or not, but, uh, I won't be joining you. After I see my mother, I'm going back to Manhattan."

"What are you talking about?" I say, horrified.

"A war is starting, and I can't leave the Convenes behind. So many of them are sick or dying. It wouldn't be right."

"We don't know for sure that there's a war," I say, hating the neediness in my voice. "That was just Rayna—"

"You can't tell me you haven't thought about going back to help the Laurel Society and your Nana," he says.

I look away. Of course he's right.

"You can't go back!" Mary says, as loud as she dares. "It's too dangerous."

"It's not like the Unbound have treated us so much better," he says with bitterness.

"No one wants to *kill* you," she says.

"Are you sure about that?" Juda says. "I think Jeffrey in session would be pretty happy to see my head on a spike."

Luke Tanner made it clear he didn't want any of the Manhattan Five in Kingsboro, but I'm not about to tell Juda about him.

People in the cafeteria begin to look at us.

"This is a useless argument," I whisper. "We aren't even free yet." I'm too overwhelmed to consider that Juda might want to go back to the island. We went through *so* much to escape it. Once he sees Rose, he won't be able to leave her, right?

"How about you, Mina? What will you do?" Silas asks.

"I don't know," I say. It's been one day at a time for so long. Seeing Juda is all I've cared about, and he's here beside me. I don't know what else I want.

"You don't have to decide right now," Mary says with a gentle smile.

"What about you, Mary?" I ask.

She shrugs, smiling. "Upstate? I don't know. As long as I don't have to wear khaki."

THIRTY

Mary and I wait as late as we can to return to the dorm, determined to avoid a fight with Connie and her cronies. We can't afford any trouble tonight.

Mary is convinced we'll be able to go to sleep without any harassment, but I can't see how this will happen after our fight this morning. Connie was ready to rip my head off when we left.

When we arrive, Connie sits on a top bunk with both her friends.

"Gross. It's back," she says when she sees Mary. "And it's caught a disease." She means me.

The girls giggle like Connie is a genius with words.

Mary ignores her, going to her bed and pulling back her blanket.

"Are you sure that bed can support you, Meatball?" says Connie. "I'd hate for you to get hurt."

Mary is breathing steadily, and I know she's repeating one phrase over and over: *I'll never see her again. I'll never see her again.*

We have about five minutes until lights out. Neither of us

plans to change out of our clothes. Mary says the other girls won't think this is odd since she never changes in front of them with the lights on.

Mary helps me climb into my bunk, using her hands to take some of the weight of the backpack. I land with a thud on the mattress.

A ball of something hits Mary in the back of the head. "Hey, Meatball! I'm talking to you!" Connie says, laughing.

You'll never see her again, I try to transmit with a look.

"Hey, woolie!" says Connie looking at me. "Is this lezo trying to hook up with you?" She turns to her friends. "What do you guys think of a woolie/Meatball sandwich? Gross!"

The three of them shriek with laughter.

Mary turns to them, face red, and I hold my breath. "Shut your mouth. I'm warning you," she says.

"Doesn't look like you've *ever* shut your mouth, huh, Meatball?"

Mary walks to Connie's bunk.

Don't do it, Mary. Please.

She puts her hands on her hips. "Connie, since the moment you arrived in the Forgiveness Home, you've been lying about why you are here. You want these vapid friends of yours to think it's because you blinkered your lady bug with Daniel Holmes, but I happen to know from my brother that you were caught feeling up Diana Flaunder. So maybe think again before you start calling other people 'lezos.'"

Connie's face goes from very pale to deep purple. She makes a choked sound, like *kuh.* She turns to her friends, saying, "The Meatball is a lying cow, right, guys?"

They stare at her in silence.

"She's just saying that because she *wishes* I was a lezo."

The girls climb down from her bunk and climb into their own beds.

I stare at Mary in awe. Is she telling the truth?

Waiting to hear Connie rail and scream, I watch instead as she climbs under her blanket and turns her face to the wall.

Mary gets into her own bed, and instead of the look of triumph that I expect, she looks sad. She was telling the truth. All this time, she'd been keeping a secret that she knew would shame and humiliate Connie, and she chose not to share it despite how nasty Connie was. She only revealed it tonight to protect our plan.

I've learned something big tonight, but it wasn't about Connie. I learned Mary is a better person than I am.

I'm sure I'm too nervous to sleep, but the next thing I know, Mary is nudging me awake. She doesn't say anything, and she doesn't have to. She'll go to the bathroom and, five minutes later, I'll follow.

The moments after she leaves feel interminable. I'm paranoid every other girl in the room is awake, ready to start screaming the moment I get out of my bunk, but when it's time, I carefully step down the ladder and don't hear a sound. I tiptoe out of the room.

I debated a lot on whether or not I should bring the backpack with me. I decided the extra weight would cause the ladder steps to creak, so I left it behind. If I get caught in the hallway without it . . . I can't bear to think what Solomon would do.

I step into the hall, looking both ways for Sentries. When I see the coast is clear, I hurry down the hallway and around the corner.

With relief, I step inside the restroom, which is enormous. Rusted lockers line one wall, and our showers are down a tiny corridor on my right. They're moldy and old-fashioned, but I prefer them to the one at the Dixons.

I approach the toilet stalls, where Mary is supposed to be waiting. I knock on the door at the end, and she knocks back, both of us too nervous to speak.

I go into one of the other stalls, lowering the toilet seat to sit. And then we wait.

Juda and Silas are due here by 12:30 a.m. It can only be 12:05. Why did we come so early? Waiting is torture.

We had argued about whether or not Mary and I should meet the boys in the kitchen, but it was finally determined that it would be too dangerous for us without StickFoot, and they needed to come get us.

I don't regret the decision. I really don't want to run into Solomon or Kalyb in a dark hallway.

Mary whispers, "I'm scared."

"Me too," I whisper back. "What will they do if they catch us?"

"I don't know," she says, "but I have a feeling none of us would remember each other when Solomon was done."

A chill runs through me. What he did to me was awful—I now remember screaming and screaming—and the idea that it could get worse is terrifying.

I hear a rattling of the door. I hold my breath and raise my feet, in case another girl has decided to use the toilet.

I hear Juda's voice. "Mina?"

I exhale. "Yes."

"It's about time," says Mary.

When we exit our stalls, Silas and Juda are standing in the bathroom. Seeing us all in our tan uniforms, I wish we had the Smokers to camouflage us a bit.

"Any problems?" Mary asks them.

"Not yet," Silas says. "Lift your feet."

We do as he says, and, one at a time, he sprays our shoes with the StickFoot. Then he sprays our hands.

"Remember when you walk to step lightly and push your foot forward or you'll activate the adhesive," he says.

We all nod. He gave a long tutorial this afternoon.

"How's your wrist?" I ask him.

"It hurts, but it's major worth it," he says, grinning.

Juda leans in, kissing me lightly on the forehead. "You look better."

"So do you," I say. His swollen lip has calmed down.

"Can we get out of here?" Silas says.

"Chill," Mary says.

Juda pushes the bathroom door with his back, then peeks into the hallway. Once he's sure it's safe, he nods at us, and we file out. Silas quickly climbs up the wall and onto the ceiling. I want to laugh because he moves like some sort of bug.

"You next," whispers Juda to Mary.

Mary grimaces. "Nope. I don't want you staring at my butt."

Juda laughs but then realizes she's serious. He signals for me to go.

Putting my hands on the wall, I begin to ascend just like Silas taught me. My body feels like someone else's—my back and shoulders throbbing with the memory of hulking rocks.

When I get to the ceiling, I panic. Looking at Silas, I know that the StickFoot will hold me, but convincing yourself to place your body upside down is a whole other thing.

Juda is soon next to me on the wall, smiling. He and Silas crawled across the ceiling to reach Mary and me, so he's already done this. Was he nervous too?

He attaches one hand and one foot to the ceiling, and then the other hand and the other foot. I imitate him, and the next thing you know I am hanging upside down on the ceiling. *Wow*.

Mary climbs up quickly, and she is impressively graceful, but then she grew up using StickFoot like Silas.

Silas creeps across the ceiling toward the cafeteria while the rest of us follow. I try to focus on Juda's feet so that I don't look at the floor, which will make me lightheaded.

Walking on the floor through the hallway, the cafeteria seems close, but now it feels miles away.

The halls are deathly quiet except for the slight *hwwwick hwwwick* of our hands and feet sticking and unsticking from the ceiling. It sounds as loud as car horns to me, and I can't imagine that the sound isn't waking up Solomon, Kalyb, and the Sentries.

Silas suddenly stops, and I'm so surprised I almost lose my grip. He listens for a moment, frozen. I'm about to ask him what's wrong, when I spot it—a Sentry coming up the hallway to our right. I swallow the cry that surges up my throat.

The Sentry moves casually, making rounds that he's made a hundred times. He hasn't spotted us yet, which seems absurd, since we're hanging only a foot above his head.

He passes beneath me. I could reach down and touch his sandy blond hair. I hold my breath, starting a counting loop, hoping it will keep me calm.

1000. 999. 998.

He strolls toward the dorm, where we've just come from. Turning the corner, he passes out of sight.

I barely have time to exhale before Silas is moving again. He must be thinking the same thing as me: will the Sentry notice our empty beds?

My heart races like a hummingbird.

After several more turns, we reach the kitchen. Silas attempts to open the door from the ceiling, but the angle is too awkward. He has to shimmy down the wall and open it from the floor, which feels reckless. The rest of us return to the floor and hurry through.

The kitchen is huge, with long counters covered with crates of vegetables and grains. The air is thick and hot with the memory of active ovens and stoves. I hear a horrible crack and look over to see Silas biting into a raw carrot. "Sorry," he says, putting it down.

I understand the urge. I'm so nervous, I need to do something and eating seems like a great idea. I spot a jar of nuts and consider filling my pockets, until I realize they'll all fall out when I'm upside down again.

I watch Juda, who paces. We're all nervous, but he's got an extra level of anxiety. He doesn't even know if his mother is alive.

I feel guilty that I've seen her and he hasn't. I pray she's okay.

I worry about all the "ifs" in our plan. I wonder about Mary's brother's house—if it will be safe, if we'll be able to find food. Will Dr. Rachel help us see Rose? If so, will Rose be well enough to travel? Will Juda really go back to Manhattan?

There are so many questions. Have I really thought this through? We're setting something huge in motion here, and we won't be able to undo it once we go out the panel doors. We'll be escapees and no longer subject to the good graces of the Unbound. Am I ready to be on the run again? *We just got here.* The last time was hard enough and it ended in the death of two people.

My hands tremble. Has the Sentry already noticed we're gone?

"Juda, maybe this is a bad idea," I tell him.

"What?" he says, confused. "What's wrong?"

"Someone might get hurt."

"I have to go, Mina. I have to see Ma."

"I know you do, but maybe I should stay. Maybe I should profess my sins, go back to the Dixons, and—"

A noise comes from above, a buzzing that sounds like a Bee but then increases to a vibrating rumble, like a car engine.

"It's time!" says Silas.

"We have to go," Juda says, grabbing my hand and leading me

to the wall. Silas and Mary scurry up and perch by the panel doors.

Juda looks at me. "You're coming with me, Mina Clark. Don't even think about saying no."

I smile weakly.

I climb up the wall, so nervous I can barely remember how to place my hands.

An enormous *clank* fills the room as the panel doors open, but instead of dropping straight down and stopping, like we anticipated, they keeping moving and lifting to the sides. They continue toward the ceiling, straight for us. "Out of the way!" says Silas.

I manage to get out of the way just in time, but the door catches Juda's ankle, and the next thing I know, he's tumbling to the ground.

He lands with a horrible thud.

As I wait for him to move, I hear a terrifying sound. Food is dropping into the kitchen, and it's about to land right on top of Juda.

He opens his eyes, and they grow huge as he sees an enormous crate aiming straight for his head.

He rolls out of the way the second before it lands.

I scramble back down the wall.

"No, Mina!" he cries. "Go! The door will close!"

"I'm not leaving you!" I say, reaching the floor.

The creaking of metal signals the panels beginning to close.

"Come on!" says Mary.

"Go!" I tell her and Silas.

I run to Juda, forgetting to step lightly. The StickFoot on my shoes adheres to the floor and I trip immediately.

By now Juda is standing, and he helps me up. Silas and Mary are gone and the doors are halfway closed.

"Hurry!" I say.

Running to the wall, we shimmy up like monkeys avoiding a flood. We scurry across the ceiling and reach the panels just as they're about to close. Juda shoves his body in between the metal slabs, blocking them from closing any further. The huge gears grind in protest.

"Go!" he says.

"How will you—?"

"Just go!" he says, and I can see that the pressure of the doors is causing him pain, so I hurry through as quickly as I can. As I grip the metal door, my feet dangle for a horrifying moment, but the StickFoot holds, and I'm able to hoist myself onto the roof, where Silas and Mary wait to lift me.

I look down at Juda, still wedged between the doors.

"How do we get him out?" I ask Mary, frantic. "If he releases those panels, he'll be crushed."

Mary lifts her shirt and whips off the belt she's been wearing for six months. She holds one end down to Juda. "Grab on!" she says.

Silas gets behind Mary and wraps his hands around her for support. Mary doesn't like to be touched, but she seems to be making an exception.

Bracing one panel with his shoulders, Juda grabs the end of the belt. I pray the StickFoot on his hands will bind him to the thin strap.

Mary gives the belt one hard yank, and Juda comes surging upward. As he grabs onto the roof, the panel doors slam shut underneath him. Mary and Silas fall backward as Juda worms his way onto the flat surface.

Mary rolls off of Silas and begins to laugh.

What's wrong with her? Doesn't she realize how close Juda just came to losing a leg?

She turns her head to look at Juda. "You should be seriously grateful right now that my waist is not smaller."

He grins, breathless and exhausted. "I am seriously grateful for *everything* about you right now."

I lie down next to them, worn out by the stress. I've never been so happy to see the night sky. Juda squeezes my hand. I squeeze back.

"Are you hurt?" I ask him, picturing his fall.

"I was too scared to feel a thing," he says.

I breathe in the fresh air. The night is hot but not as hot as that kitchen. I want to lie here and celebrate a while, but of course we've only accomplished a small part of our plan.

Slowly standing and stretching, Juda examines the stars.

"Which way?" Silas asks, antsy.

"That's north," Juda says, pointing toward the trees. "If you squint, you can see the island, there." He points west.

The rest of us stand to see tiny fuzzy lights in the distance. During Time Zero, Manhattan would have blazed like a million Promise Proms.

"Okay, then," Mary says, "Let's quit this freakin' nuthouse already."

THIRTY-ONE

The roof seems massive—wide, flat, and covered in hundreds of solar panels.

We follow Juda to the edge and look down. It's much higher than I'd anticipated.

"This looks like three stories, not two," I say, trying to sound casual.

"It's fine," says Silas. "Totally safe."

"Maybe we need more StickFoot," I suggest. "A fresh spritz?"

He shakes his head. "It's good for six hours." He looks over the ledge again. "Just make sure you have a nice solid connection with your hands before you lower your body. And don't swing too much or you'll cause an upward motion that could unstick your hands."

This is not comforting, but we watch him go first, and, even with his injured wrist, he makes it look easy.

Mary goes second this time.

"You next," I tell Juda.

"No way. You," he says.

"I can't watch you fall again," I say.

"You'll have to watch if you're up here or down there," he says, chuckling.

"It's not funny," I say.

"We'll go together," he says.

"Deal," I say, relieved.

We place our hands on the edge of the flat roof, making sure they're good and stuck, and then drop our legs over the side. I hang there for a moment, the roof's edge cutting into my arms, as I wait for the StickFoot to fail and for me to fall to my death. But I continue to hang, so I lift my feet to attach them to the wall.

When I look over, Juda has done the same. We scamper down as quickly as we dare.

Reaching the bottom, I push my feet and hands up to release the StickFoot. I'm learning to hold my balance and not fall backward, but it's tough.

We land in grass. Silas and Mary are already searching the area. We face a small forest of oak and birch trees.

Juda walks straight for the trees, and I understand the instinct. I want cover as quickly as possible, Bees or no Bees.

The sounds of the forest keep making me jump: Twigs and branches snap nowhere near where we're walking; I'm sure I hear a girl moaning—Mary explains it's an owl. All four of us nearly start running when we hear a desolate howl.

"Coyote," says Silas.

At times I *hate* being outside of Manhattan.

I'm dying to speed up, but we can only move so fast with the tree roots and decayed street pavement at our feet. I'm ready to give my left arm for a flashlight.

None of us speak, even Mary. Silas guessed we have about thirty minutes until our Bees start tracking us. That means thirty minutes to sort out everything that's happened before our minds have to become "empty vessels."

I don't know about the others, but my mind has never seemed so full.

Besides the coyote and the idea of Solomon hot on our trail, I can't stop thinking about Juda's proclamation that he'll be returning to Manhattan. Now that I'm over the initial shock of it, I can't say I'm surprised. After he fled the Ashers' house, he was tortured by the fact that he'd left me behind. He couldn't forgive himself. Now he feels he's left behind *all* of his people.

So much could go wrong. He could be killed in the war. He could be arrested by Twitchers and charged with murder. He could be unable to escape the island for a second time.

After obsessing on these thoughts, I have to admit that I'm thinking about his plans because I have no idea about my own.

Do I go with him? Go west to some unknown paradise with Silas? Go upstate with Mary? And if I'm completely honest, there's a small part of me that wonders if there's still time to repent and stay with the Unbound. At least I know what to expect now, and the Dixons aren't that bad, right?

The Unbound will feed and shelter me. The other options could leave me dead in the wilderness or shot in the streets of Manhattan.

Goose pimples running up my arm, I tug Juda's shirt. "Hey," I whisper.

"Hey." I hear the tension in his voice.

"Can you talk to me a bit? I'm going crazy back here."

He slows down and strokes my arm. "Do you think it's safe?"

"We still have a few minutes left," I say, hoping I'm right.

"What do you want to talk about?"

"Ummm." I reach for a topic that doesn't involve the future. "Why were you in the Forgiveness Home?"

"I had some, uh, disagreements with my host-family," he whispers.

"Like what?" I ask, knowing I had many moments of wanting to be impolite with Tabby.

"They were just . . ." He pauses to find the right words. " . . . very condescending."

"What did you do?" I ask, thinking that there are a lot worse things than condescending.

"There was an eldest son, Beauregard, who thought it was his duty to teach me how the world really was. He treated me like an animal who didn't even know how to use a fork."

"Sounds familiar," I say, thinking of Phoebe's question about Propheteer fathers being able to sew our mouths shut.

"And then he started talking about the Prophet, calling Her a fraud and a sham."

"Did you hit him?" I ask.

"No. I, uh, put a snake in his toilet."

I laugh. "You didn't! Dead or alive?"

He grins wickedly. "Alive. He probably won't go into his bathroom ever again."

"Wow. No wonder they locked you up."

"At first I was relieved. Anything seemed better than being with that family—until I met Solomon, of course."

"How bad was it?" I ask, picturing him with a backpack.

"Bad. I didn't tell him anything for a very long time. He wouldn't let me eat, drink, or even sleep. He kept me standing at that wall for days. I thought I was going to die. He made me keep talking and talking, until it was just gibberish." His voice is bitter. "He made me apologize for things that I have no regret for, things that weren't mistakes."

"Juda, what did you tell him?"

"It doesn't matter anymore."

298

"It might, if we get caught," I say, panicking. "I need to know everything Solomon knows."

He's quiet for so long, I think he's dropped the subject, but then he says abruptly, "I told him about the day in the bunker, on the stairs, when we almost . . ."

"When we almost what?"

"I told him about my desire for you, okay?" he says with hostility.

"Are you mad at me for what happened?" I ask, taken aback.

He stops walking. "Of course not. I wish we were still there."

"Then why do you sound so angry?"

"Because he made me talk about it as if it were a sin, as if I were wrong to want you, and I hate him for that."

We start walking again.

I don't know how to feel. "Didn't we stop *because* it was a sin?"

He shakes his head. "I don't know anymore. I don't know what's right and what's wrong, which God is the 'right' God. I just know that everywhere I turn someone wants to punish me for something I'm doing or thinking. I don't know about you, but that's not the God I was raised to believe in."

Mother threatened me with God's judgment almost daily, but she also talked about the beauty and deliciousness of Paradise. She lives her life similarly to the Unbound waiting for their Ascension—suffering in this life, assuming that the next one will reward her tenfold. She once told me that as much as a husband doesn't appreciate his wife in this life, he will adore her and dote on her in the next.

"Mary and Silas were both in the Forgiveness Home for being sinners," I say, "but I think they're good people, don't you?"

After a pause, Juda says, "Is Silas homosexual?"

I stumble, I'm so thrown. "How did you know?"

"My friend Shad was a molley, and Silas kind of reminds me of him." He sees my shocked face. "In a good way."

"You had a homosexual friend? Why didn't you tell me?"

"It's never been relevant," he says.

I'm almost angry. "But I . . . I . . ." I didn't even know what a molley was, and here Juda has known about them his whole life? "You left me out."

"Out of what?" he says.

"Parts of your life."

"My life? What does my life have to do with why Silas was in the Forgiveness Home?"

"I don't know. It just does." I sense I'm being ridiculous, but I can't stop myself. Juda has made me feel ignorant, and I'm mad at him for it. Then a conversation we had long ago enters my mind. "Is Shad your friend who died in the plague?"

He nods.

"I'm sorry, Juda. I'm being a dook-wad." Am I using Mary's word correctly?

He laughs. "I don't know what that means, but your apology is accepted. And I'm sorry I thought something was going on between you and Silas. I realize how ridiculous that was."

"Yeah . . . ridiculous." I'm embarrassed to think how convinced and flattered I was that Silas was attracted to me. Even when I was mad at him, it felt good to know he had feelings for me. Is that pathetic? Or weird? Maybe I can ask Mary.

Ahead of us, Silas announces, "Time to go blank, friends. Loop-it-up."

I have to empty my head.

The Bees are coming.

THIRTY-TWO

1000. 999. 998. 997.

When will we see the first Bee? *Stop it, Mina!*

996. 995.

If we all do this correctly, we shouldn't see any Bees at all. *Count, dammit!*

994. 993. 992.

I focus on my steps and the numbers.

991. 990. 989. 988. 987.

Breathe in. Breathe out. Feel the breeze on your skin. Listen to the sounds in the air.

986. 985. 984.

I trip on a large rock, and Juda grabs my arm to stop me from falling. His touch brings my mind back to reality, back to him, and where we are.

A buzz appears in my ear. Is it a Bee? Are they coming? I don't look around.

983. 982. 981. 980.

By the time I've reached 960, the sound has disappeared. I

either imagined it, or the Bee got confused and flew away. I keep counting.

959. 958. 957. On and on. I don't look at anyone else because I'll think about how they're doing with their own loops. I have to stay within my own brain.

I stray many times but only for less than a second, which, according to Silas, isn't long enough for a Bee to synch.

Mary's in the lead now, leading us to her brother's house. Silas' theory is that since she's never walked this way before, her Bee won't recognize these particular thoughts. So Mary has the difficult job of thinking about the direction she's walking without thinking about her brother or her family.

Each of us has a backup loop. If I stray from counting, I have to think about something I've never thought about before. I can't look at Juda and think about his face or his thoughts, because I do this all the time. But I can contemplate Silas' hands or Mary's feet, because these are new impressions.

We walk about fifteen minutes without sighting any Bees, but as soon as I feel a smidge of relief, I force myself to start counting again. I can't get careless.

I've counted down to 86 by the time we emerge from the trees into a clearing. When Mary takes a sharp left, we follow, and I spot crumbling buildings from Time Zero in the distance.

That's where her brother is building a house? I want to ask Mary about it but can't risk it.

I sink back into my counting loop, watching my own feet tread through tall grass.

We enter the old city, which looks even worse close up. I'm staring at the leaning buildings and the bombed-out apartment buildings, when Mary stops in front of an old shop.

Looking less confident than usual, she opens a black door. Like most other stores on the street, the window of this shop is covered in a huge wooden board, but I now realize that this wood looks new.

After she passes through the entrance, we follow her with trepidation. We're greeted, not by rubble, but by a brand-new living space. As the door shuts behind us, we exhale with relief.

"I can't believe it worked!" Silas says, eyes wide.

"It was your plan," Juda says with gratitude.

"Yeah," Silas says, "but it was mostly based on theory."

We smile at one another, totally exhausted by the concentration of the last hour. I never knew I could be so happy to let my brain fill with whatever it wanted.

"What's that smell?" I ask, noticing a scent that's earthy, bitter, and satisfying in a way I can't explain.

"Coffee," Mary says. "My brother is obsessed with the old-school stuff."

Silas closes his eyes, inhaling. "Does he have some?"

"No, but this used to be a coffee shop, so it must always smell like this."

"Niiiice," Silas says.

Beautiful dark wood floors extend in front of us into a generous living room. One wall is brick while the others are a deep hunter green. A kitchen area on my right shows exposed pipes and an uninstalled sink.

Despite the lack of furniture and the unfinished fixtures, the place feels cozy and welcoming, exactly like a place I would like to live. Its one-room design contrasts sharply with the huge formal homes that all of the Unbound seem to inhabit.

"This is great, Mary," Juda says.

Mary beams. "It is, isn't it? Just like he described it."

"Your brother did all of this himself?" I ask.

"Yeps. He's quiet but talented." Acknowledging the empty space, she says, "Sorry there aren't any beds yet."

"I'm so tired, I could sleep in a pit of screaming babies," Silas says, yawning.

Chuckling, Juda says, "Me too."

"Okay, then," Mary says. "Choose your spot on the floor, and I'll see if I can scare up some pillows.'"

While she searches the room and various bins, Silas studies a mural on the far wall. "What is that?" he asks.

Juda and I join him.

"It looks like a queen," I say, looking at a faded painting of a woman wearing a crown.

"Why is she holding fish?" Juda asks.

"I think they're tulips," Silas says.

"I found some rags," Mary says, coming up behind us. "They seem unused." She sniffs them.

We each take a few, but mine are completely unnecessary. I curl up against Juda and am asleep within seconds.

THIRTY-THREE

When Juda wakes me, his eyes are bloodshot and his hair sticks up as if he's been running his hands through it all night. Did he sleep at all? The sun hasn't risen yet, but I get up, knowing how anxious he is to see his mother.

"I need to find that doctor," he says.

"We need Mary or Silas to find her house," I say, so tired my head won't rise completely.

"I'd rather go alone," he says.

"Why?" I say with a yawn.

"You've already put yourself in too much danger. Any new risk should be mine alone."

"I understand, but I have no idea where Dr. Rachel lives. I'm sorry."

Rubbing his head, he looks at the sleeping figures of Mary and Silas.

He nudges each of them awake as gently as possible. Mary groans and swats him away with her hand. Silas flinches like Solomon has entered the room. "Sorry!" Juda says. "I need to talk to you."

"Go back to sleep," Mary mutters.

"What is it?" Silas asks, yawning and sitting up a little.

"He needs one of you to take him to Dr. Rachel's house," I say.

"Let me sleep another hour, and I'll take you," Mary says, her eyes closed.

"We can't risk walking around in the daylight," Juda says.

"You're right," Silas says, rubbing his light hair. "I should take you now."

"Or you can draw me a map," Juda says.

"It's safer for me to lead you. I can keep us out of view."

Juda hesitates. "If you're sure."

"It's why we're here, right?" Silas says.

Juda smiles gratefully. He stands, ready to go immediately. I've never seen him so jumpy.

"Silas, you can have five minutes." I pull Juda's arm. Once we're a few feet away, I say, "I'm coming, too."

"No, I—"

"Don't argue. You don't know Dr. Rachel," I say.

"Silas does, right?" he says.

"It's different. Dr. Rachel and I, we talked about you. She understands that Rose needs to see you, and I think she's more likely to say yes if I'm with you."

His shoulders slump. "If you really think it will make that much of a difference, then . . . okay."

"I'm not asking for your permission," I say.

He gives me a rueful smile. "I'm starting to learn that."

When Silas is ready to leave, I ask a groggy Mary, "Will you be safe here alone?"

"Safer than you out there," she says. "If my brother comes by, he won't hurt me."

"Okay," I say, although I don't like the idea of splitting up. "See you soon." I give her a huge hug as she wishes us good luck.

Dr. Rachel lives in a purple house, which doesn't seem to suit her at all. When we reach her door, I can't spend even a moment thinking about what I'm doing or why we're there. I knock and then resume my counting. 1000, 999, 998.

I've counted to 792 by the time the door opens. Dr. Rachel, wearing cotton pajamas, her hair loose and tangled around a sleepy face, looks us up and down. "Silas Dixon? Mina? What are you doing here?" she says, confounded.

Without an invitation, we brush by her into the house.

"What's going on?" she asks, distress entering her voice.

"We're sorry to be so rude," I say, "but we can't have any Bees listening to us right now."

We have no idea if the rest of the Unbound know that we've escaped, or how Dr. Rachel will respond if they do. She could panic, sound the alarm to bring all the Sentries running, and all of this will have been for nothing.

My instinct tells me she won't. She seemed to really care about Rose. If she thinks seeing Juda will help Rose, I think she'll bend the rules to make it happen. I'm risking our safety on this prediction.

"I found Rose's son," I say, pointing to Juda, "and he needs to see his mother right away."

"You can come to the hospital this afternoon," she says, looking at us like we're lunatics, "during visiting hours." She gestures toward her front door.

"Wait!" Juda says.

Dr. Rachel squints at him with suspicion.

"We can't do that," I say. "We, uh, don't have a lot of time. Juda was staying, uh, somewhere complicated, and they will want him back there very soon."

She looks Juda up and down and seems to notice only now that we're all wearing tan.

"You'd better sit down," she says, motioning toward the kitchen.

I could burst from relief.

"What made you think you could bust out of the Forgiveness Home and just walk into my hospital?" Dr. Rachel asks.

We sit around her kitchen table greedily eating toast with jam and drinking hot tea.

Silas, mouth full of bread, says, "You have a better idea?"

"Juda could have petitioned Ram to see his mother."

"We don't have access to Ram," Silas says, swallowing.

"We only have access to starvation and torture," Juda says, looking her square in the eye.

"What are you talking about?" Dr. Rachel says, putting down her tea.

"Don't act like you don't know what goes on in the Forgiveness Home," Juda says, voice hard.

"Counseling and prayer for troubled youth," Dr. Rachel says.

Juda laughs nastily. "Is that what you call it?"

"Is that true, Silas? Were you being tortured?" Rachel asks.

Silas looks at her, then at both of us, then back at her. "No one is hitting us, if that's what you mean."

Juda and I look at each other, flabbergasted.

Dr. Rachel looks gently at Silas. "Torture doesn't always mean physical contact. It can be anything that leads to physical or psychological pain."

Silas looks at her, misery creasing his face. "I don't know if they *torture* us, but I do know that the Forgiveness Home is the most horrible place on the planet, and the idea of being there one more day makes me want to kill myself."

"It's what I would call 'endurance reeducation,'" Juda says. "They take away food and sleep and test your tolerance for pain until you break."

Sitting there, trying to find a way to sit that doesn't hurt my back, I know that my tolerance for pain wasn't going to last much longer.

Dr. Rachel looks teary. "I'm so sorry this happened to all of you. If I'd had any idea—"

"You'd what?" Silas says with bitterness.

"I would've tried to do *something*," she says.

Silas rolls his eyes. "I'll believe that when I see it."

"Silas, why are you being so nasty?" I ask. "She's trying to help."

"Plenty of kids, myself included, have gone home and told their parents what happens at the Forgiveness Home, and nothing has ever changed. Why would this be any different?"

"I'm not saying it will be. I'm just saying that I can try," Dr. Rachel says. "The next time I meet with Ram, I'll ask him about it."

"He'll lie," Silas says.

"I'll ask for a tour and see for myself. How about that?" she says.

Silas stares at his mug of tea. Finally, he says, "That would be good."

Dr. Rachel smiles.

"What matters right now is my mother," Juda says.

"Of course," Dr. Rachel says, gathering our plates.

We spend the next twenty minutes coming up with a plan: Dr. Rachel will drive to the hospital with Juda in the passenger seat disguised in different clothes. As they enter the hospital, they will pretend he is a very sick patient. After he's seen his mother, he'll follow the map that Silas drew to return to our hiding spot.

Once the details are clear, Dr. Rachel disappears upstairs to fetch what she and Juda will need.

"How do we know we can trust her?" Juda asks in a whisper.

"Because she would've sounded the alarm already if she wanted to turn us in," I say.

When we hear her coming down the stairs, we stop talking. She enters the kitchen with blue pants, a blue shirt, a coat, and a hat, for Juda.

"Do those belong to your husband?" I ask, realizing with a start that he could be sleeping upstairs.

"I'm not married. These were my father's."

"I've never known how you managed to stay single, Doc," Silas says. "Every woman I've ever known has a husband."

Rachel smiles ruefully. "Once I announced my intention to be a doctor, the suitors stopped coming, which was all right with me."

"Being a single doctor sounds pretty great," Silas says, and I agree with him. Dr. Rachel lives in a huge house with no one telling her what to do, what to cook, or how to behave. It seems pretty dreamy.

"Can I take a look at your wrist, Silas?" she asks. After examining it, she tells him, "It's pretty swollen. Maybe you haven't been letting it rest like the doctor told you?"

Sheepishly, he says, "It hasn't been a top priority."

"You'd better make it one, or it'll fuse incorrectly and cause you pain for the rest of your life."

Silas looks startled. "Okay."

He's been acting as if the wrist were completely healed, but what was he going to do? Stay in the Forgiveness Home?

"Juda and I should leave," Dr. Rachel says. "Where will you two go?" she asks me and Silas.

"We're fine," he says. "Our hiding place is safe."

"You can't hide forever," she says. "I hope you have a plan."

"We do," Silas says, a grin spreading across his face.

I wish I was as confident as he was. What we have is less of a plan and more of a rough intention.

Taking my hand, Juda says, "Be careful. Don't make me break you out of the Forgiveness Home a second time."

"*You* broke *me* out?" I ask. "I think I was helping you."

"I think Mary technically *yanked* me out," he says, smiling.

Smile disappearing, I say, "Be careful. Really."

"I will." Leaning down, he kisses me on the forehead, on each cheek and then on the mouth. My nerve endings all seem to buzz at once. When he pulls away, I'm giddy with longing.

"See you soon," he says.

"See you soon," I echo.

THIRTY-FOUR

I wonder what time it is. Five in the morning? Six? People will be waking up soon.

Silas guides me back the way we came, but with the rising sun we seem so much more exposed. He leads us deeper behind trees and shrubbery.

I've counted so much tonight that I decide to switch to Kalyb's method of focusing on different parts of the body. I start with my forehead, nose, and mouth, picturing Dr. Rachel's lasers scanning me from top to bottom.

Prowling around behind Silas reminds me of the night we snuck out of his house, when I thought I was going to see Juda. A lot has happened since then. A wave of distrust washes over me, and, for a second, I wonder where Silas is taking me. I have to remind myself that I know his secret now, and I didn't then.

Concentrate, Mina. Shoulders, chest, belly button . . .

Silas is different to me now. I can see the cracks where his father made him feel unloved and also the little boy who had to face Solomon alone. He seems more vulnerable and more powerful at the same time, if such a thing is possible.

Back to your loop! Thighs, knees, ankles . . .

Silas has been more honest with me than I've been with him. I have lots of secrets he still doesn't know about.

My mind flashes to Solomon dragging me into a room full of cables. A gurney. Screaming. "All of us! Everyone!"

Oh my God. My confession. *I told Solomon about Damon.*

How could I have forgotten that? I confessed my own sin, but I also betrayed Juda, Rose, Dekker, and Grace! *What have I done?*

I'm so upset by the memory, at first I don't notice the whirring sound. I spin around, looking for the source, and when I don't see anything, with dread, I look up.

And there is a Bee.

Nyek.

It hovers only two feet above my head. I take a quick step to my right, and it mimics my motions. It's synched me.

Without moving my head, I look around and spot Silas, who's continuing to walk. I see his lips counting. No other Bees are in sight. I run in the opposite direction of Silas, and the Bee dutifully follows.

What was I thinking? I wasn't omming *at all!* I was thinking about Solomon and Damon like an *idiot.*

Too late now. I'm caught. I wish I had a giant fly swatter so I could smash the Bee into a thousand pieces.

By the time I've run three blocks, I hear the shouts of men behind me. I pray I've given Silas enough distance to escape.

"Freeze!" screams an angry, male voice. I stop running. I know what happens if I try to escape: nets and needles.

"Get on the ground and put your hands on your head!" a second man yells.

I drop to my knees in the grass and do what he says.

My heart thumps from sprinting, but also from fear and disappointment. I wasn't even free twenty-four hours.

Footsteps approach, and when I twist around, my stomach turns. It's not a Sentry. It's Mr. Tanner.

He gives me a nasty grin. "Not too bright, you woolies—walking around in the daylight."

Another man comes to his side. He has a weaselly face and tiny shoulders. His slight build is counterbalanced by the enormous shotgun he holds in his hands. He smiles, just like Tanner, as if he's shot a holiday pig—or worse—is about to. "Nice one, Luke," he says.

"I told you it was worthwhile holding onto last year's Bees." Tanner opens up his jacket, makes a chirping sound, and the Bee flies into an inside pocket. "No one's watching us now. Let's take her back to where we caught her."

The little man nods.

Tanner tells me, "Let's go," but I don't budge. Without warning, he kicks me in the stomach.

Wind knocked out of me, I fall to the ground, gasping for air and grabbing my belly in pain.

"You ready to come with us now?" Tanner asks.

I stand with difficulty, and the men lead me by gunpoint back to the edge of the woods where I first noticed the Bee.

"This is the spot," says the little man, who must have been watching through the Bee.

"Okay, Samuel," says Tanner. "Let's say I came running around from behind that house over there, saw her, saw her gun, and then saw her pointing it at you."

"Sounds good to me," says Samuel, grinning widely.

What's happening? I don't have a gun. Panic shoots through me as I try to catch up to what they're saying.

"Okay," Tanner says. "That means I'll have to shoot her from way over here." He walks to the edge of the house, and points his shotgun right at my head.

I almost faint thinking he's going to pull the trigger.

"Wait for me to get out of the way!" Samuel says.

"Wait! No!" I plead. "I don't have a gun!"

"Of course you don't, dearie," Tanner says. "That's why Samuel brought one for you. But sadly, you won't be getting it until you're dead." Sticking out his lower lip, he mocks a sad face.

What happened to Ram's special protection?

What should I do? What *can* I do? My mind races for an action—any action that will delay them.

Is Silas still here or did he escape when I gave him the chance?

I spin around, turning my back toward Tanner. "You're going to have to shoot me in the back. Everyone will know I wasn't aiming a gun at Samuel."

"Whatever you prefer," says Tanner. "I'm good at improvising." I hear the cock of the gun. "Time to meet the Devil, you woolie trash."

"Put it down, Mr. Tanner," growls a deep voice.

Mr. Tanner goes rigid. I spin around, searching for the source.

Jeremiah comes around the side of the house in his Sentry uniform. I can't believe how relieved I am to see him. He holds up the same large gun he held the first time I saw him.

"It's time for you to go home, Mr. Tanner. You, too, Samuel. We'll talk about this with Ram tomorrow."

After the two men mutter disgusting things at me, they slowly walk away, chests puffed out, trying to let Jeremiah know that they aren't afraid of him.

Once they're gone, Jeremiah asks, "Are you okay?"

I still can't breathe fully since the kick Mr. Tanner gave me, and my body is so full of adrenaline I may pass out. I sit down in the grass.

"We'll get you some help," he says. He blinks quickly, awakening his Tact. "I need an ambulance at Eleventh Street, behind the Folsom house."

Ambulance? I think. Will it take me to the hospital? Will Juda be there? What if we arrive right when he's trying to escape? That sounds bad.

"No," I say. "I'm fine. I don't need an ambulance."

"You sure?" Jeremiah says, skeptical. He comes over, kneeling beside me.

"Yes, I'm sure."

"Okay, then. In that case, you're under arrest."

Of course I am. I nod.

After he cancels the ambulance, he says, "Before I take you in, I have one question."

I'm surprised. I've never heard Jeremiah speak this much. His blue eyes are full of anger, but I also detect anxiety.

"Where is my sister?"

"How should I know?" I ask, confused.

"Don't play dumb," he says, standing. "We know Mary broke out with you. So where is she?"

Mary is Jeremiah's sister?! How could she neglect to tell us that her brother was a Sentry?

"I don't know. We got separated," I say.

He takes a deep breath as he produces a long piece of hard plastic to tie my wrists together. "I don't believe you, but we'll get the truth out of you. One way or another."

THIRTY-FIVE

Jeremiah leads me to a van exactly like the one that I was forced into on my first day—black with black windows. I'm confounded when not only does Jeremiah not sedate me, but instead of throwing me in the back, he tells me to get in the front seat.

He doesn't say where we're going, but he doesn't have to: the Forgiveness Home and Solomon. My back begins to ache at the thought, while my heart accelerates with fear.

"Is she okay?" Jeremiah says, jolting me out of my thoughts.

I stare at his profile. Mary's brother? I still can't believe it. Mary is full of opinions and sarcasm and is one of the funniest people I've ever met; Jeremiah is such a . . . big lump of cooperation. You wouldn't think he had an opinion in his head.

"Last time I saw her," I say.

"That's what I meant," he says, frustrated. "How was she doing in the Forgiveness Home?"

What should I say? She was far from happy. She was being tortured by a barbaric belt around her waist. The girls in the dorm treated her like dirt. I know that Jeremiah was writing her letters, but I also remember her saying that her whole family thought she was disgusting, and I have to guess that that included Jeremiah.

I'd love to tell him the truth, but I'm nervous I could make things worse for me *and* Mary. I'm preparing some sort of neutral answer about Mary's "continuing faith in God," when Jeremiah says, "How did she *look*?"

My temper flairs. I blurt, "She was miserable. It's a horrible, horrible place where they treat people like freaks and criminals, and you shouldn't have left her there for even one day."

He looks at me briefly, hatred in his face. Staring back at the road, he says, "I should have known better than to ask a woolie for the truth."

We don't speak again for the rest of the trip.

Having expected the Forgiveness Home, I'm surprised when we pull up to the front of the Leisure Center.

"Get out," he tells me.

After I open the door and climb down from the seat, I'm confronted by an enormous figure.

It's Gilad.

He points at my face with a chubby finger, saying, "You ruined my son! You ruined my daughter! You ruined my family!" He lunges for me.

I raise my tied wrists to block my face, but Jeremiah is right next to me, shoving him back easily.

When he's regained his balance, Gilad looks at him with disgust. "I thought better of you, Jeremiah," he says.

"And I thought better of you," Jeremiah says, grabbing my shoulders and pushing past him.

I'm mortified to see hundreds of faces peering out from behind the glass of the Leisure Center. I'm sure everyone watching will be telling their neighbors each detail—my hand-cuffs, Gilad's accusations—as soon as they can.

Jeremiah leads me up the stairs to Ram's office as Gilad howls behind us. Why is he so angry? Does he think I talked Silas into breaking out? When I ruined Promise Prom, did I somehow "ruin his family"?

Before I can begin to formulate answers, we enter the waiting area to Ram's office, the cold air making me shrink into myself. Marjory sits at her desk, glaring at me like I'm her cat that went feral.

I glare right back, happy to stop pretending that I like everyone.

We don't linger long. I seem to have become a priority. Ram's office door pops open, and Marjory looks at it, not deigning to speak to me.

Jeremiah unties my wrists, and I walk inside the office.

Ram sits in a chair, not on the floor. For the first time since we met, he's not smiling. Even Jezzie stays in her bed, unwilling to greet me.

"Sit down," Ram says.

I begin to sit in one of the beanbag chairs, when he says, "No. On the floor."

I lower myself and cross my legs. I look up at him and wait.

"This is unacceptable," he says. "I have been nothing but generous to you and you have repeatedly paid me back with rudeness and insubordination. I gave you room and board. I offered you an education and a beautiful future. I presented you with God's light, the ultimate gift. And you have spit in my face. Why?"

"I haven't meant to—"

"I'll tell you why," he says, his high-pitched voice intensifying in an uncharacteristic way. "You are a selfish, vain, spiritless girl. God could no more move through you than a cement block."

I look at the floor. Have I been selfish? Or vain? I've been so focused on seeing Juda, I haven't been able to see much else around me.

"What if we hadn't taken you in? Have you considered that? Where would you be now? Starving in the woods! Gunned down by vagrants! So desperate that you have to return to that trash heap you call a city!"

He's spitting he's so angry. This is a completely different man than the one I met before, the sweet, laughing, boyish leader who soothed me at every turn.

With his high voice and pointy little ears, he now reminds me of some sort of demon. "Where are they?" he says, eyes narrowing.

I stare at Jezzie chewing her paw in the corner. "I don't know."

"Don't be silly," he says, "and don't waste my time."

I keep watching the dog, trying to keep an even tone. "I got separated. I don't know where they are now."

"I feel confident that you know exactly where they are, and you already know that I'm not the only one looking for them."

My chest tightens.

"I preach tolerance at every service, but as you know, I've been unable to reach Mr. Tanner and his flock of Purists. They're convinced that your people are an infestation that will destroy us. Their search party found you, and I'm sure it's only a matter of time before they find your friends. And this time Jeremiah might not reach them in time."

A chill runs through me.

After my continued silence, Ram says, "If you cooperate, you will save your friends from Mr. Tanner, and then you will be free to go."

I laugh at the lie.

"No one has forced you to stay with us," he says. "The Forgiveness Home is nothing but a training center, a way for you to gain God's forgiveness so that you might assimilate and live among us in harmony. If that's not what you want, and it's not what we want, then perhaps the experiment is over, and the five of you should be on your way."

"But Rose—"

"Is ill, yes. That's regrettable. She'll stay here until she's well enough to travel, and then she can join you."

"You're really going to let us just walk out of Kingsboro?" I can't imagine after our break out that Solomon won't want retribution. "What about Mary and Silas?" I ask.

"I'm afraid there's nothing I can do there. They are Unbound born, and here they will stay."

"Either we all go, or I won't tell you where they are."

He grins. "You're acting as if you hold all the cards, when it's your friends' lives that are in danger. I'm only trying to help you." He crosses his legs.

I don't think he's as relaxed as he looks. Mr. Tanner will look very clever and powerful if he reaches the runaways before Ram, and Ram can't have that.

"All of us or no deal," I say, trying to hide my anxiety.

We stare at each other and his delicate features betray nothing. He could be frustrated; he could be furious; he could be about to nap.

He bursts out laughing. "Fine. When you leave, Silas and Mary will go with you, and they'll have you to thank!" He stands. "I'll give you a minute to think about it." He strides across the room. "Don't take too long. Mr. Tanner works fast." He closes the door, and the second he's gone, Jezzie gives me a little growl.

What am I supposed to do? I can't imagine opening my mouth and saying the words "They're hiding in Jeremiah's house." Yet I saw the loathing in Mr. Tanner's face and felt the blow of his boot. He and Samuel would have happily killed me. They failed because they delayed too long, so they won't take their time with the others. They'll just walk in shooting.

I want to throw up.

Can I trust Ram? Will he really let us leave? It seems so unlikely, and yet why would he force us to stay? We've caused nothing but problems since we arrived. Our exit would be a great relief to so many people. In fact, Ram probably *needs* us to leave, and he's only shaping it as a huge favor to me.

People never straight out tell you what they need. They have to manipulate and blackmail, just like Juda said.

If Ram is lying, and Juda, Mary, and Silas hear that I gave them away, they'll hate me forever. But isn't that better than them being dead?

Will Juda be back at Jeremiah's? He's probably still at the hospital with Rose. If I don't mention this to Ram, could Mr. Tanner find him there? Mr. Tanner was using some sort of reconstructed Bee to search for us. Juda is safe inside the hospital, but if he's already left, he'll be vulnerable like the others.

Slumping, I bury my face in my hands. This is awful. Why did I have to be the one to get caught, to make this decision? If only I could warn them all to leave Kingsboro and never come back.

Minutes later, the door opens. In walk Ram and Jeremiah.

"What have we decided?" Ram says in a light voice, as if I were choosing between cake or pie.

Jeremiah ignores me, standing against the wall at attention.

I sit up, my brain still searching for an alternate choice. I glower at Ram. "I hate you for this," I say.

He sighs. "But God still loves you, which is His majesty. Where are they?"

My whole body tensing in protest, I whisper, "They're at Jeremiah's house."

Jeremiah's head snaps in my direction. "What?"

Ram laughs. "How ironic. I love it."

"I apologize, sir," Jeremiah says. "I—"

"No, no. You've been much too busy searching to even

consider it. Forest for the trees and all that." He produces his sickly sweet smile. "Why don't you take Jezzie with you?"

Jeremiah nods. In a clipped voice, he says, "Jezebel, come!"

Jezzie jumps up at once to join him.

"Use her well," Ram says, "but make sure to stop her before she does any real damage."

"Yes, sir," Jeremiah says, and I see the unease in his face.

Mary is his sister, and Ram has just told him to hunt her down with a dog. Silas warned me that Ram was the cruel hand behind Solomon, and I didn't want to believe it. Now I know Silas was right.

THIRTY-SIX

After Jeremiah and Jezzie leave, Marjory comes to fetch me. Ram sits on his beanbag, staring at the wall. He doesn't say goodbye.

Without a word, Marjory takes me by the elbow and leads me out of the office. As soon as we're back in the waiting area, another handleless door swings open. She takes me into a room with no furniture and one window. It's cold and empty, except for a girl curled up in the corner.

Still silent, Marjory leaves me inside and exits. Even though I know it's futile, I push on the closed door. It's locked.

A familiar voice says, "Of course. I should have known things could get worse."

I turn to see Tabby glaring at me from the floor. She looks pale and tired, her beautiful hair unbrushed and tangled.

"What are *you* doing here?" I ask.

She doesn't answer.

"Was it us? Because of me and Silas and what we did? I'm so sorry." At home this is standard, that when a person does something sinful, other family members are punished.

She plays with her hair, so I assume I'm right.

"The Forgiveness Home is a terrible place, Tabby. They were doing horrible things to Silas. He couldn't stay there if—"

"That boy-suck has made his own bed."

I don't know what to say. Silas told me that Tabby knew his secret, but I didn't expect her to be so cold about it. But why am I surprised? When has she been anything but a block of ice?

"He would never have wanted you here," I say. "He didn't mean to hurt you."

"Not everything is about him, and not everything is about you, okay?" She turns to face the wall.

"So what happened?" I ask.

"What do you care?"

I don't really, but I need information about what's going on and who knows what. "I like you," I say.

"Ha!" she says. "Please. No one likes me."

"You have lots of friends," I say.

"I have girls who are afraid *not* to be my friends," she says tightly.

"Is that why you're upset?"

She shakes her head like I'm an idiot.

I keep talking. "I'm in here because I screwed up again, and now other people are about to pay for my mistakes. Again." She doesn't turn around. "I'm really scared. What if Mr. Tanner finds Silas and Mary? He could kill them. And Juda . . . What if he doesn't get to see his mother? That will be my fault. If something happens to him . . ." I slump against the wall.

She stirs. "Silas is in danger, like, for real?"

I nod. "Mr. Tanner and Samuel have guns."

Tabby's brow furrows. "I hate Silas but I, like, love him, ya know?"

I do know. I hate Dekker, but I don't want him dead.

"Does it really bother you that he's . . . ?" I'm not sure which word to use.

"A molley? No, not really." She sits up. "He just makes things hard on my family. Some people have wanted Dad to resign from the Elders because of Silas, and now they'll get their way for sure. The only reason we took you in was to gain favor with the Elders."

Oh. That explains why Gilad screamed at me. I didn't exactly save his position, did I?

"My friends don't say anything to my face," she says, "but I know they laugh at my family behind my back. Now they're going to have a field day."

"Because of the breakout?" I ask.

"If only," she says, staring at the floor. She sighs. "Whatever. Everyone will know by tomorrow anyway." She looks at me. "I twittled my lady bug."

"What?" I say, perplexed.

"My lady bug? I set it off."

The pellets the girls got during Promise Prom—Grace said they could detect any surge in hormones to signal inappropriate interactions with boys. Sure I've turned pink, I ask, "Was it that boy? From the Prom?"

She nods. "Adam."

"Do you love him?" I ask.

The softness leaves her face. "Does it matter?"

"No, I just thought—"

"My parents and Ram don't care about love, so why should I? They just care about my precious virginity. Let me ask you a question: if the only thing that's valuable about me is my virginity, does that make my mother worthless?"

"I don't know," I say, confused.

"She may not be quite as priceless as an untouched girl, but she's got value because she's a *mother*. So during the time when you're not a virgin and you're not a mother, what are you?"

"I—"

"You're a useless piece of manure is what you are," she says, as if this were the obvious and only answer.

I don't know what to say. I had no idea that the women of the Unbound could feel useless. With their education and confidence, they seem so free. But if men are deciding women's worth, women will always feel they are worth less.

"So you don't love Adam?" I ask.

"I didn't say that. I said it didn't matter," she says, the venom leaving her voice.

"So what happens now?"

Her eyes grow watery. "I'll tell you what's *not* going to happen. I'm not going to become some freaking trash lady. I'm going to get out of this."

"Can you repent?" Maybe she can walk on water, like I did.

She raises an eyebrow. "You don't know much, do you?"

"Not really," I say. I don't know anything about her situation, and I can't pretend to. "How did you meet Adam?"

She hugs her knees. "When I was little, I thought the Savior would be my boyfriend one day. The idea that He was always watching me—it was really soothing. My parents paid a lot more attention to Silas than me, so God was like my third parent. I felt warm knowing He was in the room.

"At some point, I can't remember when, it started to feel claustrophobic, a big eye of judgment I couldn't escape. Adam was the first one I told that to. He said he wasn't sure God was in the room at all, which was major outrageous. The more we talked about it, the more I wondered if maybe he was right."

I'm amazed that Tabby is speaking to me like this.

"It's not that I don't believe in God. I'm just not sure that He's in every room, every single second, of every day, judging us for every single thing. How could He possibly have time? And why would He want to? We're His chosen ones. There are so many sinners doing things *far* worse than us. Your people probably sin, like, more in five minutes than we do in a year."

I squirm, trying not to get angry.

"Adam and I first started talking because of God. It wasn't flirtation or anything, and I wasn't thinking of him in a romantic way. He sat by me at the Worship Hub one day, and I saw him roll his eyes at something Ram said, which seemed major blasphemous. I wanted to ask him about it. I cornered him at the Spring Festival. He was really surprised, which I get. He's not exactly my league, I guess. Or Phoebe and Deb wouldn't think so. If I'm honest, I didn't used to think so either. His skin isn't great, and he's kind of skinny, but he has these really beautiful brown eyes and big, sexy hands. I kinda can't believe I never noticed him before.

"He says he noticed me, all the time, but he never had the nerve to talk to me. I thought he meant because I was so beautiful, but he said it was because I was such a bitch. Ha!"

I suppress a smile.

"He's right," she says. "I was never nice to him. I'm never nice to many people. I don't see the point really. I seem to get what I want more often if I'm mean. Adam says this isn't a very good way to live. He thinks that kindness is important, and that even if God isn't watching us every second, He's looking at the big picture. Adam thinks I'd be happier if I were kinder. *He's* kind, and he makes me happy. It actually makes me feel good to do nice things for him. I don't really see how that would extend to other people. I don't like other people. Why should I do things for them? When do they do things for me? But this is exactly the attitude Adam has been working on with me." She rolls her eyes. "It's hard."

Touched by her desire to make him happy, I say, "You do love him."

Face hardening, she says, "Do you believe in God?"

I pretend to examine my knee, which got scraped when Mr. Tanner captured me. Do I want to have this conversation with Tabby? The answer feels complicated.

"I always thought I did," I say. "I had faith in the Prophet— She seemed the same as God. I loved that She was a woman. The Teachers could take away our rights, but they couldn't take that away, you know? I loved Her story, and Her presence made me feel, um, warm, like you said. Then I came here, and everyone said She was a fraud. It was heartbreaking, like losing my Nana again. I've always been able to count on the Prophet's presence, and now She couldn't be my guardian anymore.

"I felt this loss, but Ram made up for it with promises of safety and education. And after I pledged myself to the Savior, I walked on water! It was so incredible. I don't know that I've ever felt anything like it. I've always had faith, but I never expected to *perform* a miracle." My body thrills at the memory.

Tabby scoffs. "Please. You don't actually believe that twaddle."

"What do you mean?"

"You didn't walk on water. It's a *trick*."

My body twitches with anger.

"Ram uses resin or, like, something in the water, so that you can step across. You can't really be such a twit that you think you *walked on water*."

"Why was everyone shouting and clapping if it was such an obvious trick?"

Raising an eyebrow, she says, "People believe what they want to believe." The Tabby I know has returned, spiteful and superior.

"You mean like you and Adam thinking you could *not possibly* set off your lady bug?" I say, feeling cruel.

Her eyes go dark as she leans forward. "Mr. Tanner is right.

You're nothing but a parasite and your people should be wiped off the planet."

She turns toward the wall, and we don't say another word.

An hour later, Marjory opens the door, and I bolt up, assuming there's news about the hunt for the others. She says, "Ram is ready to speak with you, Tabby."

Tabby stands. She's shaky as she smoothes her hair and pats her wrinkled yellow clothes. She gives me a look of bile and hatred as she passes, but by the time she reaches Marjory, she looks as demure and virtuous as an angel.

THIRTY-SEVEN

I sit on the hard concrete, my rear end aching, dying to know what's happening. Tabby has been gone for hours. Is she coming back?

Occasional murmuring seeps through the door, but I can't hear anything distinct, and it's maddening.

Did I make the right choice? Are the others safe? Will Jeremiah reach them in time?

The time alone gives me plenty of time to think. Being locked in this room, hearing about Tabby's impending punishment, learning my walk on water was a hoax—I now know that I cannot stay with the Unbound, and I cannot return to Manhattan.

I'm tired of being told what to do by men. I thought the Unbound were different, but they're not. They want their girls to be genteel, modest, and docile, just like at home.

And I love Juda, but I can't return to the island with him. I want to help the Laurel Society, but what could I possibly do? I'm just one person. Nana wants me free. She would be furious if I returned. At least, I think she would be.

I want to go west with Silas, find out if there's another way to live.

How can I possibly tell Juda? We never talked about it, but I know, deep down, he hopes I'll decide to help the Convenes. Will he forgive me? Maybe I can convince him to join us. If Rose has improved enough, she can join us, too.

I feel better thinking this is my next problem, convincing Juda to travel west. I refuse to believe that anything could've happened to him or the others. They're safe, and Ram will let us go wherever we want, just like he said. *They're safe, and I did the right thing.* This becomes my new loop: *I did the right thing. I did the right thing.*

The door opens, and a Sentry I've never seen before walks in. He's absolutely massive—like he could pick me up with his pinky.

"Come with me," he says, pulling out another plastic cord to tie my wrists in front of me.

After my hands are secured, he leads me straight through the waiting room and out the front door. Marjory and Ram are nowhere to be seen. Stranger yet, the crowd inside the Leisure Center has disappeared.

At the base of the stairs is a black van like the one I arrived in. The Sentry opens the back doors. "Get in," he says.

I look inside, and my breath catches. Mary, Silas, and Juda all sit inside. Juda's face lights up when he sees me, and Silas grins.

My wrists are tied, so I'm not sure how to get in the van. I attempt to raise my leg high enough to step into the cargo hold, and after I fail, Juda and Mary rush forward to help.

Their hands are cuffed as well, but Juda can still grab my hand and hoist me up. My entire body is barely inside, when the Sentry slams the doors shut.

Mary throws her secured wrists over my head and hugs me, while Juda gives me a once over, making sure I'm uninjured. Once Mary has released me, he hugs me hard.

"I was getting worried," he says.

"Me too," I say.

He kisses me.

They don't know yet that I ratted them out.

Silas is the only one who doesn't stand to greet me, and I'm startled to see his ankle is bandaged.

"What happened?" I say, sitting next to him.

"Jezebel," Mary says.

"We heard the Sentries coming and made a run for it." He frowns. "We didn't count on Jezzie being with them."

"Is it bad?" I ask. First his wrist and now this.

"No. Jeremiah stopped her before she did real damage." He looks at Mary. "Good thing she was with your brother, or she might've chewed my foot off."

She rolls her eyes. "Yeah. Good thing my brother betrayed and arrested us."

The word "betrayed" hangs in the air.

With a lurch, the van starts moving. "Where are we going?" I ask.

"I was hoping you knew," Juda says.

I shake my head, but Ram made me a promise. Now's the moment when I'll learn if he was telling the truth. When the van doors open, will we be at the edge of town or back at the Forgiveness Home? I hate that my hands are cuffed, because they're shaking, and I can't hide them.

"How's your mom?" I ask Juda, trying to focus on the reason we escaped in the first place.

He smiles slightly. "She's stable. She was really happy to see me, and Dr. Rachel said that after I arrived, Ma looked better than she had in days." He looks at the three of us. "Thank you. I can never repay you. I know it wasn't worth it for you, but it was for me. No matter what happens now, at least I got to see her."

"What are you talking about?" Mary says. "It was totally

worth it for me. I got to breathe outside air, scale a wall, and save you from being ripped in half. I exercised more than I have in a decade. And I got to see my brother, even if he was just there to arrest me."

Silas laughs.

Juda smiles, grateful for her kindness.

I want to laugh, but I'm too on edge—wherever we're going there's a chance that these three will hate me soon, and the thought is devastating.

"Where's Jeremiah?" I ask Mary.

"He didn't pick you up?" she asks, surprised.

"No," I say. "Just the big guy."

"He drove us to get you. That's weird," she says, looking concerned.

"Do you think he's in trouble?" Silas asks. "Because we were at his house?"

"No, of course not," she says, but her voice is shaky. It hadn't occurred to me that Jeremiah might be in trouble. He had no idea where we were hiding.

The van stops sooner than I would like. We haven't traveled far enough to be outside the town. When the Sentry opens the doors, I don't recognize our location—an empty parking garage.

"Let's go," says the Sentry.

We climb out of the van, and the dark silence puts me on edge. We seem to be deep underground.

"Where are we?" I ask the Sentry, but he doesn't answer.

I look at Silas and Mary, but they shake their heads. They don't know either.

The Sentry leads us through the creepy garage and then up dank stairs. The space feels old and decaying, like we're back in Manhattan. Our footsteps echo through the abandoned stairwell; none of us says a word. Silas limps a bit on his injured leg.

Several flights up, the Sentry bangs open a metal door, and

we're assaulted by the sound of people. Men in headsets rush around carrying clipboards. They dodge the cables and lights that lie on the floor.

I exhale. *The Worship Hub.*

"Maybe we're here for a service," I say to the others.

"Some public repenting?" Silas guesses, sounding as relieved as I feel.

"Maybe we're just here to see Ram," Mary says.

"I have a few words to say to that guy," Juda says, and it occurs to me that he's never met Ram. He's probably picturing someone very different than the man he'll eventually encounter.

The Sentry leads us adroitly through the mayhem. It's hard to imagine the last time I was here—the joy and pride I felt as I walked through this hallway, fresh off of my "miracle." I was so full of hope about Ram and the Unbound: the promise of a gentle God and Savior, a reunion with my friends, school and an education. Now my best-case scenario is that they will let me and my friends run off into the wilderness to starve to death.

We've almost reached the stage, when the Sentry stops us. "We'll wait here," he says.

We're hidden behind curtains, but we can see into the auditorium, which is flooded with people.

"What's going on?" Mary asks.

"I don't know," Silas says. "It's not Sunday. Maybe it's another Revelation Day, like last week?"

Everyone in Kingsboro seems to be arriving—men, women, and children. This is why the crowd was gone from the Leisure Center. Everyone is here. Something big is happening. My skin prickles.

Sitting in the front row with her family is Susanna, Silas' friend. She looks completely different than the day I met her, sitting with her hands crossed delicately in her lap. Her face is vacant and bland and not at all passionate. As if feeling my eyes upon her, she looks up and spots us off stage. Seeing Silas, she sits up straighter. She gives him a sad little wave. He waves back.

"She's been a good friend to you," I say.

"My only one," he says, smiling at her. Susanna's parents notice her distraction and scold her. "Maybe my last one," he says, backing away from the curtain.

Resting my hand on his back, I say, "Don't be silly. We're your friends."

"There's no chance Solomon and Kalyb will let us near each other again," he says.

He's right, but if Ram keeps his promise, we won't have to worry about them.

All of a sudden, Ram is standing at our side. "Well, well, well," he says. "Welcome back, my prodigal children." Mary and Silas glower at him.

"Juda," Ram says in his squeaky voice. "So nice to finally meet you. I'm Ram."

Juda's eyes bulge, as I anticipated. How could this little boy of a man control this entire community?

"Mina cares very much for you, so you must be good people," he says with a huge smile.

Juda, over his initial astonishment, scowls at Ram. "You seem to enjoy locking up children for no good reason, so I can't say I care very much for you."

We stand in flabbergasted silence. Juda grew up poor, but he grew up a poor *boy*. He will always have a boldness I lack.

Ram breaks the tension with a laugh. "Wonderful. Exactly how I imagined you." He turns to the rest of us. "Thank you for joining us here today."

Mary guffaws. "Like we have a choice."

"You would have been sad to miss it, I assure you," Ram says. "I'm making a big announcement, one of the biggest in Unbound history." When none of us react, he says, "And you all have a part to play in it, so I need you here."

We look at one another. What on earth could he mean?

"We'll speak more when the service is over." He gives us a wink as he grabs his headset and walks on stage.

Juda and I lock eyes. This can't be good.

If Ram plans to fulfill his promise and let us go, why would he involve us in some big announcement? I stumble a bit to my left.

"Are you okay?" Juda asks.

I'm not. I've made a horrible error, and I'm about to find out how catastrophic it was.

THIRTY-EIGHT

The second Ram walks on stage the congregation goes wild. They continue to applaud until Ram raises his hands, motioning for them to be quiet.

"Good afternoon! How wonderful to see you!" he says into his headset, his voice booming throughout the auditorium. "I know you're wondering why I called you here today. What a special occasion it is! My heart dances, not only for you, but for your beautiful souls. Our dreams are about to come true!"

His arms open wide, and someone yells, "We LOVE YOU, Ram!"

He continues, "You know that I've been working on a treaty with the Propheteers, a treaty that will lead to wonderful things, and I'm here to tell you that today I have been successful. We have finally done it!"

Some members of the Unbound applaud, while others whisper among themselves. A few people are angry, Purists obviously.

"Beautiful people," Ram says, smiling larger than ever, "don't be afraid. This is the best of news. This is the path to our redemption, the path to our Ascension. As long as there is hatred and bitterness between us and the Propheteers, the Savior will not come, and is anything more important than His return?"

"NO!" someone yells.

"I am always looking forward, toward the light, toward His return. You know that," he says, exuding calm on his angelic face. "I will never lead you astray."

His words act as a sedative. The whispering crowd grows still, a pond that's absorbed the ripples of a troublesome stone.

"And now for the best part. I knew that we had many things we could offer Uncle Ruho: fuel, medicine, food. However, I wanted to offer something that would make our bond everlasting. So I am bonding our two people not just with resources, but with blood."

People look at one another in confusion.

Ram throws out his arm, gesturing to the other side of the stage. "Ladies and gentlemen, I introduce you to the new divine first lady of Manhattan, the future wife of Uncle Ruho, Tabitha Dixon!"

My head whirls toward Silas, whose mouth has popped open.

Tabby walks onto the stage wearing a floor-length purple gown, her hair curled and flowing down her back. The smile plastered on her face, her wide eyes, and stiff waving hand make her look more like a mannequin than a girl.

"What in Hell is she doing?" says Silas.

I shake my head, too stunned to speak.

"Who is that?" Juda asks.

"His sister," Mary says, pointing at Silas.

Juda looks at Silas. "You can't let her do it."

"I'm not really standing in a position of power, am I?" Silas snaps.

"Shhhh," I say, trying to hear what Ram says next.

"Miss Dixon will act as a diplomat of the Unbound," Ram

says, taking her hand, "and once she has children, our two societies will be connected by blood, in peace, forever, and then the Savior will be happy to liberate us all. Let's hear it for the Queen of the Propheteers!" He raises her hand to the ceiling, and everyone cheers.

"Queen?" I say. "Uncle Ruho isn't a king."

"I don't think he cares," says Mary. "The crowd loves it."

She's right. The congregation is in a frenzy.

Tabby holds her impossible grin.

"Why would she do it?" Mary asks, astounded.

"She, uh . . ." I look at Silas, embarrassed. "She triggered her lady bug."

Silas' eyes grow huge

Mary whistles. "Whoa."

"What are you talking about?" Juda asks.

"I'll explain later," I tell him.

Ram keeps the crowd clapping for Tabby and praises the treaty several more times. When the audience seems enthusiastic beyond return, he says, "Go out and celebrate with your neighbors and loved ones! Praise God and let Him see your joy! And I'll see you here next week, when we'll discuss the royal wedding!"

He dismisses them with a "So be it," and people rise to leave. Even from off stage, I can hear the crowd buzzing with the news.

Ram and Tabby exit on our side of the stage. Glancing at us, Ram says, "Follow me." The Sentry tells us to obey the order. Still stunned by the new development, the four of us look at one another and comply.

Ram walks quickly through the backstage corridors, nodding and smiling at his staff. Silas and I catch up to Tabby, who's struggling to walk in high heels.

When we're directly behind her, Silas whispers, "Tabby, are you okay?"

She glances at Silas' bandaged ankle but says nothing.

"You can't do this," I say, voice as loud as I dare. "What about Adam?"

"It's this or the Fallen," she hisses under her breath. "Easy choice."

Before I can respond, she catches up with Ram, whom she towers over in her heels. She adoringly loops her arm through his. What lies has he been feeding her?

I'm so caught up in figuring out how to get Tabby away from Ram that at first I don't notice that Juda and Silas have gone rigid. Mary emits a squeaking noise.

I scan the hallway, and there's Solomon, walking straight for us.

Is this it? Is now when he takes us back into custody?

He leers at us with disgust.

I prepare to run. *I am not leaving here with that man.* Looking at my friends' angry and determined faces, I know they feel the same way.

Approaching us, Solomon says through gritted teeth, "Didn't get very far, did you?"

And then he keeps walking!

Only now can we see that a Sentry walks behind him. The Sentry gives him a shove, causing him to stumble as he moves forward. His head whips around, and we can see he wants to throttle the Sentry, but this is not the Forgiveness Home, and he's no longer in charge.

Mary's jaw is about to hit the floor, and I'm sure my face looks equally astounded.

Ram calls to us from the top of a spiral staircase. "Up here, boys and girls. Shake a leg, please!"

We walk up the stairs, taking our time. Our Sentry stays at the bottom.

"Is Solomon being punished for letting us escape?" Mary whispers.

Silas smiles. "If there is a God, Solomon will be wearing a rock backpack for the next ten years."

I giggle as Juda says, "So be it."

I savor this brief moment of relief. Knowing we don't have to face Solomon makes me feel like I can survive what lies ahead.

When we arrive at the top of the staircase, Ram opens a door for us. "My dressing room."

Thoughts of Solomon are washed away as I see the lavish room. Blue velvet couches and chairs sit atop exotic rugs. Sparkling gilded mirrors hang from the walls. Fresh yellow roses adorn every available surface, making the air smell decadent and delicious. An oversized gold and black dressing table is piled with powders, pallets, and silver brushes. Susanna was right! Ram does wear makeup.

"Have a seat, everyone," Ram says, plopping onto a velvet chair and removing his headset. Tabby sits regally in the chair next to him.

Juda, Mary, Silas, and I all sit on one couch, making Ram laugh. "Spread out, for Pete's sake! No need to act like you're chained together."

I'm not sure why he thinks this is funny, considering we're still wearing handcuffs. Juda and I move to the second sofa.

"You've heard the exciting news about Tabitha and—" Ram says.

"You can't let her do it!" I interrupt. I look at Tabby. "You can't go! You have no idea what you're getting into!"

"I'll be fine," says Tabby. "It's God's will, and God will protect me."

Ram beams. "Of course He will."

Silas looks desperate. "Ram's using you, Tabs. Why can't you see that? You're going to be miserable and—"

"No!" she says, losing her smile. "He's not using me. Ram is helping me. If I stay *here,* I'll be miserable. I will collect garbage on the streets. In Manhattan, I'll be like royalty. I'll be married. I'll have children. I'll be respected by everyone!"

Juda shakes his head. We both know that to enter into a marriage on the island as a woman is to guarantee respect from no one.

"Do you know what the penalty is for talking back to your husband?" I ask her. "A beating. For reading a book? A life sentence in the Tunnel. For adultery? Death by stoning. NO ONE would CHOOSE to live that way!" I can't believe how angry I am.

"Can we be honest here?" Mary says. "This is all about your stupid lady bug. Who cares what happened? Who cares if you had sex? A couple of dried-up old ladies and clueless men."

Tabby has gone pale. She says hoarsely, "Everyone cares. My life here is over."

"Well, then that's on you, Ram," says Mary. "You've created a world where if a girl seeks any physical pleasure, her life will be over. Congratulations."

"We are not here to debate the moral standards of the Unbound," says Ram, clearly growing annoyed.

"Good!" says Mary, who's on a roll. "Because then we'd have to discuss why in your utopian-fantasy-world kids who don't conform to your ideals have to be locked away where they're tortured, starved, and told they're worthless."

"Tabby, you love someone else!" I cry. "Uncle Ruho is an *old man!*"

"Enough!" says Ram, hitting the arm of his chair. "Can't you see that this is bigger than any of us? Tabitha is giving herself over in service to God, in service to us, so that we might be reunited with our Savior. Nothing is more important than that—we must stop being selfish, stop thinking about ourselves, and start thinking about the group as a whole."

"How does that even work?" Mary says. "The Savior won't come if Ruho is married. He will only come if he is dead."

"The Savior will come if Ruho stops claiming he is divine," Tabby says, with a superior smile.

Ram reaches out and strokes her hand. "Tabby's job is, over time, to convince Ruho that he is just a man." They beam at each other, their secret revealed.

"That will never happen," Juda says. "You are giving her a death sentence that—"

"I'm glad you're so concerned about Tabby," Ram says, looking at each of us, "because you will be helping to keep her safe." He takes a dramatic pause. "You will be going with her to the island and acting as her privy council."

THIRTY-NINE

I feel as if Solomon has shocked me with his cables again. I may be sick. Ram, this man who looks like an innocent boy, who offered me a home with his people, and who once said, "I am always here for you," is nothing but a monstrous, backstabbing liar. Standing, I say, "You promised we could go free!"

"I said you could leave Kingsboro, and you will," he says, grinning at his own cleverness.

"I'm not going anywhere," says Mary, standing up as well. "I'm just a girl who likes chocolate cake too much."

"Sit down," Ram says. "You are a girl who broke the law when she escaped from the Forgiveness Home, trespassed on her brother's property, and then resisted arrest. Plus, Mina said she would not give up your location unless you *all* left Kingsboro."

Mary and Silas look at me in disbelief.

"That's not fair!" I shout at Ram. "That's not what I meant, and you know it!"

He shrugs.

"I'm so sorry," I say to Silas and Mary, who turn their faces away.

"You didn't say anything about this, Ram," says Tabby, trying to maintain a smile.

"I'll go," Silas says quietly. "I'll go look after you, Tabby."

Instead of looking grateful, Tabby looks disgusted. "I don't need any of you to look after me. I'm not a baby."

"You don't know anything, Tabby," I say, "and you *are* a baby." I turn to Ram. "And I am NOT going back there." I sit down and look at Juda, who hasn't said a word. His fists are clenched, while his eyes search the room. I have to assume he's looking for a weapon.

"The thing is," Ram says, ignoring our outrage, "my vision was very clearly about five people who would help the Unbound, and we only have four here."

"What about me?" says Tabby, indignant.

"You're more than a person, darling. You're a bride."

She smiles smugly, settling back into her seat.

Ram lifts his headset and speaks into the mic. "Send them in."

The door opens and in walks our Sentry, followed by Dekker and Grace.

"Thank you," Ram tells the Sentry, who quietly exits.

Grace and Dekker take in the room: Ram, Tabby, and the four of us sitting on couches. Dekker raises an eyebrow. "Weird party."

"Sit down, please," Ram says.

Grace hurries to sit by me on the couch.

"I think I'll stand," says Dekker, leaning against the wall by the door. He wears white and looks weirdly puffy. He seems to have been enjoying the food here. Besides that he looks healthy, which is a relief.

Grace, also in white, takes my hand the second she sits down. I'm sure she heard about our escape. Was she in the audience just now? She gives me a timid smile.

"Good," says Ram. "We're all here. Dekker, Grace, as I was explaining to the others, I am creating a small private council to send with Tabitha to Manhattan. I had originally planned to send the Manhattan Five, but sadly, one of you has fallen ill, and you became four. The good news for you is that Mina has volunteered Silas Dixon and Mary Benjamin, so now we have six!"

Grace looks at me in horror. Unable to say anything, I throw my arms around her. She sobs into my shoulder.

"Mina," Ram says, "I once told you that the Unbound all have the same job. That job is to ensure the Ascension transpires without delay. The time has come for you all to play your part, to do your jobs as members of our community."

Lurching forward, Dekker approaches Ram menacingly. "You've got another thing coming if you think I'm going back to that Hellhole."

"Aaron," Ram says into his mic, "please join us again."

The Sentry is back in the room within seconds.

Dekker looks him up and down. Dekker is tall, but Aaron obviously bench-presses a car every morning.

"Do we need Aaron here?" Ram asks Dekker. "We're just having a discussion."

Dekker licks his lips. He looks at Juda, silently asking if he'll help take Aaron down. But Juda doesn't move. He's as rigid as a statue.

Dekker's eyes flick to mine, while I shake my head slightly, sure I'm thinking the same thing as Juda: We can't defeat these people, not here. If Dekker beats up Aaron, there are a hundred Sentries to take his place.

Dekker doesn't step back from Ram. He seems stuck, unable to admit he's helpless.

Ram smiles. "I would like to speak with the Propheteers alone please."

This isn't what Dekker was expecting. His adrenaline is

pumped and ready to go, and if he doesn't hit something, he might fall over.

"Yes, sir," says Aaron.

He opens the door and gestures for Tabby, Silas and Mary to leave.

Tabby is not pleased. She's enjoying her new position of importance. "Do I have to leave?"

"Yes, darling, but only for a minute," Ram says. "Then you'll be the center of attention again."

Understanding this as an insult, she leaves the room with an aggressive flip of the hair. Mary and Silas march out after her, their faces frozen in distress and confusion.

Once they're gone, Ram sighs, taking the four of us in. "It's not as bad as you think," he says.

"Then why don't *you* go live with her?" Dekker says.

Grace is still crying.

"It's not permanent. Once you've completed your assignment you can stay there, you can come back here, you can go live on Mars for all I care."

"Our assignment?" Juda asks.

Grace sniffs. "We just have to take care of her for a little while?"

"The four of you have a much higher purpose than aiding Miss Dixon. I told you that I had a dream about the Manhattan Five months ago. I knew you would be of extreme importance but the vision only became clear recently." He stands, placing his hands in a prayer position under his chin. He walks behind his chair and looks at the sky. "You will go back to Manhattan as Tabitha's private council, live with her, and aide her in her transition, and when the time is right, you will kill Uncle Ruho."

I'm too dumbfounded to respond.

"You want us to do what?" Dekker asks, almost laughing. "You are truly out of your nut!"

"You have an entire army of Sentries at your disposal," says Juda. "Why would you send children to do a soldier's job?"

I find my voice. "You have weapons. Drop a bomb on his head!"

"Yes! Great idea!" says Dekker, pointing at me.

"Why do you think we would kill someone?" Grace whispers.

Ram gives her a look of feigned shock. "Because you already have! The five of you killed Damon Asher. You are the most ruthless children I have ever met!"

Solomon told him everything. He tortured me, making me believe I'd offended God, when all he really wanted was information to feed Ram.

"You have not answered my question," Juda says, temper swelling. "Why are you sending untrained children to do an assassin's job?"

"I'm not a child!" says Dekker.

"Shut up!" I say.

Sitting back down, Ram crosses his legs. "Do you like Uncle Ruho? I thought you left because you didn't."

"That's not the point!" I say.

"I know why he wants us to do it," says Grace, her voice barely audible.

Our heads all turn to her, but she keeps staring at Ram. "A member of the Unbound *can't* kill him. The Savior won't return if one of *you* has committed murder. But a Propheteer can, right? And then your Ascension can occur?"

Ram giggles and claps. "You have become quite the little student, haven't you, Grace? Very good. What an honor you're all receiving—to be our hand. To lead us to our mighty Ascension, finally!"

Dizzy with rage, I drop my head into my hands. This horrible, disgusting act that has haunted me every waking hour, that I thought had been forgiven by the Unbound's God—they want me to do it again.

"I can't do it," I say. "I won't do it."

"Yes, you will," Ram says. "Or I will blow your entire island to smithereens."

Juda, Grace, Dekker, and I look at one another. We are going to have to go back. And one of us is going to have to kill our Divine Leader.

End of Book Two

NOTE TO READER

Gay "conversion therapy" or "ex-gay ministry" (what happens to Silas in the Forgiveness Home) is a discredited psychotherapy method aiming to change a person's sexual orientation or gender identity that happens all over the United States. A backpack of rocks is a real example of a conversion technique used by a Mormon "clinic" in Utah. Electrocution and electroshock therapy are also methods used on children as young as twelve. As of March 2017, only five states, as well as Washington D.C., have formally banned conversion therapy. Survivors of conversion therapy are 8.9 times more likely than their peers to consider taking their own lives.

To read more or to help survivors, please visit conversiontherapysurvivors.org and follow #bornperfect

"Purity Balls" (Promise Proms) in which a daughter pledges her virginity to her father occur in 48 states and are spreading to other countries. Statistically, pledge-takers have premarital sex as often as non-pledge takers, but the pledge-takers are much more likely to have unprotected sex, leading to STDs and unplanned pregnancies. Teaching a girl that her value lies in whether or not she abstains from sex reinforces stereotypical gender roles and can negatively affect her sexual and emotional health.

Learn more here:
https://www.youtube.com/watch?v=Hvcb_JRHJyY

More than 40% of Americans believe in the Rapture (the Ascension), the idea that one day Christ will return to Earth and good Christians will be beamed into Heaven, while seven billion people are left to suffer and die. As a result, many families do not save for their children's education or for their own retirement.

Learn more here:
http://www.nytimes.com/2011/05/20/us/20rapture.html

**To learn more about all of the rules and practices
in the *Time Zero* trilogy, please visit
www.timezerobook.com/religious-rules**

Want to be the first to know
about the release of Book 3 in the Time Zero trilogy?

Go to **www.timezerobook.com**
for series news, bonus content, and sneak peaks.

ABOUT THE AUTHOR

Carolyn Cohagan began her writing career on the stage. She has performed stand-up and one-woman shows at festivals around the world from Adelaide to Edinburgh. Her first novel, *The Lost Children*, became part of the Scholastic Book Club in 2011 and was nominated for a 2014 Massachusetts Children's Book Award. Her YA novel *Time Zero* is the winner of the 2017 Readers Favorite Award and the 2017 International Book Award. She lives in Austin, Texas, where she is the founder of Girls With Pens, a creative writing organization dedicated to fostering the individual voices and offbeat imaginations of girls ages 8-14.

@timezerobook
#findtheleaf

ACKNOWLEDGMENTS

I'm extremely happy to acknowledge all the young people who helped this book come to fruition: Evan Allbritton, Kailen Cohagan, Kaissa Doichev, Becks Konradi, Lena Konradi, Sasha Konradi, Helen Randle, Katie Simmons, Pippa Sims, Vivian Quinn, and Lucie Young.

I would also like to thank Amy Elliott, whose consistent feedback and availability kept me from pulling out my hair on many occasions. My appreciation also goes to Lynn Cohagan, Katherine Catmull, Elisa Todd Ellis, Josh Jackson, Emily Klein, Shelley Reece, Steve Schrader, Andrea Eames, Robert Toteras, Roberto Cipriano, Martin Skea, Ingrid Powell, Karen Nalle, and Natalia Sylvester. Thank you to The Writing Barn for your peaceful and always productive space; and thanks to the brilliant ladies of LLL and the Loma Linda writing retreat, who keep me inspired and even better, keep me laughing.